Marius' Mules XI

Tides of War

by S. J. A. Turney

1st Edition

"Marius' Mules: nickname acquired by the legions after the general Marius made it standard practice for the soldier to carry all of his kit about his person."

FOR PAUL AND CHARLENE

I would like to thank Jenny for her sterling work in making Marius' Mules eleven what it is with her editing. Thanks also to my beautiful wife Tracey and my children Marcus and Callie for their support.

Cover photos courtesy of Paul and Garry of the Deva Victrix Legio XX. Visit http://www.romantoursuk.com/ to see their excellent work.

Cover design by Dave Slaney.

Many thanks to the above for their skill and generosity.

All internal maps are copyright the author of this work.

Published in this format 2018 by Victrix Books

Copyright - S.J.A. Turney

First Edition

Also by S. J. A. Turney:

Continuing the Marius' Mules Series

Marius' Mules I: The Invasion of Gaul (2009)
Marius' Mules II: The Belgae (2010)
Marius' Mules III: Gallia Invicta (2011)
Marius' Mules IV: Conspiracy of Eagles (2012)
Marius' Mules V: Hades' Gate (2013)
Marius' Mules VI: Caesar's Vow (2014)
Marius' Mules: Prelude to War (2014)
Marius' Mules VII: The Great Revolt (2014)
Marius' Mules VIII: Sons of Taranis (2015)
Marius' Mules IX: Pax Gallica (2016)
Marius' Mules X: Fields of Mars (2017)

The Praetorian Series

The Great Game (2015)
The Price of Treason (2015)
Eagles of Dacia (2017)

The Damned Emperors Series

Caligula (2018)

The Knights Templar Series

Daughter of War (2018)

The Ottoman Cycle

The Thief's Tale (2013)
The Priest's Tale (2013)
The Assassin's Tale (2014)
The Pasha's Tale (2015)

Tales of the Empire

Interregnum (2009)
Ironroot (2010)
Dark Empress (2011)
Insurgency (2016)
Invasion (2017)
Jade Empire (2017)

Roman Adventures (Children's Roman fiction with Dave Slaney)

Crocodile Legion (2016)
Pirate Legion (Summer 2017)

Short story compilations & contributions:

Tales of Ancient Rome vol. 1 - S.J.A. Turney (2011)
Tortured Hearts vol 1 - Various (2012)
Tortured Hearts vol 2 - Various (2012)
Temporal Tales - Various (2013)
A Year of Ravens - Various (2015)
A Song of War – Various (Oct 2016)

For more information visit http://www.sjaturney.co.uk/
or http://www.facebook.com/SJATurney
or follow Simon on Twitter @SJATurney

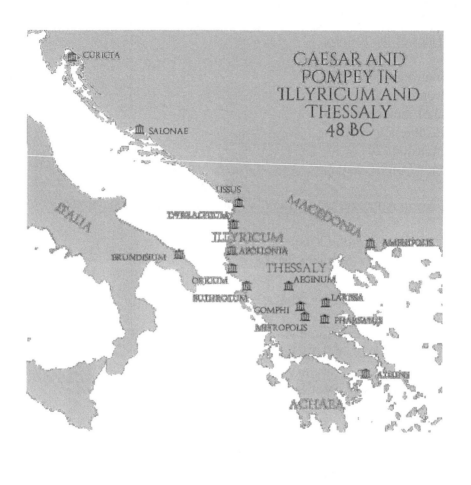

CAESAR AND
POMPEY IN
ILLYRICUM AND
THESSALY
48 BC

CURICTA

SALONAE

ITALIA

MACEDONIA

LISSUS

DYRRACHIUM

ILLYRICUM

APOLLONIA

BRUNDISIUM

AMPHIPOLIS

THESSALY

ORICUM

AEGINUM

BUTHROTUM

LARISSA

GOMPHI

METROPOLIS

PHARSALUS

ATHENS

ACHAEA

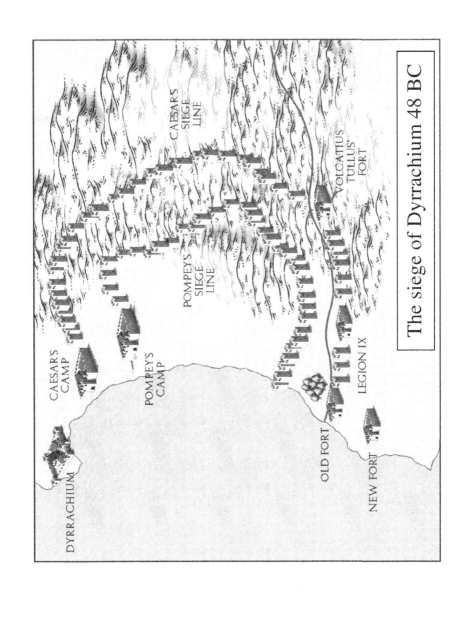

The siege of Dyrrachium 48 BC

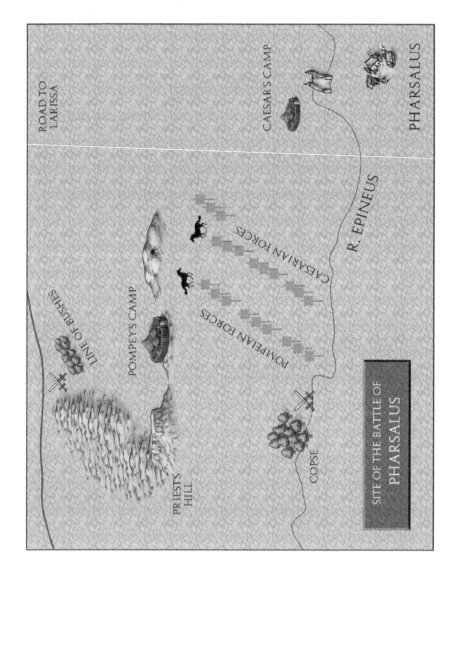

ROAD TO LARISSA

CAESAR'S CAMP

PHARSALUS

R. EPINEUS

CAESARIAN FORCES

POMPEIAN FORCES

LINE OF BUSHES

POMPEY'S CAMP

PRIEST'S HILL

COPSE

SITE OF THE BATTLE OF
PHARSALUS

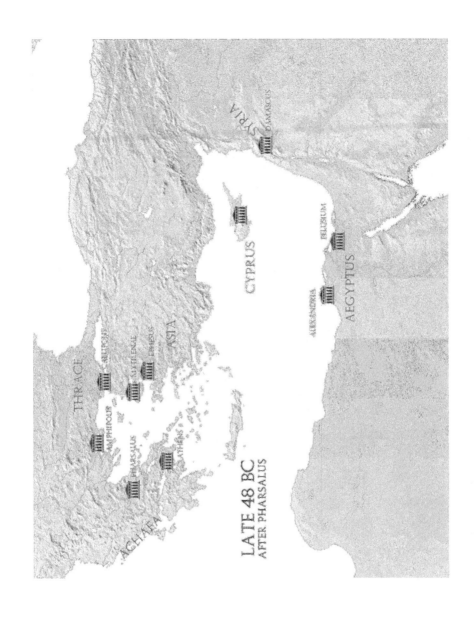

LATE 48 BC
AFTER PHARSALUS

THEBES, AEGYPTUS, WINTER 49 BC

The room was warm and filled with the heady aroma of a dozen expensive spices burning in braziers. In an alcove surrounded by white curtains and gold cords, a leopard rolled over languidly, letting out a stifled rumble of satisfaction, the collar around its neck tinkling as it moved.

A figure approached slowly.

'Your husband has issued orders for the devaluation of coins once more, Majesty, though it is a common belief that this is simply a move to issue new coinage with only his likeness on, removing your noble self.'

The queen turned inscrutable, kohl-rimmed eyes upon the functionary, one of the increasingly few willing to support and serve her in the volatile court. She sighed and shifted in her throne, rearranging the exquisite green chiton that she had ordered from her favourite seamstress in Athens the previous month. She noted the servant's disapproving gaze and made a mental note to have him flogged for such insolence once she was fully in control. So many of the low-born clung to the ways of the people of the black land from ancient times. They should have accepted long ago that they were a conquered people and that they had been under the rule of Macedonian blood for centuries. Ptolemy played to their native style, but then he had always been a vacuous turd.

'My *brother*,' she said acidly, redefining their relationship in a word, 'thinks only in the short term. A solution for now that cripples the future. Do not speak to me of him again. Have you a message from Achillas?'

The functionary shook his head, his eyes meeting hers, displaying doubt in abundance. Yes, a flogging for sure. 'The

1

general has refused your overtures, Majesty. He clings to your husband-brother.'

It was irksome how so many fawned around an ineffectual boy simply because they were more comfortable serving a male fool than a female intellect. This cold war they enjoyed was most certainly warming up.

'What is the latest news of Rome?'

The servant shrugged. How insolent. 'It is said that Caesar is still ascendant, but that his days are numbered. He remains in the capital resolving troubles while his men fail and his armies revolt and fall apart, and while Pompey builds a vast force in the east. The scribes are outside, ready to pen your letters, my queen.'

She nodded, tapping a finger to her chin thoughtfully. 'Tell them to depart for now. This is not yet the time.'

'Your husband is preparing to open negotiations with Pompey. He is of the opinion that showing support for the stronger candidate will pay dividends when their war is over, and, given your father's links with the Roman general...'

'My *brother* is an idiot. It is too early to back a horse in this race, though if I were to do so, I believe I would place my coins on Caesar.'

'Majesty?'

'My brother has no opinion of his own. It is Achillas that favours Pompey and he does so with only a soldier's eye. He sees only Caesar fighting fires in Rome and a large force awaiting him in Greece. But I have watched these men for years. Pompey is clever enough and certainly a strong commander, but Caesar has been trapped, beaten, captured, threatened with legal trouble, and betrayed, and yet who stands in Rome with a senate of his own choosing? The man is watched over by gods. As I am Isis, so he is the grandson of Venus. Yes, Caesar is the one to watch, not Pompey. But I will not ink my pen until we see how this coming spring falls out. Now leave me.'

The functionary bowed low and retreated from the room.

Yes. It was going to be interesting to see how Caesar wriggled out of his latest predicaments, but the queen was certain of one thing. Wriggle out of them, he would.

PART ONE:

TITANS

DYRRACHIUM

48 BC

CHAPTER 1

Rome, 5th December 49 BC

Fronto hurried through the atrium, nodding absently at Hirtius, who stood in tight, hushed conversation with a senator. The dismounted cavalrymen of Aulus Ingenuus' unit standing to either side of the door, looking oddly out of place without their swords and armour, straightened at the sight of the senior officer approaching. Both men's fingers touched the tip of the club at their side, but remained still.

'The general is free?'

One of the men nodded. 'He is, sir. Not in the best of moods, though.'

'I can imagine.' Fronto strode in between them, clacking along the connecting corridor in his nailed boots. With the family still safely out of the way in Tarraco, he had fallen back easily into old military habits, foregoing the soft leather shoes he had taken to wearing in the city. Painted marble faces of the Julii going back a hundred years watched him with frowns of disapproval.

He hurried past them, trying not to feel judged by their implacable features. Yes, the general would be in a bad mood. The news was all over Rome, if only as a dozen vague and often conflicting rumours, yet it seemed certain to be true in basis, if not in the detail. While he visited Caesar, Galronus waited outside, absorbing every new rumour that passed.

The general was seated in his office, wrapped neatly in a purple-bordered toga, worn over the top of a military-cut tunic of plain white. His fingers were drumming on the arm of the curule chair, which was a clear sign of his irritation, even if Fronto hadn't been able to recognise the look on the man's face. His eyes were shadowed with dark circles, too. Caesar slept little anyway, so to acquire this colour, he must barely touch the bed at all before he was back up and working. He was beginning to look slightly unhealthy to Fronto's mind. The sooner he was back out in the open air on a horse, the better. Some men were not born to be inside.

Fronto cleared his throat.

The greatest figure in the republic turned to the new arrival, and Fronto instinctively bowed his head in respectful greeting. His history with the general had had its highs and lows, but no one now could deny the man's greatness. Conqueror of Gaul, restorer of Hispania, master of Rome, but so much more. His consulate, so long sought in Gaul and the reason for crossing the Rubicon last year, had been confirmed. In the new year he would share the consulate with Servilius Vatia Isauricus, a pliable nonentity who owed Caesar much. And more impressive than the consulate even, the senate had voted to make Caesar dictator, a move confirmed by the present consuls, with a remit to restore the republic and repair Rome and Italia following the depredations of the previous year.

Much of that work would be at the root of the general's stress and sleeplessness, and it seemed likely to Fronto that as soon as Caesar could, he would see that remit fulfilled and the position resigned in favour of more pressing matters.

It was all very impressive and, to the average man on the streets of Rome, would seem a full vindication of Caesar and all he had done. Those with more political savvy would remember that any senator who might consider standing against the general had fled with Pompey to the east, and the men who sat in the curia now, white togas like a sea of wool, were each and every one Caesar's creatures, many from his province of Cisalpine Gaul. The senate did what Caesar wanted, for Caesar told the senate what to do. Somewhere deep in his soul, Fronto recognised the danger his old friend posed to the very republic he was serving. Rome would never countenance a king again, but how close could Caesar come before he went too far?

He shook away such thoughts.

'Is it true?' he asked.

The general nodded, lips pressed tight, and Fronto sagged. 'At least we hold Sicilia still,' he said, 'so the east is not closed to the fleets. What were the losses?'

'Total.'

Fronto blew out an explosive breath. 'The African governor must be clever, then, because Curio was no fool.'

'It was blind bad luck by all appearances. From what I understand, Curio located a small Numidian cavalry unit and went for them, only to discover they were merely part of an enormous force. By the time he managed to bring up all his troops they were already in trouble. The governor had him trapped. They were utterly annihilated. A junior tribune escaped with just a handful of men and managed to make it to the coast. He is back on Sicilia where he is requesting reinforcements in case Attius decides to cross the water from Africa and come for him.'

'You turned him down, I presume?'

The general – *The consul? The dictator?* – nodded. 'Attius will be content with his success. Pompey will be pleased with him, and his position is now secure. Crossing and attempting to invade my territory is a whole different proposition. Attius will not leave Africa now unless ordered to do so by his master. Besides, I cannot spare the men.'

'You could send him the Ninth,' Fronto snorted, earning a black look from Caesar.

The Ninth were something of a taboo subject among the staff, and mention of them clearly angered Caesar, though that mattered little given how angry he already was at the odds mounting against him and this latest slew of ill tidings. The Ninth, based at Placentia in the north, had mutinied the previous month over an unpaid bonus the general had promised them. The threat of decimation when Caesar arrived in person had been enough to shock the legion out of their rebellious mood swiftly, though, and in the end the general had confined his punishments to the execution of the twelve men at the root of the mutiny. Now restaffed with loyal officers, the Ninth were once more part of the preparations for the coming year, though their name had been blackened, possibly for good.

And as if the trouble with the Ninth and Curio's defeat in Africa were not source enough for the general's anger, Marcus Antonius had suffered a defeat at the hands of Pompeian troops in Illyricum where he and his brother had been tasked with securing the territory and creating a safe bridgehead for the coming campaign.

It was nothing compared to Curio's heavy losses, but it still made the impending crossing that little bit less certain. With Antonius and his brother on the back foot in Illyricum, Pompey's huge navy was at liberty on the Adriatic Sea.

'The Ninth are at Brundisium with the rest,' Caesar said, leaning back in the chair. 'I am confident that the force gathering there will be adequate to begin pressing Pompey in the coming months. I will not see this struggle with my former colleague extend past another winter. We will find him, trap him, and defeat him in Illyricum. With luck, he will see sense and offer peace when he knows I am coming for him.'

'How many are at Brundisium now?' Fronto had listened with interest at every new report of a unit being sent to the mustering point, wondering when he would be assigned to one of them. With the bulk of the senior officers being in the south and Rome largely the province of politicians, Caesar had ceased his regular briefings for the time being, and all Fronto's information came second-hand from a variety of sources.

'Twelve legions,' the general replied, still tapping his chair arm, 'along with a strong cavalry wing and sundry auxiliaries. My principle fear now is whether we can gather enough ships for the voyage.'

'That and the possibility of running into the enemy fleet mid-crossing,' Fronto added, regretting it instantly. Everyone knew of that potential disaster, and reminding the general of it would only sour his mood further. He glanced back at the doorway. They were more or less alone. The two guards on the door could hear, but the murmur of distant conversation confirmed that other ears were too far away to listen in. He moved close to the general.

'Can we do it?'

Caesar rubbed his temples and sagged back. 'It will not be easy. In fact, everything we have achieved in Gaul and Hispania will feel like a walk in the forum compared with facing Pompey. The man is a lion on the battlefield, and reports suggest that his army already outnumbers us considerably. We are not facing disorganised tribes now, or even the timid and argumentative generals from Spain. In fact these men will be harder to deal with even than the rat Ahenobarbus. The only real advantage we have is that few of their legions are veterans. Most will be raw recruits with little training and discipline, while every man waiting at Brundisium is a trained killer.'

'That and good officers,' Fronto added. 'Curio notwithstanding, I've been looking at the lists of commanders and there is some of the finest military talent in the republic there.'

'And some with Pompey, too. I still lament the defection of Labienus. He had been my right arm for so many years in Gaul, and he knows me well. I do not relish the thought of facing him in battle. Between him and Pompey, we will pay for every foot of ground we take.'

Fronto rolled his shoulders. 'We'll deal with Labienus in due course.' In truth he had even less desire to meet his old friend across the field of battle than did Caesar. 'When we win, what will you do with the officers and men?'

'Disband his legions, settle veterans and incorporate any willing to take the oath into my own forces for now until we have dealt with all other Pompeian armies. Once the old fellow falls into our hands, we shall still have to deal with Attius in Africa and undoubtedly other smaller groups. As for the officers…'

'Yes?'

'They are largely good noble Romans, many of whom I once called friend and who have only been driven to this course by loyalty or patronage to the enemy. Pompey was my *son-in-law*, after all. Safe, quiet retirement, I think, for most. An example will have to be made of a few – the rabid dog Ahenobarbus, for example. But for most, I think they will have lost their claws in defeat. They can be relied upon to sink into obscurity and cause no further trouble for the sake of their family's future.'

Fronto felt a wave of relief wash through him. He'd heard good men among Caesar's advisors advocating a stance of execution without trial or mercy for any rebel officer that fell into Caesar's hands. Fronto had hoped that the general's policy of clemency that had earned him good grace throughout Italia would continue. The bulk of the enemy officers were Romans of principle, who truly believed they were doing the right thing for the republic. Executing them out of hand would have been wrong.

'When do we move to Brundisium? Will you wait until the new year for your consulate first?'

'No. We move in days. I have a few small tasks to complete here under the remit of my dictatorship before I can leave Rome in the hands of Servilius Vatia. There are vast numbers of outstanding loans and creditors across Italia since the outbreak of this war, and I need to have them arbitrated and settled, else we will leave behind a land in a disgruntled mood. Plus I need to restore a few key figures to their former strength since Pompey and his friends whittled away their power. Various small tasks that will set the state upon an even keel once more. Once those things are done I can resign the dictatorship and set my focus on more important business. As soon as possible I intend to ride for Brundisium and join the legions. Pompey has had long enough. He will not expect us to move on him until the spring, so we must make good use of the winter.'

'Which brings me to the question that's been burning for some time,' Fronto said, trying to keep a note of impatience out of his voice.

'Your role in all this?'

He nodded. The general had intimated back in Massilia that he needed Fronto on the battlefield and yet every legion had been assigned an officer and sent to Brundisium while Fronto remained in Rome with a few staff officers and a lot of the general's secretaries and clerks.

The general smiled. 'I could not leave the Ninth in the hands of Caelius Rufus. I have concerns about the man's loyalty, and have decided to leave him in Rome as a magistrate.'

Fronto's spirits sank. The Ninth. Recently rebellious and punished. Wonderful.

Caesar's smile became sly. 'No. Not you. I need someone a little more rigid and humourless in charge of them than you. I cannot afford to allow any leeway for the Ninth until they have redeemed themselves and proved their loyalty once more. I have moved Publius Cornelius Sulla to that role for now. Which means...'

'The Tenth.'

'Yes. In our days in Gaul, the Tenth under you were my strongest legion. They were lucky. I need that strength and fortune again. Take your old legion. And I'm assigning Salvius Cursor as your senior tribune, too.'

Gods, why?

Caesar's eyebrow rose quizzically at the look on Fronto's face. 'I know you and he are not the best of friends, but he *is* effective, and the two of you proved to complement one another well at Massilia. I am sure you will do the same in the coming days. I am not in the business of creating families, but of placing excellent officers in the correct position to maximise their value.'

Fronto nodded, his face twisting with conflicting emotions. Although he had grumbled and complained to his friends about remaining on Caesar's staff and his desire to return to his family, there was a certain satisfaction to be found in the notion that he would be there now until the end, seeing the conclusion of this stupid war and the restoration of the ordered republic. If there were to be heroes made in his generation, this would be the time they were made. And while self-aggrandizement was not a large part of Fronto's soul, he was becoming increasingly conscious of the age and awareness of his boys. His own father had bequeathed him little of which to be proud, and he was determined to leave something of import for the twins. One day they would be the voice of the Falerii in the republic, and it would stand them in good stead if their father had been one of those heroes who had brought peace and order back to the republic. And to be given the Tenth, too. His own veteran legion.

But it was bittersweet. Most of his old comrades in the Tenth were gone. Priscus, Velius, Florus, Fabius, Furius, so many names carved in cold stone. At least there would be Atenos. Carbo had been transferred to the Thirteenth, according to a report Fronto had caught, but the huge, blond, Gallic centurion would still be primus pilus of the Tenth. He would perhaps help keep the unrestrained violence of Salvius Cursor in check until it was time to unleash him.

'You had better put things in order in Rome, Fronto. It would be worth you leaving for Brundisium early. I would like the legion familiar with you by the time I arrive, and without Sulla in charge any more, they are currently under the command of the camp prefect.'

Fronto nodded and excused himself, assuming that to be a dismissal.

Moments later he was back through the corridor, across the atrium and out of Caesar's townhouse. Galronus leaned against the wall opposite, excavating something from his teeth and looking suitably bored.

'Well?' the Remi nudged as Fronto crossed to him and gestured for them to walk. He fell in alongside the Roman, still rummaging in his mouth.

'I'm assigned to the Tenth and sent to Brundisium straight away. We're to embark even in the heart of winter.'

'You had best write to Lucilia.'

'Can you not let her know? You'll have time on your hands.'

Galronus' brow creased. 'She will want to hear from her husband, not his friend. Besides, if you think you're off to face Pompey without me, you're a bigger fool than I thought.'

Fronto huffed. 'We all have our roles to play. I'm Caesar's terrier. You're his iron gauntlet in the senate.'

'I have no intention of sitting in that room full of musty old men telling them what Caesar wants them to do while you march across Greece.'

'Galronus, Caesar will be irked if you leave Rome. He put you in the senate for a reason.'

'Lug's bollocks,' said the Remi with a snort. 'Come on. I need to dig out my sword and lose this stupid wool wrap. How Rome conquered half the world wearing this ridiculous garment, I have no idea.'

Fronto laughed. 'He'll he extremely peeved with you when he gets to Brundisium.'

'Let him be peeved. He knows how useful I can be.'

* * *

Brundisium

'Reminds me of the old days,' Galronus said with a smile, peering at the huge mass of men and tents ahead, corrals of horses, of pack beasts, of cattle and goats, splayed out like a vast temporary city before the walls of the city.

'Reminds me of the last time we were here,' Fronto said sourly. 'So close to stopping Pompey's flight I could almost see his bare arse as he ran. If we'd caught him at Brundisium it would all have been over last year.'

Galronus rolled his eyes at his friend's gloomy appraisal and continued along the road. The pickets at the periphery of the massive camp were polite but firm in preventing access without the day's watchword, and a summoned centurion took note of the baton of command and accepted Fronto's sealed scroll case containing Caesar's orders.

'Apologies, Legate,' the man said with deferential determination, 'you will understand I'm sure that Pompey may well still have men in Italia, and we have to be extremely careful with security.'

Fronto nodded and they rode on into the camp. A few yards out of earshot, he snorted. 'Security. I know they have to look like they're trying, but I can guarantee that Pompey has at least a dozen pairs of eyes and ears in this camp. We don't have that luxury, of course, as most of his legions are new-raised in Illyricum, and the rest departed before we arrived here. But Pompey's wily enough to have left plenty of men behind to infiltrate this force, and even though we're commandeering every vessel that can transport troops, odd little boats will be crossing with intelligence all the time.'

Two legionaries and an optio discussing some matter on the main road hurried out of the way as the new arrivals rode towards them, and Fronto slowed.

'Where can I find the Tenth, soldier, and where is the current headquarters of the staff?'

The optio gestured off to the left. 'The Tenth are on the shore of the northern harbour, sir, and the headquarters is in the city, by the port. Can't miss it, as it has Caesar's flag all over it.'

'Thank you.'

They rode on between the massed lines of legionary tents, each one made to hold eight people. Fronto lost count of the number of grass streets between them, let alone tents. The vexilla of four different legions were visible from the road alone. He kept an eye out for anyone he recognised, but there was little chance of spotting a friend in this sea of humanity.

'Where first?' Galronus muttered, pointing to a wider avenue leading towards the northern branch of the harbour where the Tenth would be quartered.

'Command, first. Confirm our positions, catch up with the latest news and see who's about. And I want to have a look at the fleet they've gathered. You know how much I love the sea. I want a big, steady boat.'

'Ship.'

'Whatever.'

Their orders were checked once more at the gate to the city, the centurion displaying just as careful and officious a manner as the picket officer. Once inside, Galronus noted with a smile how both men had accepted Fronto's orders but neither had questioned his companion, who was not mentioned in them.

Brundisium was an ancient town full of tightly packed housing, but over the years of Roman rule it had gradually changed to display a more grid-like street plan, so finding the forum and then the port was not difficult. He had been to Brundisium once, a year earlier, and on that occasion had only passed inside the walls on one occasion. The place seemed remarkably well-ordered, given that twelve legions had been billeted here.

The headquarters building was every bit as easy to identify as they'd been led to believe. Facing the port, it was a large building, probably something to do with the city's council. Three gigantic red banners hung from the eaves of the building, each displaying Caesar's bull emblem in gold, and two legionaries stood on guard at the main door. Fronto began to make for it, though his eyes strayed across the vessels moored at the port and he frowned.

'I thought a fleet was gathering. This looks more like a fishing expedition.'

Galronus nodded. 'Not a lot of room aboard that lot.'

Fronto could not easily count the ships, as they were moored several deep, with more anchored in the centre of the harbour. Numerically there might be as many ships as he'd expected to see in a fleet for an army this size, but the majority of them were small traders and working boats, and only half a dozen large warships sat among them. They were clearly inadequate for the task, even at first glance.

14

Moments later they had left their horses hitched at a rail outside with a soldier tending to them, and were striding into the main room of the headquarters. Half a dozen senior officers were present, discussing matters, poring over maps and lists, but one figure at the desk in the centre rose and smiled at the sight of them.

'Brutus,' Fronto said warmly, striding over to clasp the man's hand. 'Thank the gods. Can you explain the fleet?'

'And hello to you too,' Brutus replied with a half-smile. 'Explain?'

'Caesar told me he was gathering a fleet here to take us to Illyricum. He didn't say *you* were here, but I should have assumed. How are you planning to fit this army on those paltry ships?'

Brutus sagged. 'It's a problem. And I anticipate only half a dozen more arriving before Caesar is here and wanting to leave.'

'Where are all the big ships?'

Brutus glanced momentarily towards the window. 'Greece and Illyricum. Pompey took every ship he could find when he left last year. There aren't many in this entire region. Half the ones you see out there have come a hundred miles. We set a minimum size limit, and most ships above it are with Pompey. His navy is reportedly enormous.'

'What of Caesar's fleets in the west?'

'Fronto, they're busy. Squadrons assigned to Hispania to keep things settled there, some at Sicilia. Others guarding the grain shipments. Very few are coming through the straits below Sicilia for fear that the governor of Africa will sink them as they try. He has a small fleet of his own. All we have is what we can gather from the eastern Italian coast.'

Galronus leaned in. 'Could you not have built ships? You had twelve built in thirty days at Massilia.'

Brutus nodded. 'With adequate supplies and skills, we did. There we had shipyards, veteran sailors and shipbuilders and everything we needed, including good wood. Here we have nothing. Before Pompey's force departed they ravaged the area. The shipyards are bare. All equipment was taken with them, and it appears he took every able bodied shipbuilder with him too. The man might have run, but he was thorough in doing so. He took everything he needed to build and maintain and left us nothing. It would take months to bring in the manpower and equipment and

15

put the shipyards to rights. We don't have that time. Caesar wants to sail while there's still frost on the world.'

Fronto nodded gloomily.

'So,' Brutus sighed, 'all we can do is load on as many troops as we can and take them blindly into a sea patrolled by a vast enemy navy, then have them return and repeat the journey as many times as necessary to transport the army.'

'Joy abounds,' Fronto said with a sour face. 'I'm beginning to dislike Brundisium.'

'On a brighter note, you're here to command the Tenth?'

Fronto nodded.

'And Galronus? The cavalry?'

'We're not quite sure yet. He's supposed to be in the senate battering senators into line, but doesn't want to miss the fun.'

Brutus laughed. 'Caesar will be pleased. Anyway, I suggest you head to your command and then join me and the others for the evening meal and we can tell you all, while you can update us on what's happening in Rome.'

A quarter of an hour later, Fronto and Galronus emerged from the city gate once more and angled to the north. The camp of the Tenth was well-ordered and Fronto nodded with satisfaction. Offering the password that he'd been given at the port, they were admitted to the camp and made for the headquarters.

The large, rigid tent was dimly-lit with two oil lamps, and as Fronto stepped inside he had to take a moment to allow his eyes to adjust.

Lucius Salvius Cursor rose from behind the desk with a stiff, formal salute.

'Legate. Welcome to Brundisium.'

Fronto returned the gesture with a vague wave of the hand. 'Shitty to be here. Have you been in camp long? What's the state of the legion, and who're the senior officers?'

Salvius Cursor drummed his fingers on the desk below him. 'I arrived two days ago to find the legion in good condition. Current manpower is considerably below the mark, as expected, with a total headcount of three thousand eight hundred and twenty seven men and officers, and a little over thirty of those on the sick list. I have put in for extra men from command, and Domitius Calvinus has consented to a reserve of four hundred men for the Tenth. Senior centurion is Atenos, other than that, the cavalry commander and the junior tribunes are all new arrivals from Rome who I do not know. Their names are written down in the ledger there. I hereby relinquish command of the Tenth to you. What are your orders.'

'Gods, man, but you're bloody stiff.' Fronto rolled his eyes. 'Let's get something straight, Salvius. If we're going to command the Tenth, we need to be seen to be in concert at all times. If you ever feel the need for one of your violent little outbursts, you need to hold it in until we're alone. If you'll extend me that courtesy, then I'll treat you like a trusted second at all times. Do we have a deal?'

Salvius Cursor saluted with a nod.

'Good. As for orders, I have no intention of running anything until I have had a meal, a bath, and a night's sleep. But if you really need something to do, find whoever is in charge of assigning ships and secure the biggest, most stable one for the Tenth and her officers. If we're going to sail blindly out into a sea filled with enemy warships, I'd rather not be in a small fishing boat.'

As Salvius Cursor returned to his work, Fronto and Galronus exited the tent once more and paused in the afternoon light, looking around them.

'I might have wanted to return to the family,' he said, 'and the gods know I'm not looking forwards to seeing so many Romans butchering one another, but nothing feels like home quite so much as standing in the middle of the Tenth.'

Home.

CHAPTER 2

Mare Adriaticum, 5ᵗʰ Januarius 48 BC

The sea-sickness was like an old friend – albeit an unwanted and fairly unpleasant one – compared with Fronto's main worry. The fleet, a grand moniker that hardly did the ragtag flotilla justice, had embarked the previous day at Brundisium, after Caesar had left as long as he dared for further vessels to arrive. In the end some fifteen thousand legionaries and five hundred cavalry were crammed aboard, featuring vexillations from seven different legions.

The overnight journey had been one of the tensest times in Fronto's life, though at least the constant anxiety had left him little time to bother about the contents of his stomach and their repeated casting over the side of the ship. In the fleet of mostly wide and shallow mercantile vessels, only twelve warships had been summoned and most of those were smaller examples, only four having an upper deck. A paltry escort for a cargo of this size and importance.

There had been a freezing fog when they departed. The officers had bandied about a number of opinions over the wisdom of the timing. There was, for a start, the distinct possibility of collisions in the thick mist; then they would have very little warning if they bumped into an enemy ship, and keeping on course would be extremely difficult, too. On the other hand, the sea would be at least as troublesome for Pompey's vast fleet, and the fog would hide Caesar's crossing well. It was a toss of the coin whether the decision was good or bad, but it was made anyway by the general, and Fronto had stood at the rail with ever-watchful eyes in a green face as they set sail.

That day had been terrifying. Every man on every ship had been silent and subdued, the dense fog suppressing what little sound there was. All Fronto had heard for hours was the creak of wood, the splash of water around the hull and the occasional low commands and calls from the crew. Sometime after noon, the fog began to dissipate, leaving thousands of men soaked through and freezing. The rest of the day was not much of an improvement. With the fog lifted, they could see many miles across the open water, which meant that any passing trireme of Pompey's could do the same. The journey was a two-day sail and until they were within sight of the Illyrian coast, should they be spotted, there was a good chance that they would find themselves surrounded by a vastly superior fleet long before they disembarked.

Every eye watched the horizon unceasingly. Gods were beseeched, meals eaten with sullen silence. Always the creaking and splashing. Yet despite the collective nerves, the afternoon brought only empty sea, and as darkness fell Fronto had expected to feel relieved. He did not.

Each ship was obliged to hang a lantern at the prow, the stern, and amidships at intervals, so that collisions in the darkness could be avoided. While that helpfully prevented the Caesarian fleet from shifting and crashing into one another, it would also make them visible for miles, like a huge swarm of fireflies just above the water's surface.

Few men slept that night for more than an hour, and those who did slept badly. Still, it seemed Fortuna, Mars and Neptune were all with them, for they passed that long, nervous night safe and unmolested.

The morning brought clear open seas and icy air, and once more every eye studied the horizon.

To Fronto's knowledge the first time a soldier had laughed or raised his voice happened after noon on the second day when the call went out from the lead ship that land had been spotted. At first Fronto thought they must be dreadfully off course, as he peered myopically at the coastline approaching at speed. He'd assumed they would be making for one the large ports. He'd heard the names Apollonia and Dyrrachium tossed about in briefings, though he'd been only half-listening to the plans for the landing. It was the journey and the stages that followed disembarkation that he was focused upon: puking and fighting.

Instead of one of the great port cities of Illyricum, what faced them on this foreign coast was a line of high, green hills, dotted with small signs of life, bordered by a stunning beach of white sand that stretched more than a mile in each direction.

It took four hours to disembark the army onto that stretch of white beach, using rowing boats to ferry men from the larger ships that could not come too close for fear of becoming grounded, and the afternoon was already acquiring a tint of dusk when the full force was ashore. Once the Tenth, or at least the thousand men drawn from the Tenth on that trip, were all ashore, Salvius had them form up. The sense of relief was palpable. Every man had at least half expected to be attacked and drowned on the journey, yet here they were on a deserted beach under a chilly winter late afternoon sun.

Fronto was inspecting his men, checking for signs of illness or trouble after the crossing, when a call went up from one of the scouts at the edge of the landing site. The entire beach leapt to action, centurions shouting and whistles blowing before it became apparent that the force the watchman had sighted was friendly. Such was the trouble with a civil war: being certain who was who.

The exploratory army relaxed at the news and fell back into their formations awaiting further orders as a small cavalry force emerged through the greenery at the edge of the beach and began to plod across the white sand towards the small knot of senior officers. Fronto left the Tenth to Salvius and Atenos, who was busy berating a legionary, apparently for not being perfect, and hurried across to the staff. He smiled at the sight of the column of horsemen. They showed signs of hardship, wounds evident and eyes rimmed with tired red, but they looked strong and confident regardless, and none more so than the officer at their head: Marcus Antonius.

'Well met, Caesar,' he said wearily as he slipped from his horse's back and handed the reins to one of his men, stamping his feet in the soft sand.

'Antonius. Ill tidings still?'

'Mixed, in truth. We have suffered several small defeats in trying to clear out Pompeian forces and secure the Illyrian coast. Only small sections are under our control. My brother was forced to surrender an entire army at Curicta following betrayal by one of his officers – Titus Pullo, no less. One of your old heroes from Gaul, the treacherous bastard. We still have small forces here and there, but nothing like this. Thank the gods you're here and we can turn things around.'

'That doesn't sound very mixed,' Fronto huffed.

'On the bright side,' Antonius said, 'you've got here safely and now we have a chance. The local section of Pompey's fleet is split. The nearest grouping is at Oricum about twenty miles north, but round a huge headland, and they're of little or no use. Rufus and Vespillo seem to be terrified of the Adriatic in winter. They've eighteen ships that haven't been out of port in months. The main force is with Bibulus at Corcyra about thirty or forty miles south, but he's had his ships all over the place and his crews on shore leave. News of your fleet sighted out at sea spread pretty quick, but it'll take Bibulus a while to gather his fleet together.'

'Will we have time to send the ships back to Brundisium?' Brutus put in. 'The rest of the army awaits collection there.'

Antonius shrugged. 'It's a guessing game. If Bibulus waits long enough to gather his full fleet you'll have time. If he just put to sea with whatever ships he had in port as soon as you were sighted, he could already be just around the next headland, and would probably still have enough ships to stop you. Bibulus is a dangerous one. A nasty piece of work.'

Caesar nodded slowly. 'I remember him well. We served as aediles together and the man blocked and vetoed my every move. He has been at worst an enemy, but at best a thorn in my side for decades. We need to get the ships back out to open sea fast and gone to Brundisium before the enemy arrives. And if we bring the men inland, that fleet will not be able to pin us down. Brutus? I need you to take the ships back to Brundisium. Antonius, you go too. You are my eyes, ears and fist. Bring me my army.'

The two officers nodded their acceptance.

'Calenus?'

The staff officer turned in surprise from where he'd been discussing pickets with a tribune. 'General?'

'Take two hundred of our best men as marines. Split them between the warships of Antonius and Brutus and make sure they get back to Brundisium safely. There is always the possibility of bumping into a lone enemy trireme who might try their luck, and despite Pompey's great achievement, we all know that he didn't *completely* clear the seas of pirates. A poorly defended convoy of merchant vessels will look attractive.'

Fufius Calenus saluted and began to give orders to his men, then he and Brutus rushed off to begin preparations with the fleet, who had been preparing to anchor until first light.

Antonius snorted. 'I was hoping to have a bath and a hot meal before anything else. I shall have to make do with a damp cloth and a jar of Chian.'

'The day a single jar of wine lasts you, the gods will end the world,' Caesar said flatly. 'What news of Pompey, other than his fleets?'

Antonius pursed his lips. 'There are two main winter quarters on the coast, both currently defended. Both have enough forces that we've not tried to break them, and I think they would even stand against this lot, though things will change when the rest get here. That's Apollonia and Dyrrachium. Pompey himself, with the bulk of his army, has been off inland, in Macedonia, though there are reports that he's headed back this way. I would say you've got sufficient force now to take Oricum, or one of the smaller cities in the area. Perhaps we can take command of the local towns, but it's not worth trying for Apollonia or Dyrrachium until I return with the reserves.'

'With luck you can bring the rest of the army over unmolested and we can dig in before Pompey gets here. If we can create a strong bridgehead, maybe with these towns of which you speak, perhaps we can wrest control of the region from him and force him back.'

'Perhaps,' Antonius replied, 'but one thing I've learned out here is never to rely on a plan working out.'

With that, Antonius clasped Caesar's hand and strode away towards Brutus and Calenus. The ships were already beginning to come about with some difficulty. Acilius, one of the staff loitering nearby, cleared his throat. 'The wind is coming in off the sea, General, and it's picking up. There's a storm in the offing, and even now there will be an adverse wind for departure. And we're already starting to lose the light. I wonder if it might be better to wait until morning?'

Caesar's jaw twitched slightly. 'And if Bibulus arrives with two score heavy warships before then? Then we shall have a beach full of kindling and no way to bring across the rest of the army. No, they must depart now and move with all speed.' He turned and addressed the officers in general. 'Have all your forces move from the beach up to better ground and fortify for the night. We shall set up signal stations on the shore's highest points, and there we shall await the rest of the army. For myself, I want to find the best viewpoint to watch proceedings.'

Fronto left them to it and strode back to the Tenth. Salvius Cursor was busily berating someone for the quality of their kit, which earned Fronto's rare approval, and so the legate singled out Atenos, waving him over. 'Have the Tenth move up into the hills behind the beach and settle in for the night. Have a fence of wattle put up if you can manage it but dig in however you can. Get moving straight away, because seven legions will be on their way looking for the best position and I don't want the Tenth camped in the latrine because we were late to the party.'

Atenos grinned. 'I'll have this lot in place by the time you can say "bollocks", sir'

Fronto chuckled as the primus pilus turned and gestured to the men of the Tenth.

'Listen up, the lot of you. We're heading for that hill up there,' he pointed to a nice, flat-topped hill a thousand paces or so from the sand. 'And I want to be camped there before another legion finds it. The first man up there gets a jar of wine. The last gets a week's latrine duty.'

There was a murmur among the men and Atenos waved his hands. 'What are you waiting for?'

With sudden shouts the legionaries burst into life, their centurions alongside as they broke all formation and began running for the greenery behind the beach in eight-man units at best. Salvius Cursor turned to Atenos and Fronto. 'Poor discipline. What if they are ambushed?'

Fronto shrugged. 'Scouts have been crawling around those hills for the last four hours. If they were dangerous we'd know by now. If you're so concerned, go with them.'

Atenos saluted and jogged off after his men. Salvius threw his commander a last, bitter, disapproving look, then followed. Fronto smiled at the rest of the units moving off the beach in an orderly manner. All well and good, but someone there would end up

24

camped on a thirty degree slope among prickly plants. Not the Tenth. Leaving it all to Atenos and Salvius, he turned and made for the small corral of officers' horses, where an equisio was busy brushing down Bucephalus. He could see Caesar and a few of the others already mounted and heading off the beach towards a high spur to the north that should grant a commanding view of the coast in both directions.

Retrieving his ageing black horse and mounting with only a couple of groans, Fronto walked him off along the beach after the officers. It took almost half an hour to reach the vantage point, where two of the legions' scouts were already in position. Dismounting and handing over the reins to a legionary who tethered the mounts, the small knot of nine officers moved to a high, flat rocky outcrop that jutted from the bushes and trees. The view was excellent. To the north, the beach swiftly petered out and became a rocky shoreline, with the hills dropping right down to the water's edge. To the south, the sands stretched some three miles before disappearing around a promontory, the next bay and headland just visible in the failing light. The beach was all-but empty now, a few small units busy there, but the bulk of the legions busy setting up camp in the hills behind.

The wind blowing in off the Adriaticum was cold and becoming stronger all the time, and was considerably more noticeable up here in such an exposed location. Fronto turned to look out to sea. The fleet was a mess. Not through lack of command ability, for certain with Brutus on board. But with such a disparate group of vessels of different sizes and capabilities, it was almost impossible to keep them working in concert. Some of the vessels were designed to rely on wind in the sails far more than any oars, and with an adverse breeze blowing in off the sea, they were having some difficulty making headway. Despite Caesar's persuasive argument, Fronto was beginning to think that Acilius had been right in advocating a delay.

Something ruffled the hairs on the back of his neck and he shivered. He knew something was wrong even before the call went up, and was already moving forwards, his eyes raking the sea's surface.

'Ships sighted,' bellowed one of the legionaries on sentry duty, pointing away to the south.

The man had damn good eyes. Fronto took some time to locate them, but when he did, a cold stone of certainty settled in his belly. Disaster was about to strike. Even as he peered into the distant evening light he could see more and more of them. Perhaps fifty ships, perhaps even more. All good, strong and well-equipped warships, too. Bibulus' fleet. The ragtag flotilla leaving the beach stood no chance, even with the dozen warships escorting them. It was like watching a pack of wolves racing towards a panicked flock of sheep.

'Can they make it?' Caesar breathed.

Acilius, apparently a man with some naval experience, sucked in cold air through his teeth. 'No, Caesar. Perhaps the fastest and strongest will be able to outpace them and make it to the relative safety of open sea. The slower ones are doomed.'

Fronto nodded unhappily, watching the disaster unfold. The commanders of the fleet had clearly come to the same conclusion. At an unheard command, far out to sea, the twelve warships and the fastest of the civilian fleet began to pick up pace, abandoning the slower ships. The flotilla resembled a frayed rope giving and then breaking. The lead vessels raced away, making for the dark waters of open sea, risking sailing without lights, which would increase the danger of collisions, but make them much more difficult to spot at a distance in the fading light.

The nearest, slowest vessels clearly decided they could not make it out to sea and would be prey to the enemy. Some dithered in open water, still heading west, but too slow, too late. Others were turning, but again indecisively and far too slow. Bibulus' fleet was cutting through the water like a sharp knife at an astonishing speed. A small collection of ships were making for the beach now, a large group out to sea and rapidly disappearing, a few unable to either race away fast enough or retreat in time. They were clearly lost.

Fronto performed a quick count. Twelve ships were coming for the beach and would probably make it. Surprisingly, one of those was a small, fast warship, a liburnian that could quite reasonably have made it out to sea, but had decided to herd the vessels back to land like a sheepdog. Even as Fronto watched, the small, fast warship closed on two of the dithering vessels and there was a brief exchange, following which both began to race for the beach, jettisoning anything they could to lighten the vessels and speed them up. So, perhaps fourteen ships would make it back to the beach. Twenty or thirty were in the dangerous area and easy prey for Bibulus – it was hard to take a true count with the way they milled about in panic and passed one another. All had now decided that the beach was their only chance and were coming about and making for the coast, but it was too late. They would never make it. The only positive was that the numbers Fronto counted meant that more than fifty vessels must have made it out to sea.

Tense, he watched the pack of sea wolves bearing down on their prey. For good or ill, Bibulus had focused on the easy target. His entire fleet had set a tangential course that would bring them straight to that gaggle of ships that would never reach the beach in time. Fronto threw up a quick prayer that the enemy and the sea god would both show mercy, for those ships would all fall. Yet in doing so, they had bought time for the rest, a small flotilla returning to the beach and a larger fleet out in the dark sea, racing into the safety of night and open water.

Fronto kept his eyes on the ships as the enemy triremes closed. With a sinking, disgusted feeling, he saw golden flame beginning to spring up among the Pompeian fleet. A moment later fiery missiles began to arc through the air as the lead ships closed on the doomed vessels. The first shots fell short, but Bibulus knew what he was doing. His fleet began to fan out into a wide front, and bow-mounted artillery joined a myriad of archers launching burning matter at the Caesarian ships.

The arrows and bolts and jars of pitch began to strike timber, and instantly the beleaguered merchant ships caught fire. Fronto watched, sick, as men leapt from burning vessels into the water. Seemingly heedless of the danger they too faced from the flames, the lead ships of Bibulus' fleet picked up their pace, racing into the doomed vessels at ramming speed. Smaller, flaming ships were smashed in two by the large military ones which continued to launch their missiles at the remaining vessels. Men in the water would be being battered by floundering hulls and smashed into by enemy warships in for the kill, and any sailor who'd jumped overboard and survived the immediate clash would inevitably die anyway. It was Januarius and the water was almost ice. No man could last long enough in that sea to make it to shore. Every soul on those thirty ships would die, either by fire, drowning, freezing or a deadly flaming iron point.

'I will see Bibulus die for this,' Caesar said quietly, and Fronto and the others nodded as one. Caesar was renowned for his clemency, but there were times when mercy had to be pushed aside in favour of justice. The Pompeian fleet could easily have captured those vessels and taken their crew. Even if they had no use for them, they could have scuttled them and saved the men. Instead, Bibulus had charged in with the clear intent to kill and destroy everything in his path. Did the man not remember that these too were Romans he was killing?

This was precisely the sort of thing Fronto had anticipated after Massilia and which had led him to the initial decision to retire once more. He'd agreed, under duress, to serve for another year, and had almost fallen into the trap of the comfortable military life once he'd been back with the Tenth. Now, watching Roman sailors burned, crushed and drowned by other Roman sailors, the sickness of it all came back in wrenching waves.

Thirty or so ships were now little more than burning kindling in the water, the enemy vessels circling them and adding to the carnage whenever they spotted a survivor. There was no sign of the escaping ships that had made it out to sea. At least one of the senior officers would have been aboard them. And another fourteen vessels were even now pulling up onto the beach, grounding themselves as their crews leapt ashore and raced for the perceived safety of the hills and the military camps therein.

'Once Bibulus has been made to pay, though,' Fronto said quietly, 'we need to make a last attempt to end this all with words. What's just happened down there is like a bar fight compared with what's coming on land. If we can avoid the slaughter of thousands and thousands of Roman lives, it's our duty to do just that.'

Caesar nodded seriously. 'Quite so, Fronto. But not at the expense of laying bare our belly to Pompey and handing him the knife.'

Men were rushing across the beach now and Fronto could just, in the dim light, make out two senior officers with a troop of legionaries having left the liburnian, hurrying towards the high place where the officers stood watching.

'Who, do you suppose?'

'Calenus and Brutus,' Caesar said quietly.

'Why not Marcus Antonius?' Fronto replied.

'Because Calenus would have accompanied one of the others, so one must be him, and Brutus is always concerned about his charges. Only Brutus would have chosen to stay when he could have run, and help the rest reach safety. And you know Antonius. The moment a decision had to be made, he would focus on pushing forwards, his eyes set on Brundisium and the rest of the army. No, that was the work of Brutus and Calenus, bringing back what they could to safety, and the vision of Antonius forging out into the darkness.'

Fronto nodded. There was no denying that summary of the two men. The burning wreckage of the ships was now beginning to thin out as what remained sank beneath the icy surface, joining the bodies of the frozen crewmen. Bibulus and his commanders seemed to have decided that there was no further use in hanging about with the wrecks and already the fleet was moving off. Fronto half expected them to close on the beach and attempt to fire the ships that had escaped, but they did not, presumably nervous about the forces already on land and what might happen to the ships if they came too close to a shore controlled by Caesar. Similarly, they made no attempt to race off into the growing dark in search of the ships Antonius was taking back to Italia. The captains, once safely out of sight, would have drawn the fleet together and performed several course changes, making it almost impossible to track them across the water. They were safe unless they happened to bump into trouble by accident.

'Looks like we're in for a long stay,' Acilius said quietly as the enemy fleet split up and began to disperse both north and south, a few vessels seeking good position in the locale.

'What?' Fronto muttered.

'They're not leaving. They're moving into blockade position.'

'What?'

'With a fleet like that he can control the water all the way from Pietas in the north to Buthrotum in the south, especially when he retrieves the other vessels under his command. Antonius suggested this was just the ones he could get his hands on immediately. With perhaps double this fleet or maybe more, he could stop anything

29

coming in or going out for well over a hundred miles, plenty more if he stretched himself.'

Fronto shivered. 'Could he stop the reserves getting through?'

'Without a doubt. There will be few warships among them, even if extras have been found. With the pride of Pompey's navy here, we might just be on our own from now on.'

'You paint a bleak picture, Acilius,' Caesar said quietly.

'Apologies, Caesar. Staius Murcus and myself both served in Pompey's navy against the pirates of the east some twenty years ago. We were only young men then, but I doubt there are two men in your army who know Pompey's navy as well as we do.'

'Congratulations, Acilius,' Caesar said with an iron-hard expression. 'You just bought yourself and Murcus the command of the Illyrian shore. If Bibulus thinks he can pen us in and keep the reserves out, then let's besiege him at sea. See how long his fleet can last if they cannot put to shore for food and fresh water. See to it that the land is denied him all along the coast.'

Acilius grinned. 'A pleasure, General.'

'Won't he just resupply from one of his cities? Dyrrachium, for instance?'

Caesar nodded. 'Dyrrachium in particular is a thorn in the side. Taking it would be advantageous. But for now, if Bibulus truly has that sizeable a fleet, supplying it from a city via merchant ships will be a slow and laborious business. I think his ships will go hungry and thirsty much faster than he will be able to supply them.'

'Can we take Dyrrachium with the men we have?' Publius Cornelius Sulla asked quietly.

'Perhaps. But we are not ready for it, and we have no siege equipment, and Antonius seemed to think not. Besides, Pompey is on the way there with his army. And if there is any hope of securing a peace with the man, taking his winter quarters out from under his nose will shatter that hope. I think... I think we need to meet Pompey in open ground and neither of us atop the walls of Dyrrachium. It's time to send him a message.'

He turned from the scenes below, full of purpose.

'Find me Lucius Vibullius Rufus.'

CHAPTER 3

Illyricum, Martius 48 BC

'Still nothing?'

Fronto turned to see Galronus strolling up the path to the now well-worn lookout point. He shook his head. Of course there was nothing, he thought irritably. He came here every morning in the hope of discovering something that might change the situation, yet met with only empty sea and disappointment each time. Not *empty* sea, he corrected himself. *Empty* sea would bear hope. This was a sea dotted with powerful ships, just not the ones Caesar's army longed to see.

After the initial rush to command a position on the shore and the disaster with the returning fleet, everything had come to a stop.

With just fifteen thousand men, a fraction of the number they had commanded in Gaul, it would be foolhardy and extremely dangerous to begin prosecuting any kind of major action. The hotter heads among the staff – and Salvius Cursor too, of course – advocated moving in an attempt to take Dyrrachium or Apollonia, the two city-fortresses that still dominated the coast in favour of Pompey. Fifteen thousand men, though, was not enough to besiege such a great city with any real effectiveness, especially when the defenders could be resupplied easily by sea. At least in the siege of Massilia they'd had Brutus' fleet to blockade. Here it was Pompey's ships that created a cordon all along the Illyrian coast, effectively sealing the Caesarian army in and preventing any hope of reinforcement.

Bastards.

Two months.

Two months with no sign of Antonius and the rest of the army. No news had come from the west. Had Antonius made it back across the Adriaticum? Had he met with disaster from pirates or storms or even more of Pompey's seemingly endless navy? If he *had* reached Brundisium, had he been unable to gather enough ships to bring the men across? Given Pompey's blockade it would be an ill-judged move to attempt a breakthrough for the sake of just a few men. It would have to be the rest of the army to make it worthwhile.

And that army had not come.

There had been a report early on, while the officers were still making initial plans, that a Caesarian ship had limped into the harbour at Oricum and there been burned by the Pompeian garrison, but it seemed unlikely. Why would one ship come alone and, if it did, why would it attempt to put to port in an enemy stronghold?

The army had not arrived, and with the relatively meagre numbers at Caesar's command there was no point in trying for one of the coastal strongholds. The forces here and there left from the army Antonius and his brother had brought across the sea last year were few enough that they'd barely hold a bridge, let alone fight a full campaign. No, without the rest of the army from Brundisium, Pompey's fortresses were safe and Caesar was incapable of securing the solid bridgehead he needed to face Pompey.

Which was not to say they had done *nothing* in those two months of misery, or that nothing else had changed. Indeed, Acilius and Murcus, with six thousand men drawn from the Tenth and Ninth, had denied the enemy fleet any stretch of coast for countless miles, and the ships guarding the shore were beginning to starve. Fronto had watched from this high point over the days as merchant vessels from Dyrrachium and Apollonia had come and gone carrying supplies, but even Apollonia was a day's sail from here, and the main source of supplies – Dyrrachium – was several days further. Acilius had estimated the volume of supplies being delivered by each ship and their frequency and had announced with satisfaction that at best the Pompeian ships were on quarter rations, and even then probably some vessels were getting nothing at all. Pompey's fleet may have them guarded and penned in, but it was the ships that were under siege, starving and weak. On land, though, rations were running low too, and soon Caesar's legions would join those poor sailors in starvation unless they could secure a supply route or adequate local sources of food. But while that was a looming worry for the invaders in the coming days, the fleet were hungry now, and already getting desperate. A few small engagements had broken out where desperate Pompeian ships had tried to land and resupply despite the legionaries dug in and waiting for them. Each attempt had ended in disaster for the sailors.

The fleet was beginning to weaken. When Antonius came, *if* Antonius came, he would at least have a chance of breaking through to the coast.

And despite their inability to take on either of the great coastal bastions, once the forces were distributed and plans laid, Caesar had moved decisively. Leaving Acilius and Murcus with their men to hold the coastline, the general had marched on the lesser, more local port of Oricum and taken it without a wound inflicted or received. The capture of Oricum gave the army a secure local region from which to work, and so Caesar had begun a campaign of conquest through fear and respect rather than blood and steel, much as he'd done in Italia the previous year. By the time the first month had passed, cities began to change allegiance through fear of Caesar, or possibly hope of being freed from Pompey's control. Not the important cities, which remained Pompey's coastal fortresses and granaries, but smaller cities here and there. First came Salonae, north along the coast, way past the danger zone. Salonae declared for Caesar, earning a chastisement from the local Pompeian forces, who besieged that ancient city but were routed and forced to flee. Byllis, Amantia, Antipatria, and numerous other cities of which Fronto could not remember the name all declared for Caesar.

Still not the critical coastal fortresses, though. And it would make only a small difference in the grand scheme of things controlling Illyrian regions if the fleet still secured the coast and the twin bastions of Pompey's power here remained untouched. No matter how many towns declared for Caesar, if Pompey arrived with his full force and Antonius had not brought across the reserves, they would be crushed. Much relied on those two great cities.

Apollonia was something of a problem, for there would be no controlling the Apsus River without holding that fortress, but Dyrrachium was worse. Well-manned and well-stocked, supplying the ships even as Caesar's legionaries began to starve on the beach,

Dyrrachium was an ancient fastness on the coast that would be harder to crack than a marble egg.

In an attempt to tip the scales and persuade Pompey's great bulwarks to see sense, Caesar had now taken seven thousand men south along the coast to the cities of Buthrotum and Phoinike. With Salonae and the north now for Caesar, if the south could be nudged that way, then things would look worrying in Dyrrachium. Even that great bulwark of Pompeian power might start to dance to a different tune if the whole Illyrian coast except them were Caesar's. Especially since Pompey had yet to put in an appearance. Perhaps it could still be ended without a fight.

Briefly, Fronto wondered what had happened to Vibullius Rufus. Caesar's chosen ambassador had been a Pompeian officer in the early days. He had stood against them at Corfinium and been one of those magnanimously pardoned by Caesar. He had the perfect credentials for carrying an overture to the enemy commander, and had set off the day after they landed with a small cavalry unit, making for the reported location of Pompey's force in the mountains some sixty miles east. His message was a last hope, a last attempt, at peace. An offer that both commanders stand down their forces and return to Rome to allow the senate to settle the affair in court rather than on the battlefield. There was little chance of Pompey submitting to a senate that owed everything to Caesar, of course, but slim chance had to be better than none. And there would be important influential men in Pompey's retinue that would see any refusal as Pompey's desire to waste Roman blood rather than confer with Caesar. A typically shrewd political move from the general. Still, nothing had been heard of the messenger now in two months. Had the deputation even made it to Pompey? If they did, had they met with death at his hands? Had Vibullius returned to his old allegiance, perhaps, and gone over to the enemy? All Fronto and his friends knew was that it was said Pompey was still coming west across the Candavii Mountains, heading slowly but surely for the coast and his winter quarters.

'They will come,' Galronus said quietly, interrupting Fronto's gloomy train of thought. For a moment he thought the Remi prince meant Pompey, but then realised they were still staring out to sea and he'd meant Antonius and the other half of Caesar's army.

34

'I hope so,' he replied with a sigh. 'We can't live forever on the supplies we've gathered from local towns. Even Oricum gave us little. We need the supply base of Dyrrachium. Or Caesar to return with a wagon train from Buthrotum. At this rate, ambrosia falling from the sky is more likely.'

The two men fell into silence once more, watching the empty sea. The waves were noticeably calmer than they'd been when they first arrived. Spring was around the corner. Silence reigned until Galronus finally cleared his throat.

'I almost forgot why I came up here. News has arrived from Calenus.'

'Oh?' Fronto turned with interest. Calenus, with a force of two thousand, all that could be spared from the thinly-spread army on the coast, had gone north several days ago in an attempt to secure positions along the Apsus River, despite the fact that at its mouth remained one of Pompey's fangs: Apollonia. Perhaps the crossings could be secured in preparation for when the enemy finally arrived.

'Apollonia is ours,' Galronus said as though reporting the latest results at the race track.

Fronto blinked. 'You almost forgot to tell me the most important news in over a month?'

Galronus shrugged nonchalantly. 'The Pompeian commander, I think his name was Stabbus...'

'Staberius. Lucius Staberius. I know him of old. He owes me money, the shit.'

'This commander bolstered the garrison with locals when Calenus was reported nearby and when they argued against it, he took hostages from them. They cornered him with his men and told him into which dark passage to shove his siege, then opened the gates to Calenus. Stabbus...'

'Staberius.'

'Stabbus just ran with his men. Fled down to the port and disappeared on a ship into the midst of the blockade fleet. Ridiculous really. He had three thousand Pompeians there and strong walls and plenty of food. But he was so worried about the arrival of two thousand of us that he cocked it all up, relied on the locals, and they bent him over and did him from behind.'

Fronto rolled his eyes. Sometimes you forgot that Galronus was one of the barbarians. And then sometimes you were reminded...

'You just can never trust natives,' Fronto smiled slyly. Galronus nodded and began to agree, then stopped with a frown.

'Your mouth's going to get you into trouble, Marcus.'

'Not for the first time. Well, assuming Caesar is successful in the south, and I think we can leap to the assumption that he will be, then almost the entire Illyrian coast is ours. The only real hiccup will be Dyrrachium holding out for Pompey. Of course, all that changes when the knob-nosed shit actually arrives with his army.'

'Why?'

Fronto shook his head. 'If we gather together every man we have in this land, including the fragments left from Antonius' campaign, we'll still have less than twenty thousand men. Pompey will have far more than that. If he turns up and draws us into open battle, then I reckon Caesar's run of luck might just end. And we might control most of the coast now, but he still controls the sea, until they all starve and we're blockaded by ships full of skeletons. Unless Antonius arrives with the rest of the army, we're still in the shit deeper than a midget in a latrine trench.'

'So it's a race of sorts.'

'Eh?'

Galronus gestured at the ships out to sea. 'If they starve first, and Antonius arrives, we walk off with the wreath. If Pompey and his men get here first, then he does.'

'Succinctly put. I'm not sure why Pompey isn't already here, to be honest. He's only been sixty or so miles away. If he'd been determined, he'd be in Dyrrachium by now laughing at us. My only assumption is that his army has been scattered and he's gathering it before he comes, preparing to face us.'

'Something's happening with the ships,' Galronus said suddenly, gesturing out to sea. Fronto followed his extended digit and spotted two smaller boats departing one of the larger warships, heading for the beach.

'Must be an officer. Might even be Bibulus. Let's get the Tenth ready to receive him. Better warn Acilius and Murcus.'

* * *

By the time the two small skiffs were close to the beach, Fronto and Galronus were lined up, along with Sulla, commander of the

Ninth, their tribunes and a small cadre of other officers. Two cohorts stood at attention on the beach, one drawn from each legion, all that could be spared. Acilius was in Oricum, in command of the walls, but Murcus had remained based at the landing site and he now stood with the other officers.

As well as the oarsmen, the boats contained two men wearing the uniforms of senior Pompeian officers and a number of heavy marine bodyguards. The two officers, their noses held high and haughty, almost tumbled into the water as the boats crunched into the beach, recovering themselves with difficulty, and their dignity not at all.

'The scrawny one I don't know,' Fronto murmured, 'but the one with the jowls is Bibulus.'

'The scrawny one is Libo,' Murcus replied. 'An old comrade.'

Neither officer left the boats, and the Caesarians kept back from the shore. Forty paces of sand separated them.

'Say your piece,' Murcus shouted, taking the lead as was his right, given his command of the shoreline.

'We starve,' called the scrawny officer. 'And you cannot be far behind. This situation is idiotic.'

'Agreed. Cease your blockade and return to your base and then we can all relax.'

'You know we won't do that,' snapped the fatter one. Fronto thought he did not look particularly well. Even at this distance he could detect a grey, waxy sheen to Bibulus' skin.

'Then we are at an impasse.'

'Murcus,' the smaller one called. 'It's me, Libo. Listen, man, the sailors are so thirsty they're gathering the night dew from the leather covers on the ships for water. This is insufferable. We want to come to an agreement. We need to discuss matters with Caesar.'

'Caesar is not here.'

Bibulus waved an angry arm. 'Then send for him. And while we wait, have some pity on your fellow Romans and let our sailors have water. A little forage. A short landing.'

'Have pity?' Fronto bellowed suddenly, stepping forwards. 'As you did on the empty transports and their crews? Sailors burned and drowned just to make a point. You know how forgiving Caesar can be, but I wouldn't expect much personally if I were you, Bibulus.'

'Please,' Libo said. 'This is not war. We are not fighting. With luck we will not have to, and yet hundreds of good Romans are dying while we wait. A truce. A temporary truce to prevent too many unnecessary deaths. While Caesar can be summoned and a deal struck.'

Fronto gestured across to Murcus and huddled the officers a little further back up the sand. Keeping his voice low, inaudible to the boats, he addressed the man in command of the coastline.

'You say you know this Libo?'

'Of old.'

'Would you trust him?'

Murcus shrugged. 'In the days we served together I would have put my life in his hands. Obviously things are different now, but Libo is a good man. Noble sort.'

'I'm of a mind to agree to a temporary truce and allow water to the ships.'

Salvius Cursor shook his head. 'Fronto, that will undo everything we have achieved. We have them on their knees.'

Fronto nodded. 'We do. But it's easy to forget that those men are Romans. Caesar is prepared for a last attempt at verbal resolution. We may not have heard back from Vibullius, but if he were here, Caesar would grant them the opportunity to talk. Besides, granting them a little water is hardly going to bring them back up to strength. They will still be weak. But every death among his fleet will make Pompey that bit less inclined to come to an agreement.'

Murcus nodded. 'I will have riders sent south. Buthrotum is only forty miles away. At a push Caesar can be back here in a day. Do we grant them water?'

Fronto nodded. 'I say so. What about you, Sulla?'

The slightly equine features of the other legate, a nephew of Rome's famous dictator of old, turned to him with a nod. 'Give them water, but just enough to keep them alive. No more. One barrel per ship until Caesar confirms our next move.'

'Agreed.'

Salvius Cursor was almost vibrating with irritation. 'Let them die. Don't pander to them.'

'They are Romans, Salvius,' Fronto snapped.

'They're still the enemy.'

'But a *Roman* enemy.'

'Caesar would not agree to this. You are taking matters into your own hands, sirs,' he gestured at Fronto and Sulla, who regarded him coldly. 'This should be Caesar's decision,' Salvius pressed. 'One more day makes little difference. Even two. Delay giving them anything until the general comes.'

Fronto flashed a look at the tribune that suggested he had seriously overstepped the mark, which had about as much impact on the man as usual. 'Salvius, a good commander relies on the men under his command. How do you think we fought across Gaul on such a grand scale for nine years? Caesar did not make every decision. He trusted his officers.'

'And now half those officers have turned their back on him and serve Pompey.'

'That is enough, Tribune. Return to the men.'

As Salvius Cursor turned with a sneer and stumped off across the sand, Fronto gestured to the shore.

'Shall we?'

Libo remained in the prow of his boat. Bibulus had sat down, still looking exceedingly unwell.

'Pass the word from ship to ship,' Murcus bellowed. 'If they send a boat to the shore, the legions based there will grant them one barrel of water for each vessel. This is a gesture of goodwill in anticipation of a full parley. I am sending a rider to bring Caesar here for a conference. With luck this can all be resolved tomorrow.'

* * *

The afternoon and evening passed swiftly, every ship in the blockading fleet sending a boat and receiving one barrel of water. It would not make a huge difference, but as a gesture it would worm its way into the heart of every thirsty sailor and it would at least prevent a few unfortunate deaths. The morning dawned without the ubiquitous damp chill, suggesting that spring might finally have sprung. Trouble started with the dawn, though, as ships sent out boats to the shore to collect a second barrel of water and were refused.

'But your centurion said we'd get one a day,' was a common argument, to which the standard reply was 'it has not yet been a day.' Scuffles broke out, though fortunately with no mortal consequences. In Fronto's opinion, every officer did a sterling job of keeping control, from senior staff right down to the optios on the scene, and indeed most of the men too.

As noon passed and the incidents became fewer, the ill feeling along the coast growing, Fronto could feel trouble looming in the sweet spring air, and it came as a balm to hear that an outlying scout had spotted riders bearing Caesar's banner. The man must have moved like Mercury himself to arrive so soon. But then if ever a man was capable of strategic and logistical miracles, it was most definitely Caesar.

Within the hour all the men available were assembled with the officers as a party of a hundred cavalry appeared at the beach's edge and began to trudge through the fine white sand. Amid them were half a dozen men in senior officer's uniforms, including the general himself. The *consul*, Fronto reminded himself. Moments later boats began to leave the ships once more. It would appear that the conference was imminent.

'Thank the gods, Caesar,' Fronto sighed as the general reached him and reined in ahead of the rest of the riders. The old man looked even more tired than usual, yet his ageing frame wore his uniform and cuirass well, and the legate doubted his old friend would baulk even now, with no sleep, at the need to dive personally into a fight.

'I am informed that Bibulus wishes a meeting?'

Fronto and Murcus both nodded, the latter stepping forwards. 'Their blockade weakens as they starve. They requested a truce and to resupply. In the hope of still securing a full conference and potential peace we thought it prudent to agree, at least in part.'

Caesar's head tilted in question.

'We gave each ship one barrel of water to prevent deaths, but that is all.'

The old man nodded. 'There will be no meeting beyond this.'

'Sir?'

Caesar gestured with a drooping arm to the east. 'Pompey is little more than a day away, according to my scouts, with a solid force. The simple fact that Vibullius has not returned and that

40

Pompey is finally moving at speed suggests that he has little intention of considering a treaty. He knows his coastline is in danger and now races to occupy Dyrrachium. If he can do that, then he can field his forces with a good supply line and sea support and likely ever more reserves will arrive by the day from his training camps in Macedonia. The man has no desire for peace. You *know* him, Fronto. You know his soul.'

Fronto nodded sadly. That fire-hearted warmonger he had come to know in Rome would hardly be prepared to place his life in the senate's hands, especially when he still held all the dice in this game.

'No. We will see what these sailors have to say, but once I have assured myself that they are merely self-serving and attempting to secure their own survival, we will move. I will leave just enough men along the coast to deny the worst-hit areas of his fleet, such as this right here, and the rest of the army will move en-masse, meeting up with my forces returning even now, and combining. We will cross the Apsus River and block it against Pompey. We will deny him Dyrrachium. Only that way can we hope to hold him. If he reaches his supply base we might as well flee back to Rome, and that would be the end of us.'

Certainly of Caesar politically, anyway, Fronto mused.

'Here they come,' Murcus muttered, and the entire officer contingent stepped towards the beach, ready to address the boats. They came as they had before, two officers, each in a boat with marines and oarsmen. As they crunched into the sand, at least this time they managed not to fall over. It was only as they straightened themselves in preparation that Fronto realised the man in the left hand boat was not Bibulus, but some naval officer with a gorilla build and a face like a pomegranate.

'Bibulus not well?' he shouted in a jocular tone. Caesar gave him a look that was unreadable, but most likely bad.

The unknown officer cupped his hands to his mouth, somewhat unnecessarily given the huge voice that emerged. 'The admiral is gravely ill and near his tomb, we think. Lack of water,' he snapped accusingly.

'Should have prioritised those ships from Dyrrachium better eh?' Fronto prodded with a malicious smile.

Caesar gave him a warning glance, and Fronto nodded his acquiescence. He cared little how much Bibulus suffered, but he'd got in his barbed comments, so that was fine.

'Say your piece,' Caesar called to the boats.

Libo gestured oratorically. 'Caesar, we have no wish in truth to fight against you. You are a consul of Rome. Pompey has lured us into a war no sane man would seek, against our brothers and countrymen. But you know the general. He is glorious and clever. Persuasive. You listen to him and do what he asks, even when you wonder at yourself for doing it. Pompey convinced his officers that Caesar had conquered Rome like some modern Brennus and that you would not stop until you were a new king.'

Fronto shivered. There was perhaps a little more truth in there than he'd expected. Right down to the monarchic reach. Libo coughed and went on.

'He told us that you would never settle. That you would never enter into treaty. But the truth is now evident. It is clear that such words were lies. You *are* willing to entreat and settle. And so let us be the olive branch of peace. Let us, who know how to persuade him, talk to Pompey and bring him to the table. Then, perhaps, we can end this dreadful war and resolve everything.

'He sounds surprisingly genuine,' Sulla murmured. 'And his arguments are persuasive.'

Caesar was inscrutable atop his horse. He gestured to Murcus, who hurried over, and then bent low to him. 'You know Libo well, I believe.'

'I do, Caesar.'

'Has he ever suffered a critical injury to his arms?'

Murcus frowned. 'I am not aware of such, General. Why?'

'Because he holds his hands clasped at his side and they both quiver as though he has a palsy, and trust me, I know the symptoms. If Libo has not had a wound that might cause it, and he is hale and well, then he is suffering a great deal of tension. In fact, I would wager the contents of the Temple of Saturn that every word that passes his lips is a lie, and that it is almost killing him to do so. He is a good man?'

'He is.'

'And a good man hates lying. Libo is fabricating, probably at Bibulus' behest. And you know why? If we agree, the fleet

42

strengthens. And while we are busy dealing with them here, Pompey arrives from the east and occupies Dyrrachium. No. In fact, the very idea that they are willing to sink so low as false treaty suggests how important it is that we dally here with them. Pompey's army must be closer than we thought. They are working to slow us and cripple us.' He looked up at Libo. 'My last messenger seems not to have reached Pompey.'

'We will send messengers, Caesar. And while they ride to secure a future for us all, perhaps the great and magnanimous Caesar will permit us sustenance?'

Even Fronto could see now how the man was quivering with the stress of his position and argument.

'No,' Caesar said in a flat and far-carrying tone. 'There will be no sustenance and no further water. Return to your ships and become cadavers, for better to end now with hunger than in the cataclysm that is coming. This meeting is over. There will be no further truce.'

He turned to the other officers and said loudly 'At the count of sixty you will have your men gather their pila and hurl them at the boats unless they are already out at sea and heading home.'

Fronto almost laughed at the comic desperation as the sailors hurried to get their boats moving once more, the officers bellowing at them in panic. Once the boats were out on the water and far from earshot, Murcus gestured to Caesar.

'They will become more desperate now, Consul, and they have no reason not to fight. They will send landing parties all along the coast to resupply.'

'There will be no fights,' Caesar replied. 'Our army will not be there. We cannot fight every front of this campaign at once with the men we have. We have to relinquish the coast and hope that in weakening them we have done enough. We gather every ally we have and race to the Apsus. It is now utterly imperative that we secure the best crossings and prevent Pompey from linking up with Dyrrachium. We move now. Have every unit along the coast ordered to march to the Apsus with all haste and muster there. Pompey must be close, and I will hold that river against him.'

'And Antonius?' Fronto urged.

'What?'

'We might be able to hold Pompey at the Apsus, at least for a while, but without the rest of the army victory is a fool's dream. It is critical to deny Pompey Dyrrachium, but it is all for nothing without the rest of the army. Any hope of success relies on Antonius arriving, and now we are allowing the blockade to begin their recovery.'

Caesar nodded. 'Sadly we are not given the luxury of choice, Fronto. We fight a desperate campaign here and must deal with what dice the gods throw as they fall. If we finish the starvation of the blockade, we let Pompey consolidate. We'll never beat him then. No, we race to the Apsus and we hold him there, with words if we can, and steel if not, until Antonius arrives with the reserves. And you know Antonius. Hades and Neptune might stand in his way, but he will find a way around them. He has never failed me.'

There's always a first time, thought Fronto as he saluted and stepped away.

CHAPTER 4

Banks of the Apsus River, Martius 48 BC

Fronto reined in Bucephalus and threw out a finger, pointing into the misty middle distance.

'The scouts were right. Look.'

Galronus and Salvius Cursor followed his finger and peered myopically into the grey. Then they saw it. A lone rider looped out of the blanket of mist and circled wide, unhurried, until he saw the activity on the north bank of the Apsus. Then he turned and hurtled back into the mist.

'How long do we have?' Galronus murmured.

Fronto huffed. 'Standard practice will have the riders anywhere up to a day ahead of the main column, but Pompey knows we're out here somewhere and he'll want regular reports. The column won't be more than six hours ahead of the army at most.'

'Considerably less,' Salvius corrected. 'When he's facing someone dangerous, Pompey keeps his riders circling on no more than a two hour circuit and they rotate constantly. His army will be less than an hour away.'

'Then I think we need to thank all the gods that we got here first,' Galronus sighed. They turned in unison and peered at the enormous camp in the early stages of construction. Already legions were billeting in the enormous rectangle, putting up their tents in ordered blocks while the engineers and architects drew out the plan and pioneers worked on the one line of fortification already underway, facing the river, a rampart rising rapidly while other men cut timber in the woods nearby, the sounds oddly dulled by the mist.

'It's going to be something of a race, mind,' Fronto muttered, turning back to the bridge. A few thousand men remained on the south bank, pushing hard to cross the Apsus to perceived safety, along with the artillery wagons and the meagre collection of supply carts. By Fronto's estimate it would take roughly an hour to get them all across and into the camp. And if Pompey's army was roughly an hour away...

His eyes drifted off to the southeast again. Somewhere behind that blanket of white was an army larger than their own, commanded by a snarling wolf. The enemy scout had vanished once more, but Fronto had marked a lone dead tree standing like some dreadful portent in the veil of mist as the direction from which the scout had arrived and whence he returned.

'Will he attack as soon as he gets here?' Galronus asked.

Fronto glanced to Salvius Cursor as the expert, a man who had once served with the general and knew his mind better than many. The tribune chewed on his cheek. 'I don't think so. He won't risk it. By now he knows we've sealed Dyrrachium to him so there is no need to rush. His column will be strung out over a distance, just as ours was, and it will take time to bring up sufficient forces to face an army our size. Given the obstacle of the river, he won't risk it. My guess is that he'll encamp opposite us while he decides his next move. We control a lot of territory now, but he still has the edge while Dyrrachium is his and his ships prevent supplies and reinforcements reaching us.'

Fronto nodded. 'In fact, with the sea to the west, Dyrrachium to the north, Pompey to the south and unknown barren hills to the east, we have a limited time here before we begin to starve. Pompey will recognise that straight away and he'll have solid supply lines out towards Macedonia. He might just sit there and watch us die of hunger.'

'Unless the fleet starves first and gives up the blockade,' Galronus mused. 'Looks likely.'

The others nodded. The fleet might still have the coast secured, but they were definitely weakening and failing. Even before the army had been on the march, while men were still stationed at the coast, rumours had begun to filter in. Bibulus had been ill, and had died in agony aboard his command ship. In his absence, he being the strong, violent commander who kept the fleet functioning as one, there had been fragmentation. There seemed no clear successor for overall command, and each high-ranking officer had taken control of the ships he had commanded before the blockade. The worst-affected had left the blockade altogether, hurrying for

Dyrrachium to resupply, or to Pompeian cities far to the north or south. Fifty ships under Libo had vanished entirely. It was suggested that they had hurried west to carry the blockade to Brundisium. With the disappearance of more than a hundred ships in total, the remaining fleet had reshuffled to maintain their cordon, though now they were well spaced and a wily commander might be able to break through.

So once more it had become a race. With their securing of the Apsus crossing and denying Pompey his base, that first contest was over, but now it was a matter of who would starve first: Caesar's army, trapped in hostile lands, or the reduced fleet that kept his reinforcements away.

They stood in silence for a while, the sounds of axes, saws, mattocks and grunting and huffing the only noise, rising from the works all around them. After almost half an hour a timber platform went up above the rampart, some twenty feet from ground level, and the three men climbed atop it for a better view, though all it really offered was a panoramic vision of the sea of white. A pair of soldiers brought a small folding table and placed jugs of water and wine and a bowl of buttered bread on it, all of which was ignored while the officers peered expectantly into the mist.

The Tenth's legate had not realised just how tense he'd become until the last of the carts rumbled from the dirt road onto the solid bridge, a rear-guard of a hundred men gathered on the far bank for protection. He exhaled noisily. They had done it. And with only moments to spare. Barely had the rumble of cart wheels died away with that vehicle's passing onto the north bank than a new noise filled the weird, white world.

Horns.

Fronto's breath caught again and his eyes rose from the bridge, where men were now jostling in a desperate hurry to be across, to the southeast. The noise came again. A cascade of notes that resolved in the damp, dull mist to become a traditional marching cadence.

Fronto took a deep breath. 'Here we go.'

Shapes emerged from the mist. Speculatores and exploratores, scouts who peeled off into a wide arc ahead of their compatriots. Then came the cavalry. Fronto felt his heartrate increase at the sight. They came in perfect formation, eight riders abreast, the column disappearing seemingly endlessly back into the mist. These were not the scarce regular Roman riders or Gallic allies like those Galronus had commanded. These were Illyrian or Macedonian riders, armoured in bronze and with spears and shields that depicted myriad colourful designs. Some had crests or long flowing plumes. They were heavy cavalry and, from their perfect formation and their equipment, experts and veterans.

'Shit.'

'Shiny helmets and bright paint do not make a warrior,' Galronus snorted.

Fronto rolled his eyes. You could plaster civilisation on the Remi as much as you liked, but Belgic pride always lay deep within. 'They will be good. Very good. The peoples of these lands have been training as cavalry for centuries. Have you ever heard of Alexander of Macedon?'

'I'm guessing he's not a poet,' Galronus grunted.

'Macedonian king about three hundred years ago. Using riders like that and phalanxes of spear men he forged an empire larger than the republic is now. He even beat Persia, and no one beats Persia. They ended Crassus, if you remember?'

'If he was so good, where's his empire now?'

Again, Fronto rolled his eyes. 'No heir. A king without an heir means trouble. When he died young, his generals carved the empire up. Seleucus took the east, Lysimachus the Achaean peninsula and Ptolemy took Egypt. There were other smaller successors, but those were the big three.'

'And what happened to them?'

Fronto sighed. Was this really the time for a history lesson? But then Galronus was a cavalry commander and it might help him to know a little about the people they might yet face. Certainly he needed to be less sure and cocky than his Belgic pride demanded.

'The Selecuids were around for a while. Lost a lot of territory gradually to the Parthians, then they were finally finished in Syria about fifteen years ago, by Pompey no less. The Antigonids ruled from Macedon and they were finished off by Aemilius Paullus over a hundred years ago. And the Ptolemies? Well they still rule Egypt. There's a brother and sister ruling together at the moment, but it's said they hate each other, so their marriage won't last long.'

48

'And will you be the Roman to end the Ptolemies?' Galronus said.

Fronto frowned at him, not sure whether the Remi was joking or serious. 'Rome has no designs there. Not of which I'm aware, anyway.'

'Rome has designs everywhere, Marcus.'

Fronto turned away, unsettled by the notion, and peered at the cavalry. They had split into two groups now and moved off to each side. The legions were emerging from the mist now, and the sight made Fronto feel queasy. Chain shirts over russet tunics, gleaming bronze helmets and long red shields, they could so easily be Fronto's men. The knowledge that they were facing their own people, brothers and cousins, surfaced unpleasantly once more. Those men now marching out of the mist could quite possibly be the same First Legion who had served under Caesar against Ambiorix.

He stood, continuing to feel disgruntled and unhappy, watching Pompey's army arrive. Gradually the legions moved into place and formed ranks. Some were clearly new and untried, gleaming and not quite as sharp as the others, but they were well-equipped and strong. More cavalry appeared, light, skirmishing riders, then rank upon rank of native auxiliaries, with archers, phalanxes, slingers and more. Finally, as the vast ranks of men stood silent across the churned grass to the south, the commanders arrived with a bodyguard unit of horsemen.

Pompey had perhaps two dozen senior officers with him, clerks and musicians, standard bearers and even lictors following on. Then came the start of the long line of supply and artillery wagons, along with yet more legionaries who'd been the rear-guard.

Galronus whistled through his teeth. 'How many?'

Fronto rubbed the back of his neck, his other hand rapping repeatedly on his hip. 'Best part of fifty thousand, I'd say.'

'And how many have we got?'

'Not much more than a quarter of that, I reckon.'

'Not good odds.'

'No. Though to be honest, I'm surprised there aren't more. Rumour put his numbers higher. He must still have men out east that he left behind in the hurry to get here. There are rumours that

Scipio rushes to his aid from Syria with two more veteran legions, as well.'

'If he decides to attack,' Salvius muttered, 'then the river will nullify his advantage.'

'Maybe. Pompey's no fool, though. If he does come, it will be because he knows how to gain the advantage. This is a man who's had three triumphs in Rome. A man whose reputation was built solely on military success.'

They had not noticed the other observation platforms going up along the south rampart, so fixated were they on the view across the river, and it was only when a horn blew that they realised the others were now occupied. Caesar had arrived to take in his opposition's number and position. The general, along with Sulla and Calvinus, stood on the next platform.

'Impressive, eh, Fronto?' the general called out, sounding almost jovial.

Fronto threw him a sour expression. 'I'd rather they were less so, Caesar.'

'Fear not,' the general said loudly, 'there is still time for a diplomatic solution.'

'Not unless you intend to show him your belly in submission, General.'

Caesar chuckled. 'Remember, Fronto, that Pompey and Crassus and I kept things perfectly functioning for some time. There is little we cannot achieve if we manage to come to an accord. I'm sure that deep down Pompey still harbours some affection for his father-in-law.'

'I think there's more chance of Crassus coming back from the dead than Pompey coming to a settlement.'

'Is there really no chance?' Galronus muttered, as Caesar turned to answer some question of Sulla's.

'Neither of them is going to be willing to surrender to the other. Both will only accept a conclusion to their advantage. Caesar will not relinquish his consulship or disband his legions. Pompey will not accept a judgement from Rome, for the senators favourable to him are almost all in his army now. Neither can truly back down. Something nasty is coming, and soon.'

The Remi noble frowned. 'I thought you still hoped for a solution. I was under the impression you still thought one possible.'

'No. Not any more. And neither does Caesar.'

'But he said…'

'Yes. He said it can still be resolved. And he said it nice and loud so that some of the men at the front of Pompey's force will have heard. That will filter through the ranks. Men might think twice if they believe they enemy are willing to seek peace. Pompey will never submit, but there is always the possibility that the men serving him might. Men like Labienus and Afranius. Men who have been Caesar's friends before now, or pardoned by him. There is no hope for a diplomatic solution with Pompey, but he could still be undermined.'

'Not from that distance,' Salvius grunted and gestured at the officers. Pompey and his men had stopped way back from the river to the south, out of earshot and, perhaps tellingly, out of artillery range. Even as Fronto watched, whistles blew and orders were called, and the legions of Pompey began to construct camp ramparts on the south bank, echoing those rising on the north.

'They seem to have no fear,' Galronus noted. 'They're not only working in artillery range, but a good archer could even hit them with an arrow from here.'

'I think there is still some confusion as to whether we're truly at war here. No spears have been thrown and it's just been a lot of running around and posturing.'

'Tell that to the sailors Bibulus killed,' Salvius spat.

Fronto's expression darkened. 'True. But the vast majority of souls on these banks want nothing more than to come to an agreement, avoid a conflict and just go home. No soldier looks forwards to a fight…' he looked Salvius Cursor up and down and corrected himself. '*Few* soldiers look forwards to a fight, but even fewer want to fight their own countrymen. No one will launch a missile until all other avenues have been closed.'

His attention was drawn rather suddenly to a shout from below, and he peered down to see a legionary with a loud voice cupping his hands to his mouth.

'You want a hand?' the man bellowed across the river. Half a dozen legionaries busy cutting earth sods on the south bank paused and straightened. 'Not really, but if you've got too much wine, we'll take that off your hands!'

There was a small explosion of mirth across the water and the soldier below Fronto replied. 'You're not cutting that straight sober. A jug of wine and you'll be swerving down into the river.' This initiated a burst of laughter from the Caesarian ramparts, and in moments half a dozen exchanges had begun in loud, shouted tones across the river.

A centurion appeared from somewhere and blew a whistle, snapping out orders for quiet and decorum, but Caesar, a twinkle in his eye, leaned down from his viewing platform and gestured at the officer. 'Let them have their camaraderie, Centurion. They are all brothers under the eagle, after all.'

Fronto smiled. 'Another tiny reminder for the enemy that Caesar is understanding and generous.' He was, to an extent, but the more he appeared so to Pompey's army, the better the chance of a rebellion among the enemy legions and officers.

'Vatinius,' Caesar called to an officer on the next platform along.

'General?' called the legate of the Fourteenth.

'I need to do some planning. See if you can arrange a conference with Pompey or his officers, will you?'

Vatinius smiled. 'My pleasure, General.'

Caesar nodded a goodbye to Fronto and descended, making for his command tent that was now in place some way to the north and would already be fully furnished.

'Who is the ranking officer over there?' Vatinius bellowed. His calls had to be loud enough to cross the river and be heard well, and so were equally clear to Fronto and the others, two observation platforms along.

A tribune emerged from a small group of officers and men gathered around a huge stack of timber that was being unloaded from a cart, and strode towards the water. The broad stripe on his tunic identified him as the senior tribune of a legion, second only to a legate.

'That would be me, sir. Regulus, senior tribune of the First.'

'What say you to an exchange of envoys, Regulus?' Vatinius said jovially.

52

'Any such request will have to be passed to the general,' the tribune replied with a sigh. 'And I do not think it likely he will agree just now.'

'Come on, man,' Vatinius shouted. 'Envoys are always permissible, and guaranteed safety. Even fugitive slaves and pirates are allowed to send envoys. Exchange of envoys is always sensible. Especially when the objective is to prevent citizens killing one another.'

There was a thoughtful silence at that, for every man held those thoughts close to his heart.

'Will you agree to an exchange of envoys?' Vatinius pressed. 'Myself acting on behalf of Caesar and you speaking as the ranking officer there?'

Regulus opened his mouth, but a new voice cut in, and men parted like waves before a trireme prow. A hawk-faced man in immaculate uniform with a general's ribbon knotted around his midriff strode forth from the enemy between the parting lines of men.

'I am the ranking officer here, now. Get back to your legion, Regulus.'

The tribune, chastened, stepped back as the senior Pompeian officer came to a halt and placed balled fists upon his hips. 'Aulus Varro, of the general's staff. It is an honour to meet you again, Legate Vatinius. And a cause of dismay that this time it should be under arms rather than ample voiced and loaded with records.'

Vatinius laughed aloud. 'Varro, by the gods. I never imagined you returning to the field. Why are you not arguing cases in the basilicas of Rome?'

'The same reason as you, Vatinius. Sadly Rome has fractured and we all must leap to a side for survival lest we disappear down the crevasse.'

Fronto leaned forwards. 'Some of us, Varro, should have taken the hint when Caesar pardoned us in Hispania and not run east to take up another command.' Though he'd been at Massilia at the time, it was common knowledge that Varro had commanded half of Hispania on behalf of Pompey and had been pardoned upon his capitulation.

The humour sucked out of the air, Varro sighed as he addressed Vatinius once more. 'Apologies, old friend. Pompey is reluctant to arrange a conference. He believes that should he show his face in person some Caesarian hopeful will put a javelin in it even if ordered not to. But perhaps even great decisions do not require the commander to be present. You say you can speak for Caesar? Then I shall speak for Pompey. Of course, anything I agree to would have to be ratified by the general.'

'Of course. The same holds for me.'

'Then we should meet. Tonight is too late – we are all tired, and both armies are engaged in the slinging of turf and the slinging of insults – but tomorrow morning? A small party of senior officers from each army, with an escort of, say, a dozen guards? We meet on the bridge?'

Vatinius nodded. 'On the bridge. But at the *second* hour of day. I am getting old, and I like to break my fast in a leisurely manner.'

Varro laughed. 'If I remember rightly you did that when you were young, too!'

'Til the morrow.'

'The morrow.'

Both men turned and moved away from the river and, entertainment over, the legions returned to their back-breaking work. Fronto beckoned to the other two on his platform and they descended, passing the lookouts who had been waiting patiently for the officers to leave so that they could take up their posts. Hurrying across to Vatinius, Fronto beckoned to his fellow legate.

'Yes?'

'You know Varro?' Fronto asked. 'And he's a reasonable man?'

Vatinius nodded with a smile. 'Best advocate I've ever faced in court. Could talk you in a spiral if he wished it. Makes me look like an infant. But he is noble and his heart is most definitely in the right place. He will do whatever he can to de-escalate the matter. In fact I would wager he is now bound for Pompey's tent to try and talk sense into the man. If anyone can, it's Varro.'

'You know that Caesar won't accept a deal in which he comes out wanting?'

'Fronto, I'm not a complete idiot. Caesar has made his terms clear all along. A mutual laying down of command and a mediated settlement between them in which both men can return to Rome without losing honour, position or power. It sounds impossible, but believe a man who has spent half his life arguing in the forum, it isn't. There are ways this can be achieved still, ending the conflict, no matter what anyone says. But it requires cool heads in charge. I imagine that Pompey would have quite intended to attend any meeting, but that Varro has argued him into not going. Pompey would take offence at something and negotiations would fall apart. Similarly, Caesar can display a temper, and so I will persuade him not to become personally involved. We must make sure our parties are formed of the most reasonable, even-tempered and peace-seeking men among the command. And the bodyguard too – all veterans with an outstanding record. No hot-heads. We have a real chance here, Fronto, so long as we can keep things amicable. Varro and I can seal a deal, with appropriate input from an able council of wise minds.'

'Do you object to me being one of them?'

Varro raised an eyebrow. 'You've not the most calm and accepting of reputations, Fronto.' He chuckled. 'Still, I know you for a man who seeks peace. By all means join me. You may very well be the most grounded of us.'

Fronto felt Salvius Cursor almost vibrating with tension beside him. He turned with a flat expression to address his senior tribune as the other officers walked on. 'No, Salvius. Before you even ask.'

'But I know Pompey and his army, Fronto. I know them well. I have insights that will be of use.'

'You heard Vatinius. Cool heads. I have never in my life met a man more prone to fits of insane violence and angry outbursts than you. Don't get me wrong. I think we see eye to eye sometimes now, and I know you have a solid place in this army. But that solid place is at the leather-grip end of a sword, coated in someone else's blood and screaming curses.'

'You're soft, Fronto.'

'And you are more dangerous than a lunatic with a blade. What am I saying? You *are* a lunatic with a blade.'

'Fronto…'

'No. Besides, I doubt anyone below the level of legate will be in attendance. Now go and stick a sword in something and calm down.'

Salvius Cursor flashed him a nasty glare, then stumped off towards the camp of the Tenth.

'That one is still going to cause you trouble,' Galronus noted.

'Undoubtedly. But I was serious about his place in things. I don't want to rely on him thinking or talking, but if things all go to shit, I will be more than happy to watch him screaming, covered in blood, and pushing forwards to tear Pompey a new rectum.'

* * *

The following day, the mist had dissipated, and there was spring in the air once more. The officers gathered at the forwards command post, between the camps of the Tenth and Eleventh. Vatinius, Calenus, Fronto, Sulla and Canuleius. Galronus watched them from a short distance away. Fronto had been tempted to try and argue for his friend's inclusion, as a holder of a rather unique viewpoint, outside Roman life, and as a senior cavalry officer. Galronus had not been remotely concerned at the lack of invitation, though, unlike Salvius Cursor, who had already thrashed three soldiers for minor infractions due to his intense irritation. The bodyguards, Fronto noted, were all formed from Caesar's own praetorians, including Aulus Ingenuus himself, his three fingers circling the pommel of his sword quietly.

'I half expected Caesar's presence.'

Vatinius looked up at Fronto's comment. 'He did expect to come – took some persuading otherwise, in fact. I fought him down with the argument that if Pompey leaves it to his officers and Caesar does not, the matter would weigh in Pompey's favour in the minds of the staff. He seemed to accept that. It is entirely true, of course.'

'Of course,' smiled Fronto. 'Shall we?'

Moments later they were striding through the opened gate in the rampart and towards the ancient, heavy, stone bridge across the sluggish grey waters of the Apsus. Right on cue, the horns across the camp blew the second hour's call, followed two heartbeats later by the same from Pompey's camp. A small party of men emerged from the Pompeian gate and walked down to the bridge.

Fronto felt the weight of history crushing down on his shoulders. He'd been in many a tight spot in his military life, but only once before, at the Rubicon, had he felt that he was part of something that might either make or break the republic. Despite his and Caesar's misgivings, if Vatinius was right, this next half hour could heal the republic and avert a cataclysm, or at least begin to do so.

The two groups of officers came to a halt on the bridge, facing one another, with Varro and Vatinius at the fore. Fronto's eyes danced across the other officers in the Pompeian party. He was grateful that Ahenobarbus, that vile dog, was not among them. Clearly Varro had done the same as Vatinius, selecting the best men for the job. He recognised the aristocratic lines of Marcus Junius Brutus' face, of Afranius, the man they had faced at Ilerda the previous summer, of…

Labienus.

Titus Labienus, once Caesar's trusted right hand. A good friend of Fronto's in his time. One of the ablest, most sensible commanders he had ever met. But something about Labienus unsettled him. Gone was that calm demeanour of the old days. This Titus Labienus had eyes like pools of tar and a face not given to laughter.

'It is clearly the desire of all worthy men to see this war averted and a reconciliation of our opposing forces,' Vatinius said first. 'As such, I believe we can come to a sensible agreement that is acceptable to both sides in short order and have it in writing on the desks of the two generals for ratification before we pause for the noon meal. What say you all?'

Varro lifted his hands, preparing for oratory, but Fronto felt a chill of the blood as the man was rudely sidestepped by Labienus, who took the fore.

'You believe you can deliver terms here that are acceptable to Pompey?' Labienus snapped. 'I am not convinced. And more importantly, I am mystified as to how you can propose terms acceptable to *me*.'

Fronto noted the horrified look on Varro's face. He had clearly miscalculated in bringing the great commander with him, for Labienus did not look remotely like a man planning for reconciliation.

'Titus…'

Labienus swung round and held up a warning hand to Varro. Since the older man fell silent instantly, Fronto could instantly see how things stood in the Pompeian camp, and remembered Salvius telling him something about this once – how officers in that army worked in a strict chain of command with little give and take. Labienus was senior to Varro, and had instantly suborned control of the conference. Damn it. Fronto wondered if there was any way he could somehow side-track Labienus and take him away from the meeting.

No. Labienus turned back to Vatinius with a cold sneer. 'The problem is that I have seen Caesar's handiwork first-hand for a decade. I know what the man is capable of. I served him as loyally as I could, but the consul is intent on shattering the republic and wrapping himself in a monarch's robes. I for one will accept no terms unless one of them is that Caesar stand trial in a neutral court of law for his many crimes and injustices. And we all know, no matter how you might try and fool yourself, how that will end. So I do not see you agreeing to it. Tell me, then, how terms can be reached?'

Fronto felt ice forming in his stomach. The conference was doomed as long as Labienus had any input. He had to do something. He locked eyes with Vatinius, who clearly thought the same, and in desperation, Fronto hurried forwards with a friendly smile, hand raised ready to place it reassuringly on Labienus' shoulder. The moment he moved, though, the guards flanking the Pompeian party bellowed warnings. A pilum swished through the air and clattered across the bridge stones, miraculously missing everyone. The guards thought he was making an aggressive move! And now, with missiles flying, anyone could be wounded or killed. Fronto hit Labienus in the midriff, ploughing him to the ground just as two more missiles swept through the air where the angry officer had been standing.

'Betrayal! Treachery!' bellowed the Pompeian guards, and rushed forwards. Fronto heard Vatinius and Varro both shouting orders to hold back, but now arrows and stones were clattering against the bridge sides, launched by men from both armies believing their officers to be under attack. Chaos erupted, and the officers dropped to the ground, some taking glancing blows from stray missiles.

Fronto was suddenly thrown back as Labienus roared 'Get off me,' and rose like the ascent of some Tartaran monster.

'Shoulder weapons,' Labienus bellowed, so loud that it cut through the noise and amazingly reached even the men on the banks. The missile shower died away, a last arrow clacking against stone and falling into the water with a 'plop'.

Fronto rose and stepped back, taking in the situation. Two officers were clutching wounds among the Pompeians. One among the Caesarians. Shit, but that was not good. A peace conference with three woundings was hardly an ideal starting point.

'Everyone stay calm,' Fronto said, stepping into the middle of the chaos and holding up both hands in a gesture of peace, but Labienus stepped out again to meet him. Varro protested, though Labienus pushed him away and thrust an accusatory finger at Fronto.

'Cease then to talk about a settlement,' the furious officer bellowed, 'for there can be no peace for us until Caesar's head is brought forth!'

With that, he turned and thundered away. The guards and most of the officers hurried after him, though Varro lagged for a moment. He said nothing, but the apologetic expression on his face said everything. Fronto turned to Vatinius, who was aghast.

'That's it, then,' Fronto sighed. 'We're at war.'

CHAPTER 5

By the Apsus, Late Martius 48 BC

N othing had happened for days. Following that dreadful, abortive conference on the bridge, Pompey's officers had returned to their camp, as had Caesar's, but the atmosphere had changed entirely. Gone was the shouted camaraderie across the river, to be replaced by gloomy mistrust. Each camp's ramparts bristled with men and weapons.

War loomed, yet no move had been made.

Caesar's army, lacking the desperately needed reinforcements from Antonius, had insufficient strength to even consider launching a campaign without an expectation of awful loss. Pompey's army might have vast numbers, but any attempt to press Caesar across the river would be extremely costly, and the old bastard was wily enough not to try it. So the two armies sat glowering across the Apsus. Pompey's army continued to resupply with wagons from the east, and also with ships from the coast. The fleet was now thin enough that they were no longer suffering their own supply problems, but was also weak enough that a wily or strong admiral might be able to rout them and break through.

Yet still Antonius had not come and the army continued to grow hungry, rations becoming ever scarcer.

Fronto sighed and turned to Galronus. The two of them stood on the shoreline, watching the shapes of the enemy ships out there across the water.

'I worry that he's starting to lose it,' he said with a sigh.

Galronus nodded as both their gazes dropped to the small jetty at the mouth of the river. They were far enough from the main camp that there was little fear of a stray missile coming their way, even if the enemy suddenly decided to begin the violence. A few of Pompey's scouts remained in position on the far bank, bored and listless. Nothing could easily be done unobserved, but at night…

That was where Caesar's lunatic idea had taken root.

'Something must be done,' the general had said. And he was right, of course. The army was weakening through starvation and not strong enough to attack either the city to their north or the army to the south. They were pinned and fading. Something had to be done. But Fronto had not been convinced *this* was the answer. Oh, it wasn't the only bowstring Caesar had. The general had also sent Quintus Tillius and Lucius Canuleius off with a small highly mobile unit. They had gone east, far enough to circumvent even Pompey's pickets, with orders to then turn and race south for the allied lands around Buthrotum and gather in any supplies they could. It was a desperate measure, for there would not be much, and the escapade was extremely hazardous. But it was still better than this.

At the jetty sat two small boats, one a native fisherman, the other a merchant of the sort used by smugglers who wanted to appear legitimate but also favoured a vessel with enough speed to outrun the majority of larger ships. It was this sleek, fast vessel upon which Caesar had set his sights. And he would personally take charge. With local sailors at the helm and steering oars and a couple of his own guard for safety, the general had conceived of the idea of setting sail suddenly and silently at night, slipping past the watchmen and out to sea. There, with this vessel and good sailors he hoped to slip through the Pompeian blockade and out onto the Adriaticum. He would race for Brundisium and find out what had happened, perhaps manage to bring over the fleet himself. And he would trust no other to the task. He would do it himself.

It was an insane idea, of course, conceived in desperation, and it had the unusual merit of uniting the entire, commonly disagreeable, staff in one opinion: against the plan.

'Would that boat even make it across the sea?' Galronus asked, eyeing the smuggler vessel warily. Fronto smiled. He hated sea travel more than almost anything, for every wave and dip brought fresh nausea, but Galronus was of the Remi. The closest his land-locked tribe ever really came to sea travel was small fishing boats on wide rivers. It had only been since Caesar had turned their world upside down that men like Galronus had experienced a voyage across the sea. He had no ill effects from it, but he clearly still mistrusted it as a method of transport.

'With good sailors, fine weather and sufficient supplies, yes. If he doesn't get attacked by pirates. If there's not a storm and the water is calm enough. If he can slip out past the ships out there.'

Fronto's finger jerked up at the blockading fleet and their gaze followed it.

He frowned.

'What's that?'

They peered past the ships. A smudge on the horizon was gradually resolving into a smattering of black shapes.

'Ships.'

Fronto chewed his lip. 'But what do they mean?'

Galronus threw him a nonplussed look.

'Ours or the enemy's, I mean.'

'It must be Antonius,' Galronus said with confidence.

'Perhaps. But Libo left here with fifty ships or so. And another smaller fleet returned to Dyrrachium. And there are still parts of his huge fleet in the east. It could be anyone.'

'It's Antonius,' the Remi said again.

'I wish I had your confidence.' He turned and waved to one of the pickets nearby. 'Ride back to the camp as fast as you can and get Caesar. Ships sighted.'

The man saluted and mounted the single horse that had been grazing happily on lush grass. At least the beasts weren't starving here. Putting heels to flank, he raced off for the camp less than a mile upriver.

'It will be maybe a quarter of an hour before we can make out anything useful,' Fronto muttered.

They stood, tense, watching as the line of black dots grew until the vague shape of ships could be made out.

'Are they big warships or merchants?' Fronto said irritably, 'My eyesight's not that good.'

'I can't really tell the difference until I'm on one,' Galronus replied.

Fronto's fingers climbed his front until they found the twin figurines hanging on the leather thong around his neck. He grasped the shape of Fortuna and brought her up to his lips, kissing her reverently. *Let them be ours*, he prayed fervently.

The shapes grew, closing. Fronto had not felt quite so tense in some time, and even Galronus was fidgeting.

Slowly, things began to move. A motion caught Fronto's eye and his gaze dropped to the Pompeian warships. He grinned.

'It is. It is Antonius.'

'I know,' Galronus said confidently.

'The warships are preparing to stop him, so it must be him.'

They watched nervously as a dozen heavy triremes with upper fighting decks manoeuvred and turned, beginning slowly to come about and form up.

'Will they make it?' Galronus said suddenly.

'There's a lot of ships out there. But if they *are* Antonius', then most of them will be merchants with no armaments, built for capacity, not speed or strength.'

'Then you know what's about to happen.'

Fronto nodded unhappily. If the fleet just came on as it was, many vessels would be sunk before the first few broke through and reached the shore. The thought of just how many soldiers would drown in the process was not a nice one.

'Our reinforcements might not end up as numerous as we thought.'

A thunder of hooves announced the arrival of others and Fronto's head snapped round to see Caesar, Calenus and Sulla dismounting.

'No, Antonius,' Caesar said as he strode forwards and stopped next to Fronto. 'He cannot be that foolish. Where are the warships, my friend?'

Fronto nodded. If Antonius had any hope of breaking through to the shore with an intact fleet, he needed to put his few warships out front to engage the Pompeian triremes and buy the merchant ships time to slip past and unload the army. Yet there was no such move.

'Who has good eyes?' Caesar said. 'Tell me what you see out there?'

Sulla peered into the distance. There was a long pause. 'Thirty two ships, by my count, and not a warship among them.'

Caesar took a deep breath. 'Then something drastic has occurred. I had wondered why he delayed so. But if he attempts to land with no warship support, we will lose half the ships and men at least. And with only thirty two ships, that cannot be the whole army, and certainly no supplies.'

Fronto nodded again. What was Antonius' intention?

Horns and whistles sounded from the Pompeian ships and the group of a dozen triremes, now fully prepared and in formation, began to surge forwards, aiming for the ragtag flotilla.

Then, almost as one, like some great school of dark brown fish, Antonius' fleet tacked sharply to the left. In moments the fleet was no longer aiming for the shore, but had swung round and begun to plough north, parallel with the coast.

'What is he doing?' Calenus murmured.

'He has clearly decided, very sensibly, that he cannot get through,' Sulla replied.

'But he must have known that before with no warships. So why come so close to engaging the triremes?'

Caesar smiled. 'Because he needed to get our attention. He needed us to know he was here, and where he's going. He's beckoning to us. Something has happened that has robbed him of his military escort, but he has men and needs to join up with us. He cannot land here, so he needs us to move to wherever he can land safely.'

Fronto pursed his lips. It made sense, but it also opened up a whole new danger.

'Caesar, if we break camp and run to meet Antonius, we lose the advantage of the Apsus. Pompey will be able to follow us with impunity. And Antonius will not be able to land anywhere between here and Dyrrachium, because of the blockade.'

Sulla nodded his agreement. 'He will have to land somewhere north of Dyrrachium, and if we go to meet him, we allow Pompey access to the place. I don't think we can afford to let the man have Dyrrachium. It's too strong and well supplied.'

Caesar drummed fingers on his arms as he watched the allied ships disappearing off to the north. 'I take your point, and you're quite right, but answer me this: how long can we last in our current situation?'

'Not more than a month for sure,' Calenus conceded.

'Antonius will land and come south to us,' Sulla put in.

Caesar's drumming fingers became a touch more frantic, a sign that he was considering a path and working through all possibilities.

'If we stay here and Antonius does not come for us, we begin to starve until Pompey decides we are weak enough to make pressing across the river viable. If we stay here and Antonius does come south with adequate troops, we will have a decision to make. Do we attack a superior force across the river? We will essentially be in the unenviable position in which Pompey has been thus far. Or do we wait it out, but then we will starve twice as fast with a larger army.'

The general huffed irritably. 'If we leave this strong position, we cannot afford to pass Dyrrachium and allow Pompey the city. So we still will not meet up with Antonius. But that city is a veritable granary waiting to be plundered. I think the decision is not a hard one. Here, we will inevitably fail. To the north, we have a chance. We break camp and move the army north. With luck, Antonius will be coming south and we can combine the armies. Then we will be a force Pompey might not want to face. And north of Dyrrachium we have allies. We can perhaps improve out supply situation.'

'Antonius will need to know. It is no good him fortifying a beach and waiting for us,' Sulla said.

Caesar nodded. 'Galronus and Fronto? Take a hundred horse and ride ahead. Find Antonius and bring him south to meet us.'

* * *

Fronto and Galronus thundered across the giving turf, a hundred Gallic auxiliaries at their rear. Somewhere far behind, Caesar and the army would be pressing north. They would have the advantage of speed, for they could simply break camp and move en-masse, while Pompey, in pursuit, would need to cross the Apsus to follow. But they would still need to stop and draw the line of defence somewhere between Pompey and Dyrrachium.

The spring sunshine held more warmth every day, now, and had the circumstances been somewhat different, it could have been a glorious day. Away to their left the low waves of the sea crashed against the clear, sandy beach. Ahead, north-west, the heavy walls

66

of Dyrrachium sat on a promontory, daring them to come too close. They were at sufficient distance that they could not see the artillery atop the city's towers, but Fronto was in no doubt that they were there, and that the defenders would have no compunction in loosing great deadly iron bolts at the riders if they came anywhere near the walls. Any cavalry this close had to be Caesar's, after all.

They had covered the thirty miles from the Apsus to Dyrrachium in record time, though the light was beginning to fade, and soon dusk would fall.

'Do we make camp for the night when it gets dark, sir?' asked a decurion, riding forwards to join the two officers. Galronus looked to Fronto for an answer.

'No,' the legate replied. 'We ride through the night. Whenever we need to stop and rest the horses we'll do so, and the men can tuck into their rations then, but we're not making camp. Short breaks only. Combining the armies before Pompey catches up is of prime importance. If Pompey catches Caesar and decides to strike before we return, we might be returning to a cemetery rather than an army.'

The decurion saluted and dropped back once more.

Although they skirted the great bastion of Pompey's power at a good distance and remained solidly out of artillery range, Fronto breathed a sigh of relief once they were safely past that city and riding on north. On the understanding that wherever Antonius had reached Illyricum, it had to be on the coastline, they veered west once more and continued along the shore. A little north of the city they broke their ride for an hour by a small and easily crossable river. While the men ate a light meal of bread and salted meat, the horses were allowed to graze and rest and drink from the clear waters of the river. Then, with complaint from both men and beasts, and a whispered apology from Fronto to poor, ageing Bucephalus, they were off once more.

The light gave way early to an indigo evening, clouds rolling in across the sea and blanketing the world. They rode on into the darkness, skirting a wide, marshy area, and had another break perhaps fifteen miles from their last position in the lee of a range of high hills and bare peaks that cut across their path from the east down to the sea. As the men rested and the horses recovered once again, Fronto and Galronus lit a small oil lamp and perused their small map.

'There are several passes through these hills,' Fronto noted, stabbing the vellum with a finger. 'The only one that's suitable for carts is way inland. The two this end of the spur are an unknown quantity. They're certainly navigable on foot. It's a gamble for cavalry. Do we trust to them or delay and take a sweep inland for the sensible route?'

Galronus peered at the map. 'Inland.'

'You're sure? I'd hate to miss Antonius' landing site.'

'These peaks go right down to the sea. Antonius couldn't land there. And the horses are close to exhaustion. You've asked a lot of them. Testing them on a poor pass through there is asking for disaster. Take them the lower, easier route.'

Fronto nodded. Speed was important, but they would be entirely unstuck if they tried one of the passes and discovered it was unsuitable for the horses. He looked back down at the map. 'According to this, there's a lot of marshland along the coast north of the hills. That's as unsuitable for Antonius' landing as the hills are. We might as well stay inland until we reach Lissus, another fifteen miles north. They still support Pompey, but it may be that Antonius has chosen Lissus as a landing place. With the men he has he could probably overcome the town and secure a safe port. Bit of a gamble, but then Antonius has always been a gambler.'

'And what do we do at Lissus if he's not there?'

Fronto shrugged. 'There's only a hundred of us. We give it a wide berth, then come back to the coast and hope to see ships and men to the north.'

This time they allowed two hours for the horses, which were already showing signs of fatigue and would not manage a great deal more without a proper rest. Fronto constantly returned to the map in worry and frustration, and it came as something of a relief once they mounted up and set off north again.

He tutted and fretted constantly at the detour and extra delay as they moved northeast and made for the pass that carried the main road north to Lissus. By the time they ascended to the height of the pass, the sun was beginning to make its presence felt in the form of a pinky-orange glow to the east. Once they reached the flat land again and the terrain opened up into grassy plains, they rested the horses once more. As the animals roved across the turf recovering from their latest ordeal, the men broke their fast with the last of their rations.

'Got to find him soon or we'll have to look for more provisions,' Fronto grumbled.

'Got to find him soon or you'll have killed the horses,' Galronus corrected him, almost in admonishment.

By the time they mounted and set off once again, the sun had risen and the world had begun to warm. This time they followed the road, making the going considerably easier, yet the horsemen set the pace slower than Fronto had expected, saving the horses as much as possible. They angled slightly west of north with the highway and continued the seemingly endless trek. Despite the unsuitable terrain for a landing, Fronto constantly worried that they'd passed Antonius somewhere. They were now close to sixty miles north of the Apsus, and thirty north of Dyrrachium.

The city of Lissus appeared on the horizon in the mid to late morning, walls gleaming in the sun. After some time the road forked, and they paused, examining the milestone standing there. The right hand road led to the city, which clung to a low slope below the hills, watching over the coast. The left veered off towards the sea, marked for a place called Nymphaeum three miles beyond. A line of blue hills ahead gradually descended to the left and must signal the point where the Illyrian coast turned northwest.

'Left?' Galronus asked quietly.

Fronto nodded. 'Left.'

They rode on, slower than ever now, horses beginning to plod and complain. After a short time, Galronus cleared his throat. 'What is that? Some kind of plantation?'

Fronto frowned and followed his gesture. His eyes fell upon the slope above the road, which separated them from the route to the city of Lissus. A small thicket of bare spires rose from the otherwise-open grass. He squinted, and his lip curled in disgust.

'Crucifixions. Gods above and below.'

He called a halt to the unit and he and Galronus climbed the slope to the grisly thicket. There was little doubt as to who they were. Some of them wore the blue tunics of sailors, and others were wearing legionary kit. They stank of death and of faeces, but also of brine. Men who had been at sea for days before their execution.

'How many?'

'More than a hundred,' Galronus replied.

Fronto nodded. 'Nearer twice that number.' He turned and peered down the slope. From here he could see the water, and it did not take long to spot the wreckage. Two ships had sunk close enough to the shore that their skeletons were still visible.

'Two ships. That means there are more. We have to hope these two just fell foul of someone and that they're not an indicator of what happened to the whole army.'

Unable to do anything about the mass execution right now, Fronto and his friend turned their back on the horrible display clearly set up by the Pompeian garrison of Lissus. They returned to the horses below and began the slow plod onwards. To the west of the road lay marshy land and large pools and small lakes until the soft, giving shoreline. To the right there were repeated thickets and ridges of green.

Fronto had become so used to the almost hypnotic sound of four hundred hooves on packed earth or gravel, and it took precious moments for him to hear the new sound over the horses. He suddenly sat bolt upright in the saddle.

'Did you hear that?'

'What?' Galronus looked around as though he might see the sound.

'There it is again,' Fronto said. 'Shouting.'

And now they all heard it. Desperate calls in Latin. Then the tell-tale shrill blast of a centurion's whistle. The lesser sounds of iron on bronze and on wood were there, beneath the shouting.

'Come on,' Fronto shouted. 'Form up for battle.' He turned to Galronus. 'You're the cavalry man. Command.'

'We don't know who they are,' the Remi muttered.

'If anyone around here is fighting Romans, I'd be willing to put money on finding some of our men there.'

Galronus nodded and began issuing orders to his riders. The decurions led their men out into a wide formation with riders forwards at the periphery, like a large crescent. At a final command they moved. The terrain here was good for the horsemen, and despite the weariness of both men and riders, they moved apace to the east, climbing the gentle slope from the road. They crested the low rise and took in the situation in an instant.

Perhaps two or three centuries of legionaries were tightly packed in the contra equitas formation, shields raised on two tiers with the upper slanted to provide protection from spears, while their own pila jutted out like the spines of a hedgehog between the shields, keeping the nervous horses of their attackers away. The shields of the legionaries bore the familiar golden bull emblem of Caesar, while their attackers were probably Illyrian, lightly armoured and bearing spears, their tunics a mass of drab colours, their shields either unpainted or bearing complex designs – those who had one, anyway. A single Roman rider sat at the higher slope gesturing with a hand, directing the attack, a native beside him with a horn blasting out the signals.

Even as Galronus and the rest appeared on the scene, the horsemen made a try for the legionary formation. The bodies scattered about, mostly in russet tunics and chain armour, told Fronto that this was far from the first attack, though likely the horsemen's clear success early on had been down to the legionaries not having managed to form up in time. Fronto watched as the Illyrians closed on the wall of shields and pila. They were far from stupid. No horse willingly attacks a hedge of spears, but the enemy riders had come in two waves. The first cast their short spears at the legionaries, then peeled off and allowed the second wave to charge. The spears mostly glanced off shields or dug into earth, but a few found targets in the narrow gaps between shields, and the damage to the formation could have been their undoing. Gaps opened up, and the second wave made for them, planning to exploit them. If the enemy riders got in through the wall of shields things would go badly for the Caesarians, especially since the Illyrians numbered perhaps twice as many. Fortunately, whoever was commanding the legionaries was worth his pay, and the gaps were closed up almost as fast as they opened. The result was that the second wave was robbed of the weakness and was forced to abandon their charge and veer off.

'Some of them have lost their spears now,' Galronus bellowed. 'Concentrate on the ones still bearing a spear. Enfold them and take them down, closing the noose on twenty.'

What half that meant was a mystery to Fronto, so he ignored it, and, reasoning that he might cock up the Remi's plan, instead made for the Roman officer on the horse, ripping his blade from its scabbard as he did so.

'For Caesar!' he bellowed as he raced for the officer. The call was echoed by the beleaguered legionaries, given extra heart and new strength by the sudden appearance of allied cavalry.

The officer turned, his eyes widening at the sight of Fronto racing towards him.

'Retreat,' he bellowed. 'Back to the city!'

And with that, he turned and kicked his horse into life, pounding away across the turf towards Lissus. Fronto made to chase him down, but the man's horse was fresh, while Bucephalus was broken, and the big black steed could do little more than canter a few paces and then slow. The same story was evident across the fight. The musician honked a call on his horn, then turned and raced off after his commander. The Illyrians broke off the fight and thundered away, Galronus' horsemen made a valiant attempt to catch a few before they fled, but the difference between fresh mounts and exhausted ones was clear, and soon the enemy were out of sight, hurtling back to the safety of their walls.

Fronto and Galronus walked their beasts over towards the legionaries, who were wearily breaking formation.

'Thank the gods,' said a scarred centurion with feeling as he stepped out from the ranks of men.

'Good day to you,' Fronto grinned. 'Nice morning for a little exercise, eh?'

Whatever the veteran centurion might have wanted to say to such levity, he was professional enough to keep to himself, and simply saluted. 'Your timing is impeccable, sir. My men are exhausted and we couldn't have held them off much longer.'

'How in Hades do you come to be here?' Fronto said. 'And do you know who the lot hanging on the crosses back there are?'

The man nodded. 'We were separated from the fleet last evening, sir. The sea swells were dreadful and we were driven in to the coast. The locals found us on the beach. The complements of both ships were given the chance to surrender. Those other lads? They were just boys. New recruits. They panicked and dropped their weapons. Look what happened to 'em. We didn't. We made a run for it. For a while we thought they were leaving us alone, but once they'd secured the youngsters they came after us. Shame. An hour longer and we'd have got there.'

Fronto frowned. 'Got where?'

'To the rest of the fleet,' the centurion said as though Fronto were an idiot, then he turned and pointed. Fronto followed his gesture and stared. They had been so busy locked on the fight and enemy fleeing east that he'd not yet turned and looked west or north.

Perhaps two miles away, around the curve of the shore, sat a fishing village, or small town, with an extensive system of jetties and docks. There, bobbing in the water were perhaps half a dozen ships, but the green land to the west of there seethed with men and tents. The legions had arrived in Illyricum.

Fronto exhaled at last.

CHAPTER 6

Near Dyrrachium, Aprilis 48 BC

The return journey from Nymphaeum had not been as fast as Fronto would have liked, though he could understand why. Necessity demanded care, and even the impulsive Marcus Antonius was playing a safe game at the moment. Not all the army had come across with him, and so the landing site had needed to be secured, which had, of course, involved capturing the city of Lissus.

Once the fleet was secure, they had left a small garrison and taken the bulk of the newly-arrived forces and the supplies they'd brought and began the slow trek south. Couriers had been sent ahead with spare horses to apprise Caesar of their imminent arrival, and to pinpoint the current location of the allied camp. So slow was the business of moving a fully equipped and provisioned army, that the couriers returned before they had even come south of Dyrrachium.

Still, at last they were here. They had passed that great coastal bastion of Pompey's power with care and plenty of distance. This might be a strong army, but there was no point in tempting ill fortune, regardless. Finally, stomping through the flat coastal lands south of Dyrrachium, they had spotted the first lines of pickets, set up to be certain there would be no sortie from the city into the army's unsuspecting rear. It had taken no watchwords or security to pass the pickets, not with the great general Marcus Antonius at the fore and legion after legion bearing Caesar's bull emblem. Rather than be met with suspicion, they were met with endless relief and enthusiasm. Tired and worried soldiers held out jars of wine that were hard won and jealously guarded, yet given freely to the men who had come to turn things around and save them from ongoing hardship.

It was fascinating to see what had happened in the few short days since Fronto and Galronus had left on their ride north. Caesar still held Pompey at bay, remarkably, still keeping him away from Dyrrachium. The army had settled in a perfect flat area, with ample ground for many legions to camp, and had already begin to fortify in earnest. They had built a camp large enough to accommodate more than twice the number building it, in anticipation of the rest of the army joining them, and a heavy embankment and palisade with towers that looked so reminiscent of those dreadful days at Alesia stretched from the camp down to the sea, where a small secure harbour had been created, even though nothing could come in or go out without passing through that distant cordon of enemy triremes.

The land seethed with men. No sign of the enemy, though from the reports the couriers had brought back, Pompey's army was encamped on a hill called Petra, some miles to the south, close to the sea. Had there not been light cloud and an odd haze to the air, they might well be visible from here, after all.

As the relief force neared the camp's nearest gate of many, Antonius distributed orders to the various officers and he, Fronto and Galronus rode on ahead with just a small cavalry escort. The weary soldiers of the invading army downed their tools or platters and cheered as the long-anticipated general rode past.

'Better hope you can be what they want,' Fronto muttered. 'They're clearly pinning all their hopes on your arrival.'

'Shows what the ordinary man knows,' Antonius snorted. 'They have Caesar in their camp. A man who can turn a disaster into a miracle, and they look elsewhere. He may have been waiting for me for safety, Fronto, but you know as well as I that the man has the luck of his progenitor goddess. He could walk out of this camp with a plank of wood, a wheel of cheese and three men and in days Pompey would be fighting for his life.'

Fronto rolled his eyes, but held his reply in. That may have been exaggeration and hyperbole, but it was based on a core of truth. Something about Caesar kept him winning, no matter what odds were thrown against him. Gods, but Fronto himself had set his personal flag against Caesar more than once, and yet here he was fighting for the man yet again. Coming back like a faithful hound. It was ridiculous, really.

Caesar's command tent was a seething hotspot. Officers were gathered around in knots outside, pointing, arguing, checking off lists and shouting at centurions, who would then run back to their units to shout at their men. Clerks rushed in and out of the huge tent in a constant flow and counter-flow. Aulus Hirtius, staff officer and Caesar's favourite administrator, stood by the door, directing the flow of wordsmiths by some arcane plan. Soldiers were everywhere.

The four riders dismounted and instantly an equisio was there to take the mounts, and two of Aulus Ingenuus' bodyguard, recognising the four important officers, created a passageway through the chaos for them to reach the central structure.

Fronto tried to fall back and let Antonius take the lead, but the flat-faced, curly-haired officer laughed and slowed similarly, keeping Fronto to the fore. They entered the tent and had to pause to adjust their eyesight to the gloom within.

The chaos continued inside, with scribes and officers all over the place. Caesar was seated on his curule chair behind a table covered in maps, lists and charts. He looked tired, but more alive and alert than usual, and he rose and slapped both hands flat on the table as he noticed the new arrivals.

'Thank all the gods, Marcus.' He turned and swept a hand expansively around the room.

'Out, all of you. If it can wait, go and eat. If it cannot, Hirtius will help.'

The room cleared in moments, sweating clerks hurrying past the officers with heads bowed. Calenus, to whom the rule seemingly did not apply, remained standing in the corner, a look of utmost relief on his face.

'We've directed the new arrivals to appropriate camping spots,' Antonius said, then by way of greeting, 'and it's good to see you, Gaius.'

Caesar laughed. 'Tell me everything.'

'You first. Your news is probably more important.'

Caesar shook his head. 'I doubt it. In a nutshell, the coastal barrage is still in place, though weaker than initially. We have sufficient supplies for the men we already have for perhaps ten more days, and even then on reduced rations. We go down to emergency rations shortly to preserve what we have. The local farmland has yielded all it can, since Pompey's men had been reaping it and storing it in Dyrrachium for months. We managed to secure some supplies from Apollonia, but a good proportion of that had to remain in the city for the garrison and the population. We need to be seen as saviours, not invaders, and I cannot afford to have them turn against me once more because we have starved them to feed the soldiers. We cannot venture too far inland, for Pompey's reserves are out there somewhere, including legions marching under Scipio from Syria. We can hardly afford to have foraging units bump into enemy legions. And, of course, north of here you know the situation. We managed to stay nicely ahead of Pompey and keep him out of Dyrrachium. Even with our relative strengths, he seems reluctant to commit. If I were to be charitable, I might think that he still hoped to avoid the coming conflict, but I think we all know that he is just trying to be certain of the least costly victory.'

The officers nodded. 'So where is he? This place called Petra?' Antonius asked.

Caesar looked across at Calenus and nodded. The senior staff officer cleared his throat. 'We've tentatively scouted Petra and decided that the man knows what he's about. Taking him off that hill would be like trying another Gergovia. The man is well positioned and well defended. His wagons continue to roll in from the east, and now he is also supplied by ship. His lowest auxiliary is eating more than our officers, and has a better wine ration, too. The man can probably sit there and watch us gradually fade away unless you have good news for us?'

All eyes turned to Antonius, who looked up suddenly from where he'd been helping himself to a wine jug. 'Fronto...'

'No, this story is yours. I'll take the wine.'

Antonius noted the sly smile on Caesar's face and reluctantly handed the wine to Fronto. Calenus made a snorting noise. As Fronto poured himself a much-desired cup of wine, Antonius rolled his shoulders.

'It's a long story.'

'Currently we have time, though if it's too long we might all starve, so skip the oratory,' Caesar smiled.

Antonius rolled his eyes. 'Well, we reached Brundisium without incident. A few new ships had been found but not enough to offset those we'd already lost. We took the fleet we had into port and began to put out calls for more vessels but the next thing we know, some pig's pizzle called Libo turns up. Cunning little bastard sailed in at night, took out our watchmen and occupied the island just outside Brundisium. Filled the damn place with missile troops and kept his military ships there, ready to shaft us up the out-pipe if we decided to try set sail. You know how few military escort vessels we had. So we were effectively blockaded into Brundisium.'

Caesar sighed. 'How shrewd. Libo reduces the need for a huge cordon of ships in Illyricum by concentrating on the source and stopping you putting to sea to join us.'

'Precisely. And his plan was good. Kept us bent over and saying yes please for a while. Had to find a way to break him. In the end I pulled the old false retreat. Never done it at sea before, but I had good men, and they translated land tactics to ships surprisingly well. We sent a couple of ships out to look like they were making a break one morning. This Libo dick noticed and sent heavy ships after them. They backwatered and drew Libo's ships into the harbour. Thing is: we'd spent half the night sending missile units out to the shorelines and other islands. The poor bastards sailed straight into a storm of iron. Five quadriremes in the deepest of shit. We sank two and captured one. The other two limped back out in a hurry. Seems they were the backbone of his fleet. Next morning, he turned tail and sailed away with that same tail between his legs. No idea where he went but we've not seen a sign of him since.'

Caesar frowned. 'So you still have your warships, and one more besides? Why were they not with you when you neared the coast close to us then?'

Antonius shrugged. 'I only brought the fastest ships to the shore to show you we were here and where we were going. The warships stayed out to sea with the rest and met us north of Dyrrachium.'

'So you're all here?'

Antonius shook his head. 'A little more than half, I'd say. We were just too short of ships. Once we'd kicked Libo back out to sea, we brought everyone we could fit. Came close enough for you to see what we were doing, then cut out north, outrunning the blockade ships. We made sure to move north of the current blockade and landed just north of Lissus.'

Fronto coughed and Antonius shot him a sour look.

'Almost all of us. The weather was bad and the sea really shitty. Two ships were driven off course and hit Lissus. They tried to surrender. The local commander crucified half of them. The other half were fighting for their lives when Fronto and this Gallic lunatic turned up and saved them. We were quite lucky in a way. The enemy were on our behind and racing to follow us in. We hurtled into the shore with the current and winds, and the moment we were secure, the whole thing changed, and the enemy were fighting both wind and current to pursue us. Once a few of them had been sunk they gave up and returned to their places.'

'And then?' Caesar's face was hungry, expectant.

'And then I sent the ships back to Brundisium to bring over the rest, warships and all. A few odd vessels stayed here, but the rest of the army will be with you in just days. Unless Libo remembers where his guts are and stops sailing around in circles in embarrassment, they should encounter no trouble in the crossing. We were slightly delayed in the march south as we had to keep the landing secure for them. We moved on Lissus, ready to take them down, but the citizens did the right thing. They overthrew the garrison and opened the gates to us. Lissus is yours. We were appropriately merciful to the garrison, given what they'd done days earlier. We crucified two hundred of them and then let the others run away. All except the commander. We made him regret his decisions. Briefly, I'll admit. But there was a *lot* of regret. And it smelled of ammonia.'

Caesar laughed.

'Then we have decisions to make. Any attack on Pompey is still dangerous and foolhardy at best. We could try and take Dyrrachium, but then we risk landing ourselves in the midst of a siege with Pompey coming up on us from behind. His army is well-fed, and I suspect if we were to halve his rations, we might bring things back into balance. Oh, that reminds me. What of supplies?'

Antonius shrugged. 'The good news is we will be able to ship supplies over from Brundisium once the entire army is here, and there will be some relief from the north, too, so the army will not starve immediately. Moreover, I've brought some wagons with me, which will relieve your current situation.'

'And the bad news?'

'Our supply routes are long and tenuous. At sea they're at risk from pirates, storms and Pompey's ships. From the north, they have to pass towns that still hold allegiance to Pompey, and after the past hard winter there is precious little to spare anyway. Normally, as in Gaul, we'd rely on forage, but Pompey's clearly dealt with that by stripping the land clear before we arrived. The upshot is that even with the supply routes I've secured the army's going to go hungry. Especially with every new body we bring in.'

'Meanwhile,' Caesar sighed, 'Pompey receives supplies from both sides. Shipped in from his huge granaries in Dyrrachium, which contain a year's worth of forage and more, and driven in from the east, from his camps and practice grounds in Macedonia. He eats well. We need to do something to redress this balance, clearly.'

'Dyrrachium?' Antonius mused. 'I know you worry about getting us caught between the city and Pompey's army, but we take Dyrrachium, and we secure his granaries. Then we have ample food and he's reliant upon the east.'

Calenus shook his head. 'We've mooted the possibility of storming Dyrrachium so many times it's giving me a headache. The place is strong, well supplied and well defended. Still, with the army we have now, we could take it I'm sure, but as Caesar said, in doing so we turn an unprotected back to the south and Pompey only has to step down from his Petra heights and plant a knife in it and the whole thing is over. We can't take Dyrrachium with Pompey looming as he is. And the sad and simple fact is that even with the increased manpower and new supplies, driving him from that hill would be a feat of godly proportions.'

'So what's the option?' Fronto muttered. 'Sit and wait for a sign from Mars?'

'We cannot take Dyrrachium and we cannot assault Pompey, yet slowly we starve while he eats,' Caesar said. 'We are used to hardship. Pompey and his men are not. We need to make them hungry.'

'But how?'

'There is little we can do to prevent him receiving supplies by sea. He has effective control of these waters, and a clear line from Dyrrachium. But if we can cut off his other supplies from the east, I believe his ships will not be able to meet the demands of his army, no matter how fast they sail, much as his fleet discovered.'

'And how do we do that?' Antonius huffed. 'Scatter our army over a fifty mile stretch of land and tell them to look for wagons?'

'No. We learn from our experiences in Gaul, Marcus. We besiege him. We begin circumvallation, as we did at Alesia. We seal off Petra with an arc of defences so that no land route remains open to him.'

Fronto's eyes strayed to the sizeable campaign map. The terrain looked appalling, and to effectively seal Pompey in would take miles and miles of defences. Unbidden, memories of that awful, cataclysmic battle below the oppidum of Alesia came flooding back. That battle had left him with nightmares that had taken years to fade. And to contemplate a repeat, but against Romans?

He shuddered

* * *

Fronto stood on a particularly lofty perch of the hill and squinted off into the haze.

'This is bloody ridiculous.'

Antonius nodded. 'That's the problem when no one really wants to fight a war. It's better to do almost anything other than actually draw a sword. I expect Pompey's army is much the same as ours. The legionaries are happy to avoid a conflict, and the only ones who itch to fight and feel the urge for booty are the foreign auxiliaries who don't care too much that they'd be killing Romans.'

'It's still bloody ridiculous.'

It had been slightly ridiculous to begin with. Caesar's forces had begun to invest the enemy with siege works along similar lines to those constructed at Alesia. A rampart of earth and rubble was thrown up in sections, with a wattle fence atop it, carefully woven, and in places timber, where terrain, time and availability allowed. Intermittent towers were raised and filled with men. Forts were created periodically along the line and manned with strong units, which had become easier with the arrival of the rest of the army from Brundisium two days earlier. One unexpected bonus had been the appearance of Mamurra, the great engineer, who had joined the army once more in Italia and shipped out to tie himself ever closer to the consul.

The master engineer sucked on his teeth and continually twitched his fingers in some sort of impatient or nervous habit. 'Had I been here from the start I would have done things differently. This is not like facing confident Gauls in their home town, like Alesia. There they were content to be enfolded, for they believed themselves impregnable and knew that aid was coming. Here, Pompey is in a temporary camp and a precarious position. He will not simply watch us wall him in. I would have begun the siege works from three or four positions, keeping the army in several vexillations such that we had him surrounded while the ramparts went up all around him. Then, the whole system might have been possible to complete in just four or five miles.'

It was all well and good to say such things, and there were difficulties he'd not accounted for, but on the whole he was probably right, and certainly the man knew of which he spoke when it came to siege works.

In actual fact, what had happened was that Caesar's army had begun from their main camp, sending the wall south in sections, gradually reaching around Pompey's position with the intention of finishing at the shore to the south of the enemy's camp. Pompey, however, had different ideas. The Caesarian siege works had arced around some two and a bit miles from camp, into the range of hills that surrounded the bay, only to be appraised by the scouts that Pompey had begun his own wall. Just as Caesar's men pushed on to seal Pompey in, Pompey was digging his own ditches and raising his own ramparts to keep Caesar out. It was almost comical in some respect. Those men in charge of the works on the Caesarian side had pushed every effort into speed, driving the defences south, claiming the best peaks they could, but Pompey's men were quicker, for they were more numerous and better fed. So every half mile Caesar's men pushed, so did Pompey. The result was that the Caesarian troops had been unable to close the arc and head back down towards the sea. Instead, Pompey's lines were forcing them to build further and further south. Instead of a solid four mile arc, now the siege line was already more than eight miles long and they were still well inland in the hills, struggling to stay ahead of Pompey's own wall, desperate to try and close the work.

'By the time we actually touch the sea again, we'll have enclosed half the republic,' Fronto grunted. 'If we keep going south with the wall like this how far can we go before we hit water anyway?'

Mamurra frowned and unfurled the map he carried, marked out with current works and projected plans. His eyes slid down the vellum roll. 'Oddly, I reckon the beach where you first landed is due south. About ninety miles, I'd say.'

'Even if we could build such a thing, we could never man it all,' Antonius snorted. 'We'll have to get ahead of them and turn the corner, close them in and head for the shore as we initially planned. It has to be possible.'

Fronto shrugged and glanced over at Mamurra. 'Well?'

The engineer sucked his teeth again and pored over the map in his hands, repeatedly lifting his gaze to the hills around them and transposing the one onto the other.

'If it is possible, then it relies upon taking several strong positions and enclosing them. See that twin hill over there that looks a little like a pair of breasts?'

Fronto and Antonius peered in the direction the man pointed.

'If you're meaning where I think you're meaning, you've met some weird looking breasts,' Fronto snorted. 'But yes, I think I see what you mean. Pompey's line will naturally take in those hills, yes?'

'The way we're all going, yes. But if we can press for that furthest hill, then his line will be forced back towards the shore. His circuit will become tighter and we can begin to press west towards the sea. There are two other places on the map I think we'll be able to do the same. If we can make a concerted push in each of those three places, we can force Pompey's wall back and enclose it.

'Looks like we're having another little skirmish,' Antonius harrumphed.

'I thought you said no one wanted to fight?' murmured Mamurra.

'I said the legions didn't like fighting one another. Native auxilia are a different matter.'

Fronto peered down at the works. In some places the lines were little more than half a mile apart, and there was the constant fear that artillery might reach across the gap. And whenever the works came close enough for worry, and the terrain allowed it, the enemy would commit their rabid oriental archers. It was happening right now, as had become an almost daily occurrence.

The work parties on the leading edge of the rampart were running from their work, dropping their baskets of stones and mattocks, leaving personal effects scattered across the grass as they dived for the cover of the great hide and felt shields that had been hastily assembled for this very purpose. Centurions' whistles blew, as well as the horn of a lookout on the walls. The man there pointed out the locations of the skirmishers only to topple from the rampart with an arrow jutting from his neck. The enemy soldiers closed on the location before coming to a halt and letting loose with full fury. More than half the workers had reached their shelter before the deadly shafts of the Greek archers dropped in a cloud, skewering men and clattering off tools and armour.

The archers stayed for a count of three missiles launched, and then melted away into the undergrowth as swiftly and unexpectedly as they'd arrived. It was an unfortunate side-effect of the terrain, with its ridges and rocks, shrubs and bushes, that small, cunning units could advance through it almost invisible to the watchmen on the walls. Naturally, the Caesarian forces responded, Illyrian auxiliaries hurrying out after the fleeing archers. They would catch a few. Maybe half a dozen, and the bodies would end up displayed on the rampart as a futile and ineffective warning.

Thus it went, and might do forever, if they couldn't seize those specific points Mamurra had identified. If they worked hard, they could occupy the first, and that might change things.

* * *

Fronto watched from the tower, tense, wishing the Tenth had been chosen rather than the Ninth, for there was nothing so frustrating for a good officer than impotently watching a peer fighting a crucial action. The men of the Ninth advanced up the slope. The task of taking the critical hills of Mamurra's had been given to the Ninth for two reasons. Firstly they had some redemption to seek after the near mutiny they had been involved in last winter, and secondly, they served Sulla, and the man had something of a reputation for pushing hard, and had asked for the opportunity. Caesar himself had remained in the main camp, attending to supply issues, leaving Antonius in charge of the main operations to the south.

Antonius stood in the next turret along, with his signallers and musicians, commanding from his optimum viewpoint.

Two cohorts of the Ninth climbed the hill under full arms, two more behind them bringing timbers and rocks and tools. As soon as they took the height, they would need to fortify and secure it so that it could be incorporated into the works. It was a dangerous push, for it was ridiculously close to Pompey's own work. If they could take that hill, then they would turn the lines back towards the sea. It was, as the engineer had noted, one of a pair of twin hills, and, though the nearer hill would be less effective, they could still begin the turn on that. Fronto had argued for that one to avoid too much trouble, but Antonius, Sulla and Caesar had agreed to try for the one closest to Pompey and save the nearer one as a fall back if they failed to take the further.

The Ninth reached the top and came to a slow halt, bristling with steel, expectant. Sulla was dangerously close to the front of his men, where he could see what was happening. Fronto, from his vantage point some distance away, could see just how close the two armies were here. Pompey's rampart occupied another ridge not more than six hundred paces from the ranks of the Ninth.

'Why have they stopped?' Galronus murmured.

'Waiting for the supplies to be brought up,' Fronto replied, pointing at the cohorts lugging huge timbers and the like up the hill.

Even as they watched, the front cohorts of the Ninth began to spread out under orders, creating an arc across the hill crest, where the rampart could be raised behind them.

'Any moment now,' Fronto muttered.

'What?'

'Should have stuck with the nearer hill. That one's too close to Pompey for comfort. If we'd been conservative and taken the nearer hill, there would have been sufficient distance still between the lines that the enemy would probably have let us. But not there. Pompey can't let us have that. It's a direct call to war, is that.'

Sure enough, a moment later, horns sounded at the far side of the enemy's part-built siege works.

'Now things will go to shit. I hope Antonius has a backup plan. Two cohorts can't hold that hill if the enemy really want it.'

'Why not commit more of ours, then?' Galronus fretted.

'Because the hill is not large enough. And if we commit a full legion there, we might just trigger the mass slaughter we've been trying to avoid. Look, he's still just committing his auxiliaries. The moment Pompey decides to field legionaries against us, there'll be no stopping the bloodletting.'

The men pouring out from Pompey's defences were clearly auxiliaries. The advance units poured forth without much call for order and discipline. Groups of archers and slingers hurtled towards the Ninth on their hill, spear men coming behind in blocks.

'Greeks, Cretans, Illyrians, Thracians. Not a Roman citizen among them,' Fronto noted. 'But they're going to cripple Sulla's cohorts.'

He watched, teeth grinding, as the enemy hurried towards the legion. A whistle blew, and the lines of Caesarian soldiers hefted their pila.

'No,' Fronto fumed. 'Don't waste them.'

But as soon as the auxiliaries came near to pilum range, another signal was given by Sulla's musician, and the legionaries launched their missiles. It was futile. By the time the first shaft was even in the air, the nimble enemy had halted and dropped back. The hundreds of iron-headed javelins crashed to the ground, bending and breaking, very few finding a target. With a roar, the natives responded instantly. Pila range was easily bow and sling range, too. Their missiles began to fly, thudding, thwacking and punching into the legionaries of the Ninth.

'Why does he not give the order to advance?' Galronus said in a near whisper.

'Because Sulla is impulsive and hard, but he recognises the danger there. If he advances beyond the brow of the hill, he's walking into a natural trap. The enemy will just pull back before him and then suddenly he'll find himself far from help, facing the spear men and within easy bow shot of the enemy ramparts. They'd be slaughtered.'

'They *are* being slaughtered,' noted the Remi nobleman, pointing.

Gloomily, Fronto nodded as he watched legionaries falling with every heartbeat, killed by arrows and sling bullets. The two cohorts were being devastated, while their companions still struggled up the slope behind them with timbers and baskets of rocks and tools.

'It's not going to work,' Fronto harrumphed. 'They need to abandon it and concentrate on the nearer hill. Gods, but this could be a mess. Sulla needs to recognise the impossibility of his position, and I damn well hope Antonius has a plan, or that lot will all die in retreat.'

They watched in cold, angry anticipation as the legionaries of the Ninth died in droves to the enemy's missiles.

'For the love of Venus, Sulla, retreat!'

As though he'd heard Fronto's imploring, the Ninth's commander finally gave a signal and horns blew. The leading cohorts of the Ninth began to flee. There was no ordered retreat here, but a desperate need to be out of range of those archers. Fronto watched, chewing his cheek, as the legionaries poured back down the slope. The archers and slingers made way for light, fast Illyrian spear men, who came flooding after the running legionaries, cresting the hill. The Ninth were now in full retreat from that rise, with spear men close behind, and missile troops following on. It looked like a disaster.

'Even the other cohorts are running,' Galronus said.

Fronto's gaze dropped to those secondary cohorts, and he frowned. 'No. Not quite. Look what they've done.'

While all attention had been on the fight on the top of the hill, those cohorts behind had not just dropped their timber and stones and tools, but had subtly, cunningly, created a wall of obstacles. Even as the fleeing legionaries leapt over it and ducked past, roaring spearmen horrifyingly close behind, Antonius in the next tower had his musicians blow a call out across the hills.

From shadowy delves, three cohorts of Hispanic archers and slingers appeared. One moment they weren't there, the next they were. And it took only a heartbeat for them to be ready. Pompey's spearmen reached the obstacles and even as they began to climb and jump, each and every one was struck with arrows and stones, their shaking corpses adding to the obstacles.

'Cunning bastard,' Fronto smiled. 'Still, he wasted good men up there.'

Sulla took up the signals again now and, at a triple blast from a horn, his men stopped running instantly, turned and began to form up. Their flight had been far more careful than it had appeared, clearly, for while the front lines had cast their pila at the hilltop, now those men were at the back, while the previously rear ranks were now at the front with their pila raised.

At the line of obstacles, the enemy spearmen were still pressing, trying to cross the timbers and bags and baskets and crates, along with the numerous dead bodies of their own fallen, and they gave a great cheer as the missiles stopped flying, and launched over the obstacles, only to come face to face with the legionaries. No longer in flight, the men of the Ninth now took the initiative; released by a centurion's whistle, they charged en-masse, punching into the lines of spear men. The obstacles provided little trouble for them as they butchered the light infantry, largely lacking armour and shields with which to defend themselves.

At the same time, the archers who had stopped loosing at the spearmen in order to avoid hitting the Ninth, now drew harder, aimed higher, and began to drop arrows among the enemy slingers and bowmen, who were still following on, ready to fall into position What had been a gleeful pursuit of the Ninth had now become a bloody rout. The enemy's officers, Roman prefects of Pompey's, were back among their own defences, hopelessly ignorant of the wholesale slaughter of their men out of sight beyond the hill.

It was over in a matter of two dozen heartbeats. The enemy skirmishers were back over the crest, screaming in panic and in hugely diminished numbers. Less than a quarter of the men who'd attacked returned to the Pompeian lines. The disciplined forces of the Ninth halted at a call from Sulla, below the crest of the hill. In moments they were back in formation, and carrying the 'obstacles' away from the carrion field, making for the second, nearer hill.

'Why do that at all, if they were happy to settle for this hill?' Galronus mused.

'Because we all know we can't hold and maintain the further hill that close to the enemy, but Sulla and Antonius just gave Pompey a bloody nose. We lost perhaps two hundred men on that hill. They lost well over a thousand. It might not exactly even our numbers, but there will be a lot of berating and punishment in the enemy camp tonight, and I think that's the last we'll see of these irritating little skirmishes for now. They've learned a hard lesson. And maybe I did too. Trust Antonius. He knows what he's doing.'

'I never know what you lot are doing,' Galronus sighed. 'The Roman way of war is so different to the Remi and other Belgae. The very idea of pretending to run away would shame any of our leaders. They would never think of such a ruse. Dishonourable way to fight.'

'But damned effective,' Fronto grinned. 'With civilisation comes deviousness. Sad, but true.'

Galronus cast him an irritated look. 'Only a patrician would think that just because we're not Roman, the Remi are uncivilised.'

'Poor choice of words,' Fronto laughed. 'Though I *have* tasted your beer, so I'm not so sure.'

The two men looked out over the hill, its grey-green summit discoloured with blood and scattered with corpses. 'With luck we can turn the angle now, and finish closing the man in,' Fronto sighed.

'And then what?'

'Sorry?'

'What happens when the lines are finished?'

'We try and starve them into submission. And if we fail, it won't be Illyrian spearmen we face next time, but Pompey's legions. Pray to your gods for sense to prevail, Galronus.'

CHAPTER 7

Near Dyrrachium, Late Maius 48BC

The three men looked down from the viewing platform on the last of the low hills. The final stages of the defences had been messy. The Caesarian forces had succeeded in turning the corner finally and had raced Pompey's construction to the sea, sealing them in, but it had involved more than one little skirmish along the way, despite Fronto's earlier words. Then, as they closed on the coast, it had been dangerously close to opening up into full warfare. The Ninth Legion had constructed a fort at the water's edge next to a small river, while the men building the defences made for it to seal the gap. However, defended by only a few engineers and pioneers, freshly constructed, the small fort had fallen to a surprise attack through the local woodland by Pompey and had instead been incorporated into the enemy's defences, forcing Caesar's men ever further south.

Still, they'd managed in the end, and Caesar's legions instead constructed a new camp in their own defence line, close by. Galronus and Salvius Cursor peered into the flat land, trying to make out the end of the siege lines and the water there, but it was almost impossible. The low land here went on for miles with scattered areas of woodland, the hills too far inland to be of any further aid in the siege works.

From Pompey's main camp at the Petra hill, his fortifications covered a distance of perhaps fifteen miles, sealing in a good area with plenty of flat land for his numerous cavalry mounts and beasts of burden. The Caesarian lines covered a distance of almost twice that, at their furthest no more than a mile from the enemy line, and at the closest perhaps only a third of that.

Now came the crucial moment. Would Pompey sit and suffer, believing that Caesar's army would submit first, or would he snap and decide that war could no longer be avoided? While almost everyone hoped for the former, they generally expected the latter. Pompey would starve first if it came down to that, for though he still had more supplies available than Caesar, delivered by ship to his protected harbour, he had more men, many more animals, and his extra supplies from the east had been cut off. Caesar had fewer supplies, but fewer mouths to feed and, crucially, as the spring rolled on into summer the crops would begin to ripen and the men would be able to forage freely without fear of Pompey's forces interfering. Those crops could not come soon enough, though, for the legions had been on half rations for some time, and two days ago even that had been further reduced.

'The men are beginning to lose the will for this,' Salvius said quietly.

'What?'

'The fight. It's hard enough at the best of times to motivate Romans to fight Romans, but this privation and hardship is wearing their patience and spirits. If something doesn't happen soon, the hunger will get to the men and we'll be looking at insurrection across the entire army.'

'I'm not sure that opening hostilities just to take the men's minds off their empty bellies would be the most prudent course,' Fronto grunted.

'We all know it's going to come down to a fight. The faster we accept that and deal with it, the stronger the legions will be. If we let them wither away with hunger, do you really think they'll stand against Pompey's men?'

'Pompey's men are largely untested new recruits,' Fronto countered.

'But strong and confident ones. Give me an untested man like that over a starving, weak veteran any day'

'Hmm.' He'd have liked to argue the point, but sadly, he couldn't find a way. Though he hated to admit it, Salvius had a point. 'The men are eating barley gruel; meat too. They might be lacking in bread, but at least they're getting sustenance.'

'Fronto, the men are digging up some kind of spiky root and mashing it up with milk, stuffing it down their gullets as though it were nectar of the gods. That is not a good sign.'

'Hmmm.' Damn it.

Dam it.

Dam it? A slow smile spread across Fronto's face as he watched the twinkling surface of that narrow river that ran down through the woods and past the old camp of the Ninth now occupied by Pompey's men.

'Water.'

'What?'

'We're all starving but despite the fact that the weather has dried out, we all have plenty of water. At least no one is dying of thirst.'

'So?'

'Remember how bad things got aboard Pompey's ships? Libo said they were sucking the dew from the canvas they were so thirsty. It was probably that thirst that did for Bibulus. They couldn't ferry water from Dyrrachium fast enough to keep everyone supplied. It would be so much worse in a large army than among naval crews.'

'But as you said, we all have plenty of water.'

Fronto's grin widened. 'But *we* have control of it. All the streams and rivers that run through Pompey's territory come from hills out here. We can dam the flow, divert the water courses. We would still have access to them, but we could dry up the supply for Pompey's men.'

Salvius Cursor also grinned now, though Galronus looked troubled. 'I do not like this method of war. It is not a way to treat warriors just because there are political differences between you.'

'There he goes with his Gallic honour thing again,' Fronto smiled. 'If it means we might be able to force them to submit without a proper fight, I'm all for it.'

'If victory is important at any cost,' Galronus said, 'then why not just poison the water and watch them all die?'

Fronto's face slipped into a sour expression of distaste. 'Some things are too low even for war. Come on. Let's go see Caesar.'

* * *

Days passed as the new plan was put into action. The tension on the Illyrian coast built slowly with each passing day as Pompey's forces watched the plentiful water supplies begin to fail. Rivers and streams became shallower and narrower until finally they halted altogether. The entire enemy army shifted its focus to what water sources remained, until they too dried up and finally, after half a month, there was no source left.

The Caesarian army worked feverishly, damming rivers and cutting new courses for them, diverting the flow into other valleys that skirted the system of siege lines and emptied into the sea safely behind Caesar's lines. Deep defiles were sealed with vertical piles driven into the solid ground, covered with horizontal slats and then built up with mounds of earth, sending the rising waters into new outlets.

The balance was beginning to tip. The men of Caesar's legions looked north hungrily towards the fertile plains around the Ardaxanos River, where young wheat was beginning to turn gold with the promise of provisions. They might be on less than half standard rations, but ample food was looming closer and closer, and at least they had plentiful water supplies. In fact, legionaries had taken to bringing buckets of water to almost within bow shot of the enemy lines and there stripping naked and bathing in full sight of an enemy that had not seen clean water for some time.

The enemy had reputedly resorted to digging shallow pits in the low, marshy ground near the sea and desperately sucking down the dank, filthy water they could sparingly find. Disease would soon become an issue for Pompey's forces. They had certainly begun to sacrifice animals they could no longer afford to keep supplied with water. Meat was plentiful among the enemy, at least, though it was not only pack animals that were given up, but even the weaker of the cavalry horses.

Fronto was in his accustomed place, at that last hill in the range, overlooking the flat lands and the dry river bed that ran down to the lost fort by the sea, Galronus and Salvius Cursor at his shoulders as usual. Here, given the terrain and the excellent vantage point, one of the numerous forts along the system sat squat and heavy on the rise. Three cohorts of the Seventh under Volcatius Tullus occupied the fort, which remained one of the most critical points in the system.

Fronto's gaze strayed from the flat ground before them back to the interior of the fort behind the platform. Tullus was visible leaning over a trestle table outside his small headquarters and stabbing a map with his finger as half a dozen centurions nodded soberly. A good man, Tullus. Not one who had made a grand name for himself, nor become rich through his association with Caesar as some had, but a veteran officer and a good, dependable man. Years earlier he had commanded the bridge across the Rhenus with great success. He had led a wing of cavalry at Alesia and commanded a legion at Ilerda. A man who Caesar trusted implicitly.

As if drawn by Fronto's gaze, Tullus looked up and nodded. Fronto returned the gesture and then spun back to the grand view before them. Something was happening at the Pompeian line some half a mile away.

'Do you see that?'

Galronus nodded. 'A gathering of men. That's not just a defensive force, is it?'

Fronto shook his head. 'Salvius?'

'A full legion, I'd say, and armed for a fight.'

'Why, though? If we've pushed Pompey far enough and he thinks it's time to open hostilities, why not field his whole army and try and swamp us. You were quite right about numbers over experience. It would certainly not be a guaranteed win for us. So why field just a single legion?'

The answer came to him in a trice as his eyes once more caught that long, dry riverbed that passed close to this fort. 'He's going to try and restore the water, isn't he. This isn't a full scale battle at all. He's trying to break through and destroy the dams.' He turned to the fort. 'Volcatius? Have your men fall in. The enemy are coming.' Then to one of the legionaries on the rampart below. 'Run to the next fort and tell the commander we need aid.'

The soldier saluted and ran off north, along the earth bank, but his mission would almost certainly be fruitless, for even as horns sang out from that gathering of Pompeian men, similar calls went up a few miles away to both left and right. Fronto's rising gaze could just make out in the great distance a force of men gathering closer to the coast, preparing to sally out against the Caesarian lines. Similar was undoubtedly the case off to the north, further into the hills. There would be no aid from the other forts and the bulk of the Caesarian reserves remained in the north at the main camp.

They were on their own.

'We're about to test your assumption on the strength of fresh recruits, Salvius. Three cohorts against a legion. Think Tullus' legionaries can each kill three men?'

'I'll make up any difference,' the tribune replied, jerking his sword from its sheath with a well-oiled hiss.

They watched, tense, as the Pompeian legion issued from a gate in that timber line half a mile away, forming up on the outside, ready to move. Moments later, Tullus was with the three officers, climbing the ladder and exhaling deeply as he took in the mass of enemy legionaries in a huge block beginning to move at the sound of the buccinae.

'They're coming for the dam?'

'I figure so.'

'Then they'll have to secure this fort, but they have enough men to concentrate on the river too.'

'Yes, I'd say so,' Fronto replied. 'You think they'll try and break through the siege line as well as taking this fort?'

'I would,' Volcatius shrugged. 'Time is essential for them. If they delay too much, reinforcements will come down from the north and begin to support the lines. They need to hack apart the dam and get the water flowing.'

'But what use is that if they don't press and secure the walls?'

'They only have to have the water flowing for a day and they can fill enough barrels to keep them going for months. It won't matter then if we damn the streams again. They'll have ample to last them until Scipio arrives with his Syrian legions and stabs us in the back.'

'So we need to protect the dam.'

Volcatius nodded and turned to his signaller, who had just climbed the ladder behind him. 'Have the Third Cohort leave by the rear gate and hurry down, forming up in the riverbed. Make sure you do it quietly. I want the enemy to think we're all still in the fort as long as possible, so they commit fully to what they think is a weak spot.'

'Cunning bugger,' Fronto grinned. 'Glad you're on our side.'

'Care to command the river bed, Fronto?'

He answered with a grin. 'Salvius? Galronus?'

The three of them followed the garrison's commander back down the ladder into the small fort, then nodded their farewell to him as he prepared his officers, distributing men along the western rampart and the flanking sections of the defensive circuit. One cohort, led by a senior centurion, was already departing the rear of the fort without the usual signals and calls, and they hurried after the men. The rear gate led to a long slope that they hurried across for the former course of the river. The bed was dry as dust now, and Fronto could see the massive earth dam just seven or eight hundred paces away, diverting the flow so that it now disappeared down a valley to the south, meandering far from its original course. The section of rampart through which the river had originally flowed had been in-filled since the dam's creation and was only identifiable as different work from the clear dip of the dry river bed that ran beneath it.

Fronto could see the lines of men from the other cohorts shuffling along the wall top, strengthening the defences. They would focus on the fort, but had to keep the flanks secure also.

Fronto and his friends scurried around to the front of the gathered cohort, where the six centurions were deep in conversation, and all six broke up, turned and snapped out a salute at the appearance of the three officers.

'Sirs.'

'Centurion. You're in charge here?'

'Yes, sir. Cincius Laeca, sir.'

'What's the plan?'

The centurion frowned. 'We split the centuries up to act as individual units and prepare for any breakthrough. That way we're highly mobile and can commit to more than one spot if we need to.'

Fronto nodded. 'Sound plan. But I'd split into groups of two centuries. Stronger units but still mobile enough to react.'

'Yes, sir.'

'Select your two most veteran centuries and put them in the centre, on the river bed. The others can be placed on the banks to left and right. Galronus here can help with the left, Salvius with the centre and I'll join the right.'

'Sir, it might not be safe to...'

Fronto waved him aside. 'Every blade is crucial when the odds are more than three to one, Centurion.'

97

Grudgingly, the centurion nodded, and distributed the orders to his fellow commanders. Fronto scanned the men atop the wall until he spotted a centurion's crest, then called out for him. When the man turned, looked down and spotted Fronto, he saluted. 'Give us a wave when it starts to look like trouble, and point the weak spots out.'

Another salute, and the man went back to preparing.

Fronto moved off to the gentle slope of the river's right bank and fell into position there with two undermanned centuries. The army may now all be here, but each legion was still short of manpower. The three units defending the dam would each number a hundred and sixty men on parchment, but in reality they would be lucky to number a hundred and twenty. Fronto fell in between the two centurions, sword out and ready. The two men gave him a polite but disapproving look, unhappy at the presence of a senior officer at the front. He glanced over to the left and could see Galronus in a similar position on the left bank and Salvius Cursor slightly out front at the centre, almost vibrating with the need to plant his blade in something.

It seemed strange being here behind the ramparts, unable to see what was happening, but the arrival of Pompey's force on the scene was clearly audible. They listened to the distinctive tromp of thousands of caligae as they closed on the Caesarian defence. Then there was silence. The enemy had drawn up their lines a little distant.

More silence. Fronto felt the tension creeping across his skin, making the hairs stand proud.

A whistle.

The thunder of thousands of men charging.

Another whistle. A few shouts from the wall top and the din of clatters and grunts as men hefted pila and threw them down at the advancing enemy. Screams, muffled, from the far side. Fronto's heart lurched as a pilum, clearly launched by an insanely powerful arm, cleared the parapet above, passed between two of the defenders and plunged down towards the hidden defenders within. The centuries behind Fronto scattered, leaving a wide circle into which the javelin fell, plunging into the earth and bending on impact. To their credit, they had not shouted or even uttered a word beyond low grunts. A man yanked the pilum out of the ground and tossed it away onto the grass and the lines re-formed.

Here and there, more missiles came over the top, each time with plenty of warning for the watchful, waiting soldiers. Over the next quarter of an hour it became clear that things were becoming more perilous atop the wall. The shouting became more desperate. The sounds of timber on timber was indicative of siege ladders. Bodies started to fall, rolling down the internal turf slope of the rampart to lie as grisly warnings to the waiting men.

When the first breach came, they needed no indication from the centurion above. Somehow the enemy had managed to haul the fence outwards, the timbers and the wicker screen falling away and leaving a gap. The officer that was supposed to be warning them managed a strangled cry and then rolled to a halt some twenty feet from Fronto, gouts of blood still pumping from his neck.

Men rushed along to defend the breach from both sides of the rampart, but it was simply too wide and broken to plug with simple shuffling of men. There would be no other breaches now. There wouldn't need to be. Fronto had expected them to come over the top piecemeal, but this would be a full push, and probably by three or four cohorts. They expected, however, only the defenders on the wall top. Fronto turned and waved at the other officers, pointing to the breach above and drawing a line across his throat with a finger. Then he nodded to the centurions beside him and they began to jog up the slope, the two centuries following without the need for an official signal.

It was the work of mere moments to climb the rear of the rampart, and as they emerged at the top the centurions beside him gave a great warlike roar and invoked the name of Mars, the centuries of men joining in. With a huge cry of fury, the reserve force filled the gap where the timbers and fencing had been pulled away with ropes. The enemy were pushing into the gap like a sea of men, climbing the far side with a triumphant rumble which turned to cries of shock and panic as they met a wall of iron and bronze in the form of fresh reserves.

'For Caesar,' Fronto bellowed as the enemy renewed their attack and pressed into the gap.

'Pompey Magnus,' bellowed someone among the enemy, drawing the bellowed name of Caesar from every voice among the defenders. Then the names were lost beneath the din of combat.

Fronto felt the familiar simplicity of war washing over him. He could see in the faces of many of those they faced how raw they were. The sheer terror of their situation widened their eyes and made their sword arms tremble. They had yet to learn that surrendering to the simplicity of it all removed the horror. It was a simple game of 'me or you'. You killed until they were all gone, or until you failed to stop a blade in time.

A young legionary with the swarthy look of a southern Greek came at him, raising his shield in preparation to smash the iron boss at Fronto's face. A standard move, and often a good one, but not against a man who'd been the aggressor and recipient of that move so many times he could no longer count. He allowed the man to come, then took a half step to the right at the last moment. As the boss smashed out in the wrong place, the young soldier unaware of the failure, the fingers of Fronto's left hand grasped the shield's shiny new edging and hauled it outwards. There was the sound of a breaking bone as the soldier's grip meant his shield hand was jerked painfully sideways. Fortunately he did not suffer long, for Fronto's blade sank into his armpit even as he raised his sword in desperation.

The man fell away and a gangly legionary behind him attempted to throw a lunge at Fronto, He over-extended himself and Fronto ducked to the side and then simply took a step forwards so that he was inside the reach of the man's arm. With calculated precision, he aimed the brim of his helmet and butted the man in the face, his strike perfectly accurate, The blow bent the cheek pieces of the poor man's helmet so that they cut painfully deep into his cheeks, though his shattered and flat nose would concern him more. The soldier howled and was gone in a moment as another man made to swipe at the legate. Fronto caught the blow with his own blade and pushed it aside. This man was more of a veteran, but still he was unprepared, and before he could recover for a second strike, Fronto lifted his foot and slammed it down on the other man's, shattering the bones and mashing the toes with the hobnails. The soldier screamed and fell, but Fronto managed to get a blow in at his arm before he disappeared from sight.

He looked around for a moment during a heartbeat's respite, and spotted Salvius Cursor close by. Galronus was just visible in the press, too. Everyone was at the party now.

'I've done my three,' Fronto bellowed. 'How about you?'

'Five,' roared Salvius as he plunged his blade into a thigh, then rose, fresh blood all down his front.

'Show-off,' grinned Fronto.

'Six,' replied Salvius, as he jumped up, threw his free arm around a man's neck and jerked his head down to meet a rising knee encased in bronze greaves. His victim screamed as the bronze tore his face, and blood and eye matter washed the metal leg armour.

'You're an animal, Salvius.'

'Aren't we all? Look to your left.'

Fronto returned his attention to the fight before him just in time to parry another blow and deliver a devastating slash to the neck.

The dance went on for perhaps a hundred heartbeats more, then a horn blew a cadence somewhere out by the fort, and the enemy began to turn and run. A few took blows to the back as they fled, but the legion of Pompey's, recent recruits from the Greek lands, were on the run. Fronto, weary but unhurt other than a few scratches and bruises, climbed up to the surviving wall walk and took in the scene. The enemy was in full retreat. They had lost a third or more of their number and were in flight back to their own lines.

Untried and untested no longer, they had been found wanting.

Volcatius had held the fort, and Fronto and the men of Volcatius' cohorts had held the river bed.

Salvius Cursor joined him, wiping gore and liquid from his face.

'A very solid victory, that. Pompey will be furious.'

'But the gates of Hades have just opened,' Fronto sighed. 'Thus far we've danced around each other, trying not to truly start the war, but it's done now. That's just the first fight. It won't stop now until either Caesar or Pompey bend their knee. The bloodshed has only just begun.'

CHAPTER 8

Caesar's camp, Junius 48 BC

It turned out that the day of the attack had been brutal all along the siege lines. Pompey had been careful to launch a number of attacks simultaneously in order to prevent the Caesarian forces from being able to strengthen any point or bring their main reserves to bear. In addition to the attack on Volcatius' camp, which had been driven off despite horrendous odds, there had been a similar push in the south, near the coast, where the Ninth had fought like lions, once and for all removing any stigma that remained from their insurrection at Placentia. Further north, in the high peaks, Calenus had struggled to control small installations against concerted attack by a sizeable force of both legionaries and auxilia. Close to Dyrrachium itself, Sulla had been the senior commander present and had brought up every man available, throwing two extra legions into the defence of the lines, where three different Pompeian armies had pushed, attempting to break through, presumably hoping to resupply from the city.

Miraculously, or at least a credit to the officers and men of Caesar's army, each of the six pushes had been contained and driven back. Losses had been high on both sides, but it was generally agreed that the Pompeians took the brunt of the body count. Hirtius, updating Caesar's accounts of the war to be published back in Rome, somewhat extravagantly numbered the enemy fallen at two thousand, and Caesar's men at less than twenty. Heroism had never looked so unbelievable.

One bright side of the push was the six Pompeian standards that had been captured, two by men of Volcatius Tullus' command. These six had been reverently packed, given an escort, and sent to the ships to transport back to Rome, where they would be prominently displayed to remind the populace of their consul's strength and divine support. And of their own loyalties, of course.

Caesar, recovering from a minor illness that had kept him from the action, spoke to the legions at the main camp, his face a little pale and drawn, but exhibiting all the strength and presence expected of him. He praised Sulla for his powerful actions and the defence of the main camps. He praised Volcatius for his heroic victory in very difficult circumstances. And he praised a centurion in particular. It was a standard trick of Caesar's, as Fronto knew well. It was all to the good lauding senior officers, but it gave heart to the men when heroics among the main fighting force were recognised.

It had brought a smile to Fronto's face, too, and had been well-deserved. A centurion by the name of Scaeva – one of only two centurions in his cohort not to have lost an eye during the fight – was invited up onto the general's rostrum. He had acquired a limp, and his leg was wrapped in linen that had already soaked through pink. Scratches and marks criss-crossed him. The men nodded their approval, but it was the piece of evidence of the man's bravery brought up for viewing that stilled the breath in all present. Scaeva's oval shield was displayed to the legions present as the sign of a man who knew no fear and was watched over by gods. There was virtually no painted linen left on the sorry item, which was more hole now than shield, punctured by dozens of arrows and spears, cut by dozens of swords. Even Fronto, no stranger to the frenetic fighting at the front line, had never seen a shield that had taken such punishment and remained in a man's possession. That Scaeva was alive at all was incredible. The man's left arm was a mass of blood and purple bruises from the blows that had penetrated the boards.

The centurion left the stand in stunned silence, eyes wide at the two hundred thousand sestertii reward the general had announced, in addition to his raising from the lesser ranks of the centurionate to the position of primus pilus.

Thus was Caesar's gratitude displayed and received.

Fronto sighed and reached for the jug of wine to top up, only to find that it had disappeared. Unsurprisingly as he scanned the gathering, the jug was in the hand of Marcus Antonius, and he felt slight irritation as he saw the jug upended into the man's cup and drained of the last drop. He needed some kind of sustenance to see him through the latest round of self-delusion among the officers.

'He will break,' Calenus said. 'He *has* to break.'

Murcus nodded his agreement. 'He now knows that he cannot overcome our lines. He has tried, and we fought him off, even with inferior numbers and no warning.'

'And that means he continues to lack water supplies,' Calenus reminded everyone. 'How long can he keep his army supplied by ship?'

'Indefinitely,' Antonius spat, waving his full cup so that the wine sloshed over the edge, adding further irritation to Fronto. What a waste.

'What?' Calenus said.

'Now that the blockade's been lifted – after all, what use is it now? – Pompey is using his entire fleet to bring in supplies from Dyrrachium and any other sympathetic source. We may have secured much of the local region, but most of Greece, Macedonia, Thrace and so on are all in Pompey's camp. Yes, it takes a long time to bring supplies that far, but he has the ships to do it.'

'He cannot produce enough water and fodder for all his beasts,' Calenus argued.

'No. That's why he fed the pack animals to his men. He's kept his core cavalry mounts and reduced the need. He can last as long as he needs to. And sooner or later Scipio is going to arrive from Syria with his legions, at which point we get done from both ends, Pompey on one side and Scipio on the other. Remember Alesia? Imagine what it had been like if the reserve army on the hill had properly committed? That's what we're facing. And these men will not baulk at coming full force. All Pompey has to do is wait. That's all. And our only chance to change things is to take Dyrrachium off him.'

The tent erupted in a wave of noise as men vented their opinions on the sense of any kind of assault on that coastal bastion.

Fronto, who had yet to say a word, stood angrily in the middle of it all, lacking wine, with a growing headache from all the noise and argument, wondering if this was how a tutor felt in a room full of unruly students.

'Quiet!' he bellowed suddenly.

The volume of his shout and the sheer anger in his tone cut through the crowd and added a great deal to Fronto's burgeoning headache. The whole tent fell silent, all officers turning to face

Fronto, even Caesar, who wore an unaccustomed expression of surprise.

'Marcus?' the general said.

'You argue over and over again in circles, never getting anywhere. I hear the same old suggestions and rebuttals going on here every day, and nothing changes. It's all repeated. Here is the situation in truth.'

Every ear twitched in anticipation, and Fronto walked over and calmly took the full cup of barely-watered wine from Antonius' hand, taking a grateful sip.

'Yes, we beat Pompey. He won't try that again. Agreed. But he is not a man to rest on his laurels. He knows that sooner or later Scipio will arrive, but he also knows that we know that, and he will expect Caesar to pull some clever little trick before then. So he will be probing, looking for a way to bring us down. Do not be fooled by this current lack of battle. It's just a drawn breath before the next fight.'

He turned and gestured to Antonius. 'It has already been concluded more than once that storming Dyrrachium stands a minute chance of success, and if we fail it undermines everything we've achieved. We cannot stop Pompey resupplying by sea, as he has all the edge in naval power. All we can do is try and diminish his sources. Caesar, send some men into Greece in the south and try and turn the coastal cities to our cause. That way his supplies from the south dry up and he is forced to rely solely on Dyrrachium. Also, while they are there, they might be able to stir up the countryside in our favour and hinder Scipio when he passes through.'

He stepped back and took a swig of wine. 'Other than that there is nothing we can do but wait and be ready. Perhaps lead out the army regularly and offer battle. But stop these interminable planning sessions where we simply argue impossible plans and the same old ideas. We sit tight, we squeeze his supplies in the small ways we can, and we wait to see what happens. Pompey is clever, but he's also impulsive. A man driven by anger. Perhaps if we squeeze enough we can cause him to do something rash that will change everything.'

He fell silent and the whole room waited, expectantly.

'There is no more,' Fronto sighed. 'That's it. Session over.'

Caesar nodded. 'Rather bleakly expressed, Marcus, but a succinct representation of our situation. Very well, I shall dismiss this meeting and another shall not be called until the Ides unless there are developments. Calenus? Take Cassius Longinus and Calvisius Sabinus and the Twenty Sixth and Twenty Seventh into Achaea and do as Fronto suggested. Take Pompey's coastal supply dumps off him and make the way slow for Scipio. You know what to do. Calvinus? You take the Eleventh and Twelfth and do the same in Macedonia. Pompey was there with his legions and training camps and that may well be the source of much of his land-based supplies. Turn Macedonia from him.'

And that was it. The officers departed, going about their own business, often in pairs, deep in discussion over the very same points Fronto had argued were pointless. Antonius crossed to Fronto with a raised eyebrow, and the legate held out the cup to its owner.

'Keep it. Seems you need it more than me.'

And he did. Right now, bogged down in an interminable siege with no great hope for a successful conclusion, with a headache and listening to the officers arguing like children, all he wanted was to be back in Tarraco with the family. Somewhere warm and comfortable where he could splash around in the water and drink his own wine while the boys cavorted and laughed and his wife smiled at him.

Gods, but when would this war finally finish?

* * *

And nothing did change. Days came and went with no appreciable difference to the situation. One minor point of interest came in the form of news finally of Vibullius Rufus. The man Caesar had chosen as his envoy to Pompey and sent thence with horsemen had apparently gone over to the enemy, for rumour emanating from Rome suggested that he was behind some stirrings of political trouble there. Closer to hand, Calenus and his cohorts disappeared off south and east to secure Achaea, but there was no sign of a reduction in the number of supply vessels coming in to feed and water Pompey's army. Indeed, if anything, it seemed that Pompey was settling in for the long run, which picked at Fronto's nerves, for he was still certain that the old bastard would try something sooner or later.

In the south, facing the defences manned mostly by the Ninth where there had been brutal fighting that day, Pompey's siege works were strengthened. The walls grew higher and new towers sprouted here and there along the ramparts. The former camp of the Ninth that Pompey's forces had manned was now abandoned, perhaps as being too difficult to protect, protruding from the main lines as it did. Its gates were blocked and the men pulled back to the main wall leaving woodland and open ground aplenty between the lines.

It all appeared to be indicative of a man happy to be besieged, knowing he would win in the end.

'He's not, though,' Fronto said, leaning on the fence, musing quietly.

'Who's not what?' asked Galronus, strolling up beside him and leaning next to him on the timber.

'Pompey. He's not content just to wait it out.'

'It does look that way.'

'But it isn't. I know how his mind works. And while I trust Salvius Cursor's opinions about as far as I could shit a trireme, he served with Pompey and he seems to know the man well, and he shares my opinion. This is all too easy. Something nasty is coming. Pompey's preparing something, I'm sure. And I wouldn't be surprised if it happens in the south.'

'Why?'

Fronto tapped his fingers on the timber. 'The lion's share of our forces are in the north, between him and Dyrrachium. But we can't be certain where his are. We have no intelligence, which I know is a joke in its own right, by the way. He's abandoned the old camp in the south and drawn back, consolidating his ramparts there.'

'So?'

'So our officers will get complacent. They see the south as being secure. Pompey's withdrawn his forwards position, so no trouble can come from there, eh? But what if Pompey's army is concentrated in the south?'

'No,' Galronus countered. 'They can't be. Every few days Caesar marches the men out and lines them up in the north, offering Pompey a fight, and he responds by bringing out his own men, never outside the protection of his missiles, but we can see them. They're in the north.'

'Pompey has a huge army, Galronus, with a lot of shiny new recruits. I'm confident that he could field a large force of impressive looking men to match Caesar's without drawing any of his veterans or the better trained troops, like those Hispanic cohorts under Afranius. No. They're in the south. I'd wager my arm on it.'

'You think he means to swamp us?'

'I just don't know. That's what stops me arguing with the officers for a concentration there. I can't figure out what he's up to. But mark my words, something will happen there.'

Galronus nodded. 'Well if that's not tension enough for you, here's some news. Scipio and his legions have been spotted in Macedonia. Calvinus is moving to intercept him.'

Fronto sighed and closed his eyes. 'That's too close for comfort. Calvinus and Scipio's forces are more or less evenly matched, but Scipio's wily. Perhaps even more so than Pompey. I fear that any direct confrontation between him and Calvinus will go badly for us. We can't really afford to lose two such veteran legions. We're standing in the latrine trench, Galronus, and the shit just gets deeper.'

'Caesar has responded,' Galronus noted. 'He's sent an ambassador to join up with Calvinus and mediate with Scipio. A mutual friend, apparently. He's hoping that Scipio can be turned from Pompey's side rather than coming into conflict with Calvinus. Let's face it, if the Syrian legions joined us, then we'd have the edge. And now that we've started harvesting the crops we could feed the excess.'

Fronto snorted. 'When did you become an expert on Roman strategy?'

You're talking to a senator of Rome, remember, Fronto?'

They both laughed for a moment.

'Let's hope this loyal envoy is more loyal than Vibullius Rufus was, eh?' Fronto sagged. 'I'm going to take Bucephalus and ride out to the south to see what I can turn up,' Fronto declared. Care to join me?'

'I might. I need to go and see Volusenus anyway. The cavalry have not been doing much more than helping gather crops these past months. I think it's time they went for a little exercise and remember they're soldiers, not farmers.'

Fronto smiled. Volusenus was the current Prefect of Horse, and took his job very seriously. He would be more than happy to commit the cavalry to exercises, since he had been moaning in meetings for some time that his forces were being used only as glorified ploughmen.

'Come on, then.'

The bulk of the cavalry, most of whom were Gallic or German auxiliaries, were based on the periphery of the huge main northern camp. Row upon row of plain tents marked out their accommodation, the cavalry standards, both Roman and native, standing in position at the end of each unit's territory. The horses were neatly corralled in large fenced areas with only peripheral guards, generally several units' steeds kept together. The officers' horses were largely kept according to their owners' wishes, which meant that most were privately stabled by their master's accommodation. Fronto, aware of Bucephalus' advanced years and the need for social animals like horses to have company, allowed his to stay with those of Galronus and Salvius and a few other officers' in a paddock of their own near the main cavalry steeds.

The two men were sauntering contentedly towards that small paddock, and the quarters of Volusenus and the various staff, when the sound of angry shouting insisted itself upon them. The two peered in the direction of the noise. A small group of Gauls were pushing and shoving towards the far end of one of the lines of tents.

'Trouble?'

'Could be,' Galronus said. 'Not one of my units, but I can't let things like that go unnoticed. Go see to your horse. I'll find out what's going on.'

Fronto nodded and, leaving his friend to it, went over to the corral, where his great black steed was happily munching on lush green grass with the other officers' horses. An equisio hurried over.

'Make Bucephalus ready,' Fronto said. 'I need to take him out for a while. And can you saddle Galronus' horse too?'

The man saluted and scurried off into his store room, returning with Fronto's saddle and tack. It took surprisingly little time for the expert horse handler to make Bucephalus ready. He was just back inside, gathering the gear for the bay mare when the Remi nobleman stormed into view once more with a face like thunder.

'What's happened?'

'Two Allobroge chieftains causing trouble,' Galronus snapped. 'They've been helping themselves to their units' pay chests. Quite blasé about it, they were, too. Didn't deny the accusations of their men. Seem to think it's their right as commanders.'

'Arseholes,' Fronto sighed. 'What did you do?'

'They're not my men, so it's not right for me to discipline them. Told them I'd report the matter to Caesar, so I've a change of plan for the afternoon. You still going south, or coming to command with me?'

Fronto nodded and caught the equisio's attention as he emerged once more from the hut.

'Sorry, soldier, but belay that. We don't need them now.'

The soldier saluted, and Fronto only just caught the irritated rolling of eyes as the man turned, but ignored it. Instead, he spun and hurried off after Galronus, marching through the lines of cavalry tents until they reached the end of the horse barracks and closed on the ramparts marking the start of the Tenth and Thirteenth's base, where the main command tents were to be found. Giving the daily password, they were admitted to the main camp and strode up the long, straight road to the large cluster of important tents at the centre. The guardsmen of Ingenuus' praetorian unit stood at attention in a cordon around the headquarters area, but accepted the password and allowed the two officers entry. They passed the headquarters of the camp prefect and made directly for Caesar's tent. Outside a guard bade them wait, knocked at the tent door and entered. A few moments later he reappeared and gave them permission to enter.

Caesar's tent was still strewn with maps and records, and the general himself was deep in conversation with Marcus Antonius, though they broke off and both looked up as the two men entered.

'Marcus. Galronus. What can I do for you?'

'We have a problem with some of the Gallic cavalry,' Fronto replied, then gestured to Galronus.

'Two Allobroge commanders by the names of Egus and Raucillus, General. Are you aware of them?'

Caesar frowned as he dredged his impressive memory, then sat back, the frown still in place. 'Yes. Chieftains. Been with us since the middle of the Gallic campaigns. They've been decorated and rewarded for valiant service a number of times. Is there trouble?'

'Definitely, Caesar. These two have been helping themselves to their units' pay chests for personal use. I gather it hadn't been noticed until the chests ran too low to pay for a funeral for one of their men who died recently. They've been almost bled dry by two men for wine and women.'

'Difficult.'

'With respect, Caesar, I don't think so. They should be punished. I don't know in whose wing they serve, but they need to be brought under control. Their men are spitting feathers over the matter.'

Caesar sighed. 'But Gaul is still settling after a decade of war. The peace is fragile and it will take time for it to become a steady province of the republic. These two men are important. Moreover, their fathers are even more important. Egus and Raucillus have been granted land and position among the conquered regions, and they're earmarked for senatorial position next year. I don't doubt that they've done wrong, but a careful and measured response is in order, I think.'

Fronto snorted. 'A proportional response is appropriate. They stole from their own men. Whoever their daddies are, they need their bollocks kicked for behaviour like that.'

Caesar flashed him an irritable look. 'It is not unusual for an officer to file false records and walk off with part of his unit's pay. It is reprehensible, but it is also surprisingly common. If we started charging everyone for such misdemeanours, we'd have few officers left. Worse, we'd have to arrest almost every governor the senate appoints, for they all do the same thing on a much grander scale. This is not the critical incident you seem to imagine, gentlemen.'

'*Misdemeanour*? With respect, General,' Galronus pressed, 'this is drawing divisions in their units. Soldiers at odds with their commanders do not perform well in war. Something has to be done about it.'

Caesar sighed. 'To an extent, I agree, but this is not the time to drag these two men through the mud and ruin them. It sets a dangerous precedent. The matter will be deferred for now.'

'General…'

Caesar held up a warning hand. 'I will speak to the two men privately and make my displeasure known. I shall take them to task and make sure they are aware of my opinion on the matter. They shall cease their larcenous ways, believe me, but without a public condemnation.'

'That is your final word?' Galronus asked coldly.

'It is.'

'Then I shall take my leave.'

* * *

The two men returned to the corral and gathered their steeds, to much eye-rolling once more from the tired equisio, and rode out, heading south on Fronto's scouting trek. As they left, they saw two of the general's praetorians marching determinedly through the lines of tents towards where the Allobroge officers were quartered.

'I hope he makes them shit their trousers,' Galronus snarled, and then they turned and rode off.

They spent the rest of the afternoon around the southern defences, peering at the enemy positions from the few high points, checking out the terrain, some of which was appalling, riding out into the no-man's-land between the lines on occasion to get a closer look, but making sure not to get within range of an opportunistic artillerist or archer.

In the end, after four hours of riding and observing, they were none the wiser, and Fronto had to conclude that there was no way of knowing what the mad old bastard planned without any kind of inside knowledge of the enemy, which was next to impossible to even contemplate. They rode back to the main camp in a sullen silence, and Galronus watched his friend with a level of worry. Fronto seemed to be hovering on the verge of distress and anger all the time at the moment. He was never the most relaxed of men, but the last time Galronus had seen him like this had been in the aftermath of Alesia. In the end, the Remi, some decade and a half younger than the Roman, had to conclude that if even *he* was beginning to feel too old for all of this, how must Fronto feel? Fronto might call Caesar 'the old man', but in truth there were surprisingly few years between the two of them.

They dismounted and handed over their reins in silence, and the equisio took them and hurried off with the beasts. As they moved back through the tents, they could hear conversation in the headquarters tent of Volusenus, and decided to drop in and see the Prefect of Horse, to appraise him of the situation. A swift knock at the door bought them an offer to enter, and so they did. The world was already fast slipping into evening now, and so the difference in light as they entered the dim interior was not so great. Volusenus looked tired.

'Gentlemen. What can I do for you?'

Galronus pursed his lips. 'There was a spot of trouble today. If I give you the names of unit commanders, can you tell me to whose wing they belong?'

'Easily. Probably without even needing the records.'

The Remi opened his mouth, but paused. 'Did you hear that?'

Fronto and Volusenus shared a furrowed expression as they looked at him, but a moment later they all heard it. The sounds of fighting and raised voices close by.

'Shit. Come on.'

The two of them raced back out of the tent, Volusenus right behind them. The noises were coming from one of the main corrals, and the three men hurried in that direction, the Prefect of Horse moving out in front with a speed and agility that belied his apparent age.

An altercation had broken out at the gate of the corral, where an equisio was lying on the floor, motionless, a spear standing proud from his back.

'Shit,' Fronto said again.

Volusenus was enraged. Out front, he raced towards the trouble, but Fronto's eyes, even old as they were and peering into the dim evening, could see the trouble the prefect was headed for.

'Volusenus, come back.'

But the prefect had ripped a *vitus* vine cane out and was bellowing for the scuffling soldiers to stand down. There was no chance of that happening, and Fronto knew it. He could see the shapes of the two disgraced Allobroge nobles, Egus and Raucillus, already on their horses in the corral, and they had perhaps two score men with them, all Gallic horsemen, all armoured for war, and those who weren't mounted already were in the process of doing so. Only the five men at the gate, who had overcome the Roman guards and butchered them in short order, remained afoot.

'Volusenus,' Fronto bellowed again, but the prefect was already there. Unnoticed by the scuffling men, he had walked up right behind them and, reaching back, thwacked his heavy stick across the nearest man's back. The Gaul yelled, then turned and swung his naked blade. Fronto saw the prefect fall, and then the two rogue Gauls were in the gateway and making for open ground. They had with them more than a dozen spare horses, and the men at the gate grabbed at beasts as they passed and hauled themselves up into the saddle. Fronto stared. Half a hundred Gallic cavalry revolting? Damn it.

Galronus was shouting now, too, and the Gauls turned, spotting the two men on the path. Recognition passed through the two chieftains as they took in Galronus, the man who had reported them to Caesar, and with bellows of war, they rode towards them. Galronus drew his long blade and set himself ready to face them, and the only thing that stopped him being churned under a hundred hooves and ground into the dirt was Fronto, who hit him in the midriff and knocked him out of the way, the two men falling to the grass behind the corner of a tent.

He half expected the Gauls to pause and deal with them, but clearly the rebels were working to a time and a plan, and they raced off, whooping, their saddles laden with bags that shushed and clinked with the sound of many coins. Fronto felt around for his sword that he'd lost in the fall, and instead found a heavy rock. Rising and stepping out into the street, he hurled it.

Fortuna was clearly enveloping him today, for the makeshift missile struck the rearmost rider directly on the back of the skull with a crack that was audible even over the hooves. The two men were running, then, as the dead Gaul lolled around in the saddle, his head smashed. The rest of his mates ignored him and continued to ride off towards the defences.

'They're not just deserting,' Fronto breathed in huffs.

Galronus shook his head. 'They're going over to Pompey.'

A moment later the Remi was at that dead Gaul's horse, pulling him from the saddle and then hauling himself up in the man's place.

'You can't stop them,' Fronto shouted, as Galronus kicked the mount into life and hared off after the defecting cavalry. Fronto jogged slowly, a little out of breath, until he was out in open ground and could see what was unfolding. The plan had been more subtle than simply grabbing horses and running. They had stolen a great deal of money in the process, taken a solid unit of veteran Gauls, and had sent men ahead to clear the way. That last was certain, for the nearest gate in the siege lines lay wide open and unmanned, a dozen Gauls swarming around it. They grabbed free horses as the renegade unit reached them, and all of them rode out into the evening light, into the barren, dangerous ground between the two armies. Galronus looked for a moment as though he was prepared to chase them through the gates of Hades if he needed to, but as he reached the defences, he reined in and turned, his horse dancing impatiently.

What difference could half a hundred Gallic cavalry make in the grand scheme of things?

Fronto hated the fact that they answers came quick and easily, and each was more worrying than the last.

The sense of foreboding was building. A storm of shit of gargantuan proportions was coming…

CHAPTER 9

Caesar's camp, Junius 48 BC

'One legion is not enough,' Fronto said fiercely, slamming his fist down on the chair arm. The force of his words brought out a mix of responses among the other officers, from surprise and agreement to shock and anger.

'I'm not sure whether you've noticed, Fronto, but we do not have an infinite supply of men. They are stretched as it is,' Canuleius replied irritably. 'The ongoing work on the ramparts drains what men are available to just stand and wait for fictional attacks.'

Fronto ground his teeth for a moment, glaring at Canuleius. 'The south is weak. The Ninth are a good legion. We know that. We've seen their response to Pompey's attacks already, but they are dangerously under strength, and they are the single sole legion controlling the southern end of the works. They are not enough. Let me take the Tenth there, or at least move the Seventh further along, since they're the nearest legion.'

'No,' Sulla replied, though Caesar's eyebrow rose a little at senior command decisions so clearly being made without his consultation. 'No. It doesn't matter what legion you intend to take to bolster the Ninth, it will mean shuffling the men around and losing a legion from the main camp.'

Fronto growled. 'The main camp is over-full. There are so many legionaries here the latrine pits fill on an hourly basis. Two thirds of our strength is here, with the rest strung out around the defences., and Pompey is not going to come here. It's pointless. Pompey is gathering in the south.'

'What evidence do you have of that?' snapped Canuleius.

'None, as you damn well know. But regardless, that is what's happening.'

'Yet we see his troops parading in the northern region the same as ours every time we lead the men out and offer battle. All the evidence points to Pompey's army being gathered mostly in the north.'

'Yet I tell you they are in the south. You might not have seen them, but they are there. Believe me.'

Canuleius snorted, and Sulla shook his head. 'You cannot drain the strength of the north for some perceived potential threat. The prize is here. Dyrrachium is here. Keep your eyes on the main goal. If we send men south, the forces that we know full well he has here will simply roll over the main camp and reach Dyrrachium. If he gets into Dyrrachium, we'll have more chance of opening an oyster with a loincloth than prising him out from those walls. No. Caesar?'

The general tapped a finger on his lips. 'I appreciate the danger you suspect Fronto, but there really is no evidence to support it. I cannot sanction the draining of men from a location that we know to be critical against the vague possibility of action elsewhere.'

'When have I been wrong, Caesar?' Fronto snapped.

'Would you like a list? I have one somewhere.'

Fronto threw an angry glance at Hirtius, who had chuckled at the jibe.

'It will happen. And if you're not prepared, then we might as well just open the gates and hand him our weapons.'

'The answer is no, Fronto,' Sulla said. 'You heard the general.'

The argument was clearly lost. The officers en-masse were arrayed against him. Earlier, when it had been just Canuleius and Sulla denying him there had been possibilities, but now that Caesar had spoken, the rest of the officers had sided with him. Only one figure crossed the room and stood next to Fronto. Marcus Antonius took a sip of his wine and cleared his throat.

'I think I stand with Fronto on this.'

Caesar's eyebrow jerked upwards again, and Antonius shrugged. 'Fronto's gut tells him we face trouble there, and his gut has a tendency towards prophecy, I find. And eye-watering wind. But mainly prophecy. If Fronto says there will be trouble in the south, I say bolster the south.'

Fronto nodded, but there was still a distinct air of refusal in the room.

'Sulla, the Ninth are *your legion*,' Fronto snapped. 'Does it not concern you that it's your men who face any danger? No, of course it doesn't. Now that they've been blooded and redeemed themselves you're not bothered about them anymore. When was the last time you set foot in their camp? I notice that you command the Ninth from a comfy chair ten miles away and under Caesar's wing.'

Sulla stepped forwards angrily. 'Watch that tongue, Fronto, or I might be tempted to rip it out.'

'Who *is* commanding your men, though,' insisted Antonius.

'The Ninth are in the care of the capable senior tribune, Lentulus Marcellinus.'

'A man who's suffering some kind of dreadful illness and is bedridden for much of the time I understand?'

'His mind and his mouth still work, Antonius.'

'So while he's sweating out his commands from his bedsheets, who's striding around the place actually telling people what to do?'

'The camp prefect, Fulvius Postumus, is a veteran and a good man. The Ninth are in good hands, Antonius.'

'The Ninth are going to get their arses handed to them by Pompey's legions soon,' grunted Fronto.

'Clearly this is going nowhere,' Caesar put in, cutting through the building tension of the argument, 'Fronto, your instincts are good, but the evidence suggests that on this occasion they are wrong. Without some sort of supporting evidence I am not willing to weaken our position in front of Dyrrachium and tempt Pompey to walk over us. What I will do is have the number of lookouts and couriers all along the defences doubled, so that messages are guaranteed to be passed quickly, and I will make sure that every unit's commander and ever position's senior officer is aware of the possibility of trouble in the south and ensure that they are in a position to react in the shortest possible time. That is the end of the discussion. Hirtius, I need you to remain here. We have correspondence to complete.'

Summarily dismissed, Fronto was the first to leave, throwing out an almost insolent salute and then turning his back on them all and stomping from the tent into the late afternoon air, with the hum of bees and the distant calls of birds disturbed by the ongoing works. He stopped some twenty paces from the headquarters where he was unlikely to be caught up swiftly by the other officers, and balled his fist, pounding it on a wooden stake that formed part of a fence.

'Blind, stupid bastards,' he snarled.

'Blind, not necessarily stupid,' Antonius said at his shoulder, making him jump a little.

'I disagree.'

'That's because you're angry.' Antonius passed him a cup of wine. Where did he get the damn things from all the time? 'In truth, few officers would support your gut over the visible evidence. You know they're just being cautious and sensible. I think they're probably wrong, but I can understand their position.'

'Their position will be *bent over and begging* if they don't listen.'

Antonius laughed. 'Caesar has spoken. You won't change that. So do what you can within the bounds of his orders.'

Fronto frowned. 'What?'

'The Ninth are commanded by a sick tribune and an old camp prefect. Both men are good enough at their jobs, but neither of them is in a position to storm ramparts or swing a sword. Yet that's your forte. It's what you're good at. Go to the Ninth and hang around. With luck you'll get the evidence you need to persuade Gaius. If not, when the shit starts to fly at least they'll have a healthy veteran commander there.'

Fronto nodded. 'You're quite right, of course.'

'And I have no specific command. I am simply Caesar's sword arm right now. The nearest positions to the Ninth are manned by the Seventh and the Tenth. I shall make my presence felt among them and make sure they are, let's say *extremely mobile*.'

'You'll be ready to support?'

'As fast as I can. Bear in mind we'll still have four or five miles to cover once we've got the two forces together, but we'll be ready for it, and we'll come as fast as we can. Make sure you have a rider ready at all times.'

'If you lead the legions away to help me, you'll leave six miles or so of the lines more or less undefended. Caesar will be furious.'

'Let me handle Gaius. I know how to deal with him.'

Fronto smiled. 'Tell Salvius Cursor to sharpen his sword, then. He'll get to use it again soon enough.'

Shaking hands with Antonius and thanking him for his support, Fronto strode off towards the animal pens to retrieve Bucephalus. He'd hoped to spot Galronus on the way and encourage the Remi to come with him, but the man was nowhere to be seen. Since the flight of the Allobroge deserters, Galronus seemed to have taken the matter personally, as though it were somehow his responsibility. Consequently, he had spent all his time among the other Gallic and Belgic and Germanic auxiliary horse, encouraging their loyalty and vetting their commanders. Useful, but Fronto missed his friend's company. The equisio handed him the reins of the great black steed and, mounting up, Fronto rode off along the siege lines.

More work was being undertaken all along the ramparts from the bay below Dyrrachium, past Caesar's camp, all along the hills and down to the camp of the Ninth and the last stretch of walls to the sea in the south. Caesar had sent overtures of peace to the approaching army of Scipio, but that sour faced and staunchly traditional commander had no great love of the general or his friends, and success seemed exceedingly unlikely. Consequently, the entire defensive system had taken a leaf from the book of Alesia, preparing a second set of siege works, facing outward from the extant ones, ready to repel a second force when it arrived. The legions all along the system were at work raising more towers and ramparts, digging more ditches. The more Fronto thought about the immediate future, the bleaker it looked.

Last year it had seemed so positive. Oh, he'd had his doubts and had been distressed at the very nature of civil war, but it had seemed possible. They had crossed the Rubicon and defied Pompey and the senate and yet met little resistance, securing the whole of Italia in short order and watching Pompey flee with his tail between his legs. Hispania and Massilia had been difficult propositions, but still, Fronto had simply felt that it had been a matter of pushing through and succeeding.

Then they had gathered for the last push. Pompey had run like a coward and raised weak, untrained legions in the east. All they had to do was cross the Adriatic Sea and catch the old knob-nosed bastard and they'd bring him to heel, accept the surrender of the senate, then they could all go home. It had seemed to simple.

Then they had suffered all the problems with crossing and putting to shore. Then they had spent months with half an army, beleaguered by Pompey's navy. Then they had finally met Pompey and realised that his men might be untested, but still there were so many of them, and they had good veteran commanders. They had managed to get the army back together but still they were outnumbered. They'd had to suffer through to the harvest and even now they were not in any real position to push Pompey and attempt a victory. The coming days would only see at least two veteran legions added to the enemy's strength. The likelihood of easily walking away with Pompey's surrender had never seemed more remote.

He was watchful as he rode. At least the men of Caesar's legions were true experts at siegecraft after all their time in Gaul. The extra line facing outward had risen at an incredible rate and only small areas were yet to be completed, which was a relief, with Scipio not far away.

He rode past the camp where the majority of the Tenth were based, their men all along the defences to either side of the hilltop fort. He felt a moment's guilt over accusing Sulla of abandoning his command when in truth Fronto had spent hardly any time with the Tenth since they had begun the works here. Still, he knew they were well-looked after, and swore he spotted Atenos atop the wall yelling into the face of a startled legionary. Somewhere in there Salvius Cursor would be dreaming about standing in a lake of enemy blood, pulling the arms and legs off Pompey. Good for him. The man might be an insufferable lunatic, but he was *Fronto's* insufferable lunatic, and unleashed and pointed towards the enemy, he was as useful as any cohort of veterans.

On past the fort of Volcatius Tullus, scene of the last brutal fight, and he was pleased to see that the breach at the riverbed had not only been repaired but strengthened, with a spike-filled ditch along the front. The defences were every bit as strong as they had been at Alesia. They had to be. This time they were facing Romans, men with as much experience of siege warfare as they themselves.

A rampart ten feet high and ten wide, topped with timber and wicker defences, dependent upon terrain and available materials, with towers and observation platforms. Spikes and lilia pits, and all with a ditch fifteen feet wide in front of it. A formidable line. And behind it a no-man's-land six hundred feet wide before the new, outer defences. Similar in design, though with a lower rampart due to the sheer work involved and the limited time before Scipio's legions hove into view.

Down from the hills, with a wave of recognition to the men of Volcatius' fort, and onto the flat lands. He raced along between the inner and outer defences, heading for the fortification of the Ninth. They were doing well, he decided as he approached. Their legion had been seriously undermanned in the first place, and that was before they had been hit hard by Pompeian forces. They had fought like lions and upheld their honour, which pleased Fronto, given that they'd once been his own legion, long ago in Hispania. He doubted a single soldier remained in the legion who remembered his tenure as legatus, though some would remember and still mourn Longinus, who'd died on the battlefield against Ariovistus a decade ago. And now their current commander lounged leagues to the north in luxury while they struggled. Sulla was a good commander in his way, and certainly the man to keep control of an unruly force, but he ever sought fame, and having rebuilt the Ninth and achieved his goals, he was looking for something new to win at. And he saw that as coming in the north, before Dyrrachium. Sad, really, since Fronto was utterly convinced that if Sulla really wanted to make a name for himself in war, at the head of his legion was where he would get the best chance.

The Ninth were busy completing their own siege works, despite having fewer men to cover more miles than most other positions, despite the absence of their legatus and the illness of their senior tribune. It was a testament to their professionalism. The bulk of their works were complete, with just the outer ditch to dig, and the final enclosing section to add at the end, where it would run along the sea shore and seal in the defenders.

Very nicely done.

It was almost dark now, the sun sinking towards the glittering water of the sea beyond, and Fronto could almost hear the sighs of relief as the centurions blew their whistles and released the men from their labours. The workers, lathered with sweat and with aching muscles, hurried to the sea to dip in the cool water and reinvigorate themselves before retiring for an evening meal.

Fronto gave the daily watchword and passed through the solid watchful lines of the Ninth into their domain. He made his way to the camp centre and the headquarters tent pitched there, introducing himself to the two men guarding the doorway. One moved inside to announce him and then returned, ushering him in.

The tent was dark and stuffy, sultry warm to an uncomfortable level in the summer evening. His eyes took some time to adjust and finally he realised that there was no one in the seat at the table, the senior tribune instead lying on a cot bed to one side, his face waxy grey. Fronto hadn't realised he knew Marcellinus, but he recognised the man from somewhere, some engagement in the past they'd both fought in, and though he couldn't remember the details, the impression he had was one of a solid professional. Not in the best of health right now, though.

The man gave a rasping cough and started to pull himself up into a seated position. Fronto crossed quickly and pushed him back down. 'Don't be daft, man. You're in no condition. Stay there and get better. The medicus says you will *get* better, yes?'

Marcellinus gave a short bark of laughter, which initiated a coughing fit that lasted some time, then sighed and slumped back.

'I can't stay here, sir. The men need me out there.'

'You wouldn't make it past the door. But I have to commend you on your work here. Without Sulla's helpful input you seem to have achieved as much as any other position commander, and from your sickbed, with a diminished legion, no less. Quite an achievement.'

Marcellinus nodded his thanks. 'Credit has to go to Postumus, though. Couldn't have managed without him.'

'I'm here to lend a hand.' Fronto took a deep breath, ready to broach a potentially troublesome subject. 'Do you have any concerns about the south?'

Marcellinus laughed again, then coughed for some time. 'Yes, sir. Dreadfully so. I think the enemy are building their forces ready for something similar to last time. Yesterday there were the distinctive sounds of artillery test-firing inside their lines. They're getting ready for something. And I tell you this…'

But he didn't, because he spent some time instead coughing relentlessly. When he finally settled into ragged gasps, he steadied himself. 'The ships.'

'The ships?'

'I've been counting them, sir. The supply ships that come in to the harbour there. More come in than go back out. Why's that then, sir?'

Fronto frowned. 'He's amassing ships? Maybe he's planning to run?'

Marcellinus shook his head. 'He'd need every ship in his fleet to move that army. No, he's got something else planned.'

Fronto nodded. 'I've done my best to persuade command that you're in danger here, but they won't help. On the bright side, Antonius and I are working to have reserves on hand at short notice. Best we can do with the orders we've been given.'

The man smiled. 'Thank you, sir.'

'Get some rest.'

Fronto left the headquarters, sought out the camp prefect, Postumus, and introduced himself, and then spent some time at the ramparts watching the enemy lines like a hawk before deciding there truly was nothing to see and finally locating a free tent and settling in for the night.

* * *

Fronto knew something was wrong before the warning came. The hair stood proud on the back of his neck. His dream changed, and even in his sleep his fingers twitched, reaching from a sword that wasn't at his hip. In his unconscious mind the great ship had been ploughing through the waves and somehow had been miraculously blessed by the gods so that it failed to make him sick. He had revelled in being able to enjoy sea travel and had been at the prow, above the ram, feeling the salt spray in his face and loving every moment.

Then the salt spray had turned warm, and he had looked down. Homer had called it the "wine dark sea", and in his dream so was Fronto's ocean. A sea of blood, deep and rolling, gleaming dark red waves splashing against the timbers.

He awoke suddenly, those grasping fingers instinctively dropping from his hip to the pile of clothing and equipment he had left beside the bed the night before. They closed on the sword as his salt-encrusted eyes blinked groggily open. When the soldier entered, Fronto was already half-upright with his sword drawn.

'Sir, there's… oh.'

Fronto nodded. 'Where?'

'Everywhere sir. Shit from every side.'

Fronto returned to full consciousness with the ability of the career soldier, and moments later he was shrugging into his mail shirt. Somewhere back among the Tenth in his proper tent was his burnished officer's cuirass. But he'd long since decided that unforgiving sheets of bronze were not the most comfortable option on a horse, and so had adopted a regular soldier's chain shirt whenever he anticipated a day spent largely in the saddle.

Fastening his expensive belt around the shirt, he sheathed the sword once more, slipped his feet into his boots, which came up to mid-calf, and grabbed his helmet with the sorry looking, limp red plume. Moments later he was emerging from the tent into the light of pre-dawn. Soldiers were running everywhere. The night-time torches were still burning, and all was chaos.

He hurried down the alley between tent groups, heading for the main siege works, where he would be able to see the Pompeian lines and get the best idea of what was happening, and halfway there almost fell over a junior tribune running the other way. The man stopped for a moment, unaware of who Fronto was and somewhat confused by the common chain shirt. Finally, seemingly swayed by the plume and the expensive sword and belt, he saluted.

'What's happened?' Fronto barked.

'We're under attack, sir.'

'No shit. Where?'

'Both sides, sir. Somehow they've managed to get outside the lines. Some of the men say it's Scipio, sir, but they're carrying Pompey's standards.'

Fronto nodded. It couldn't be Scipio. He was still too far away. But that explained the damn ships. The twisted, cunning, knob-nosed old fart had used the darkness to ship men past the lines to the south. Then, as dawn cracked, he'd launched a simultaneous assault against the defences of the Ninth from both damn sides, forcing them to divide their meagre strength. He'd damn well told Caesar. He'd warned him. Arseholes, the lot of them. And now the Ninth were neck deep in the latrine pit.

He hurried to the northern ramparts, and his breath caught in his throat as he climbed the bank and took in the view. Pompey's army was huge. The ground seethed with men, pouring out of the woodland on the far side of the dry river bed. Five legions? Six? And that was only here. How many men had he dropped outside the lines to fight at the other side?

Even as he felt the cold dread of facing a vastly superior force, the artillery began. With thuds and cracks, Pompey's engines began their bombardment. Huge rocks, pots of flaming pitch, iron bolts two feet long, stone balls the side of a big man's hand. They rained in on the fort of the Ninth like deadly hail.

'Shit.' He turned and was somewhat surprised to see that the tribune had followed him. 'Find a courier. No, find two. Tell them to ride around the lines and beg help. They will get it from two places. Volcatius Tullus in the next main fort, and Marcus Antonius at the one beyond. Tell them Fronto needs help. They will come, and they'll bring the Seventh and Tenth. We just have to hope they get here before we're all dead.'

The tribune saluted and hurried off, perhaps grateful at being given something useful to do that didn't involve watching a missile coming for his face. Fronto peered at the array of men and weapons before him. That constituted a proper threat, let alone what was probably happening at the far side. His gaze swept around the indigo morning, and stopped somewhere in the middle, pointing a little north of west.

'Oh, shit.'

'Sir?' enquired a centurion close by, who was overseeing the mounting of scorpion artillery along the rampart.

'More ships.'

'Hardly makes a difference at this point, sir.'

'Yes, it bloody does. They're not heading south. They're coming for the gap between the walls. The unfinished stretch. If they get between the two walls, they'll tear this place to pieces and leave four thousand corpses in an hour. Gather every man you can spare and make for the shore, centurion.'

And he began to run, heading along the wall as rocks and bolts whispered and hummed past him on their deadly trajectories. As he ran, he gathered men. It was something he'd seen happen before. An officer running with purpose somehow picked up men as he went, and as he left the fort and hurried out into the no-man's land between the walls, he already had almost a century of men with him.

He ran on. The ships were closing on the shore. They would get there first. They would land. If they each carried perhaps two hundred men, then that would be at least two thousand on their way right now. Bearing in mind that the entire Ninth Legion numbered less than twice that, it spelled defeat in ten-foot-high, blood-streaked letters.

Glancing over his shoulder, he was relieved to see that same centurion emerge from the fort gate with another large group of men at his heel. Perhaps they would still be dangerously outnumbered, but at least there would be enough to give him a faint chance.

Fronto waved on his century of men, and they ran for the shore as though Hades himself were behind them, Cerberus snapping at their heels. The enemy ships were now grounding, their keels crunching into the gravel and the vessels tipping to one side as they beached. Men were leaping from them and howling.

Fronto did a quick calculation as he ran. All in all there couldn't be more than a cohort of men defending the walls to either side. They would be overrun in moments. Even if Fronto and the helpful centurion could double those numbers, the chance of holding their own against the enemy was dropping with every heartbeat. They were being forced to fight enemies at both ramparts, and now more of them were in between the two lines.

Somehow, despite the fact that he and his men had been running full pelt for the enemy, the centurion and his support had managed to catch up with them, soldiers running and panting, sagging and yet determined and with expressions of furious defiance.

Fronto was proud to fight alongside men like this. Pompey might have the edge in numbers, but men like this had conquered Gaul.

The shore was closer and closer. More and more ships were landing. Already Pompeian legionaries were swarming to either side, running up the banks and the steps, taking on the soldiers on the ramparts from behind their own lines. It was chaos. Impossible to tell which legionaries were part of the Ninth and which were Pompey's unless you happened to catch the design on their shields.

This was a disaster. Unless they got help, and damn quick, it would signal the end of the siege in the most brutal and unpleasant way.

Screaming defiance and with half a thousand soldiers at his back, Fronto threw himself at Pompey's army.

CHAPTER 10

Pompey's legions gleamed. Caesar's soldiers had by and large served a decade or more now in the general's army, fighting across Gaul, Italia and Hispania with a dozen or more victories to their name, and their equipment and appearance was correspondingly grimy. Their gear was pitted and marked from a hundred engagements, their leather goods worn-in and dark, their tunics dulled with endless wear and wash and more than a fair share of blood stains. In short, they were veterans. Pompey's army gleamed with the shine of burnished iron and bronze, of freshly-made and recently dyed madder tunics, the leather still bright and unyielding. And their faces were likewise fresh and unmarked.

That was the only really simple way to identify the enemy, and Fronto latched onto it straightaway, shouting as much to the centurions around him. Ships continued to beach, disgorging men into the slaughter while the sailors grunted and hauled the empty vessels back out to sea to make room for the next ones. It was not ordered or neat. It was not a feat of logistics, such as might have been expected had Caesar planned the attack. This was more indicative of Pompey's style. Headlong and forceful, with the simple objective of dropping as many men into the gap as possible in the shortest span of time.

There was going to be a disaster here, and Fronto could see it unfolding. Already the defending forces were hopelessly outnumbered. Oh, they'd been outnumbered at Volcatius Tullus' camp, but there they had had ramparts to defend. Here the enemy were now inside the lines, and there was nothing to defend.

Lightly armed auxiliaries poured up the banks of the new, barely-complete, outer works, and the tired, beleaguered men of the Ninth turned to meet the new threat with professional calm and a hopeless determination to make the best stand of it they could. Perhaps a third of their number remained at the parapet, holding off the auxiliaries that were pressing from that side, while yet more light troops ferried thence by night loosed clouds of arrows heedlessly into the press.

A similar story was unfolding on the inner defences. Men there were fighting off new legionaries coming for their unprotected backs, while trying to hold the bulk of Pompey's strength beyond. Across that dry river, men were flooding from the woodlands like a river bursting its banks. With repeated thuds and cracks, missiles struck men and defences, pulverising the former, having fortunately little effect on the latter. The packed earth of the banks defied the heavy stone missiles, and the wicker screens allowed sharp missiles to pass inside and either rip through or become entangled. Occasionally a stone would shatter a piece of the timber defences, but with little effect given that their men were already inside. Indeed, as the sea-borne legionaries began to become visible on the wall tops, the artillery and arrows died away, the soldiers fearful of killing more of their own men than of Caesar's.

As they closed on the legionaries hurrying up from the beach, Fronto allowed the soldiers with him to take the lead, slowing just a little as a young junior tribune appeared from somewhere, sweating with a new, unused sword in hand.

'This is impossible, sir,' the tribune said, using his blade to gesture at the chaos ahead.

It was. There was no hope of holding the place. In quarter of an hour every Caesarian soldier in this sector would be nothing but a mouldering corpse. It was hopeless. He nodded at the tribune.

'It is. But we have to withdraw in an orderly manner or the losses will be near total. Find musicians. Get them to blow the retreat, but make sure every tribune, centurion and optio is keeping his men in line. We form up to fall back, bringing the men down from the ramparts to either side. Form into a block. Then retreat in good order, fighting as we go.'

'Abandon the walls, sir?' barked an astonished centurion he'd not noticed.

'The walls are lost, man. We need to fall back to the fort. There we can hold them off until friends arrive.'

If they arrived.

The centurion and the tribune both hurried off to carry out those tasks, and heartbeats later Fronto heard the distinctive calls to fall back.

132

It would not be enough. The men of the Ninth were dying in droves. They were taking plenty of the enemy with them, but the problem was that there were plenty of the enemy to take. Fronto pushed forwards to where the men he had led had not yet responded to a call, engaged as they were in a fight to the death with a superior force. The centurion there clearly knew what he was doing. They were formed well and could not begin to fall back until the men from the walls to either side were doing so, else they would be overrun in moments.

Suddenly, with a cry of victory, a legionary with a Pompeian design on his shield and a cut along his cheek beneath his eye, burst through the Caesarian lines into the space behind. For a moment he staggered to a halt, uncertain what to do next, now that he was inside. Then he turned and went for the unprotected rear of the Ninth, making for one particular man. Somewhere in the midst of the press he, like Fronto, could see the silver eagle of the Ninth bobbing above the heads of the men. Killing centurions was of prime importance in any engagement like this for, without their direction, units often began to fall apart. Taking standards was a matter for unit pride. A man who captured a standard was a guaranteed hero. But a man who captured a legion's eagle was made for life, and that legion dishonoured utterly.

Fronto moved instantly. The Pompeian thrust his blade into a man, picking his armpit target easily from the unprotected rear. The man screamed, then gurgled, then fell, opening up the tiniest space towards the aquilifer and his silver eagle.

He brought back his sword to strike the next man, but Fronto was on him then. The tip of the legate's gladius punched into the man's neck between chain collar and bronze neck guard, slamming through muscle and tendon. He knew the wound well, had seen it happen plenty of times, as the helmet tipped to one side, the cords in the man's neck ruined.

The formerly-victorious legionary jerked and dropped his blade, lurching back and staggering a few feet before falling, a small jet of crimson bursting out from beneath his helmet.

Fronto ignored the man. He would be dead soon enough and little danger until then. His eyes took in the walls to either side. His heart sank. There would be no orderly retreat. The walls were hard fought, but already the Pompeians had achieved control of much of them. If they managed to secure the whole length, then Fronto and his men would be surrounded on three sides.

'Fall back,' he bellowed. To his relief, the centurion took up the call and blew his whistle.

The men of the Ninth began to step back, trying to open up the gap between them and the enemy without weakening their line in the process, but the enemy were too many and too eager, pressing the fight forwards faster than the Ninth could retreat, forcing them to fight for their very existence with each step they took. Men were falling with every heartbeat, and Fronto was dismayed to see how few there were already. Two standard bearers remained in the press, and two centurions and an optio, as far as he could see, as well as that all-important silver eagle wavering in the centre.

Still they pushed and fought. Without fully intending to, Fronto suddenly found that he'd made his way in among the combatants and was pushing towards the enemy through a crowd of his men heading the other way as best they could. It was not hard to reach the front, for men were falling to be trodden underfoot, and suddenly he was there, stabbing and hacking, wishing he had a shield. He felt a blow on his left shoulder that was dulled by the double layer of chain but would leave an impressive bruise. He felt the fire of a cut on his arm, then one on his leg, mere flesh wounds but painful. He stabbed again, and again, killing with masterful efficiency, yet never making headway for there were always two men ready to replace each one he killed.

His fight was over in a trice. Some furious, wild young Achaean with a lust for battle tried twice to take the officer before him in the neck or armpit. Fronto turned each blow, but the young man was so fast and damned energetic that the legate never had the time to return the favour. Finally, snarling with anger that he seemed so unable to kill the officer, the legionary resorted to an unexpected move.

He kicked out and struck Fronto in the knee.

The legate's world exploded in shimmering white pain. It was blind luck that he fell backwards and not forwards into the path of the young legionary's blade. For years he had been building up the strength of his weak knee, knowing it for trouble. He had reached the point where it only ached in cold winter weather, and could bear him even on the hardest runs. He had almost forgotten that it was his weak spot. His Achilles heel, as it were. But now, the joint damaged with a kick from a hobnail boot, through tears of pain, the trouble he'd had all came flooding back. In a panic, he wondered whether it was broken. Would he walk again? Somehow the present odds of being dead at any moment seemed less important than the long-term possibilities of immobility.

He felt boots kicking him in the press, then suddenly arms were under him, helping him up. The retreat had paused just long enough to secure the officer and help him from the ground. He tried to put his weight on his knee and discovered to his astonishment that he could. It hurt like the cuts of a thousand blades, but it would take his weight. Panting, wincing, and crying out, he tried not to be too much of a burden.

The legionary at one side was already badly wounded, his sword arm useless. At the other side, Fronto was shocked to see that it was the aquilifer helping him, legate in one hand, eagle in the other, sword lost somewhere in the press. They were falling back, and they had gone far enough that he could no longer see the enemy ships through the press, but they were still dying in droves, and the unit was horribly diminished. Even the most basic calculation told him they'd never reach the fort.

More men suddenly disappeared in front of them, and Pompeian legionaries were there, snarling and charging. The legionary, unable to fight anyway, continued to help Fronto backwards. The aquilifer bellowed to his compatriots for aid and began to swing the silver-tipped staff like a weapon, keeping the enemy at bay. It was a good tactic for a moment, and bought them enough time for Fronto to be hauled back out of immediate danger, but even before more Caesarian legionaries could reach him to help, the eagle bearer had been mobbed. His eagle remained in hand, but had been knocked aside, and now he held it up, as far from any grasping hand as he could. He took two, then three, then four wounds, men swiping and stabbing.

Finally, other legionaries were there, helping hold back the enemy. The aquilifer, horribly wounded, staggering and groaning, limped and shuffled back from the enemy.

Fronto was almost trampled by the horse before he realised it was there. He turned at a snort and a huge expulsion of horse breath, and stared up the nostrils of a white mare.

Three horsemen. A tribune, a decurion and a courier.

'My compliments, Legate Fronto,' the junior tribune said with weary politeness. 'Tribune Marcellinus is on his way to your relief and bids you not die until he arrives.'

'I'll try rather hard,' grinned Fronto.

'Here,' the aquilifer shouted next to the officers, staggering forwards and pressing the silver eagle on the great ash shaft to the decurion. 'The eagle is my life. It's been mine for years. Restore it to Caesar with honour before the enemy take it.'

The decurion, staring, grasped the eagle and lifted it reverentially. He glanced over at the tribune, who nodded, then turned and rode off back towards the bulk of the army, carrying the vital symbol.

With the legionary's help, Fronto limped to the nearest open space and took stock. The enemy's advance along the gap between the walls had slowed, naturally. As the distance to the fort shortened, so the number of defenders within the gap became proportionally higher, even with the dreadful losses, so their front against the enemy was becoming stronger despite men falling constantly. The standards and the eagle had all been brought back out of danger. Having redeemed themselves over that unpleasant business at Placentia, the Ninth were damned if they were going to be dishonoured now. They were the indispensable unit here, they alone holding off the might of Pompey.

Fronto sighed. He was done fighting for today, until he could get a medicus to look at his knee and strap it up. At least they were in good order now. They were still dying and being fought back, and the battle here was currently hopeless, but they could hold on for a short while now.

It was not long before the reserves arrived. More legionaries, several cohorts in fact, threw themselves into the fray and helped hold back the tide. Fronto sagged as a figure on a horse appeared close by. He looked up into the grey, waxy, sweating face of Marcellinus.

'You look like shit.'

'You're no Olympias painting yourself,' the ill tribune chuckled, then coughed briefly. 'I've brought your horse. Fortunate, it seems.'

He gestured and a legionary hurried forwards leading Bucephalus by the reins. Fronto smiled with relief, and allowed the one-armed legionary who'd saved his life to help him up. He turned to Marcellinus. 'This soldier is to be commended. Saved my life.'

A centurion close by, who'd overheard, reached out to help the injured soldier. 'I'll see he gets straight to a medicus, sir.'

Fronto nodded. 'And a reward later. Definitely a reward.' He looked around, hoping to find the Ninth's aquilifer kneeling and rocking, but sadly the man lay prone and immobile, having finally succumbed to his dreadful injuries. 'Your eagle bearer deserves to be buried with extreme honour, too.'

Marcellinus gestured expansively with a shaking arm. 'I doubt *anyone* will get much of a burial, Legate. I've brought four more cohorts and they're just getting lost in the chaos. All I'm doing is sacrificing more men. I think you had it right. We need to pull back to the fort and hold there.'

The two officers sat together as their orders were relayed, and then began to turn and head for the fort. As the line of butchery closed, men still dropping with every heartbeat, the officers entered the fort and gave orders that the gates all be closed, leaving only this one until the last men had come through and they could save no more. Having dismounted, with the aid of a legionary Fronto struggled up the steps to the wall walk above the remaining gate and leaned on the parapet next to a tense-looking soldier, Marcellinus coming to stand beside him, leaning likewise on the timber and shaking with the effort of simply being upright and out of his sick bed.

The view from this vantage point was far from encouraging.

The ramparts from this fort to the sea were lost. To the south, lightly armed and armoured auxiliary cavalry and spearmen flooded the countryside, their discipline not the match of the legions. A number of them had broken off the attack entirely to find a source of fresh water and slake the thirst that had been growing for months. Still, there were enough engaged with the Caesarians to keep them busy at the siege line, though now most of that was in their hands anyway, barring the last hundred paces or so outside the fort. On the Pompeian side of the twin defences, the legions of the enemy had triumphed, sweeping out of that woodland, across the dry river and over the walls like a mass of ants. Their artillery was arrayed on the far bank of the river bed, but had long since fallen silent, now entirely unnecessary against the disastrously beaten Caesarians.

Indeed, all that remained of those cohorts from the Ninth who had swept out in an attempt to halt the landing of troops on the shore between the walls was less than a cohort's worth of men. A few ragged centuries completely devoid of centurions now, yet still holding together in a disciplined line despite that, as they fell back from the meat grinder to the unlikely safety of the fort.

They were still dying as they came, but the Pompeians pressing them were starting to ease up a little the closer they came to the camp of the Ninth, knowing that they would soon be in range of the scorpions and pila of the defenders on the walls.

Fronto watched in bitter anger as the heroic men fighting back to safety began to pass through the gate. It was not his place to make the decision, with the Ninth's current commander present, but judging by the look on Marcellinus' face, he was hardly relishing the duty, either. Sometimes a senior officer, rather than delegating had to take on the more onerous tasks to lift them from the shoulders of his men. With a deep breath and a dark sigh, Fronto lifted his hand and, pausing until he could justify the delay no longer, bellowed the hated command.

'Close the gates.'

Below, a centurion relayed the order and two dozen men began to force the gate closed against the tide of desperate men from the Ninth still flooding through it. Men would be trapped out there, and they would die, because Fronto had sealed the gate on them, but the alternative was unthinkable. To wait and save every last man would almost certainly allow Pompeian legionaries in too, and if they gained even the slightest foothold, they could keep the gates wide for their fellows. Then the enemy would be in, and the fort would fall, butchered from within, just as they had been on the sea walls.

With some struggling, the leaves of the gate were forced closed, a last few thankful and relieved men pushing their way through the gap before the timbers banged together and the twin wooden beams were dropped across it to hold it closed.

Fronto forced himself to watch the butchering of the men he had condemned to their fate outside the gate. He counted them and wished he had names to remember. Twenty two men were killed before the gate under his sickened gaze.

But the fort was sealed tight and they were as safe as they could hope to be right now.

That very notion was challenged even as it occurred to Fronto, a pilum shaft clunking against the timbers before him, and a sling stone whipping through the air close to his ear. Both he and Marcellinus ducked back. Expert artillerists manned their weapons and began to release bolts and stones from the ramparts into the crowds of Pompeian soldiers outside. The few men trained with slings brought them to the west rampart and began to fling bullets back into the enemy, and others gathered rocks to throw. Fronto tried not to think of the odds. It was like a reedy child in a tree throwing sticks at a pack of wolves.

The two senior officers stood back, as safe as they could manage from the errant missiles whirring over the parapet, both men leaning on fencing for support, for injury or ailment's sake. The sounds of battle were furious, coming now from west, north and south ramparts, the small fort almost surrounded. They would soon have to make the next difficult decision: whether to abandon the fort and flee through the east gate – the only free side – along the line between the two walls, and as far as the next manned installation. To do so would save lives, but would be to effectively abandon any hope of maintaining the siege and to force Caesar to withdraw, for Pompey would then control at least a quarter of the Caesarian defences. Or perhaps to stay and make a heroic stand here. Very likely everyone would die, of course, and the result might well be the same, but then that way at least there was the faintest chance. As long as they held, there would always be hope.

Damn Caesar for not listening.

A rumble had begun somewhere, and Fronto realised he was hearing it underneath the din of battle. Thunder? But the skies were clear, and there had been no rain in so long.

Hooves. That was the thunder of hooves.

Limping and cursing, Fronto lurched as fast as his painful knee would allow along the rampart to the south, from where the noise was clearly now coming. As he neared the corner of the fort, where the line of the outer defences joined, he frowned. The rumble was the skirmishing light cavalry of Pompey's, who had been racing around the periphery threatening and supporting. Now they were racing en-masse back towards the shore.

The frown turned into a smile as his gaze tracked back to the east, towards that from which Pompey's horsemen were running. Caesar's Gallic horse, a German unit too, were racing along in formation outside the walls, and Fronto could make out the shape of Galronus on the lead beast, with a decurion close by, bellowing battle cries in his native tongue. The other auxiliaries there turned and fled, too, in the face of Galronus and his horsemen. Fronto's grin faltered as he realised the riders were not as numerous as he'd initially supposed. They were enough to put the enemy to flight, but if the Pompeians realised how few their pursuers were and decided to turn and face them, the engagement would probably still tip in the enemy's favour. Fronto had assumed it was the lead wing of the full cavalry, but in fact it was less than a wing.

His faltering smile returned to glory as his ears now picked up a new sound. Buccinae. Legionary calls from the east. Ignoring the pain in his knee as best he could, he now lurched along the outer wall, the Gallic and German cavalry racing past below him like some dreadful native war band. In thirty heartbeats, he reached the next corner, and was rewarded with a view east between the twin ramparts. Perhaps six or seven thousand men were coming in full battle array and tight formation. At the head of them rode a man in gleaming burnished bronze on a tall, impressive grey. Marcus Antonius. And the standards behind him were those of the Seventh and Tenth Legions.

Help had arrived. Marcellinus, who had followed Fronto round with a relieved smile plastered across his face, called out the order to open the gate and, with a sense of profound gratitude, the legionaries below threw the gates wide.

Fronto couldn't help but grin as Antonius rode through the gate with the tribunes of the two legions at his back and the men stomping along in lines. The soldiers of the Ninth erupted into cheers as the relief force surged through the gate and into the camp, Antonius' straying gaze catching Fronto and mouthing something uncomplimentary about Caesar at him in passing, with a grin. Atenos threw him a salute, and even Salvius Cursor cast him an acknowledging nod of recognition.

As they moved through the centre of the small fort, Antonius bellowed the order for the soldiers at the west gate to stand ready, then told his men to draw their blades. The officers re-formed their units ready for battle. In swift succession, Antonius gave the two orders to open the gate and to charge. Fronto's grin broadened as the combined forces of the Seventh and Tenth ran at the gate even as it was hauled open. The Pompeian forces outside let out a cry of triumph at the opening gate, which turned into shouts of dismay as they ran into the fort only to find themselves face to face with a wall of iron, bronze and painted wood in the form of fresh, enthusiastic veteran legionaries.

The Seventh and the Tenth roared the name of Caesar, invoked Minerva and Mars and high Jupiter, and began to kill, pushing the numerous but green forces of Pompey back from the gate. In mere moments they were in the open once more, in the space between the inner and outer siege works, scything through Pompey's men like a farmer through the wheat harvest. Fronto and Marcellinus lurched and staggered round to the west gate where they had started, leaning once more upon the parapet to watch the fight unfold.

The outer wall was clear. Galronus and his cavalry, though numerically inferior, had put the enemy to flight. The Pompeian skirmishers, horse and foot alike, had melted away into the countryside to the south. The Remi noble who had led the heroic charge kept a tight rein on his forces, though. A few small units slipped his command, racing off after the fleeing enemy, but returned, chastened, at belligerent calls from the cavalry horns. They had to keep order. If the Gauls and Germans raced off into the country seeking their prey they would be no further use here, and calling them back would be more difficult with every half mile they raced. Instead, they thundered along the ramparts, hurling light javelins at the Pompeian soldiers at the parapets, helping clear the way for Antonius' relief force.

Antonius, of course, had gradually dropped to the rear of his force, allowing the heavy infantry to lead the way. By the time the next stage of the battle was well underway, Antonius had dismounted and climbed the wall to stand between Fronto and Marcellinus.

'Of course, we can't win,' he said, his smile still in place.

Fronto nodded his agreement, though Marcellinus frowned.

'Why not, sir?'

'Even with my reinforcements, we number three diminished legions against perhaps seven or eight of Pompey's. And the cavalry out there are still outnumbered. They helped turn the tide, but that tide will roll back in yet. That's why Galronus has not pressed them when they fled. And the two legions I brought will not attempt to actually win here. That's not the orders I gave.'

'What orders did you give then, sir?'

'To drive them back and free the fort. I want them out of artillery range so we can consolidate once again. If we try to do more we'll just end up butchered and back in the same position as the Ninth were a quarter of an hour ago. No, we need the enemy out of reach so we can all breathe and reassess. The Seventh and Tenth have excellent men in charge: Atenos and Volcatius Tullus. Both men know just how far to go and when to stop, and both have solid control of their men. No heroics. Just a single push and then back to the fort. See how that's happening even now?'

And they could. The attacking Caesarians had reached a point some eight hundred paces from the fort walls and had given a final, terrifying, charge. Even from this distance, Fronto was certain that the figure leading the charge like some Tartaran monster of ancient legend was Salvius Cursor. The enemy broke and ran towards the sea, but the Seventh and Tenth did not follow. Instead, they began to chant their commander in chief's name and slowly pulled back in perfect order, filing through the gate.

'What now then?' Fronto breathed as the relief force swarmed into the fort and the gate was shut.

'Now we watch and observe. We add what extra defences we can manage, we heal the wounded and we bury the dead. And we hope that Gaius hauls Sulla's head out of his backside long enough to realise he's needed. I sent a message to Caesar as we marched for here. By now, hopefully, the general has gathered a sizeable force and set off around the defences to support us. There is a chance here, Fronto. Right now, we're in the shit. But if Caesar comes in force and we can come anywhere close to matching their numbers, we could force Pompey to commit to open battle at last. We could end this whole thing here, today, before Scipio and his men get here.'

'I pray Fortuna's listening,' Fronto muttered, grasping the pendant at his neck.

'Knee troubling you again, Fronto?'

'Some young knobhead in the enemy lines kicked me in it. Felt it go. At least I can still stand. I thought the runt had broken it for a moment.'

'You'll bounce back, Fronto. Never seen anyone with your power of recovery. Or your luck.'

'I don't feel especially lucky right now. Watching Pompey swarming over our walls, with a knee that hurts like bollocks and relying on someone turning up to haul us back out of the latrine.'

'You're not dead, Fronto. Given what you just went through, that's lucky.'

'I suppose. But we've lost the sea walls. Can you see? Pompey's men are already at work dismantling parts of our defences and building their own. They're making it unusable to us and turning it into their own lines. I'm starting to think this is a lost cause and we'd be better pulling back for a while.'

They all watched. Some distance away, close to the shore, Pompey's men were already beginning to construct another large camp outside the entire system. Along with that re-occupied camp the Ninth once built, that gave Pompey complete control of the coast and free passage in and out of the siege lines for forage and animal fodder. The siege had failed. Unless the general decided to leave, all they could hope for now was to force Pompey to commit to full battle and end the war here.

Hopefully as the victors…

CHAPTER 11

Caesar arrived to an atmosphere of sullen dismay. The success of the Tenth and Seventh legions in forcing back Pompey's attack and freeing the fort had given everyone time to breathe, but it had also given them time to think, which had left them pondering the inevitable. The sea walls stretch was lost, and there was little they could do about it. A rough estimate put the enemy numbers visible at perhaps ten or eleven legions in total, far too many to think about challenging. And the longer they stayed in command of that position, the stronger they would get, for they would no longer be cut off from adequate water and fodder. Though it had taken some time for the enemy skirmishers and light auxiliaries to return from their flight into the wilds, Galronus had spotted new cavalry brought in from the main camp. These were not the lightly armed auxiliaries he had terrified with his charge, but those same bright, bronze-clad horsemen of whom Fronto had spoken so highly on first sight.

Caesar had arrived with two more legions, bringing the numerical total to five now, though in terms of manpower it would truly count more like three. The Fifth, Seventh, Ninth, Tenth and Thirteenth were now crammed in the fort and the circumvallation behind it, working on the defences to improve them, largely to keep them busy as the officers pondered their next move.

'They have begun their own new systems of siege works, aimed at keeping us out and maintaining their control of the coast,' Antonius said. 'You can see odd parts of it from here, but the woods hide more. A few tentative scouting missions have confirmed the scale of their works. And with the number of men they have, their new defences are going up rapidly.'

'So we are no longer familiar with the lay of the land there,' Caesar mused.

'No. And their men are everywhere. I can't see a clear way out.'

Fronto nodded. 'There isn't one. We're outnumbered more than two to one, and I've seen the banners of a number of his veteran legions there. The First and the Third at the very least. And now he's brought out his heavy horse too, which shows he means business. We've lost our grip on him, and now he has all the advantages. Caesar, we have to accept that this battle is no longer tenable.'

The other officers turned surprised and disapproving looks on the Tenth's legate, who was leaning on a chair back to take the weight off his knee, which was now bandaged and strapped up for support. Fronto shrugged. 'There comes a time when common sense has to overcome heroism. We've managed valiantly so far, but I think we're at the end of our run of good fortune. Unless someone can conjure up miracles, I think we need to cut our losses.'

'You mean retreat?' Sulla said in disbelief.

'While we still have an army to do it with, yes.'

'Then all this will have been in vain,' Tillius put in.

'Admittedly so, but there is an old adage about throwing good coins after bad. Is it worth sacrificing the rest of our army on the altar of hubris just because we don't want to admit defeat.'

Caesar's eyes flashed. 'I will not be defeated, Fronto.'

'We *have* been defeated, Caesar,' Fronto countered. 'And there's no shame in it. Pompey is acknowledged as one of Rome's greatest military minds ever. To lose one fight against him is no dishonour, but at least if we accept that we can regroup, strengthen, and face him again with better odds.'

'No,' Caesar said coldly, with Sulla suddenly next to him, nodding his approval.

'Caesar…'

'No. We just need to break his control. We cut his forces in half and reconstitute the siege. Then we are at leisure to deal with those we trap outside while the rest return to his camp at Petra to die of thirst. We need to take one of those two forts. That would give us a stronghold in the centre.'

'Marching five legions into the midst of twice that many will not divide them and conquer,' Fronto growled. 'That is like sending them into the maw of Tartarus. They will be overrun and destroyed. And one of those legions is mine. I don't relish the thought of losing the Tenth.'

'Fronto, your defeatist input to this discussion is not welcome,' Sulla snapped. 'We are trying to work out how to beat the man, not run from him with our tail between our legs.'

'I won't lead the Tenth into certain death,' Fronto snarled.

'You won't lead them *anywhere*,' Sulla countered angrily. 'Look at you. You're hobbled, man. You can barely walk, let alone fight. Your command is up. Salvius leads the Tenth.'

'Over my dead body.'

'Close enough, yes.'

'Caesar?'

The general held up a hand to quell the arguments.

'Gentlemen, decorum please. Fronto, I owe you an apology for not heeding your warning in good time. Your instincts are good, and I appreciate your point of view in this matter. You may even be correct again, though I hope to Hades you are not. Whatever the case, I will not abandon this fight until there is no other option. You retain your command of the Tenth, Fronto, of course, but Sulla is correct that you are in no shape to lead them physically until that knee heals. Salvius Cursor will lead them in your stead for now. His particular brand of blind murderous glee is more or less what we shall need in the coming days.'

Fronto sagged over the chair back. 'Any push here is doomed. Believe me. Even with Salvius coated in blood and screaming curses at the front.'

'Your opinion is noted,' Caesar said with finality. 'Now we need to plan. What is our prime target?'

'The new camp he's built, General,' Tillius put in. 'That way we can incorporate it into our system and seal him in again with relative ease.'

'Bollocks,' muttered Fronto under his breath, earning a number of hard looks and a silent warning from the general.

'No. It has to be the inner camp' Antonius said. 'The one originally built by the Ninth. Scouts say he's enlarged it a great deal, which suggests he means it to be a major base of operations. And it lies behind the woods. Gives us a more covert approach.'

'Covert?,' Fronto snorted. 'Five legions? Might as well ring bells and blow whistles. Trees won't hide you.'

Caesar nodded. 'True. So we need to make our approach more subtle. No signals given that might attract the enemy. Just use standards and gestures for commands. We shall split the force and come against the fort in a two-pronged attack. Shuffle all the badly injured and immobile into a few cohorts and they can stay here and work on the defences, making a lot of noise and trying to look like several legions. If the enemy think we continue to work so, they will not be looking for an attack. Perhaps we can hit them by surprise.'

'What about their cavalry?' Brutus put in.

'Sorry, Brutus?'

'They have heavy cavalry there now, of a sort designed to kill a phalanx. As soon as any fight begins, Pompey is bound to field them, and they will be swift to involve themselves.'

Gaius Volusenus, the Prefect of Horse, nodded. 'We can respond with our own cavalry. Send them in behind the infantry. We've brought most of the horse up now. We're strong.'

'No we're not,' Galronus said flatly.

'What?'

'Not there, we're not. Through woodland and unknown defences. We could be trapped easily. Our cavalry are only effective in open ground.'

'You've been around your friend Fronto too long, Gaul,' Sulla grunted.

'I am not a Gaul,' Galronus replied with an arched eyebrow. 'I am Remi.'

'Whatever,' snorted Sulla with a dismissive wave.

'We will only field the cavalry once we are committed and the infantry have cleared the way,' Caesar said. He reached up to the recent map on the wall, which was as close as they could manage to accurate.

'I shall lead one force. I shall take sixteen cohorts to the left, here. We will move slowly and quietly through the woodlands. We shall sacrifice speed for silence. While we are doing that, Tillius will lead the second column of a similar number at higher speed far to the right, using this river bed as a track to move fast. They will skirt the enemy fort and come at it from the north, inside the enemy's region of control. The cavalry will follow them, for the river bed should make their approach easier. If we time things correctly, my force should hit the south and east of the fort at the same time that of Tillius hits the north. If we achieve an adequate element of surprise, we might overrun them before they can do anything about it. Once we are ensconced there, more troops can be brought in from the far lines and we can seal the gap once more.'

Galronus gave an almost insolent nod, and slipped away from the gathering as the details began to be hammered out. Fronto followed him after a moment and found the Remi standing in the evening air and breathing deeply.

'This is one attack I am grateful not to be part of,' Fronto said quietly. 'My knee may have done me a favour.'

'We are going to lose,' Galronus said.

'Yes. Don't go. You don't have to. Volusenus is Prefect of Horse. Let him do it.'

'Some of these units have been in my command for many years,' Galronus said. 'Some came through Alesia with me. It would be poor repayment for me to abandon them now.'

'Don't get yourself killed. My sister would never forgive me.'

'Is there not a chance?' Brutus said suddenly, behind them, having approached unnoticed. 'None at all?'

Fronto sighed. 'Caesar has pulled victories from the backside of defeat before now,' Fronto admitted. 'But this is different. Pompey is clever. And he's prepared. Even if Caesar takes him by surprise, he'll react quickly. I cannot see this turning out well.'

* * *

Salvius Cursor changed hands with his sword for a moment, wiping his sweaty palm on his tunic before returning the blade to the correct hand. He was more surprised than anyone to find that he was uncertain. Stupid, really. This was exactly the plan he would have suggested himself, and to find that he was one of the most senior officers engaged in it, effectively in control of those cohorts drawn from the Tenth, was an honour. Moreover he would, if everything went right, get his chance to plant a blade in a dozen Pompeian hearts and help secure the old bastard once more where he could starve. All was good. And yet a nagging little voice at the back of his mind kept telling him that something was wrong. That he needed to be prepared and on his guard. Perhaps it was just Fronto's attitude. Or worse, his last words before the tribune had led the men out of camp.

'Bring the Tenth home, Salvius. Don't get my legion killed.'

Damn it, but that had put something on his shoulders he really didn't need at a time like this.

Caesar led the column. Actually led it, as though he were a legionary himself. Admittedly there were half a dozen praetorian horsemen with him for protection, but it was still impressive, given that Pompey had never taken the forwards position in his life. In addition to Salvius, Volcatius Tullus and Sulla himself moved forwards with their legions, the latter in a more traditional position, bringing up the rear of his force. A legion approaching, let alone two, was hardly a quiet thing, and yet he'd been impressed at how subtle they were. The crunch, clonk and rattle of soldiers on the move was partially deadened by the woods around them, and he doubted anyone up ahead would have much warning of their approach.

Still, he was feeling less than confident with regard to the coming fight. Damn it, but he was starting to catch it from Fronto. At this rate, within a year or two he'd be a soft old bugger like the legate.

His attention was drawn by movement ahead, and he spotted one of the advance scouts suddenly appearing back through the trees, waving his arms. He then gestured to the right with both hands and motioned that the enemy were as yet unaware. Good. Things were going as planned. All Salvius had to do was kill as many Pompeians as he could.

And not get the Tenth killed.

Damn it, Fronto.

Caesar turned and gave his signals, which were picked up by the standard bearers of each unit, guiding their soldiers from the eight-man column into a much wider front for the attack. As he passed through one of the areas of the woods with slightly sparser trees, Salvius looked up at the sun. It was almost at the apex. The enemy would be about ready to change guard on the hour, and every man would be focused on the coming midday meal. If ever the defenders were going to be unprepared, it was now. And if all was going according to plan then the second column, closely followed by the cavalry, would be approaching the camp's north gate now.

Why, then, was he so worried?

In the camp, the blast of a horn announced the next watch. Perfect timing.

Barely had the last echo of the instrument washed over the woods before Salvius and the rest of Caesar's attack burst from the tree line to find themselves only a hundred paces from the enemy camp. Best of all, the Pompeians had been entirely unaware of the approach of the Caesarian force. The walls showed perhaps half as many guards as Salvius had expected, for it was the change of guard shifts, and men were busy coming and going.

With a bellow from the general, the entire force, fifteen cohorts strong, let loose a roar to shake the heavens. The ramparts were some ten feet high but the enemy, in constructing the new, larger fort, had been lax. They had not sheared off the rampart at the exterior, and so left a slope. A steep one, admittedly, but enough for a man to climb. Furthermore, as Salvius ran on, he noted that the wide ditch around the place had not yet been filled with spikes or obstructions. They were too overconfident in their security. The other officers and men had clearly noted all this too, for the roar only increased in intensity, and the officers all across the line directed their men to parts of the walls. Little would stop the Caesarians from crossing that line unless the enemy somehow suddenly flooded the ramparts with men and artillery.

In two dozen heartbeats he had crossed the open ground. Missiles began to fly from the fort: stones, arrows and heavy bolts, but only in small numbers and inexpertly launched. Salvius, screaming incoherently, reached the ditch and barely paused, leaping into it, swiftly followed by Atenos and the men of the Tenth. Across the wide ditch they ran, then to the steep rampart. Up they scrabbled, grasping at earth and grass and timbers to aid their climb. The enemy had managed to get more men to the walls now, and some armed with pila, but they did not throw them, instead using them like spears to thrust down at the soldiers coming at them. A quick glance to the left revealed a cohort of the Seventh hitting the gate like a wave of angry bronze and red.

Salvius did not have the luxury of time to watch their endeavours. Instead, he joined the swarm of men reaching the rampart and surrendered his will to the god of war. A legionary appeared at the top of the wooden palisade above him and reached over, jabbing down awkwardly with his gladius. Salvius instinctively ducked to one side, then, with his free hand, grabbed the man's wrist and pulled. He heard the wrench as the legionary's shoulder dislocated, and tried to ignore the screams as he used the arm as a rope to pull himself up to the parapet, where he deftly kicked the young soldier in the head, ruining his face with hobnails, and pushed him away, looking for the next challenge.

Two more legionaries were coming for him now, one from each side. They were young. Whoever the legion in charge of the fort was, they weren't veterans but young pups with a month or two's training. Salvius taught them a hard lesson. Waiting until they were almost on him, yelling their fury, he simply stepped back onto the embankment behind the walls, and the two men collided in a crash of panic. He left them no time to recover, launching a series of lightning fast blows of which probably the first two had been enough to kill, though Salvius liked to be sure. He blinked away the blood that has fountained into his face, then turned. The walls were already under control. The men of the Tenth and Seventh were surging over them, fighting off the meagre defence. The centre of the great square was largely open ground, awaiting the tents of whichever legions were destined to be based here, but over in one corner, Salvius could see the original camp the Ninth had built, occupying a quarter of the larger installation, but still separated from the rest by its own wall, and host to the tents of the defenders. There, the enemy were gathering for a more formidable contest.

Salvius knew his place. Barely had the signallers begun to give out the general's command before the tribune, followed by a group of his legionaries, raced around the walls for that next fight.

A man in a prefect's uniform was directing the fight from there, arraying his men, and Salvius marked the man as the most senior on site, and therefore the most important to target. The enemy commander was clearly a veteran, even if his men were not, for as soon as it had become clear that the walls of the main camp were too poorly-constructed and defended to hold, he had drawn back every man he could to hold the small fort within its bounds. The gate there had been shut and barred, but the smaller fort had two weak spots: it was readily accessible where its walls joined those of the larger camp, and so it was at these two spots that the defenders were massing. That would be more of a fight.

Salvius continued to jog along the wall top, dodging the other Caesarian troops as they poured over, skirting small struggles and here and there swiping his blade at the enemies he passed in a half-hearted, opportunistic manner.

He was halfway to the small fort when he realised that Atenos was running beside him. He still did not know what to make of the Tenth's huge, blond senior centurion. The man was clearly little more than a Gaul, his Latin still accented and his chin showing a beard even beneath the cheek plates of his helmet. And this barbarian was one of Fronto's close friends, which meant he was probably more given to yapping than fighting. Yet from what he'd seen of the big man in combat, he seemed fearsome. Well, they would need fearsome today.

'We punch through the defenders as hard as we can. Once we're inside that fort they're lost'

Atenos nodded. 'That prefect is mine, though, Tribune.'

'I beg to differ,' Salvius barked. 'I marked him first.'

'That's Titus Pullo. Used to be a centurion in the Fourteenth, then the Eleventh. I've fought alongside the bastard.'

'Pullo?' Salvius said in surprise. 'The man who betrayed Antonius last winter?'

'The very bastard. Cost us most of our strength in Illyria.'

'Then you'll have to race me to him,' Salvius said.

Both men put on an extra turn of speed, the legionaries of the Tenth panting behind them to keep up. As they neared the point where both walls met, Pullo, now the enemy prefect, pulled his men into a shield wall three deep. He was no idiot, and put the bulk of his men between him and the screaming officers of the Tenth running his way.

The Caesarians hit like a battering ram, punching into the enemy shield wall so hard that even the rearmost men staggered back and a few toppled away down the embankment. Not Pullo. He kept his feet and kept his place. Salvius went to work stabbing, slashing and hacking, his blade rising and falling like a butcher's cleaver, warm blood spraying out across the air. He took a couple of minor blows, which was inevitable, especially with no shield, but Salvius did not fear for his life. He knew he was protected by Mars. Had not the god of war saved him in the old days? Saved him from Pompey?

Beside him, Atenos was similarly brutal, using every weapon available, right down to feet, knees and even teeth. They were making headway, and the rest of the legionaries from the Tenth that had followed them around the walls were joining in now, but it would be slow work even then. With such a narrow point of entry it was easy to defend, and they needed to take the fort fast, lest Pompey commit men to the fight and they be swamped.

He wondered momentarily why there had been no sign yet of the second column. If they were on schedule with the plan, they should have been attacking from the north at the same time Salvius had hit the south. Yet there was no sign of them.

That sinking feeling that had been there on the journey returned suddenly. Fronto had been right again. This was a fool's errand. Almost as if he had summoned disaster, sudden calls blared out from buccinae beyond the wall. Salvius took a moment, stepped back from the fight and allowed a legionary to take his place as he shook his head to clear his vision a little. Then he crossed to the wall top, where he was looking southwest.

'Oh, Hades.'

Men were coming at speed. Fresh legionaries, in numbers that brought a touch of panic to even Salvius. What were there: four legions? Five? Veteran ones too, by the looks of it. And the Caesarian force at the fort numbered roughly a legion and a half until the others arrived from wherever they were. The odds were about to tip horribly in the enemy's favour. Unless they could do something, they were going to be trapped in this fort by forces in total three times their size. That would be it. He was sure they couldn't get out of that. And as it that were not bad enough, a thunderous rumble joined the horn calls, and he caught sight of the Illyrian heavy cavalry, clad in bronze, beyond those new, fresh legions.

His gaze slipped to the north.

'Where are you?' he murmured in a dark voice.

* * *

Galronus felt all hope slipping away like a loose river bank in a storm. The sun had passed the apex some time ago and he was fairly sure he'd heard horn calls through the woods. They were late to dinner, and soon there would be nothing left but scraps. And the worst of it was that he was totally impotent to do anything about it.

Tillius was in charge, way out ahead at the front of the force, largely made up of men from the Fifth and Thirteenth, with a cohort from the Ninth in there too. They had marched along the river bed at a more sedate pace than Galronus had expected. And though his place was with the cavalry at the rear, waiting to be given the all clear to race past and engage an enemy, he was beginning to believe that Tillius was lost and too pig-headed to admit it.

'I'm going ahead,' he said to the nearest decurion, who nodded his understanding. A moment later, Galronus was hurtling along the dry river bed alongside the column of men, raising dust beneath his hooves that drew angry curses from the men it engulfed as he passed. It took some time to pass seventeen cohorts, but finally he spotted the commanders on their horses at the head of the column. Kicking his steed for a turn of speed, he raced towards them and even as he fell in alongside Tillius and opened his mouth to speak, his eyes took in their surroundings and he blinked.

'Where the shit are we?'

Tillius frowned. 'North wall. Looking for the gate, Commander. It must be along here. Strange that there's no defenders, eh? But all the better for us.'

'That's not the fort,' Galronus said in an exasperated tone.

'What?'

The Remi turned and pointed off ahead, along the river. 'You see that blue wobbly thing over there? That's the sea.'

'I'm well aware of that.' Tillius replied in a scathing voice.

'Then we're way past the fort and near the shore. We passed it half an hour ago, I reckon. I head a horn call back then, I think.'

'If this is not the fort, then what is it?' snapped Tillius, pointing at the ramparts through two dozen paces of woodland on their left.

'I don't know,' shouted Galronus angrily, 'but the enemy have been building all sorts of new defences since we pulled back, and this goes down to the sea, so whatever it is, it's not the damned fort"'

155

'Then we'll have to turn around,' Tillius said, anger in his tone, but his face beginning to flush with embarrassment. This would not go down well with the general.

'You can't,' Galronus bellowed. 'Fifteenth cohorts, and behind them the cavalry and all along a single dry river bed? Idiot. Just getting them turned round and starting moving again will take at least half an hour.'

'Then we shall take these walls and see what lies beyond,' announced Tillius.

'What?'

'Well if we've somehow missed the fort, probably through the faults of your scout riders, then our best chance is to break through whatever these defences are and see what the terrain is like on the far side. Perhaps we can find open ground. Perhaps we will be able to see the fort and return to our primary task.'

'You're a damned idiot.'

Tillius glared at him. 'Get back to your barbarians, man, and leave this to Romans.'

'Romans who are lost?' sneered Galronus, but he knew he was in no position to command here. Tillius had control. Galronus stepped his horse back to the nearest trees at the far bank of the river and watched in disbelief as the legate distributed orders and the legions began to swarm up the far side and towards the earthen embankment topped by a fresh timber wall beyond.

There were no defenders. And to Galronus that meant the defences were latent, unused and of little value. He was half tempted to have the cavalry turn around and leave. It seemed exceedingly unlikely that anything good was coming.

With a sigh, he watched the legionaries storming an empty wall, and turned his horse, riding back for the cavalry at the rear. He had not gone far before he heard a new noise.

Horn calls. Very distant, somewhere south over the woods, but most definitely the calls of legions. And far too many to be Caesar and his sixteen cohorts.

With some certainty, he decided that Caesar and his men were in the shit, neck deep, and unless something unexpected happened here, the second column and the cavalry were going to be of no help.

The gods had better be watching over the general right now.

CHAPTER 12

Atenos lurched back as a sword scraped across the brow of his helmet with a nerve-jangling sound, creating sparks. The tip narrowly missed bifurcating his nose, and the big centurion realised how close he'd come to being an ex-centurion. In a fraction of a heartbeat, he threw a prayer of thanks to Lug, and to Jupiter, just in case. But it had been a lucky blow rather than a clever one. The soldier facing him was playing everything by the legionary training manual. Every stab, step and parry had been drilled into him by a training officer relatively recently.

Atenos, on the other hand, had the advantage of years of practice as a mercenary, fighting in more than one army, against more than one type of foe, sometimes for Rome and sometimes against it, despite his current loyalties. Consequently, he was considerably more adaptable than the average legionary.

The soldier, having overreached, did exactly as he'd been taught, putting his large shield between himself and the enemy, hunching down behind it for protection as he pulled back his blade and prepared to drive it forwards again, looking for the centurion's armpit. The problem was, he had not had sufficient practice to know how best to brace. From the angle of the shield alone, Atenos spotted the mistake. The legionary had pushed his shin at the bottom of the shield and put his shoulder into it low, crouching so that only his eyes upwards were visible above the shield. A veteran would know to brace his shoulder against the shield higher than that.

Gripping his sword tight ready, Atenos slammed out with the heel of his palm against the shield, just below the upper rim. With the brace point too low the soldier was doomed. The top of the shield simply slammed back into his face, very hard, given the massive strength in the Gaul's arms. Atenos heard the grind of the man's cheek pieces bending in and the crunch of a broken nose.

Howling, the soldier automatically lowered his shield, blinking away the pain, and for his sins received Atenos' blade in the eye. The big centurion grunted with effort as the blade grated on bone and the dying, disfigured legionary fell away.

He seized the opportunity to glance to his left. That mad bastard tribune was intent on the enemy commander, but Atenos was damned if he was going to let anyone else have him. Titus Pullo had been one of Caesar's own. A hero and a veteran centurion. He had fought valiantly for the general across Gaul, and alongside Atenos more than once. But he was a betrayer. Like Labienus and so many others, he had turned his back on his loyalty to Caesar and fled to Pompey in sick treachery. Worse still, he had been the man who had sold out the Twenty Fourth Legion to the enemy and caused the failure of Gaius Antoninus' campaign in Illyria. The man was the worst sort, and his removal would be like excising the rotten flesh from a wound.

He was surprised to note that the lunatic Salvius Cursor had backed away from the combat, moving to the parapet and peering off into the distance. Atenos wondered in passing what had so drawn the man's attention as to drag him from combat, but let the thought go. He had other fish to fry.

Three legionaries stood between him and Pullo now. More men were coming up behind in support, but the enemy prefect had clearly marked Atenos out and was not falling back behind his men. Indeed, Pullo flexed his muscles and readied his sword, clearly waiting for Atenos.

Another legionary made to stab Atenos in the groin, thrusting low and keeping as close behind his shield as he could. The big Gaul contemptuously knocked the blade aside with his own, stamped on the man's exposed foot and, as the shield dropped a little in response, slammed the hilt of his blade into the man's face. He fell, but Atenos had no time to recover, for another man made a swipe. Atenos lurched to the side and felt a line of hot fiery pain open up along his forearm where the blade just made contact enough to wound the flesh.

He roared and recovered, but had no chance to respond to his attacker, for one of his own men managed to plant a blow into the man's neck, twisting amid the sound of breaking bone and cartilage and ripping the sword back out with a huge gout of blood. The enemy soldier collapsed and suddenly Atenos was through, facing Pullo.

It was odd how this sometimes happened on a battlefield. It had something to do with the respect and fear centurions instilled in the common soldiery. Despite the fact that this was a hard-press of fighting, men pressed up against one another in a tight mass of killing, somehow none of them interfered with the two officers facing one another. The fight seethed on around them, yet they were an island of calm in the centre as the two men watched one another's eyes.

Pullo struck first. His sword dashed out with impressive speed. It was not intended to be a killing blow, understandably. The problem with two such skilled veterans facing one another was that both knew all the killing points and how to protect them. Pullo's blow was to the centre of the torso. The centurion's chain shirt would stop the point, for certain, but the blow would wind him and bruise badly. Hades, if the blow was powerful enough, it could even crack his breastbone.

Atenos twisted a quarter to his left and the point of the blade grated across the metal links with an eye-watering noise. In response, Atenos spun the other three quarters into a full circle, out of the way of his opponent's blade, lancing out with his own sword for a similar strike.

Pullo's defence was hardly noble, but it was expedient and swift. Exposed, he had no shield and could not withdraw his sword in time to parry. Instead, his free hand grabbed the shoulder doubling of a legionary's mail shirt and yanked him into the path of the blow, a human shield. The legionary yelped as Atenos' sword scraped his arm and drew blood before Pullo cast him aside again.

Once more they paused, facing one another.

'Atenos.'

'Pullo. I am disappointed to say the least.'

'I'll try and do better. Bear with me.'

'I don't mean your sword. I mean your soul. Why? Why betray your commander?'

'You have no idea what you're talking about Atenos.'

'Care to enlighten me?' There was an odd, pregnant pause, and the big centurion suddenly dropped low and slashed at Pullo's legs. The prefect stepped a pace backwards, dropping his own blade into the path of the attack.

'I didn't betray Caesar. Caesar betrayed the republic. I didn't do it lightly, Atenos. I did it for principles. You wouldn't understand. You're a Gaul. A mercenary.'

'I know I took an oath to Caesar, and so did you. Where I'm from we don't break oaths.'

The two men circled a half turn.

'Rome has to be bigger than individual loyalties, Atenos. Caesar has his eyes on a throne, man. He has to be stopped. Pompey's an insufferable arse, but he's a republican arse. It's you who fights for wickedness, Atenos, not me.'

'I guess we'll just have to agree to disagree,' the centurion spat.

'Only briefly.'

Pullo lunged again, his blade low for a belly strike, but coming up at the last moment for a chest blow once again. It was a masterful feint, and Atenos only just turned in time to rob the blow of most of its strength, though he felt a rib crack under the strike. Still, sometimes you had to sacrifice to win. It was only a rib.

Pullo's face dropped into a frown. His eyes pulled back from his sword, pressed against Atenos' side, along his extended arm, and to the hilt of the centurion's blade, clutched tight in an extended hand, all that could be seen of the sword that had punched into his exposed armpit. He blinked.

'A quick death,' Atenos said. 'A soldier's death.'

Wincing at the pain of his broken rib, he twisted the blade, ramming it in a little further, mincing heart and other organs before ripping it out.

Pullo, eyes wide, stared at the blade as it left him, then simply folded up with a sigh that sounded oddly regretful.

Atenos had no time to mourn or celebrate, which was perhaps a good thing, since he was not sure which was more appropriate. A legionary swung at him and he almost followed Pullo into Elysium there and then, saved only by pure chance. The soldier's sword glanced off the bronze hooks that held the doubled layer of chain over his shoulders and instead of shattering more bones, simply scraped away to the side, grating across iron links. The big centurion wobbled for a moment, and then stabbed the man in the throat.

The press closed in again, and Pullo's body was lost to sight beneath the mass of soldiers stabbing and hacking for both sides. Grunting at the pain of his broken rib, Atenos was forced to favour his right side and realised that he was starting to lose his strength. He only heard Salvius Cursor's shout the third or fourth time, and staggered from the line of men over to the parapet, breathing heavily.

'What is it, sir?'

But he didn't need the tribune to answer He could see for himself the serried ranks of Pompey's legions tromping steadily towards the fort.

'Bollocks.'

'Exactly. Even with Tillius and his column that would be a damned hard fight. Without him, it's suicide.'

Atenos nodded. 'I'm with you there. What are your orders?'

Salvius nudged him and pointed over towards the interior of the fort, where Caesar, with other commanders and his personal guard, was giving out orders and pointing to positions around the walls.

'Caesar's clearly not planning to leave, so we can't. I suggest we try and take this small inner fort and hold it. There's not enough of us to hold the large one. And then maybe we can survive long enough for Tillius to get here.'

'If he's coming.'

* * *

Galronus took a deep breath, preparing himself. The odd, abandoned wall had been broken down across a fairly wide section, and the legions had crossed the gap swiftly, deploying on the far side, though they had, as usual, given precious little thought to the cavalry. The men had swarmed down the ditch, up the steep bank, over the shattered fence, and off into the open. That terrain would be guaranteed to break a number of horse's legs and ruin the cavalry. It had taken some argument with Tillius before he deployed men to level out a section for the cavalry to cross securely. Even then it was only wide enough for a couple of horses with any level of safety.

The legions were beyond the wall now, the last few pioneers who'd been working on the flattening gathering their tools and running to join their mates. Word had come back that the woodland continued on the far side, but was much thinner than elsewhere making it more suitable for larger scale manoeuvres and for cavalry. Moreover, many of the trees had been sacrificed to create the forts and walls in the area, thinning it still further.

'Forwards, two at a time. On the far side, separate and move to both flanks, wherever there's adequate space to form up.'

Leaving his officers to carry out the orders, Galronus moved on ahead, walking his horse carefully across the freshly compacted earth causeway over the ditch. It was still soft when taking the weight of a horse, but considerably better than negotiating the dangerous ditch. At the far side, he climbed the low rampart where it had been brought down a little, and rode off towards the gathered legions. Between the ranks of men bent out of formation by the presence of foliage and wide stumps, and those same boles of tall trees, he could not see the officers out front, though he knew they would be at the fore somewhere. Satisfied that the route was safe enough now, he shouted as much back to the others, and the horsemen, who had been approaching the crossing rather gingerly, picked up the pace.

Galronus, satisfied that the infantry clearly were not hurrying off anywhere, fell into position at their rear, watching as his riders crested the rampart and descended to his position. As they arrived, he pointed either left or right to each one, directing them to the flanks to fall into the position favoured by a Roman general in the field. He counted the first hundred men through. It was going to take some time to get all the cavalry across, but they were managing. Given how late they were, though, he couldn't understand why Tillius was delaying so. The infantry could run to the aid of their fellows,, or should at least be looking for them. The cavalry could deploy afterwards if necessary. It wasn't ideal, but with the almighty cock up the legate had already achieved, it was the best they could hope for.

At a hundred and twenty men, he decided they were fine deploying themselves and nothing would stop them, and wheeled his horse, trotting off around the lines of infantry in search of their officers.

He found them easily enough, but it was not the heated debate going on among them that halted him in his tracks. As he emerged from the last trees and into open ground, his eyes widened at the sight that lay before him. A sea of silver and bronze and red much larger than the one they had brought. Pompey's legions lay before them in vast array, marching purposefully. His gaze slid in their direction of march and finally he saw the fort that had been their destination perhaps a quarter of a mile away. On the other side of a huge enemy force. Pompey's legions had, completely by chance, divided the two forces. There was simply no hope of Tillius' legions getting to the fort to aid their allies. Caesar and his men were doomed. Only the fact that the second army was partially hidden in the woodland had saved them. Pompey's forces had not yet identified this second threat.

For a moment, Galronus wondered whether it was possible. If they hit Pompey's legions on the flank, could they make the difference? But the answer was clear. They were hopelessly outnumbered, and as if to seal that conclusion, Galronus caught sight of a second force moving towards the field of combat. Those heavy Illyrian cavalry were out and ready. The men Galronus could see from here alone would outnumber them two to one.

Two options. Take advantage of the surprise and make a try for it. The infantry might be able to overcome the superior enemy force with enough shock attack, and then Galronus would have to pit his Gauls and Germans against the Illyrian horsemen and test Fronto's high opinion of them. It was dangerous. Perhaps even suicidal. But it was the only chance they had to help the others in the fort. Surprise was their only advantage. Or flight. Did they withdraw and hope that Caesar had given the same orders at the far side of the battle? It was the sensible option. But if they did that, the siege was effectively over.

With a deep breath and an underlying sea of anger at the lunacy that had brought them to this position, Galronus rode the last fifty paces to where the officers were arguing. They would have to make their mind up about a course of action fast and put it into play, before they were noticed by the enemy. The legions may be wholly focused on the camp, but the cavalry would spot the second army in the wood sooner or later.

He prepared himself to demand their decision between fight or flight, but before he could open his mouth, the argument erupted, and as Murcus, the legate of the Thirteenth, waved his hands in desperation, Tillius marched towards his own signallers from the Fifth.

'No!' bellowed Murcus, but to no avail.

Tillius snapped something at his signallers, and a cornicen lifted his instrument to his lips.

Galronus felt his blood chill. What was the idiot doing now? Before he could stop the man, the cornicen honked the call for the advance, which was picked up by the other musicians in the Fifth. There went the element of surprise, the only advantage they had.

Galronus' gaze slid to the enemy once more. They reacted swiftly, two whole legions turning on the flank and presenting a wall of iron to the men in the woods. Worse still, the Illyrian cavalry suddenly leapt to life, whooping and with the tooting of their own horns, splitting into two sizeable wings, one of which continued to move towards the beleaguered camp while the other raced towards the woodland.

The legionaries of the Fifth began to march out of the woodland in as solid a formation as they could manage given the obstacles, their faces blanching at the sight of the enemy awaiting them. A moment later, the world spiralled into chaos. In response to their argument, Murcus had marched over to the Thirteenth and his own musicians issued the call for retreat

While each legion had their own calls, they were all variations on a standard, and consequently, the retreat call was close enough to that of the Fifth to cause utter confusion. Half the Fifth stopped advancing and tried to turn, while the rest walked into them on the march. Some of the Thirteenth remained where they were, while others began to retreat. The cohort of the Ninth at the centre, commanded by a baffled tribune, dithered, uncertain as to the general order.

The woods were suddenly awash with men either marching forwards or jogging back, often past one another. Chaos. Horns were blowing constantly both calls to advance and retreat, and no one seemed to be able to identify what they were expected to do.

Galronus peered across the open ground. Perhaps three legions and a huge wing of heavy cavalry were now coming for them at speed. They held the slight edge in numbers, but the real deciding factor in the fight that loomed was discipline and morale. The Pompeians were moving in perfect concert, and they marched with determination. Conversely, the Caesarian force was now scattered throughout the woodland, moving in several directions at once, blowing conflicting calls and milling about. Even in a matter of heartbeats, Galronus knew what was coming. He watched the mood of the Fifth, Thirteenth and Ninth change in a trice from confusion to consternation, and then, inevitably, to panic.

The legions of Tillius broke.

Galronus recognised it in time to begin racing around the periphery. Reaching his own gathering forces, he pointed back beyond them. 'Sound the retreat. Fall back as fast as you can. Get past the rampart and don't wait for formation. Every man needs to be back along the river to the main camp as fast as they can.'

Leaving the men to it, he weaved his way between milling, panicked soldiers and wide squat tree stumps until the spotted his second wing at the far side. Bellowing the same orders, he turned and began to move back towards the rampart himself. They had precious little time before the enemy reached them. The legions in the woods were still in chaos. Some of the men were managing to form into centuries in the mess, those with the better centurions, and some were now moving in an orderly retreat, but others were still panicking. Some were even moving in the wrong direction for either attack or retreat, hopelessly turned around in the mess. One thing was certain: no one was marching for the attack any more. They would be at the mercy of Pompey's legions as soon as they got here.

The cavalry were moving fast. With the advantage of not having been given conflicting orders and no signals having been issued, they were still moving as units and with confidence, though, despite that, they were moving in flight. By the time Galronus reached the dismantled rampart already much of his force had crossed, discarding the certainty of two beasts abreast and a slow pace for a steady trot and three or even four at a time.

Legionaries were fleeing across the defences now, too, though few tried to negotiate the same path as the cavalry for fear of being trampled by the beasts. Galronus fell in with his men and crossed at speed. Back on the far side, he crossed the dry river bed and came to a halt on the far bank, turning to watch.

Probably Fronto had been right. With the speed that Pompey's reserves had responded, and the fact that there were likely still as many waiting that he could also commit if necessary, the chances were that this attack had always been doomed to fail. But even if Fronto had been wrong and Caesar's plan had stood a chance, it had been undermined and ruined by the short-sightedness and idiocy of Tillius, and he and Murcus' indecision when faced with the enemy.

The army was in full rout now, and Galronus could not blame them. No force would have held in those circumstances, when even their commanders seemed dim and Hades-bent on mass suicide.

The last of the cavalry crossed the rampart and, as ordered, immediately turned east and raced along the river bed back towards the fort. Behind them came the bulk of the Thirteenth and Fifth, and a cohort of the ever-battered Ninth. Full panic had set in, and the men were fleeing in disorder, their centurions unable to keep control, their senior officers lost in the press and less use than a lettuce javelin. Men were flooding through the breach, trying to move across the gaps the cavalry had used, but not limited to that. Others were crossing the gap the way they had initially come, clambering up and dropping into the ditch, but such was the huge press of men and the grand panic of the pursuing army that men were even hurling themselves from the unbroken parapet into the ditch, risking broken legs in the process. Indeed, bodies were beginning to pile up there swiftly as panicked legionaries snapped bones and collapsed, screaming as their tent mates crushed them underfoot in their own flight.

It was not a fighting withdrawal.

It was not even a retreat.

It was a disaster, pure and simple.

Heavy-hearted, he turned away from the flight of the legions and raced off after his cavalry. The siege was over, the battle lost. And if Caesar had not survived the fight in the camp, then the entire war was over, and they had lost.

* * *

'What's that?' Atenos said suddenly, cocking his head to try and catch a sound he thought he'd heard over the general din.

'What's what, Centurion?' said a voice from behind in cracked, strained tones. Atenos and Salvius were already saluting as they turned to see Caesar clambering up the slope to their vantage point.

'I thought I heard a call. One of ours.'

'Thank the gods,' Caesar murmured as he came to a halt next to them and leaned on the parapet. His gaze slid to the right, where there was still heavy fighting at the small camp. Heavier than ever, in fact. With the fresh knowledge that their relief was on the way, the Pompeians here had seemingly doubled in strength and confidence and were fighting back tenaciously, holding the invading force at the Decumana Gate. With heart-stopping speed, several legions were tromping towards the fort from the Pompeian lines, and beyond them the heavy Illyrian cavalry were massing for some kind of move. Without the support of Tillius and his column, all hope was lost.

'I hear it now,' Salvius Cursor said, straining to catch it, peering off to the west, into the thin woodland. 'I think… I'm not sure, but I think there are men in the woods over there. And they're sounding the advance.'

'No,' Atenos said with a frown. 'That's the retreat.'

Caesar, his face grim as he leaned on the timbers, shook his head. 'It's both. Tillius, what have you done?'

And even as they watched, they saw men emerge from the woods at a march, only to pause some fifty paces from the tree line, then turn and march back into the woods. Other figures emerged on their own, or in small groups, often at a run. Though they were too distant to make out details, the fact that they were overwhelmingly metallic and not red suggested a lack of shields. Had they thrown them away and run? Moments later there was nothing to be seen of them, as every last man had fled back into the woods. Three of the attacking Pompeian legions had peeled off and were marching determinedly in that direction, as were half the cavalry.

'They've run,' Salvius said in astonishment. 'They've panicked and run.'

'They would never have got to us anyway,' Atenos noted. 'The enemy reserves are between them and us.'

'We'll never know now that they've run away.'

'Look to your men,' Caesar said suddenly. 'Panic spreads swifter than a forest fire.'

And his words were borne out in mere moments. Other men of the Tenth, Ninth and Seventh on the wall tops had obviously observed the same disastrous events. Sounds of panicked dismay began to ring out around the fort.

'We have to go, Caesar,' Salvius said hurriedly.

'Go?'

'Retreat. Run. Flee. Or everyone here is dead. And the army cannot afford to lose you.'

Atenos nodded, but Caesar simply frowned as though he failed entirely to grasp the notion. 'I cannot run. I cannot lose this. If I lose this fight, I lose the siege. If I lose the siege, I lose Pompey and likely the whole war. I could even lose Rome. It all hinges on this. I have to be seen victorious. I sent his standards back to Rome in victory. I cannot lose. Rome will not countenance me losing.'

Atenos sighed. 'Caesar, we've lost. It's just a matter of how many men we can save. We can always fight again, but only if we survive.

'No,' Caesar said defiantly, his voice oddly hollow. 'I accepted Gergovia, but I will not accept this. I will not lose Dyrrachium to the man. Never.'

The general turned and began to march determinedly off down the slope towards the centre of the camp, where his signallers were standing in a nervous knot. The praetorian guards were still with him as he went, but even they looked tense now.

Salvius Cursor looked over the parapet. The enemy legions were here. In moments they would be claiming the ramparts, bursting through the gate. And then everyone here was a dead man.

The soldiers of the beleaguered Caesarian legions were on the run. The panic had spread in moments, like the wildfire to which Caesar had likened it. Men were fleeing now, diving over the ramparts they had taken so recently and running for the perceived safety of their own camp. Many were being killed even as they tried to pull back.

'Even you don't want to stay for this fight?' Atenos said.

'I'm not stupid, Centurion,' Salvius replied, and ducked as a pilum whipped through the air nearby. 'The general?'

168

'We've got to get him out of here.'

The two officers turned and hurtled down the turf embankment without thought of the risk of falling, hearts in their mouths. The legions were running and Caesar, like some demented lunatic, was the only man in the whole fort standing his ground, grabbing at fleeing soldiers, haranguing them to stay and fight. As the two men ran towards him, they watched in horror as a standard bearer from the Seventh, a man who had distinguished himself at Volcatius' camp, tried to run past his general. Caesar grasped at the man's standard and screamed at the soldier to stand with him. The standard bearer shouted something inaudible, but which sounded desperate, and simply let go of the standard, running for his life.

Caesar stood, wild-eyed, in the centre of the fort, clutching at the standard as though he were trying to throttle it. The last remnants of the defending Pompeians were slowly edging towards him, as though attacking Caesar might bring down some divine curse, but they were definitely moving on him, as were the fresh soldiers now pouring over the ramparts. Salvius and Atenos ran towards him.

'What's wrong with him?' Atenos said suddenly. The general was starting to shake wildly and his mouth was open, teeth gritted in a grimace as foamy saliva drooled out of the corners of his mouth. His right arm shot out, still holding the standard, which flailed and circled with his shaking.

'I don't know,' admitted Salvius Cursor, 'but we have to get him out of here.'

Atenos nodded and bent low as they ran. The praetorians around the general looked more and more panicked, unsure what was wrong with their commander and what to do about the centurion who looked set to shoulder-barge him. Atenos hit the general like a blow to a punch-bag, sweeping him up and dropping him over a huge Gallic shoulder without slowing his pace, whimpering in pain at the rib that ached all the more with the effort. The general weighed surprisingly little, but he was hard to carry while he was shaking like this.

With Pompeian legionaries in pursuit, they ran for the east gate where the legions had first entered the fort. The praetorians, relieved that at least something positive was happening, fell in defensively, making for the gate but simultaneously presenting a threat to anyone who might try and stop the general. Two of the guard fell to flying pila, but soon they outpaced the tired defenders, and the newly-arrived reserves seemed more intent on securing the fort than chasing what appeared to be three officers fleeing for their lives.

Salvius Cursor watched the centurion running full pelt with the general thrashing about over his shoulder. If he'd been a man to believe too strongly in omens it would be hard not to see this as one.

The battle was over.

They had lost.

CHAPTER 13

The mood in Caesar's command tent was sombre. The gathered officers stood waiting without the customary banter; all except Fronto, anyway, who sat to one side nursing his aching knee. The events of the previous day hung heavy over all, even those who had remained in other positions around the circumvallation and had had nothing to do with the unmitigated disaster in the south. The various units involved had been sent to positions around the siege lines for want of a better plan, and the hard fought south abandoned entirely. Everyone, officers and men alike, awaited the decision on the next move.

Finally, the door opened, and Caesar swept in with his customary energy. Fronto could not help but be impressed. A matter of hours ago the general had been recovering from a fit and had been weak and drawn. Now, he was the same old Caesar again, as if nothing had happened. *Or almost…* He strode across to the table and stood behind it, Aulus Hirtius coming to a halt beside him in his accustomed place.

'Gentlemen.'

The officers greeted Caesar politely, though with a total lack of enthusiasm.

'Let us deal with the unpleasant part first, and swiftly,' the general announced. 'Hirtius?'

The staff officer and secretary opened his wax ledger and peered myopically at the scratchings therein.

'The confirmed dead number nine hundred and sixty, with almost as many again as yet unaccounted for. The critically wounded number four hundred and thirty two, and the walking wounded who will return to duty in due course two thousand eight hundred and five. Thus, our current total strength is now down by a little over five thousand men.'

The leaden silence that greeted the figure said it all. Enough men to furnish a full strength legion. And all of them veterans. It was not a good number to hear.

'Officers?' Caesar prompted.

'Four senior prefects: Tuticanus, Fleginas, Granius and Sacratavir. In total thirty two tribunes and centurions. I do not have the specific breakdown of those yet. And, on a dark note, twenty eight standards lost to the enemy.'

There was a groan of dismay across the tent. Death and dishonour in huge quantities. This was starting to make that awful day at Gergovia look like a walk in the forum.

Caesar nodded as though they meant little more than the results of a chariot race. 'Pompey is being proclaimed imperator by his men. He was even given a laurel wreath by those exiled senators who follow him. He believes he has won.'

'Why is he still sitting there then?' Antonius grumbled, slapping a balled fist into an open palm.

'Precisely because he thinks he has won,' Caesar replied. 'He believes we are beaten, and we are, and now he awaits my capitulation and, failing that, the chance to finish us off. We can no longer maintain the siege. Summer is here and we are well provisioned through forage, but with autumn coming, and then winter, we will not be able to maintain that position for long, while Pompey can. He knows that. The sad fact is that this siege is over and we must withdraw. He knows *that* too. So he is aware that unless we simply surrender, at some point we will be forced to leave our fortifications. When we do, he can chase us down and finish us. Waiting for us to run is the sensible option. It is what I would do. Why risk throwing men at our defences when he can simply wait for us to leave and then meet us in the open? As you all know, morale plays a large part in any engagement, and our army is currently at an all-time low, while Pompey's rides high. If he meets us in open battle with a superior force at the moment, very likely we will be fleeing back to Rome with his cavalry snapping at our heels. And if that happens, we could lose Rome to him and become the exiles ourselves. Things appear bleak, I shall admit.'

He straightened. 'But what we must remember is that we have lost a battle, yet we are still here, and still strong. We should concentrate not on having lost at Dyrrachium, but on having succeeded in securing Italia and Spain, in having managed to bring an army here despite Pompey's control of both land and sea, and the fact that the war is not over. Our men need their spirits lifted, and that will have to come from their officers. I look around this tent and all I see is morose, dark faces. I understand why, of course, but we cannot afford such maudlin wallowing. The men see you feeling beaten, and *they* feel beaten. Energy. Hope. Positivity. These are what I need to see in your faces, for then the men might feel more inclined to fight on. We need to sap the enemy's current euphoria and rebuild our own morale if we are to face them again.'

'What news of Scipio?' Brutus said, breaking the uncomfortable silence. 'Perhaps we can find something to announce there that might help?'

Caesar nodded slowly. 'There is little encouraging there to tell the men, though neither has there been disaster. The latest dispatches from Calvinus arrived two days ago. It seems that there are two Pompeian forces in the region under Scipio and Favonius, and they and our own men under Calvinus and Longinus have been racing across Macedonia and Thessaly, trying to outmanoeuvre one another. As yet there have been a few skirmishes, but no battle to speak of. On the bright side, their travels have kept Scipio from our back. Not that it particularly matters now.'

Brutus nodded.

'We need to alter the entire scope and direction of our campaign, gentlemen,' the general said suddenly. 'Pinning Pompey at the coast has proved costly and difficult and, with yesterday's events, continuing to do so is impossible. I believe that at this stage a pitched battle is inevitable. We will only resolve this campaign through direct force of arms in the field.'

'Didn't you just say that was exactly what Pompey wants?' Antonius said.

'It is. Pompey wants us to abandon the lines, which we all now know we must, and commit to battle with us as we leave. He will have the strong army with the high morale, and we will be overrun easily.'

'Yet you're saying that's what we're going to do?'

Caesar smiled. 'Not precisely, Antonius. We will meet him in the field, but not immediately. We need time to recover. To get the walking wounded back into their units, to heal the fractures in command,' a black look suddenly cast across the tent to Tillius, who shrank back, 'and to restore the morale of the men. Despite the numbers being in favour of Pompey we still have the better legions, and if they are in good form, I believe we can beat him.'

Fronto rose, grunting at the pain in his knee. 'But we will not have the luxury of time. The moment we leave here, Pompey will be on us.'

'Then we must slip away like thieves in the night,' Caesar replied. 'If we achieve a good head start we can stay clear of Pompey. Our supplies have been gathered and kept with our forces throughout, and so we do not have to reply on gathering them before departure. We simply have to move. Pompey has been supplied throughout by his fleet, largely from Dyrrachium. He cannot afford to simply quit his camp and chase us, for he will lack supplies. It will take him precious time to gather everything he needs and follow on. By that time we can be moving. And if, for some reason, he has the bit between his teeth and decides to chase us down, then he will be ruining his own supply line and will put himself at a serious disadvantage in the long run.'

'Where do we go, sir?' Brutus said quietly.

'East. Or more precisely, southeast,' the general replied. 'We link up with those forces we sent into Macedonia and Achaea, adding them to our strength. If we can manage to persuade Scipio to join us, we add his forces, and if not, then we outnumber him severely. If we can pin him down, we can remove him from the game board and weaken Pompey. Most of all, those regions have largely gone over to us with the sterling work of the commanders we sent there. That being the case, we can gather further supplies, recruit more men to make up for the losses, and prepare. Rebuild and prepare. Such that when Pompey reaches us, we are ready for him.'

Fronto smiled. It was one of Caesar's most formidable talents: to take a bleak situation and inject it with hope. And he could see that hope beginning to spread to the faces of those around him, too.

'I shall require my senior staff to attend a further meeting at the fifth watch, during which we will plan the withdrawal from

Dyrrachium in detail. In the meantime, I want you all wracking your brains for the best way to pull out of the lines without alerting Pompey to our intentions. Sadly, I must deal with something unpleasant first, but I cannot put it off any longer. You are dismissed until the fifth watch, all except Tillius. I need a word.'

The officers filed out, and as they did so, Fronto found a small knot of men awaiting him not far from the tent – the men he'd sent for before the briefing. He nodded at them as he limped from the headquarters. 'Can we talk in your tent, Ingenuus?'

The three-fingered cavalryman who commanded Caesar's bodyguard nodded and led the way to his tent which stood twenty paces from his general's. Salvius Cursor and Atenos followed on, and dipped in through the door. Once inside, Ingenuus lit two lamps to push back the gloom and sat on a campaign chair, folding his arms.

'What's this about Fronto?'

'The general. I don't know what your men have said to you Aulus, but a number of them witnessed Caesar's "rescue" from the enemy camp. I need to set the record straight. Caesar has not spoken of it, but I suspect he will confer with me shortly and before he does I want things clear. Salvius? Atenos? Would you like to describe the general's last few moments during the battle to me, before you delivered him to his tent?'

Salvius Cursor cleared his throat. 'I wondered if he was going to die. There was something wrong with him. He was shaking wildly and foaming at the mouth like a lunatic.'

Atenos nodded. 'Thrashing about, he was. One moment he was healthy and yelling at the men to stand and fight, the next he was shaking. I thought perhaps he had gone mad with fury.'

Fronto nodded. Fortunately, the army had been in such utter chaos as they fled the blades of Pompey's men that the two officers and the praetorians protecting Caesar had managed to get him onto a horse and covered with a cloak so that the gathered soldiery were entirely unaware of the shaking general being conveyed past them to safety. The guards had taken him straight to his tent and laid him in his bed. Fronto had been standing at the gate as the army poured back in to safety, and had spotted the small group of officers and praetorians as they arrived, falling in with them and following. Once at Caesar's tent, he had sent them all away and held the general down, forcing a leather belt between his teeth. It had not taken long for Caesar to stop shaking and lie still. The worst of the fit had been over long before he had reached his tent. Once Fronto was content that the fit was done and Caesar was in no further danger, he'd sent for a medicus and left the general in his care, telling him he had been overrun during the flight.

Fronto pursed his lips. 'The general suffers from an illness that is somewhat sporadic. It strikes him down on rare occasions and displays itself as you saw yesterday. Foaming, thrashing, eyes rolling, inability to speak. Yet when it passes he is perfectly healthy once more. What I need you all to understand is that this is purely physical and far from critical. It is an ongoing condition that does not threaten the general's life and is not increasing in any way over time. It is not an omen. It is not a punishment from the gods. It is simply a bodily condition, like my knee, or Ingenuus' fingers. I need to be very clear on this point.'

The other three men were frowning, and Fronto shrugged. 'The general made it abundantly clear to me that his condition needs to remain a secret. Entire wars have been lost because of bad omens that infect the morale of the men. We cannot afford to have the legions even think that Caesar is cursed in some way. He is not, and if this becomes widely-known, our army could suffer. Morale is low enough as it is without them finding out about this. Do you understand?'

The three men nodded, which came as something of a relief to Fronto. Atenos he was sure of, and Ingenuus was utterly loyal, but he'd not been certain that Salvius Cursor would accept it so readily.

'Alexander,' Salvius said.

'What?'

'The illness you describe, and what we saw yesterday. They say Alexander of Macedon suffered the same.'

Fronto nodded. 'I believe so.'

'Alexander died very young,' Atenos said, frowning.

'But not from that. From a fever.'

'True.'

Fronto turned to Ingenuus specifically. 'Good. The four of us are in concord. This needs to remain between us. But what of your men?'

Ingenuus' frown deepened. 'What do you mean?'

'A number of your guardsmen witnessed it. Can you trust them to keep this secret?'

The prefect gave him a disapproving look. 'Fronto, my men are hand chosen by me. They are each and every one utterly loyal to Caesar. Remember, they do not take an oath to Rome or the senate, or to an eagle. They take their oath to Caesar alone. Their fidelity is unquestionable. I shall speak to those men involved and make sure this does not spread, but you have my word that they will keep the secret to the grave.'

Fronto sagged. 'Good. Sorry I had to have this little clandestine meeting, but you understand, I'm sure. At some point today, Caesar is going to summon me, and possibly you three, and I wanted to be sure that all was settled beforehand. Nothing awkward and no chance of misunderstanding or argument.'

A few moments later they left the prefect's tent, and Fronto and his two officers began to wander back towards the pen where their horses waited. As they passed before Caesar's tent, Tillius emerged, suddenly, marching forcefully away. He ignored them entirely and stormed past them, face pale and mouth set in a straight line.

'I fear the legate just had his backside tanned like a child,' Atenos said, once Tilius was out of earshot.

'Good,' Salvius spat. 'He deserves to be nailed up for what he did yesterday. He is the principle reason we lost.'

'Legate Tillius is leaving Dyrrachium,' said a reedy voice behind them, and they turned to find Aulus Hirtius, Caesar's secretary, stepping from the general's tent. 'The legate is returning to Italia, with his legion.'

Fronto blinked. 'The Fifth? Why?'

'The Fifth lost too many men yesterday to consider them a viable command in the coming conflict. They are being sent to Italia to recruit and train up, and they are not alone. The Twelfth and Thirteenth are also to cross to Italia and rebuild. The healthy men that remain in those three legions are being transferred to others, and those men from any legion who cannot reasonably take part in the coming campaign will be shuffled into the Fifth, Twelfth or Thirteenth and sent home.'

Fronto nodded. It was a sensible solution, really, and not the decrease in strength it appeared. And Tillius' career was over. Men had failed Caesar before, and sometimes disastrously so, yet they were usually upbraided in private, or at worst disciplined in the open. To be sent home in disgrace was an entirely different matter. By the time he reached Rome, the man would be a pariah, untouchable. Only disgraced retirement awaited him. Fronto found it hard to feel sympathy, regardless. Barely had Hirtius moved off before the headquarters door opened again and Caesar emerged, pale in the sunlight. He looked surprised for a moment to see the three men gathered together, his eyes narrowing in suspicion. 'Fronto. Good. I shall want to see you later. Perhaps half an hour before the meeting?'

Fronto nodded. 'Of course, General.'

'Good,' Caesar said again, eyes still narrowed. 'Time to discipline a few standard bearers of my recent acquaintance.' And with an air of purposeful ire, he stalked away.

'I wouldn't want to be those standard bearers for all the silver in Hispania,' Salvius said quietly, and the other two nodded their profound agreement. They retrieved their horses and set off back to the southern lines where the Tenth had now replaced the shattered Ninth as the furthest strongpoint under Caesarian control, at the edge of the hills and some way from the sea. They rode through the gate of the camp, the legionaries on guard swinging the timbers wide for access, and dismounted at the centre. There seemed to be fewer soldiers milling about than Fronto expected, and he frowned.

'Where is everyone?' Salvius Cursor asked, pre-empting his question.

'I have no idea.'

Atenos, stamping life back into the feet that he much preferred to a horse, collared a soldier who emerged from his tent in a hurry.

'Where is everyone?'

'At the west wall, sir,' the soldier said, nervously. When Atenos simply furrowed his brow and turned to Fronto, the legionary scurried off.

'Come on,' the legate muttered, and the three men strode off towards the western gate, Fronto lagging a little with his limp. As they approached the ramparts closest to the Pompeian defences, they could see legionaries crowding the wall top, peering out into the lost territory. Soldiers moved respectfully aside as the three officers climbed the embankment to the parapet, and a space opened up for them to stand in.

It took a moment for Fronto to realise what it was they were watching, but when he did, his gorge rose.

On a ridge just out of bowshot, Pompeian legionaries had amassed. Before them knelt a long line of soldiers with their hands bound behind their backs. Even as Fronto understood what was happening, a Pompeian blade slammed into the next legionary, driving down through the flesh and organs in a quick but agonising death. They were being executed. Already fifty or so men lay prostrate, the victims of the killers behind. Another hundred or so awaited their fate, trembling on their knees.

Fronto felt rage rising within him. This was not acceptable, even in war, especially not when they were all brothers under the eagle. A small, unpleasant part of his mind reminded him that at least they were dying a quick soldier's death, unlike those men who had been crucified up by Lissus, but a favourable comparison still didn't make it acceptable.

His eyes strained to pick out details. He couldn't tell what units the men were from, but they were likely from every legion who had taken part in the failed attack. That meant there would be men of the Tenth there. No wonder everyone was at the walls. It was just a miracle some hot-headed centurion hadn't just decided to launch an attack against the execution party.

'We need to save them,' Salvius Cursor said.

Of course. It was certainly a damn good job Salvius hadn't been here, or they'd all have been out of the gate and running screaming at the enemy long before Fronto arrived.

'No.'

'We can't let this happen.'

'We have to,' Fronto said. 'There are too many of them out there. We'd just end up supplying them with a few more lines of kneeling men.'

'Legate…'

'The answer is no, Salvius. I don't expect you to like it. I don't like it either, but I won't sacrifice the rest of the Tenth for revenge.'

179

The tribune fell into an angry silence, and Fronto could almost feel the man restraining his bitten-back words. Instead, they watched in wordless bitterness as good men died painful deaths on the rise before them. It was then that Fronto realised that he recognised the officer presiding over them, and he felt his own anger rise to unprecedented levels.

'The bastard.'

'What, sir?' Atenos asked, frowning.

'That's Titus Labienus. I cannot believe the bastard's doing this. That's not the Labienus I remember. What's happened to him?'

'I don't know,' Salvius replied, 'but I *do* know what's happening to *them*.'

'You're not going out there, Tribune,' Fronto said with an air of finality.

But deep down, Fronto wanted nothing more than to plunge his blade into Labienus's black heart. He could almost understand his old friend's defection. He could perhaps even understand his pursuance of war as a solution and his unwilling to countenance a peace with Caesar. But the execution of captive legionaries? This Labienus was a different man to the one Fronto had known in the fields and hills of the Belgae. A man who had lamented the near genocide of a people at the tips of Roman swords. This was a darker man. Unforgiving and cold.

Without realising it, Fronto had added Labienus to the list of those who had to go, along with Ahenobarbus.

On the hill opposite, another man died.

* * *

Fronto sat astride Bucephalus, almost vibrating with nervous energy. Perhaps the gods were with them. He had to hope so. The night sky, which had been clear for so many days, was now a high fleecy blanket that blotted out the stars and hid the silvery rays of the moon. The light cloud had rolled in late in the afternoon as if called by the general for the very purpose of obfuscation.

With difficulty he tore his gaze from the line of Pompey's fortifications, marked out in the pitch blank only by the torches burning along the parapet. Occasionally, the torches winked off and on, obliterated by the shadows of men passing in front of them. Nothing exciting was happening there.

It might yet work.

He wondered how far the baggage had got.

He heard Pompey's calls across the dark world, announcing the fourth watch and carefully positioned musicians on horseback blew the same calls all along the Caesarian lines, right down to the musician twenty paces from Fronto. Almost as if in answer to the time call, a faint purple began to show itself in the east, announcing that dawn was approaching, less than two hours away.

The baggage would move slowly, of course. It was in the nature of ox-drawn wagons and carts to rattle along at an interminable pace, and it was these that slowed any army on campaign. But they had a lead of half a night now, and each wagon had had its team doubled up at the expense of the cavalry's spare horses and any beasts that could be commandeered from the surrounding area at short notice. They would move slowly, but faster than normal, at least. Preparations having been made in secret behind the ramparts, enemy attention diverted by the judicious use of distractions and diversions, the baggage, supplies and artillery had been sent out shortly after nightfall with orders to make for Apollonia with all haste and not to stop even to rest the animals. Even then it would probably take them the best part of three days to cover the forty miles of the journey. Two at the very least. The Seventh had gone with the column as its escort, hurrying out towards the southeast as quickly yet as quietly as possible. And every man's non-critical equipment had gone with the carts to enable the legions to move swift, lightly equipped.

Now, as Fronto's gaze moved back across his own lines to the safe countryside beyond, he could see the army on the move. Following on after the distant wagons, the pride of Caesar's military was departing through every gate, merging on the road and moving with what stealth a legion could manage. Men's boots were wrapped with wool to deaden the sound. The horses wore similar overshoes. Weapons were kept tightly strapped to keep them from knocking about too much and even the eagles and standards were packed away to prevent their obvious burden. It had been done well, because he had to strain to hear the departing army, and if he couldn't hear it well here, then it was unlikely that

Pompey's army would hear it from their lines. Once the column was a safe distance away they would drop the coverings and sacrifice stealth for speed, racing for Apollonia, where the wounded would be left to await transport to Italia.

All the army had gone from the siege lines now, with the exception of two legions. The Tenth and the Ninth had been the ones left behind as long as possible in order to maintain the fiction that the Caesarian lines were still fully manned and that nothing untoward was happening. The legions would catch up with the wagons soon enough, but at least they had each been given what head start could be afforded. Even Caesar had gone with the army, along with the bulk of the cavalry, most of whom were currently on foot. Only the two legions remained behind, scattered around the defences. Dispatch riders were stationed all along the lines ready to pass the word for departure to every unit.

He watched the men of the Tenth at this camp with an element of pride. The soldiers had had not a wink of sleep, instead marching up and down the walls and trying to make enough noise to sound like ten times their number. They had even engaged in fictitious changes of watch, replacing each other and dipping down behind the walls for moments to make it look as realistic as possible. Their task was to keep the ruse going as long as possible and buy the army ample time to get far from the siege works. When Pompey found out his besiegers had gone, he would have to decide between letting them go and following on when his supplies and forces were ready, or chasing them down and stretching his logistics to breaking point. The plan was good, Fronto had to admit, though, knowing Pompey, he knew what result he would put money on.

The Tenth had been given the duty for two reasons: firstly, they remained Caesar's favourites, his 'glorious Tenth', and it was their lot to be most trusted by the general. Secondly, though it had little bearing on the truth now, they retained the title that had been bestowed on them a decade ago in Gaul: The Tenth Equestris – the *Mounted Legion*. Once, long ago, part of the Tenth had been mounted on cavalry horse for a ruse. At most a quarter of the legion would even remember those days, such had the manpower come and gone, but the fact remained that the Tenth had proved they could do it. And so they were to do it again. Fully half the army's remaining mounted cavalry had departed on foot with the legions, leaving their steeds and any spare horses with the men who remained. Every soldier along the siege lines had a horse tethered close by.

It was the best plan they could come up with. He'd lobbied against the Ninth remaining too. He'd argued that they were badly understrength and exhausted and should be allowed to move with the others. That the Tenth were sufficient for the task. That the number of horses the cavalry would have to leave with them would be drastically reduced if it were just the Tenth playing the ruse. The truth of the matter was that, while most of that was true, and the Ninth were entirely untested on horseback, more so than the Tenth, what he really didn't want was to share the command here with Sulla.

The man was good in a fight, there was no doubt about it. His battle tactics were strong, and he controlled his men with iron. But he was equally rigid and inflexible in every other respect, too, and Fronto felt that such a trait was not an advantage in this kind of thing.

He stood, still and silent, for a long time. After a while, as the purple of the sky began to make itself more noticeable, Salvius Cursor came to stand next to him.

'How long has it been?' Fronto said quietly.

'An hour, give or take.'

'Any sign of the column still?'

The tribune shook his head. 'Even the rear-guard are long gone. They're moving damn fast.'

'Caesar's army has always been good at that. We marched round the lands of the Belgae at a pace that would put any other commander to shame. We've done it more than once, too. Are the men ready?'

'As ready as they'll ever be. I checked with every centurion and marked out the legionaries who'd never even climbed into a saddle. I had each of them paired with a soldier who had at least some riding skill. They'll do. All the plodders have been having condensed lessons from their mates as they wait. I passed the word to the Ninth early on to suggest they did the same. Whether they have, I can't say.'

Fronto nodded. 'Good thinking. It might take Pompey some time to move his whole army, but his cavalry might just come out first to harry us. I want to stay ahead of those Illyrian heavy horse.'

They waited again, watching. The sky changed shades continually, and finally the birds began to sing. The dawn chorus had begun, and Fronto took a deep breath. 'Time to go. If we stay here much longer it'll be light and Pompey will be able to see how few of us there are.'

Salvius nodded and hurried over to a centurion. 'Pass the word. We move on the legate's signal.' He then moved to a courier. 'Send word to Legate Sulla with the Ninth that we're moving on the legate's signal. We need to move simultaneously.'

The rider saluted and rode off, leaving Fronto and Salvius at the parapet once more. The birdsong was growing all the time, now, becoming deafening, and the sky had lightened enough to make out a few details of the world.

Fronto jumped as a horn suddenly sounded.

'What in Hades?' He scanned the enemy lines, but Salvius nudged him and pointed away to the north. 'That was from the Ninth. Listen. They're putting out the call. They're going.'

Fronto cursed. 'Damn the man, does he not understand the first thing about subtlety?' He waved at the camp. 'Have the men mount up and send the word to all other installations. Ride for the meeting point and do it now. Sulla just told Pompey loud and clear that we're leaving.'

CHAPTER 14

Fronto bellowed for his men to ride on, hauling on his reins and guiding the weary Bucephalus out of the mass of horses and to the side. The ground was dry and dusty in the summer heat and the vast cloud of brown and white that was thrown up by so many pounding hooves made it hard to see anything beyond the immediate.

The Tenth were doing well. Those who were novice riders were being assisted by men who had spent time in the saddle, and those veterans who still served in the legion and had been in the battle against Ariovistus ten years earlier made a point of proving their ability, their pride in being Caesar's 'Tenth Equestris' palpable. Indeed, Atenos had told him that it was not unusual in winter quarters for the soldiers to take rides out on their time off duty, keeping their hand in, in an arrangement with the cavalry officers. Their enthusiasm and pride showed, and it had given Fronto no small amount of pleasure when the Tenth, racing away from the defences at short notice and gathering on the run, caught up readily with the Ninth, who had had plenty of warning and could leave in good order, and yet were something of a shambles and showing little ability to even stay in the saddle. Clearly Sulla had ignored Salvius Cursor and failed to put in place his policy of pairing the novices with the riders.

The Tenth moved well, all things considered. There had been surprisingly few falls and failures – far fewer than in the Ninth ahead and, despite the danger of pursuit, Fronto had made sure to keep a group of the most experienced riders on the best horses at the rear to catch anyone who fell by the wayside and get them settled and moving again.

It was chaotic and far from perfect, but they had done what had been required of them. They had bought an entire night of freedom for the army to depart while Pompey's men lounged behind their ramparts, entirely unaware. It did not bear thinking about what might have happened had they been caught mid-departure by Pompey's superior force.

Ahead or back? Sucking on teeth coated in dust, Fronto swiftly made his decision and wheeled the horse, trotting him back along the lines of mounted legionaries. It was surprising how quickly he could travel along an entire legion when they were all moving on horseback. Not far from the end of the column, he caught sight of a centurion's crest silhouetted grey in the dust, and made for him. The rear-guard.

'How is it?' he shouted to the centurion, who blinked in the cloud and then gave as much of a salute as he could with reins in one hand and vine stick in the other.

'Shitty, sir. They're getting close.'

Fronto nodded his understanding, and dropped a little further back. He found Salvius Cursor moments later. The tribune was bellowing at soldiers to speed up and move, move, move. It had surprised Fronto when the man had volunteered to lead the rear-guard, given how much he constantly needed to be at the forefront of things, but once they were out and running, with Pompey's men in pursuit, it had become abundantly clear. At the rear, Salvius was closest to the potential for violence. If they were overtaken, the rear-guard would become the front line. And in fairness, there was nowhere better for the lunatic to be than closest to Pompey's soldiers.

The cloud of dust here was worse than ever, stirred up by so many beasts, and it took Fronto precious moments to work out what was happening as he blinked at the shapes in the cloud. A man had fallen somewhere ahead, but had had the good – or possibly bad – fortune to keep hold of his reins. Though he had managed not to be dragged beneath the pounding hooves and pulverised, as had happened to one man early on the ride, his wrist was black and crimson, lacerated from the leather than had been wrapped tightly around it, and his legs were stripped raw and bloody from bouncing along the ground. The expert horsemen at the rear had slowed and calmed the horse and lifted the groaning soldier, slinging him over the horse's rump and guiding the beast on between them, making sure the injured man stayed in place. Such was the quality of Fronto's legion, and it gave him pride to know it.

'Where are the enemy?' Fronto bellowed over the din.

'How the f… I don't know, sir?' corrected the decurion as he realised who it was who had asked.

'Salvius?' the legate shouted, beckoning to the senior tribune. The two men moved out to one side and let the mass of horsemen pull on ahead. The two men sat in the cloud of cloying dust.

'We're doing well,' Fronto said. 'It may not feel or look like it, but we are.'

Salvius' face betrayed his disbelief.

'We've been running for maybe an hour, as fast as the horses can safely maintain. And in all that time we've not yet spotted or overtaken the infantry or the wagons. That means they moved like lightning, Salvius. We did it. And, yes, Pompey might be snapping at our heels, but we got the supplies and everything away. It's a victory in itself.'

And it was. But, as he'd noted, it didn't particularly feel like it. Running away rarely felt victorious. They must have come at least fifteen miles now.

The two men lapsed into silence in the cloud as the morning sun gradually began to penetrate the dust, which was finally beginning to settle, the column now moving off ahead. Visibility came fairly suddenly, and with it it brought shock.

'Shit,' Fronto breathed.

A huge cavalry force was closing on them, less than a mile back at most, perhaps even half that. It was hard to tell with the light and the dust.

'What are they?' he said, peering into the haze.

'Everything,' Salvius replied, shading his eyes with his hand. 'Heavy horse in the centre with skirmishers on the wings. Proper cavalry, not like us.'

'Pompey must have had the bastards ready, you know. He didn't have time to gather his horse and pursue us. He was half-prepared.'

'Half is better than fully,' Salvius noted.

'True. His legions will still be far behind, and his supplies have probably barely left Dyrrachium. His horse might be in close pursuit, but they'll be all.'

Salvius nodded. 'But they will be enough to pulverise us, Fronto. All we need is for them to catch up and we'll be fighting for our lives.'

'Let's go see Sulla.'

'You go. I'm staying with the rear-guard.'

Fronto nodded and the two men turned their backs on the huge mob of horsemen in pursuit, racing off after their own mounted soldiers. As they entered the mobile dust cloud once more and fell in with the rear-guard, Salvius Cursor peeled off and joined them, and Fronto continued to run along the side of his men. The Tenth moved at a steady canter with occasional drops into a trot, enough to maintain good speed but not break the mounts, but despite his age, Bucephalus was tough and fast, and Fronto knew his excellent limits. He moved now at a gallop for a short time, passing the legionaries and officers, many of whom cheered as their legate passed, and closing with the Ninth.

In fact, it was difficult to tell where the Tenth ended and the Ninth began, since the latter had shown little skill and organisation and had become strung out and varying in speed. He estimated that soldiers from the Ninth were probably even halfway back among the Tenth by now. He passed Atenos, who he knew would be at the fore of his men along with two of the junior tribunes who were nominally his superiors and yet who looked to him for instruction and support constantly.

On he went with a nod to Atenos, along the side of the Ninth. Finally, the cloud thinned out, suggesting he was at the fore, and he hauled on the reins in shock as visibility cleared and he almost went thundering down a scree slope.

His eyes widened.

They were at a river. A wide river. Too wide and too deep to try and cross on horse, especially for men with little skill in horsemanship. A little to their left a good road that they had been moving parallel with for some time rose where the slope fell away to a bridge that arced up and over the torrent. The bridge was a good, solid stone affair, wide enough for two carts abreast, and yet still there was a bottleneck as men pressed to try and feed onto the crossing.

Fronto found himself making quick calculations in his head despite himself and came inevitably to the conclusion that they would never cross before Pompey's horse caught them.

His gaze lifted and he squinted at the south bank. He could see the masses of Caesar's legions ahead where they had been slowed by the crossing. They had caught up with the infantry. And now, as he adjusted to the clarity, he could see a cohort of men settled to both sides of the bridge, playing rear-guard, allowing the lead units of mounted legionaries to pass between them, managing a few of the customary jibes despite the dire situation. His gaze caught on three men sitting to one side on their horses on a rise at the far side, and he squinted further. Sulla, and Caesar and Antonius.

'Pompey is here,' he bellowed.

The three men took a moment to notice the lone officer on the south bank shouting at them. Antonius made gestures indicating that he couldn't hear.

'Pompey,' Fronto bellowed at the top of his voice, turning and pointing back along the dusty lines. 'Pompey! Horse!'

The sudden frantic change in the manner of the three men told him that this time they had heard, but he had to accept that there was little they could do about it. Pompey's men were coming, The Tenth and some of the Ninth would be caught here, and no one else could help them. And with Sulla on the south bank, Fronto was the ranking officer. It was up to him.

Shit.

He tried to recall the map he had studied so many times in so many briefings. They were still well north of the Apsus and Apollonia. There was another river that ran past up here. The… the Genusus. That was it. Wide enough to hold up an army, it flowed from the eastern ranges down to the sea, crossed by few bridges. In fact this one, on the Via Egnatia, would be the lowest crossing. That meant that the next bridge or ford would be in the hilly or even mountainous land to the east. This was the only feasible crossing for cavalry. That meant there was no point in sending half the men upstream to seek another crossing and speed up matters. No. They were trapped, and they would have to fight. On the bright side, he was still convinced that this would be only Pompey's cavalry. They would not have to face enemy legions, and if they could fight this lot off, then they could buy ever more time for the army.

His gaze swept the dusty ground. If the sudden appearance of the bridge and the river had taken him so by surprise, then it would do the same for Pompey's horsemen. If he could use the dust cloud to mask his movements and could organise everything…

He rode over to the place where the riders were milling, trying to get into line to cross the bridge, and spotted a centurion.

'You! We're about to be hit by Pompey's horse. I need to organise a defence. Get all your men from the Ninth over the bridge. But anyone from the Tenth, turn them aside. I want them formed up at fifty paces to left and right in two groups.'

The centurion looked startled, but saluted and began to shout orders to the men around him. Next, he latched on to the senior centurion of the infantry by the bridge. Unlike the mounted Ninth and Tenth, they were in full kit and armed to the teeth, right down to twin pila.

'Centurion? We have to hold off Pompey's horse. Once the Ninth are past, block the route. Have your men in open lines ready to throw. The moment the enemy horse are in sight, I want each man's first pilum cast at them and as soon as the pila are in the air, drop into contra equitas formation and deny them the crossing.'

The centurion grinned and began waving to his men. Four hundred veteran heavy infantry forming the centre would be adequate, Fronto decided. Contra equitas was hard to break, especially if the cavalry were unprepared.

His squinting eyes picked out standards among the riders, and he ignored those of the Ninth, but spotting two vexilla from the Tenth he trotted towards them and gestured.

'You two. You're the hub for each wing. Get out to each side of the infantry at around fifty paces and let the men form on you. I know they're legionaries, but they're about to get a taste of cavalry combat.'

The two flag bearers saluted, and rode out to where mounted men from the Tenth were already gathering, directed there by that centurion near the bridge. The dust cloud would dissipate a little with the column's movement arrested, he realised. Frowning, he rode back and forth between the two flag bearers, the infantry centurion and the centurion from the Ninth directing the riders, and gave the same instructions to all. Stamp their feet. March on the spot. Scuff their feet if they can. Raise as much dust as they could. They needed to keep the river and the bridge hidden.

It was uncomfortable for them all, stamping on the spot, choking in a dust cloud of their own making, but Fronto smiled. If he could barely see in the cloud, then what was going on was totally unknown to the enemy following them.

He watched as the horsemen flooded past, slowing as the word spread of what was happening. The Ninth continued to be directed over the bridge to safety, though they were still gathered on this bank, waiting their turn. But their numbers were thinning, and the number of men being alternately sent left and right to form on the Tenth's flags increased. The legions were now almost separated.

Tactics.

He mused. Shame Galronus wasn't here. Or Varus. Or any man with experience of cavalry warfare. Fronto had seen his share but he would be the first to admit that he was an infantry commander. Small scale or large, but always on foot. He was about as comfortable directing mounted combat as he would be triremes.

Pompey had sent his horse out in a set formation. Heavy cavalry in the centre and skirmishers on the wings. Old fashioned, but effective. The centre, heavily armed and armoured but slower, would charge like a battering ram for the enemy column, expecting to break the Caesarians through shock and sheer force, while the flanking light cavalry, much faster and more manoeuvrable, would enfold them on both wings and seal them in. The Caesarians would be unable to rally, given that they were on horseback and could hardly form a defensive square. Then they would be systematically ground down from three sides.

Except Fronto knew they were coming, and they did not know that Fronto knew and was preparing. Play them at their own game, his mind said, maliciously. He knew enough about basic tactics. He might not have a subtle cavalry mind, but he knew what surprise and panic could do. A slow smile spread across his face.

He watched as the men continued to arrive, now all the Ninth near the bridge, preparing to cross, milling about and waiting their turn. The Tenth were thinning out as they arrived and were directed to either side in the cloud of grey.

There was someone in this cloud that was just perfect for what he had in mind.

As an afterthought, he trotted over to the infantry centurion, whose men were formed in lines now, blocking the path. 'Move forwards. I need you at the front. I need them to see you before they see us. And get those pila launched quickly. You'll have moments at best. Throw, throw, form up. By the time they're on you, you need to be ready and formed up.'

The centurion nodded and jogged his men forty paces forwards, keeping very professionally to formation as they ran. He wondered in passing what legion they belonged to. He'd have to find out and send them some wine if they got through this.

Finally, the figure he was anticipating appeared through the dust, and he trotted over, waving.

'Salvius? You ready to tear a new arsehole in Pompey's cavalry?'

The tribune's face lit up in answer.

'Good. We're at the crossing of the Genusus and things are a bit tight. I've got the infantry formed in the centre. The Ninth are back there crossing the bridge, and I'm forming the Tenth on each flank. I'm taking the left. I want you to take the right. The moment the enemy become visible, they'll realise that we're ready for them but it'll be too late. Their heavy cavalry at the centre will take two lots of pila from the legionaries and will then, hopefully, be met by contra equitas and have to stop. Their light cavalry will be expecting to enfold us and harry us, but we're going to do that to them instead. As soon as the first pilum is thrown, we need to charge like maniacs. Don't stop. Tear through their light cavalry and butcher as many as you can. Their heavy horse will be relying on us being surrounded, and when they realise that's not what's happening, they'll either fight to the death, if they're mad, or they'll run like the breath of Hades is on them.'

Salvius Cursor grinned. 'You're no cavalry tactician, Fronto. Your plan is to ride at them screaming, kill as many as possible and hope they run away?'

Fronto frowned. It didn't sound half as good when Salvius said it.

'Relax. It sounds like an excellent plan. Just my kind of plan, in fact.'

Fronto rolled his eyes. 'Then it's probably as shit as you suggested.'

With a bark of laughter, Salvius ripped his sword from its sheath. 'See you on a pile of Pompeian corpses, Fronto.'

With another roll of the eyes, Fronto turned and rode off to the gathering horsemen of the Tenth on the left flank. There he sat and waited. It felt strange being surrounded by cavalry, yet oddly comfortable, they being the Tenth. And despite his unfamiliarity with the type of warfare, somehow he felt he had the handle of the situation. He knew this was right. And gods, the men needed a victory right now. If Caesar was right and morale was half the battle, then he could help rebuild by fighting off Pompey's cavalry with a truly oddball force.

Gradually the men arriving and falling in at either side thinned out, and finally the last men arrived. Those who were wounded were sent on to join the Ninth at the bridge, but the bulk of the Tenth were gathered in two wings, flanking the infantry. All was ready. And though all present continued to stamp their feet and hooves, raising dust, he began to hear the rumble of the cavalry chasing them down insisting itself over the top.

Here they went.

He kept his eyes on the vague shapes of the infantry close by, a crowd of loosely-spaced ghosts in the grey. He could hear the senior centurion. 'Ready…'

Knowing that a lot of this rested on timing, he raised his hand for the signal. Behind him every centurion in the Tenth did the same, ready to pass the signal so that every horse moved at once. If they were too slow, they would end up mired in two lines. If they were too early, they would spoil the surprise. He felt his heart thundering.

His hand trembled with the effort of being held aloft.

'Ready those pila,' the centurion said.

There was a long, horrible pause, filled with the ever-growing sound of approaching hooves in their thousands.

Fronto's teeth ground together.

'Now,' the centurion yelled and even as he bellowed 'Pila…. Cast!,' Fronto dropped his hand and the Tenth charged.

From his position at the fore of the mounted wing, he had an unprecedented view of the results of his plan. Kudos to the centurion of infantry and his men. They had been as fast as any unit Fronto had ever seen. The cavalry suddenly emerged through the white cloud as vague shapes and even as they did so four hundred pila plunged into the mass. Horses reared, horses fell, men were thrown. Panic flooded across the enemy in a heartbeat. The carnage was impressive, caused more by horsemen riding their fellows down than the pila themselves. The cohort dropped into formation like a machine, shields locked and remaining pila jutting from between the shields like an iron hedge, an obstacle no horse would be eager to close on.

The Illyrian heavy horse charge ground to a halt in an instant, leaping their own dead in desperation and trying to haul on their reins before they fell foul of the legionaries. Any man who failed and came too close was rewarded with multiple stab wounds from the projecting pila.

Their attack had faltered, but it could still rally. Fronto and Salvius had to see it fail. Even as the chaos struck at the centre, Fronto and his men hurtled forwards at breakneck speed. The enemy suddenly emerged from the white cloud like ghosts coalescing in the firmament, and in that moment, Fronto knew he'd been right and they'd won.

The skirmishing light cavalry on the enemy flanks were barely armoured at all, many just in a grey or white tunic. Some had helmets, more hats, more still were bare-headed. Some had small, round shields and either an axe or a sword strapped at the side, but all were armed with a light ash cavalry spear. Had they been ready, those spears could have been lethal, but they were not ready. They had expected to ride along the flanks of a terrified force, hurling their spears and harrying them while the centre did its work. Instead the centre had become a meat grinder, and the men they had expected to harry were instead hurtling towards them like a battering ram. Fronto's men were all armoured in chain and equipped with pila and swords.

The two forces hit and the quality of both men and equipment became clear in moments. Though both forces were matched in speed and strength, Fronto's were heavy and determined. They carved a great gouge through the centre of the Pompeian auxiliaries, their swords rising and falling, pila stabbing out like cavalry spears, dropped as they became useless and replaced with drawn swords.

In ten heartbeats they had broken the light cavalry. The rear ranks of Pompeians, as yet uncommitted, were turning, and running. Fronto's legionaries were cutting through them like a wheat harvest. They had expected cavalry. They had found the Tenth.

It was over in short order. The flank, shattered and panicked by Fronto's unexpected charge, had turned and fled, and the legionaries killed as many with their backs turned as they had in the initial clash. Disciplined men, they kept formation and, as the light cavalry ran, they declined to follow. Fronto could hardly estimate numbers at this stage, but he'd be willing to bet they'd killed more than a third of the enemy in mere moments with minimal casualties to their own force.

He watched in satisfaction as the enemy light cavalry disappeared into their own dust cloud. The heavy Illyrian armoured horsemen were close behind, routed by their failed charge, numerous dead, and the impenetrable wall of the legionaries that held them at bay. A similar tale had clearly played out at the far flank, for a cloud of dust was all that could be made out of the light horse at that side too.

A victory. A very solid victory. It might not win the war, and it would make little difference in grand terms of numbers, but the morale that had been an all-important factor at the end of the last debacle had changed entirely. Across the north bank of the Genusus, every face wore a look of triumph and satisfaction, while utter panic would be the order of the day among Pompey's cavalry. And better, some way distant, miles to the north, Pompey's infantry would be marching slowly in their wake, and their own morale would suffer when they met their own cavalry coming the other way in defeat. Best of all, Pompey would shortly learn of it. And with Pompey's temper, he would be unrestrained in his fury, which would only unsettle his men all the more.

And now they would have time to cross the Genusus in peace.

His gaze crossed the river once more, though it was hard to make much out through the cloud of grey. There were the distinct signs of Caesar's army making camp. Whether or not that was a good idea, at least they would be across the river from Pompey, and at the worst they could demolish the bridge to halt pursuit. And every man would feel better to be in camp together, safe from enemy forces for now.

He turned at the shouting of his name, and blanched at the sight of Salvius Cursor. The tribune managed to get coated in blood and gore from head to foot every time he drew his sword, but this was the first time Fronto had seen a horse in a similar state. The animal looked horrified. Where did Salvius find so much blood?

'Nicely done, sir,' the tribune grinned. 'I think we bought some time.'

'Agreed. And now we cross and rest for a while. And we consider how much luckier we are than Pompey, for our supplies are on the road ahead of us, waiting, while his will be trundling along slowly from Dyrrachium, desperate to catch up.'

CHAPTER 15

Caesar stood, silent and watchful on the raised rampart., his officers in attendance, Fronto busily tapping his fingers irritably and impatiently on the bronzed plates of his belt.

'Give the word,' the general said, 'quietly and carefully. No music, no muster. Just have everyone ready.'

The four couriers standing at the rear of the group saluted and scattered like dandelion seeds in a breeze, leaving the officers alone.

'I still don't understand why we allowed him to camp at all, General,' one of the junior officers said, echoing Fronto's frustration with the whole situation.

'Because,' Caesar replied patiently, not taking his eyes off the Pompeian camp on the far side of the Genusus river, 'sometimes one has to give ground a little to find a better position.'

'I'm not sure I follow, sir.'

Caesar paused, eyes still on the camp before him, and Fronto heaved an impatient sigh and answered for the general.

'We beat back his advance cavalry and gave them a fright, but Pompey is tenacious and clever. It was only a brief setback. His horse would be able to cross the river close by, at one of several fordable points, and we would be fighting off attacks like that one all the way to Apollonia. And we wouldn't be that lucky every time, so we give him time to gather and believe he's going to face us properly. Now he's settling in ready to deal with us.'

'Precisely sir,' the young officer said uncertainly. 'That seems like a step backwards to me, when we had the jump on him.'

Fronto shook his head. 'He's not ready for us yet. The bulk of his army is here, but his supplies are still trundling along back there somewhere. It'll take a day or more before they're anywhere near. But what don't you see across there?'

The young man frowned and squinted, scanning the camp. After a long pause, he coughed. 'I don't know, sir. I'm not sure I follow.'

'Look at our cavalry corrals, then look over at Pompey's.'

The man did so and his brow creased further. 'They're half empty.'

'Exactly. Pompey thinks we mean to deny him the crossing. He thinks we're going to face him here. He's under the impression that we're settled in. And because his supply situation is so thin right now, he's sent every man he can spare out foraging, gathering supplies and cutting timber and the like. Probably the equivalent of a legion of men have been sent out since dawn to the nearest good woodlands, and to any farm that still has crops ripe and ready or any town or village with a bulging granary. And his cavalry are out, too. They are spread far and wide along that bank looking for supplies and heading back north to locate the wagons and hurry them along. Pompey's about to hit the roof with irritation when he sees what's happened.'

'Because we're moving, sir?'

'Precisely. Just as we dropped and ran unexpectedly at the siege lines and he was taken unawares, we're doing it again. We don't have to worry about our supply wagons because they're already way ahead, closing on Apollonia, along with the wounded. And our men are equipped light for a fast march. As soon as Caesar's next word is given, our army will move fast. Pompey's, on the other hand, is spread all over the countryside. It'll take him half a day just to call back his cavalry. By the time he's got his legions across the bridge to follow and brought in all his scattered men, we'll have at least a day on him.'

'If you understand what we're doing,' Antonius said, flicking a glance across at Fronto, 'why are you so twitchy?'

'Because I understand it, but I don't like it. The idea of running away from him, even tactically, doesn't sit well with me. Pompey's clever. It's all well and good pulling a fast one on him, but there's always a good chance he'll anticipate something and have a surprise ready for us. This isn't like facing Gauls or ordinary commanders.'

'You sound like you admire him,' Sulla said dismissively.

'Of course he does,' Caesar cut in. 'And with good reason. Pompey has had more military success than any living Roman, including myself. He is not to be taken lightly. And whether we like him or not, he is a Roman hero and deserving of both admiration and respect. When this is all over, and we have put his army in place and removed those rebel senators in authority, Pompey will be allowed to retire with every honour of a Roman general intact. But first we must beat him. And as Fronto noted, he is clever. The only way to beat him with our inferior force is to continually throw him off balance and push him into doing something precipitous of which we can take advantage. His temper may be his undoing.'

Fronto nodded. 'And that's why I don't like this plan. Fall back river by river. Sooner or later he will tire of following us as we plan and he'll do something unexpected.'

'We fall back as far as Apollonia,' Caesar replied, 'and there we garrison the place with the wounded, while we turn and head southeast into Achaea. Pompey will have two choices then. Either he launches a desperate, badly-provisioned attack, which will be difficult and costly, or he gives up the chase. His distance from his supply line will be too great and he will not be able to follow further.'

'Either way, we win,' Antonius added. 'If he tries to stop us, his troops will be hungry, unhappy and playing catch up, while we will be well provisioned, in good morale and able to choose the ground. If he turns away, he gives us time to heal and strengthen.'

'Be prepared for a surprise,' Fronto said darkly. 'Nothing with Pompey is quite so simple.'

Caesar turned, peering out across their own camp. The legions were ready. The tents had all been taken down and what was required stowed for transport. All that could be seen from the Pompeian camp would be the ramparts, which were still manned, and the corral full of horses. They were about to get a surprise.

'Give the order to move, gentlemen,' Caesar said, and turned, dropping down the rough steps cut in the earth bank and crossing to his horse that stood nearby, held by a soldier and close to the mounts of each other officer.

Fronto saluted and limped down the steps, wincing, then over to Bucephalus, where he mounted at the wrong side in order to favour his good knee, helped up by the soldier who'd held the reins. Fifty heartbeats later, he was at the head of the Tenth, alongside Salvius Cursor and Atenos, giving the signal. Across the camp the silence was suddenly broken by a multitude of centurions' whistles and the legions began to move at double pace from the outset, swarming over the low south rampart and racing away towards Apollonia. The men at the walls facing Pompey's camp across the river dropped and ran, falling in at the rear of their legions as they moved off. Out to both flanks, the cavalry surged into the corrals, mounting with the professionalism of natural horsemen and immediately riding off, falling into their units on the move for speed.

Thus did Caesar's army break camp at the Genusus and move off without warning, leaving Pompey's army taken by surprise, unprepared and scattered far and wide.

* * *

Fronto passed through the north gate of Apollonia with a sense of tense relief. It seemed that Caesar's plan had unfolded just as anticipated. Following their flight from the Genusus, leaving Pompey to flounder around desperately and shake his fist in anger, they had force-marched eight miles and crossed a lesser river – one of the numerous such in this wide, flat agricultural region – and camped on the south side once more.

Pompey's vanguard had arrived on the far bank once dark had already begun to fall, tired and dispirited. They had made camp there, opposite Caesar's, digging and building in the evening and into the night, foraging only locally to prevent the same trick being pulled once more. The result would be a drop in the enemy's morale and certainly in their fighting readiness as they collapsed, exhausted, into their tents long after dark, eating a small meal mostly of hard rations, their supply train strung out far to the north, increasingly distant from the army that desperately needed it.

Conversely, the legions of Caesar, who had moved at speed but with a strong head start and for just eight miles, had been safely encamped, fed and sheltered before even Pompey's scouts had arrived at the river, and had sat at leisure and watched the enemy struggle into the darkness. Fronto had to concede that Caesar's actions were having just the desired effect: making Pompey's position weaker and his men less content with every mile travelled, while Caesar's army continued to follow their supply line, well-fed and with continually improving morale. The disastrous rout at

Dyrrachium no longer loomed over the men's heads like a tombstone. Now they were healing, while Pompey's men suffered.

Once more, the legions of Caesar had abandoned their camp before dawn and moved on to Apollonia. While Pompey had kept his men from becoming too scattered this time, it would still take them precious time to funnel the huge force across the river, and when they did, the enemy legions would be exhausted, malnourished and in poor spirits from their late night and early start on emergency supplies.

And yet, despite everything seemingly going according to plan, something was nagging at Fronto. It was all going *too* well. Too easily. They had become confident and complacent at Dyrrachium, believing Pompey contained and settled, and the dangerous old bastard had caught Caesar in the latrine with his subligaculum down, destroying the siege that had taken so much work to put in place. Fronto had that strange feeling that something was not going right, though he'd not been able to pin down what it might be, so at every briefing or meeting, he had constantly warned against overconfidence, reminding them of Pompey's shrewd military mind.

As the men of the Tenth moved off to camp just south of the city along with the bulk of the legions, Fronto ignored the rest of the officers making for the heart of the urban sprawl to settle into comfortable quarters, instead dropping from Bucephalus with a grunt of pain, tying the great black beast to a rail and limping up the steps of the gatehouse to the wall top.

He was alone there, apart from a couple of men on guard, the officers having all moved into the town. Apollonia was garrisoned by those wounded who would heal fully in due course and could still function in the meantime, but whose inclusion would slow the ongoing march if they remained with the column. Fronto nodded at the two men, who saluted and stood carefully to attention in the presence of a senior officer. Ignoring them further, he leaned on the parapet and peered out to the north. The view was unrestricted hills or forests for miles, the flat farmland stretching out before them as the last of Caesar's army closed on the city and settled into camps. There had been no rain for some time, and the dust cloud raised by the army continued to billow in their wake, the only thing that marred the panorama from the wall.

Just the settling dust cloud.

Fronto pursed his lips. The dust cloud. He needed a better view. Turning, he looked up at the city behind him. Apollonia was built on the slope of a great hill at the southern edge of the flat farmland, the river Apsus looping along nearby, cutting through that lush green land to the north. At the top of the urban conglomeration sat an archaic citadel, an acropolis of the ancient Greek city. Given the hill and the large walls, it would be offer the best views of the plain.

Trying not to curse the pain in his knee, Fronto shuffled back down and mounted Bucephalus once more, trotting along the cobbled road up the slope of the town, past the seemingly endless side streets and tightly packed housing built to the contours of the hill in an old Greek manner rather than an ordered grid of Roman design. He passed a grand nymphaeum with colourful and graceful statuary, and finally reached the acropolis. The fortification was no longer used as such, housing a solid-looking temple and a few warehouses that had been built up against the ancient defensive walls. He found a set of steps that led up and dismounted once more, tethering Bucephalus and grunting and wincing his way to the wall top.

By the time he leaned over the ancient, crumbling parapet and overcame a moment of dizziness at the impressive drop on the far side, the legions had largely arrived and moved into their positions to make camp, just the last few cohorts closing in. The dust cloud was slowly settling across the landscape, but from this lofty position the dust was little more than a carpet.

Here he could see beyond it for some way, much further than from the more recent city walls below. In fact, he was willing to bet he could see almost all fifteen miles to the river where they had camped last night. He could certainly see the wide saddle between two ridges that they had passed through in the mid-morning.

And the thought that had occurred to him down on the lower wall was confirmed with this view.

There was no dust cloud to the north.

A quarter of an hour later, he limped into the bouleuterion, the city's council chamber that was serving temporarily as Caesar's meeting room. The general was seated in a curule chair facing the semicircular seating rows, half a dozen of the other officers in place around that arc. Whatever they were discussing, they fell silent as Fronto stepped into the chamber, his nailed boots slipping, scraping and clacking on the exquisite, ancient marble.

'Fronto?' Caesar's drawn face turned to him.

'Pompey has abandoned the chase.'

The general nodded. 'I had a feeling he would. He is fighting his own instincts now. He would want nothing more than to press the attack, but he knows at what a disadvantage that would put him, so he breaks off the chase. Good.'

'I don't think so,' Fronto replied. 'At least when he was following us, we knew where he was and that he was getting weaker. Now we have no idea where he is going or what he is up to. I warned you that he would be unpredictable. He's clever.'

'He *is* clever, Marcus, though I am far from foolish myself.'

Fronto frowned, and the general smiled that infuriating smile. 'You've not been paying attention to the numbers as we marched, clearly. Even now a cohort of ours that slipped back north past Pompey will be closing on Lissus where they will cut off any of Pompey's support and supplies from the north. Three cohorts are now in residence ahead of us at Oricum, securing a landing point for further supplies and men that is much more convenient for crossings from Italia, should we need to make use of it. We leave four cohorts to hold Apollonia and at dawn tomorrow we march into Achaea to collect the forces that are at work there under Calenus and Calvinus. With them we will be strong again, and by that time, our legions will be ready for the fray. Then we move on Pompey once more.'

'If we can *find* him,' Fronto muttered, 'and if he's not got any surprises for us.'

'Really, Marcus, you are such a pessimist. We have taken the most disastrous defeat since Gergovia and in a matter of days we have turned it around, making Pompey hungry and miserable while our men strengthen by the day ready to fight him.'

Fronto nodded. 'All the same, I don't think Pompey is going to settle back into Dyrrachium now. I'd prefer to know what he's up to.'

'Get some rest, Fronto. We'll be moving out early.'

* * *

The journey from Apollonia was interminable. Seemingly endless stretches of brown and grey mountains and sparse vegetation, hot, searing days and steaming nights all overlaid, for the officers, with a layer of tension and uncertainty.

Caesar had relented to Fronto's pleas and sent out small groups of fast, highly mobile scouts garnered from the local towns and with good regional and geographic knowledge to track Pompey's movements. The best they could ascertain was that the enemy had returned to the north bank of the Genusus River and followed it east, deep into Macedonian lands. Whether he meant to link up with Scipio or find a convenient place to turn south and cut off the Caesarian march no one could say, for with the ever-increasing distance between the two forces, the value of scouts rapidly became nullified.

So Caesar's army pressed on southeast into the great world of Achaea, seeking the forces operating there under Calenus and Calvinus, less aware even of *their* location than of Pompey's. Rumour put Calenus far to the south near Athens, securing the ancient powerhouse states of Greece against Pompey. Calvinus seemed to have ranged far and wide, and word of his location was nebulous, placing him in a dozen places across the land.

Taking the most secure and direct route to the heart of Greece, the irony was not lost on Fronto that Caesar's legions were marching up the Aous valley, just as those of Titus Flamininus had done a century and a half ago in pursuit of Philip of Macedon. He wondered on occasion whether Caesar saw himself as a new Flamininus, a new saviour and conqueror. But Fronto was no fool, and he knew Caesar of old. Among the old man's more prevalent faults was an unshakable self-belief, bordering on egomania. If anything, Caesar would already see himself as surpassing Flamininus in his achievements.

The Aous did little to diminish the tension. Its gradual deepening, with the peaks to each side becoming high and oppressive, left the officers under no illusion that they were safe. Somewhere to the north lay Pompey's army, and the man was ever tricky. If he had managed to anticipate Caesar's plans and sacrificed strength for speed, his men could be hidden by any of these peaks even now. It was a little like walking into a room blindfolded, knowing there was a pit in the floor somewhere.

The men moved on heedless of the potential danger. By Caesar's explicit command, no matter how uncertain or nervous the officers might be, they were to control it and wear a mask of utter confidence in front of the men. Morale was now as high as it had been at any point since the disaster of Dyrrachium, and with the potential cataclysm coming their way, their spirits needed to remain high.

Still, tense as they were, Fronto and his compatriots marched on unmolested, ever deeper into the Greek world. They passed the wide blue span of the Pambotis Lake where the legionaries relished every break in the march, splashing and drinking, bathing and laughing, seeing only the clear, inviting waters, while the officers instead saw the distant hazy blue-grey slopes on the far side that could hide ten thousand men with ease, and the dead white trees reaching up along the shore like imploring skeletal arms thrust up through the earth.

The journey went on, the summer gradually sliding away, the men becoming aware that the height of the season was almost upon them and that after that, unless they brought Pompey to battle favourably, they would be wintering deep in the Achaean peninsula.

From the lake, they turned of necessity due east, climbing to the Katara Pass, a height that surprised Fronto, and one of the loftiest mountain crossings he had traversed in his time. Here, despite the searing sun of mid-summer, the peaks were still sheathed in glittering white, foreboding and lofty. Despite the best efforts of the officers to keep morale high, Fronto could feel the change in the men as it happened, sliding from easy confidence to worry and discomfort. The journey was beginning to sap the spirit from the legions, especially now, with this new troublesome terrain. Moreover, since they were now travelling with the baggage and supply wagons, the pace had gradually slowed with the incline, further dragging at every man's spirit.

Any other year, Fronto might not have been so concerned. But so much in the coming days would rely upon the mood of the men, and the spirit they had gained since the disaster, their most precious commodity, was beginning to slip. Fronto did not want to countenance meeting Pompey's army in these stark mountains with the legions in the mood into which they seemed to be descending. Something had to change soon.

Then, one morning when the sun beat down mercilessly, burning and bronzing skin despite the chill in the air from the mountainous terrain, paradise appeared before them.

Fronto had ridden ahead to join the officers at the van and, passing around a loose rock formation, the world opened up before them to reveal a new type of valley from those through which they had been passing for what seemed like months. *This* valley was wide, and the bottom flat, cultivated with green farmland. Small settlements lay dotted along the valley side, unlike the bleak timber villages they had seen in the mountains, clinging to grey cliffs as though to prevent tumbling into the chasms below.

Farms…

Farms meant that the lowlands were close and the mountains coming to an end. Fronto could feel the relief flooding out of the other officers at the sight, each man having contained his growing concern through the pass and the deep valleys. Behind them, as they began the descent into a new green and welcoming world, the front ranks of the legions gave a rowdy cheer, and even the centurions and tribunes joined in, rather than instilling professional silence. This was not a time for stilted quiet. This was a time to cry relief.

Word spread back along the army like a brush fire and Fronto felt his own heart lose its heaviest weight as the morale of the men lifted in the blink of an eye. Marching songs sprang up for the first time since they had left that lake and it was a jubilant column that descended the valley to the lush flat lands ahead. They passed another wide valley off to the right and a sign here pointed along that side-vale identifying a settlement somewhere there as Kalaia, but ahead announcing the city of Aeginium. Another sigh of relief sounded around the army, for Aeginium was an ancient, well known metropolis, and was the first true sign of major civilisation since Apollonia.

Caesar, aware that there was every possibility that the city still held for Pompey, sent off a unit of light, fast-moving scouts to inspect the city and evaluate the situation, while the army moved on sluggishly behind.

Fronto sat straighter in the saddle with the fresh knowledge that soon he might well be sleeping beneath a real roof, and possibly even sinking into a warm bath. He was not the young man he'd been when they chased out the Helvetii, and was growing to appreciate the smaller comforts. On the bright side, while such a protracted time in the saddle had numbed his arse to the texture of leather, his knee had been blessed with ample rest and, along with the ministrations and care of one of the less acerbic medici, it had strengthened a great deal. Soon he might begin to test it a little in exercise.

He was musing on how nice it would be to be able to climb and descend stairs alternately, rather than dragging his left leg to catch up on each step, when the commotion began. He looked up sharply to see the scouts hurtling back towards them. For a moment he wondered whether he'd nodded off and missed something, but he clearly hadn't, which meant that the scouts hadn't even got out of sight before they turned around, let alone reached Aeginium.

The lead rider sent his men peeling off to either side, where they began to climb the slopes, while he reined in before the officers and saluted.

'Report.' Caesar commanded.

'A large force, General, coming down the next valley to the north, not more than a mile away. Their scouts saw us as we saw them.'

'What sort of force?'

'Legionaries, sir. With cavalry escort and what looked like auxilia. Moving fast, too.'

Caesar swept the helmet from his head and let out a hiss of breath. 'Who are they?'

'Sir?'

'Is it Pompey? Scipio? One of ours? We are blind out here, and you are my only eyes. Who are they?'

The scout shrugged for a moment, but a thought struck him, and his eyes narrowed. 'The lead vexillum had a golden bull on it, General, I believe.'

Caesar chewed his lip. 'Are you *sure*, man? This is important.'

The scout nodded emphatically. 'Yes, sir. I can see it in the eye of my mind. Plain as day. Gold bull on red.'

'Let us pray to all the gods you are correct, soldier. If this is Pompey and we are caught strung out like this then I might as well hand him Rome now.'

The general's hand went up in the signal to halt the column. A new murmur of uncertainty swept along the column, replacing the marching songs like a ripple in water. The officers sat silent, horses huffing and occasionally stamping. The commanders cast pensive glances at one another.

'General?' muttered Aulus Ingenuus, sidestepping his mount closer. 'Might I suggest you bring a cohort forwards. If the scout is wrong, the entire army's staff is at risk.'

Caesar shook his head. 'Trust in the gods, Aulus. If I am suddenly enfolded in steel, how do you think the men will react? No, we need to be seen to be confident and in control. Trust in the gods.'

Regardless, Ingenuus brought his own mounted guardsmen close and kept them in two flanking pockets ready to hurry in and protect the general against any danger. Fronto smiled at the younger officer, remembering the green but eager cavalryman he had been a decade ago in Gaul. How things changed...

The other army appeared suddenly, around the edge of the northern valley, and Fronto was immediately suspicious of the scout's call, since he could hardly see the flags at all, let alone what was on them. Still, they were not arrayed in battle formation, and, as they appeared, a small knot of riders broke away from the van and pounded along the valley towards the waiting legions.

Despite the tension he felt still in every sinew, Fronto forced himself to be calm and breathe deeply. They could not be the enemy. Even to parley before battle, no one would send so many officers with such little protection.

He felt the stress drain from him as the dozen or so riders approached and slowed their dusty mounts, for he recognised even through the dirt of travel the face of Domitius Calvinus.

They had found their allies.

'Calvinus,' Caesar smiled. 'You are a divine gift for a weary and troubled general. Well met.'

The travel-worn officer bowed as low as his saddle and cuirass would allow. 'It is most certainly good to see you and the legions, sir. Once we knew of the disaster at Dyrrachium and the failure of the siege, we thought the worst. Is the army seriously under strength?'

Caesar frowned, shaking his head. 'We took losses, certainly, but we are still strong, and regrouping to fight once more. How did you hear of Dyrrachium?'

Calvinus sagged in the saddle. 'Rumour reached us a hair's breadth ahead of disaster, General. Loyal locals passed word to our native scouts, and they barely had time to relay the news to us before Pompey himself hoved into view with an enormous force.'

Caesar threw a look at Fronto. He'd warned the general that Pompey would do something, that he was full of surprises. 'Pompey attacked you?'

Calvinus snorted, then recovered and straightened, remembering to whom he was speaking. 'Apologies, General. No. We received word of his approach only from those self-same scouts. We had far too few cohorts to even consider standing against Pompey. We'd have been swamped. We cut and run as soon as we heard, leaving even the baggage and tents. We've been running double time ever since. The scouts estimate that Pompey missed trouncing us by just a few short hours.'

'Gods be praised for the efficiency of the native scouts and for your own common sense, Calvinus. But if you did not know we survived thus, how did you come to join us here?'

Again, Calvinus laughed with no mirth. 'You, sir? We rode south to find Calenus somewhere near Athens. By the will of Fortuna we simply stumbled across you on our way.'

Caesar laughed now, though his chuckle did contain that grain of humour.

'Then all is good. Pompey is still to the north, we are stronger than we were, and now we can find an advantageous position on the plains to regroup, rest and recuperate before Pompey arrives, for arrive he will. That he made straight for you when he lost us tells me that he intends to press the attack now and finish his campaign this summer. The time is nigh, gentlemen. By the end of the season we will have clashed, and one man will be master of Rome, either Pompey or I.'

Fronto felt an odd lurch in his soul at the strange shade of glee he heard in those words. *Master of Rome.* The warnings of Verginius and Labienus and so many others suddenly flooded his mind, spat words that Caesar had his eyes set on a loftier perch than the consulate.

He bit down on the worry. Pompey would be far worse for Rome than Caesar, and right now, that was what mattered. And though Caesar had not mentioned the possibility, Fronto would be willing to bet that Pompey bumped into Calvinus by chance just as much as Calvinus had done here. Pompey was not chasing shadows in Macedonia. He was joining with Scipio.

The odds had almost certainly just become worse.

PELUSIUM, AEGYPTUS.

'**D**ivine daughter of the endless river and queen of the world, your brother's forces are arrayed in key positions across the delta and in great strength here, here, and particularly here,' the general said, stabbing the map with his index finger.

The queen leaned back, still seeming languid and sultry even in a hard campaign chair in her office. It showed a certain level of progress to Cleopatra's mind that at least her functionaries and officers alike had begun to refer to Ptolemy as her brother now, rather than her husband. Months of civil war it had taken to finally change that perception. She would change it further, yet... from brother to corpse.

Months earlier their disagreement had reached critical levels and Ptolemy, maddened child that he was, had gathered troops, preparing to oust his sister/wife/queen from her throne and rule alone. Recognising her relatively poor position in the political and military game, and understanding when it was wiser to retreat and regroup, the queen had fled Thebes before her brother's army had arrived to 'deal with her'. Knowing that Aegyptus was largely in his grasp and that it would take careful alliances and wise manoeuvres to gain a foothold, she had taken her court, her small force and a wagon train of enough gold to make Midas sweat and travelled east and north, through Judea, to Syria where the wealth she carried had bought her a sizeable mercenary army.

There, she had received news of the Roman generals' movements in Macedonia and Illyricum, and had begun to form her plan even from the start. The one thing she knew as they had returned south at the head of her force, was that she still was not militarily strong enough to oppose Ptolemy, especially with his general Achillas at the helm. However, she was confident that she would be powerful enough that the wily Achillas would also be reluctant to launch an all-out attack on her. The dance of war and politics would go on until one of them had the edge.

That edge lay with Rome. She knew it and, even if her brother was too short-sighted and stupid to do so, she knew Achillas knew it too. Ptolemy and his general would be playing a careful game. They were watching what happened between Rome's two great lions so that they knew who to ingratiate their selves with in order to achieve overall ascendance. Cleopatra, on the other hand, knew that preparation was everything. She had placed her coins on Caesar and, no matter what had happened at Dyrrachium, she was still convinced he was the horse to win this particular race.

She realised suddenly that long moments had passed, and her general was waiting, looking uncomfortable.

'Have you found him?'

The officer nodded. 'Then send him in,' the queen commanded.

The man who entered as the general left offered no deference to the commander, though he bowed with relative respect to the queen. He was of middling height and had sandy coloured, short and neat hair. His skin tone spoke of a westerner who had been many years under the eastern sun. His uniform was Roman, though finessed with nuances that were clearly Aegyptian.

'You served with Pompey?'

The man nodded. His face betrayed nothing. 'And now you belong to the Gabiniani?' Another nod. The Gabiniani nominally supported Ptolemy. A Roman garrison that had been assigned to protect their father seven years ago, the Gabiniani had long since 'gone native'. An odd mix of Roman and Aegyptian. This man still bore more Roman haughtiness than most of his unit.

'Your unit serves my brother.'

'It does, my queen.'

'And yet I find you in my army, a Gabinian centurion commanding Syrian mercenaries.'

'I have my reasons, my queen.'

She nodded. She respected that. People did not always wear their heart upon their sleeve, and that did not make them less deserving of respect or trust. That he was here at all said much.

'I have a commission for you. One that I am given to understand will be much to your liking, Marcus Salvius Aper.'

CHAPTER 16

Aeginium, Northern Thessaly July 48 BC

A eginium proved to be a mixed blessing to the Caesarian army. The populace threw open their gates and made the arriving force welcome, and yet not one man passing through those portals laboured under the impression that they were either expected or truly welcome. It seemed that word of what had happened at Dyrrachium had spread far and wide, and remarkably swiftly. Aeginium had been far from unique in minting coins celebrating their links with Pompey and scratching anti-Caesarian graffiti into the wall plaster of houses, but as the general suddenly appeared on their doorstep, they made him most welcome, hurrying ahead to remove the clearest sentiment and bury the offending coins. And while the Caesarian forces were welcomed, it became clear that half a month earlier, the supplies based in the city had been sent north to support Scipio. Caesar had greeted the news with his traditional quiet acceptance, taking only what the city could still spare, which turned out, rather apologetically, to be not much at all.

They had moved on the next morning, allowing Fronto at least the benefit of a hot bath, and heading south towards Gomphi. There, at least, they felt assured of a solid welcome. Of all the cities in Thessaly, Gomphi had early declared for Caesar and had continued to do so.

And that was why it so surprised Caesar and the staff to arrive and find the city gates closed.

As the army approached and assembled on the plain below the town, which crawled up the side of a hill on the edge of a huge tract of flat farmland, just as Apollonia had, the officers sat astride their horses, watching the city.

'I thought Gomphi was ours,' Antonius grunted.

'Evidence suggests otherwise,' Fronto said acerbically. 'Allegiances change in situations like this as I'm sure anyone who remembers Labienus will know.'

'The man in command here,' Caesar said, 'and who theoretically has hegemony over the entire region, is a man named Androsthenes. He declared for us, but he is a notoriously slippery character and with news of Dyrrachium it is no surprise that he has now thrown his token into Pompey's pot. What surprises me is that we are here in force and he has had the fortitude to weather that and remain in Pompey's purse. Uncharacteristically strong, I would say.'

'The simple fact,' Fronto said, cutting through the conversation, 'is that we can't leave Gomphi behind us, and we need their supplies. We're going to have to take the place.'

Caesar nodded. 'Just so. Have a camp constructed for us, and call every senior centurion and tribune to a conference.'

The following hour was a little chaotic as the legions continued to arrive to be set to the task of creating siege camps rather than sitting in Gomphi's bars and gardens as they had anticipated. By the time the sun was reaching its zenith, the senior officers stood in lines like a plumed and crested legion of their own, watching the general and his staff on the tribunal.

Caesar stepped forwards.

'Gentlemen, I have a message for you, and for you each to pass on to the men under your command.'

A sense of odd anticipation flowed out before them, and Caesar threw out a finger towards the high walls before them.

'Gomphi was ours and they have allowed their head to be turned by our mistake at Dyrrachium.'

Mistake, indeed, thought Fronto.

'They declare against us, thinking us beaten. We are all quite aware, I think, how much of this war is based upon reputation and fear. If we allow Gomphi to defy us, then every city, fortress, village and cow shed between here and Athens will do the same, thinking us beaten. We need to prove to the world that we are still a force to be reckoned with. That we are still the armies of Rome fighting a rebel, rather than the other way around.'

There was a roar of approval, and Antonius stepped forwards to stand next to Caesar. Unsure of whether this was scripted or genuine, Fronto joined the general on the other side, where he was acknowledged with a professional nod.

'We must take Gomphi.' Fronto shouted. 'They are a well provisioned town. Taking them will make your bellies full. And this is a hub of communication. Word of our arrival will spread throughout the towns of Achaea. But only if we win.'

On the far side, Antonius similarly gestured at the walls behind them. 'Gomphi has made itself our enemy. While we treat friends well, we must instil fear in our enemies. Gomphi shall not be spared. The legions have permission to sack and plunder when the town falls.'

Fronto flashed a look of surprise at Antonius. Was that wise? He saw Caesar similarly frowning at the other officer, but the general swiftly nodded and turned back to the assembled officers. 'It is the Ninth hour, now,' he announced. 'Gomphi must be taken before darkness falls. Fall in to your ranks.'

With a roar, the centurions and tribunes saluted and then dispersed instantly, heading off to their own units. Fronto watched them go, Mamurra and Brutus leaving the tribunal and hurrying towards the flat ground where siege engines were being removed from carts and assembled. He then turned to the two men next to him.

'Sacking and pillaging?'

Caesar shrugged. 'Antonius was a little impetuous, perhaps, but I think his reasoning is correct. We need to be seen to be as strong and merciless to our enemies as we are helpful and forgiving to our friends. One night of brutality could open a hundred gates across Greece. We send a message.'

Fronto huffed. He didn't particularly like it. Letting soldiers have free rein in a defeated city resulted in serious unpleasantness. It was, in fact, the worst part of any war. But though it sickened him to think of the rape and murder that would result, he couldn't fault the logic of his fellow officers.

'What is our strategy, then, General?' he sighed

Caesar peered at the heavy, squat walls. 'Pounding them to dust with artillery would take too long. We need to be swift and merciless. How strong do we estimate them to be?'

Sulla cleared his throat. 'The last intelligence we had put Androsthenes' forces at less than a thousand.'

Caesar nodded. 'And if, like Aeginium, he has sent supplies and support to Scipio, then we may be looking at half that number. The defenders on the wall top are certainly well spaced.'

Fronto nodded. 'They are few. I suspect that if the scouts ride up and around the rear of the town on the western heights they'll find no defenders there at all, but just the odd watchman. I'd wager they've put most of their strength here to look better defended than they are. They've seen our legions and they can't hope to hold against us. That suggests they've sent to Pompey for help when they knew we were coming. They're trying to deter us and hold out for support.'

'Which makes it all the more imperative that Gomphi falls immediately,' Antonius said.

'We are agreed, then,' Caesar nodded, glancing at the others, 'that we outnumber the defenders by a vast margin?'

'I think that can be safely concluded, General,' Sulla agreed.

'Then we need not spend too much time strategizing and preparing plans. We simply swamp the walls. Give the signal, sweep the rampart tops with missiles and then release the legions en-masse to overcome the walls. And there need be no care taken to keep order thereafter. Allow the soldiers to vent their frustrations on Gomphi. Discipline can be restored the next morning when we move off and leave only ruins and dust for Pompey's men to find.'

Fronto shivered. Not at the blunt directness of the plan, but at the coming night, once the walls fell.

Nodding to the other officers, he hobbled off towards the camp of the Tenth, which lay at the northern periphery of the arc of legions arrayed on the flat lands around the hill of Gomphi. He found Salvius Cursor and Atenos engaged in a discussion, and came to a halt beside them.

'Problems?'

'Not as such,' Salvius replied. 'A minor disagreement on approach. The centurion here favours climbing the slopes and coming at Gomphi from the higher ground. I prefer the notion of a low attack, where the artillery can do its work first.'

Fronto nodded. 'Both equally workable options. The consensus of the staff is a direct, full scale assault in the belief that the defending garrison is paltry.'

The two men nodded their agreement, and Fronto sucked on his teeth, 'Very well. Atenos, you take half the men up the slope and try and take the rear walls. You will likely find them less well defended. You'll still have to take some of the siege ladders from the carts. Salvius, you get your frontal assault with the other half. Atenos, you'd best get moving into position. The signals will be given as soon as the artillerists have had their fun.'

The centurion saluted and hurried off to gather his cohorts and collect the ladders. 'Your place is back with the commanders, sir,' Salvius said. Fronto narrowed his eyes, uncertain whether this was born of genuine concern or possibly the desire to take the lead himself.

'I have every intention of moving into Gomphi and trying to preserve a few useful lives before the entire population of the city are torn apart by triumphant legionaries.'

'*Useful* lives?'

'Androsthenes was one of our men, and his staff were ours too. The idiot might have panicked and turned to Pompey, but there may be men on his staff who would willingly come back to us, and those men will have invaluable information about the area, other notable commanders, and possibly even about Scipio and Pompey's forces and movements. I'd rather have a chance to speak to such men before legionaries start jumping up and down on their faces.'

The tribune seemed to weigh this up for a moment, then nodded reluctantly. 'Sensible, sir, and I'll accompany you once we're in, but you'll never get up a siege ladder with your knee. Take a century of men and make for the gate over there. Once we're in, I'll have that gate thrown open and then you can move in safely.'

A touch of irritation rippled through Fronto at being mothered so by his second in command, but he was forced to accede in the knowledge that his knee, while improving again, would certainly make clambering over walls more than a little challenging.

'Agreed.'

As if the reminder of his discomfort was a trigger his knee began to throb a little, and he moved over to a stack of crates and settled onto one, watching the Tenth and the other legions nearby shifting into position. Atenos and his cohorts were already on the move, arcing round to the west where they would climb the slopes ready to fall upon the rear of the town. Almost certainly the commander of whichever legion held the far end of the arc would be doing something similar. Salvius moved off, gathering his own force and collecting a dozen long siege ladders, and Fronto instead concentrated on the walls.

As the siege engines were moved into position and began in their own time to hurl bolts and stones at the wall tops, he tried to make sense of what little he could see of the town behind those defences. It was extremely unlikely that Androsthenes or any of his senior men would place themselves in the greatest danger at the walls. They would be commanding from a headquarters. Very likely they would be using the city's bouleuterion – the council chamber – which was designed for meetings and would have arcs of seating. He could just make out an area high up in the town that seemed to be clear of cluttered buildings and would probably be the market place: the agora. That would be where he would find the council chamber and therefore, very likely, the more important of the enemy officers.

For a quarter of an hour the machines pounded the walls, Atenos now lost from sight with his men far off to the west, Salvius almost vibrating with the tense desire to move, his cohorts lined up behind him. At a brassy fanfare, the engines stopped loosing and units of slingers and archers moved forwards into position.

The death toll atop the walls had probably not been too horrific. Once the first dozen men in sight had fallen to the missiles, the rest had ducked back into safety, only a few being struck thereafter. Now, as the stones stopped and the creaking machines fell silent, worried faces appeared along the walls once more, then disappeared equally swiftly as a second call from the musicians unleashed the arrows and sling stones.

Once more men died, though most ducked back into safety. Fronto sat silent, pondering the coming scenes, until finally the missile barrage halted at a series of calls and the legions bristled, preparing to move. He wondered idly how many of those pale faces who now reappeared on the parapet regretted their praetor's decision to defy Caesar in favour of Pompey. Would any of them have the wherewithal to simply open the gates and let the army in? It would be defying their praetor, but only in favour of his own commander. If they did, perhaps Fronto could persuade the general not to unleash the legions in a rampage.

No. It may have been Antonius' suggestion, but it was Caesar's will. The army had seen a gradual rise in spirit ever since their morale sank to an all-time low at Dyrrachium, but the mountain passes and the continuing depletion of rations and inability of wavering towns to support them fully were taking their toll. The troops needed a surge in spirit, and the freedom to loot a town that defied them would give them that boost. This was less about punishing Androsthenes and his people than continuing to improve the morale of the legions before they came to blows once more with Pompey.

The signals were given. Fronto watched the army of Caesar begin to stomp implacably forwards, closing in on Gomphi like a noose. The lack in defending numbers was evident the moment the legions came within missile shot. A strong force in a besieged town would now be hurling bolts, stones, arrows and bullets out at the advancing lines. All that came from Gomphi were a few paltry shots. They were lacking in artillery and even in archers, seemingly.

Given heart by the lack of swarming arrows, the legions gave a triumphant roar and at the centurions' whistles broke into double time, jogging at the walls with the rattle and shush and clonk of arms and armour. Ahead, Fronto could see Salvius Cursor with over a thousand men breaking into an unrestrained charge. He could just picture the bloodlust painting the tribune's face. This was what Salvius lived for. What had Pompey done that had so drawn his ire?

Reasoning that the timing was right and that he was as safe as any man could be during a siege, Fronto waved his century of men forwards. The few arrows, spears and stones that could be raised in Gomphi continued to issue from the walls, but a small unit with an officer coming up behind the main force were of insufficient import to draw the attention of those men on the top, who continued to concentrate on the threat even now reaching the base of the walls.

As the legions slowed to a halt, siege ladders began to rise, while other men hurled up ropes with grapples, each man determined to be over that wall and taking possession of whatever he could find. It was a hopeless situation for the defenders, and the conclusion was a given even at this stage. By dark the place would be naught but a charnel house.

Veering off to the left, Fronto and his escort made for the nearest gatehouse. He could see men bearing the symbols of the Seventh not far off to his left, already climbing the walls. A glance to the right revealed men of the Tenth to be nearing the parapet, though spears lanced out, taking some of the lead men with a cry of agony and throwing them from their ladders to fall into the mass of their companions below. It came as no surprise when he caught sight of the tell-tale traditional officer's uniform near the top. Salvius was among the lead men over the walls.

His breath held tensely, Fronto came to a halt beside the gate, his men gathering around him. All of them had their faces upturned, confident that the gate would only be opened by allies, but awfully aware that a single dropped rock from above could smash a man's head like an egg, or strike a helmet so hard it would drive the bronze bowl straight through hair, flesh and bone and into the brain.

Sure enough, half a dozen missiles were dropped by panicked, opportunistic defenders, but the century of men were prepared enough that only one struck true, and that hit a man on his left shoulder, breaking the arm, but leaving him alive and grunting his pain. It seemed to take forever, though in truth it would have been less than a quarter of an hour, and finally Fronto and his century stepped back, hands gripping weapons tight when there came a deep clonk and rasping sound as the timber bar of the gate was removed, followed by metallic clanks as bolts were thrown back.

The gate opened, a dozen men of the Tenth saluting their commander as the great timber leaves crawled open. There was a cry from outside and those men still waiting to cross the wall now made for the gate and an easy admittance. Fronto almost jumped as a figure from nightmare appeared inside, stepping out of the gate's shadows, coated in blood and hair and filth, and it took moments to recognise Salvius Cursor's shape within it, though Fronto realised he should have known instantly. It was far from the first time he had seen the tribune in such a condition, after all.

The shambling gore-monster beckoned with a raised arm, and Fronto ran inside, willing his knee to hold out. Behind him came his century of men, then the masses of the Tenth and Seventh, desperately rushing to secure their cut of both victory and spoils.

The chaos in Gomphi was evident the moment Fronto emerged into the small open square behind the gate. Despite the freedom the army were to be given once they'd taken the town, the centurions were doing an admirable job of keeping their men together until the place was fully secured. Fronto saw groups of legionaries stomping off up streets, bellowing their rage, centurions' whistles echoing through the streets amid the noise. But despite their best intentions, men were taking the opportunity already to burst through doors as they passed, to butcher anyone without a legionary's red tunic who came before them, to sweep up anything of value and even snap the fingers off bodies that bore a nice looking ring.

And this was in the first moments of entry, when they were theoretically still fighting the enemy to a conclusion. The remaining Thessalians who had not been caught and butchered on the wall top were visible running one way or another in the streets, some with screams of defiance, blade in hand as they hurtled at the invader to their doom. Others were fleeing up the streets to the west, trying to escape the death and destruction.

He watched, sickened, as an old man emerged from a side door, protecting a girl – possibly his granddaughter – only to receive a dreadful sword blow across the back. The man cried out and pushed the terrified girl away. She evaded a sword blow by only a hair's breadth and fled into a narrow alley out of sight. The soldiers ignored her, concentrating on putting down the old man, and Fronto felt hollow at the sight. It would be nice to think the girl had been saved, but he knew the realities of a victorious army being given free rein. It would be a miracle if the girl survived the night.

As Fronto, Salvius and the century accompanying them jogged off up the street, trying to ignore what was happening around them and concentrating on getting safely to the agora, he was surprised to see two legionaries emerge from a door, leading a man and a woman roped together. A passing optio paused beside them and harangued them, reminding them that no one could be spared on this campaign to guard slaves, and that there were no slave traders among the inevitable followers. To put an end to their brief argument, the optio ripped free his sword and stabbed both man and woman in the chest before moving on.

They reached the agora before the bulk of the legions by simple dint of not pausing to kill and loot on the way. A small gathering of well-armed locals were forming up in the open market area, but Fronto's gaze fell on what had to be the bouleuterion at the far side. The last major push for armed defence made to take on this small force of Romans that had appeared in the square. Fronto had to hand it to them, the city was lost, and most now were running for their lives, desperate to flee the inevitable, though they would likely meet men like Atenos and his soldiers coming the other way, yet here was a small force of hard men preparing to fight to the last.

'Go,' Salvius shouted at him, pointing at the door of the council chamber even as he and the bulk of the legionaries ran, bellowing, at the enemy. Eight men peeled off from that group and followed their legate as he made for the door.

He burst through, sword in hand and ready for anything, but even as his eyes adjusted to the gloomy interior, he realised the place was empty. It had been used, though, recently and seemingly for the very purpose Fronto had supposed. A table stood in the centre and the number of cups, half-drunk, close to the jar suggested a number of people in close session.

'No one, sir,' confirmed a legionary as the eight of them moved drapes and scoured the room.

'Where did they go, then?' Fronto hissed. Moments later, he emerged back into the sunlight, to see the last of those men at the centre of the square fighting a losing battle against the enraged Salvius Cursor and his soldiers. The legate ran across to them. Even as he identified what appeared to be the most senior of the defenders, the man took an agonising blow from Salvius, who broke his sword arm just above the elbow.

'Wait.'

The tribune had delivered two more blows, snarling his anger, before Fronto reached him and grasped his sword arm's wrist even as he went for the killing blow. Salvius turned a furious look on him, but Fronto ignored it.

'Where is Androsthenes?' he asked the pained warrior. The man frowned for a moment, then shook his head.

'Tell me,' Fronto snapped, 'and I'll let you live.'

That seemed to break through the man's shell and he struggled for a moment before shrinking back and dropping his sword. 'Onesilas' shop,' he grunted in thick Greek. Fronto had to concentrate to translate. It was so rare he heard, spoke or read Greek, despite having learned it in his youth like any good noble Roman. 'The apothecary,' the man went on, gesturing at the far end of the square.

Fronto nodded. 'You have my thanks.'

He let go of Salvius' wrist at last and turned with his eight men, making for the indicated shop. Behind him he heard a shriek and a gurgle, and spun to see the tribune withdrawing his blade from the warrior's neck.

'I gave him my word,' Fronto snapped.

'I didn't,' Salvius replied, with a challenge in his eyes as he wiped his sword rather fruitlessly on the dead man's back. Mentally, Fronto added yet another incident to his catalogue of Salvius' insolence, but decided to ignore it for the time being. There would be far worse perpetrated in the coming hours, and sometimes it was just not worth the effort of arguing with the tribune.

The apothecary's shop was not difficult to find, the sign hanging outside displaying a mortar and pestle. He turned to the eight legionaries who had accompanied him. 'No killing unless we have to. I want Androsthenes alive, and anyone he might have with him.'

At an affirmative nod from the soldiers, he reached out and carefully lifted the latch, pushing open the door, sword in hand. After all, the praetor of Thessaly might not want to go down without a fight. A moment later, Fronto was hit by the smell. His gorge rising even as his spirits sank, he stepped into the dim room, his eyesight adjusting once more.

The source of the stench of gore and faeces was easy enough to spot. Bodies lay in a heap in the centre of the room. Gagging, Fronto hurried over to the window and threw open the shutters. It did little to alleviate the smell, though it did cast the grisly scene into stark illumination.

Fronto had no idea what the praetor of Thessaly, looked like, though one of those in the room was almost certainly him. At a rough count, perhaps twenty corpses lay at the centre and each was garbed in the highest quality chiton, each held in place with exquisite pins or belts with ornate buckles. All had richly coiffured hair. And all had taken blades to themselves, some digging long cuts into their forearms, others preferring the throat. Whatever the case, all were very clearly dead, though they had not been for long, as was evidenced by the fact that blood was still flowing from wounds.

'What in Minerva's name,' breathed one of the soldiers behind Fronto, who then gagged and coughed, his hand going to his scarf to pull it over his mouth and nose.

'I suspect that Androsthenes and his cronies had more than a little idea what Caesar might do to them when he got his hands on them. They took their own lives as soon as they knew it was over. Idiots.'

He turned and left the room, struggling to heave in cleansing air outside.

Caesar had wanted to send a message, and that was most definitely what they'd done.

CHAPTER 17

Thessaly, July 48 BC

Fronto rode in sullen silence. It had been bad enough witnessing the events that followed the fall of Gomphi, but he really wished he hadn't been into the city the next morning as the army prepared to move out.

After discovering the bodies in the apothecary's shop, which were swiftly identified as the leading figures of Gomphi, both political and military, he had descended the street once more until he found the first tavern. There he had pushed his way inside, along with the eight men who had stayed with him. He had promised each and every one a healthy bonus if they stayed out of the rapine and looting and kept the place clear of other crazed and victorious legionaries. In short order they had removed the sickening remains of the folk hiding in the tavern and, presumably, its owner and staff. The place had already been stripped of obvious valuables and whatever jars of wine were visible on the tables, but in-depth looting had not yet begun, since there were easier pickings to be found across the city.

Fronto had given his men orders to prevent other soldiers entering the bar, and had given them all a drink to ease their boredom, though only one, in case they felt compelled by wine to join in the chaos. He then sat in the gloomy tavern with a jug of wine, and a less important jug of water, and drank repeated toasts to the shades of all those he had known and lost, as well as to the poor folk of Gomphi. He had already lost the use of his legs when Galronus, ashen-faced, found him and without a word opened another jar of wine and joined in.

He had no recollection of the journey back to his tent that night, though vague images of the most horrific things hovered on the edge of his consciousness and were almost certainly remnants of what he'd seen on the way back, rather than mere night terrors.

The next morning, hardening himself, head pounding and having vomited copiously three times into the grass near his tent, he had gone back to the city. He felt he owed it to those ordinary folk of Gomphi whose only crime had been to be ruled by a man who defied Caesar. It had been sickening. The destruction of Gomphi had been total. This place, he knew, had something of a history of sieges. The great general Flamininus and his allies had taken Gomphi after a hard fight over a century ago, but they had simply captured and garrisoned it. Caesar's army had done to Gomphi what they had done to much of Gaul over a decade of destruction: annihilation.

Perhaps half the structures at best remained intact. Some parts of the city had been burned down and columns of smoke still twisted up into the sky here and there as visible reminders of what had happened here. The death toll had been total. The legions had visited utter carnage upon Gomphi and looted the place of every last item of worth. Here and there, as Fronto moved around, he spotted signs of acts far worse than simple killing, and tried not to think too hard on them. Gomphi had suffered appallingly.

He could see the effects in the soldiers, too. Last night they had been savage and elated and in due course, as they joked and worked hard, morale improved once more, yet in the eyes of the men, every now and then, he could see a haunted shadow of guilt over what they had done, amid their jubilation.

It was said that Caesar had taken captives, though Fronto had seen no evidence of such, so there could not have been many of them, and they were not folk of import for all those had died together by their own hands.

The army moved on the next morning just after dawn, continuing southwest towards the rumour of Calenus and his cohorts. They had moved with speed at the general's command, and Fronto had been surprised at that. He'd assumed, given the message Gomphi was meant to represent, that they would move slow enough for rumour to travel ahead of them. But no, the legions marched for Metropolis, which they reached at around noon.

The city was smaller than the name suggested and sat at the foot of a spur of land upon which clustered several ancient temples. A wall encircled the town and there was some evidence that once, a second wall had enclosed a larger area, now little more than rubble. Still, the inner wall was both intact and strong, and manned with guards along its circumference. As the officers at the head of the army, along with Ingenuus' guard, approached the city, Caesar raised his hand to halt the column.

'Another closed gate,' Antonius said quietly.

Fronto, still sullen, nodded. They had moved fast, and almost certainly word of Gomphi had not yet reached this other city, or at least, if it had, it was only the news that the place had fallen, and not of the true horror that had befallen it. Again, Fronto could not imagine why the general had moved fast enough to outpace word of his dreadful victory.

'Do we repeat the procedure?' Sulla murmured. 'Deploy the artillery first?'

Caesar shook his head. 'All is in order, gentlemen. Remain calm and seated and watch the effects of our victory take hold.'

Frowning in bafflement, the other officers remained in their saddles and watched. Metropolis glowered back at them, heavy walls, much better manned than those of Gomphi. There was no sign of the gate creaking open. After a long pause, a small detachment of legionaries appeared, jogging along the side of the column to reach the officers at the van. The scouts had peeled off ahead some time ago and were even now circling round the far side of Metropolis, checking the lie of the land.

Fronto turned his lowered brow on the detachment of legionaries as they arrived, half a century of men under an optio. At a flicked hand from Caesar they moved on ahead, making for the nearest gate in the walls of Metropolis, Now, as they passed, Fronto realised there were civilians with them. Four of them, in fact. An old man, a couple and a young girl. He only caught sight of them from the back for a moment, and dredged his memory in the hope that the girl was the one he'd seen escape harm the previous night, but he simply couldn't recall her face, and the chances of that being the case were infinitesimally small.

'Come. Join me,' Caesar said, and began to trot his horse lightly in the wake of the legionaries and their four captives. Four of the praetorian horsemen went with their commander, staying close, ready to throw their shields around him if he were to suddenly come into danger. Fronto and the other officers kicked their own steeds into movement and followed the general.

Working to some unknown but prearranged plan, the legionaries moved on until they were just three hundred paces from the walls of Metropolis that reared up golden in the sunlight before them. There they fell into two lines, pushing the four captives out before them. Caesar gestured for the others to halt their horses behind the small party, while he himself rode around them so that he was clearly visible from the walls. The praetorians moved close enough to protect him if the worst should happen, for a good archer could have planted a shaft in the general from that distance. Still there were no signs of aggression from the walls, though there was equally no sign of admittance being granted.

'Metropolis is closed to you by order of the Archon Timocreon,' called an authoritative, militant voice.

Caesar nodded for a long moment. Then he cleared his throat. 'The Archon Timocreon might want to rethink his decision. I offer one chance to change your mind, and one only. And to aid you in your decision-making, I bring you these four good Thessalian folk.'

At his words, legionaries stepped forwards and cut the bonds of the prisoners, pushing them forwards.

'Tell them who you are,' Caesar said, not unkindly, which seemed odd. 'And of Gomphi.'

Fronto felt a chill run through him as the four, who were clearly part of one family, staggered forwards into that strange, dangerous space between the Romans and the walls of the defiant city. They looked at one another, and discussed something quietly.

'Tell them,' Caesar said again, this time with a little more steel.

The discussion ended and the man, presumably the girl's father, stepped forth.

'I am Eriphus of Gomphi,' he shouted, 'a basket maker. This is my wife Astyothea, and my daughter Melinna and father Simmias.'

'Well met, basket maker,' called the man at the gate with a clear waver of uncertainty. What was this trick of the Romans?

'We are the survivors of Gomphi.'

A plain and simple statement, yet it carried a lead weight of horror, and its effects were visible in the men on the walls. The watchers immediately broke into small groups and argued or whispered to one another. There was an extended pause.

'Gomphi has been destroyed?' the speaker asked finally.

'Gomphi is *gone*,' corrected the basket weaver. 'All that remains are ruins and corpses, and those who died swiftly were the lucky ones.' The man cast a bitter look back at Caesar, who simply nodded.

There was a flurry of movement and some heated discussion at the gate.

'I advise you to make your decision swiftly,' Caesar said, his tone becoming dangerous. 'My artillery are being brought forwards.'

The pause dragged out for only four more heartbeats, and then the city gate swung open.

'Archon Timocreon has been removed from office,' called the voice, and Fronto snorted. There had been little time for such a thing. He had the private suspicion that the city's archon was probably still in his council chamber deciding how to send for help, and would react with some surprise when his officers came for him to tell him he was no longer in command.

'Gomphi is gone,' repeated Caesar, though now quietly, to the four survivors near him. 'I recommend that you become Eriphus the basket weaver of Metropolis.'

The four of them looked nervously at the general, who thrust a finger out towards the gate. 'Go.'

They needed no further urging, breaking into a run, looking back repeatedly, half expecting to be ridden down by cavalry or speared with javelins. No move was made against them and in thirty heartbeats they passed through the open gate of Metropolis and to safety.

'You, Gaius Julius Caesar, are a devious man,' grinned Marcus Antonius.

The general shrugged. 'It is an old adage to say that actions speak louder than words, but it is true nonetheless. The word of mouth that reached Metropolis would be dreadful, but second-hand news is still only second-hand. To hear from those who were there carries a great deal more weight, and even now the people of Metropolis are learning that they made the correct decision from those four survivors. I fear we would even now be bringing up the siege ladders had our friend Eriphus not been here to talk.'

Fronto nodded. 'And now the word that spreads will be not only of the total destruction of Gomphi and the horrors perpetrated there, but they will also speak of your magnanimity and the offer of peace you gave Metropolis. Sharp.'

Caesar bowed his head in acknowledgement of the compliment.

'And to further strengthen that reputation, if the former archon Timocreon survives, we shall pardon him and send him into comfortable retirement, though I suspect the good citizens of Metropolis will be rather eager to use him as a sign of their faithfulness.'

A party of officials from the city rode forth from the gate, unarmed and in wealthy civilian attire. As the officers sat silent and impressive, Caesar received them in state, accepted their oaths of loyalty and thanked them. Soon after, the commanders of the Caesarian army, under the watchful eye of Ingenuus and his men, made their way beneath the gate arch of Metropolis while the legions moved out to make camp in the surrounding countryside.

Fronto, close behind the general and with Galronus riding beside him, listened to the fawning offers of the desperate nobles of the city as they were escorted to the heart of the place. Caesar and his staff would be given the very best accommodation. Would they be staying long? The city had had a good year for produce and the store houses were full. They would make available for Caesar's men everything they could spare. The harvest would be ready soon, and it appeared it would be a good one. Perhaps the legions would like to help, and reap a great reward. And so on, and so on.

Fronto had to admit that it was refreshing to hear. Apart from a few badly-provisioned and desperate towns throughout their journey that had hurriedly turned over what they had, most of all they had endured hardship since Dyrrachium. At least they had not been pursued by Pompey, who had chosen adequate supplies over the prosecution of the campaign. It was nice to be treated well, and the men would relish the rest.

Fronto was shown to quarters in a well-appointed house that he would be sharing with two other officers. Galronus and Brutus would be good companions, he decided. The archon of the city was brought before them in chains, pushed to the dusty ground, but

Caesar magnanimously granted him a pardon for his actions and had him released.

By mid-afternoon, Fronto was once more out in the city and looking for a tavern. He found one on a gently sloping street, which had a pleasant garden shaded by plane trees, vines and climbing plants growing up trellises and across pergolas overhead. He took a seat at one of the tables and drank two pleasant, refreshing cups of watered wine before Galronus found him.

He sat there with other officers wandering past and noticing him, the odd one coming in to join in, and started as Caesar suddenly appeared outside in just his tunic and cloak, Aulus Ingenuus hovering nearby with a hand on his sword.

'Trust you, Fronto, to always find the best tavern as soon as you arrive.'

The general smiled as he passed into the tavern's garden. The majority of the officers present rose politely. Fronto remained seated, but reached out with his good leg and pushed a bench back for the general, who chuckled and sat obligingly. The innkeeper appeared with a sweat of panic running down his face and the most ridiculously obsequious grin.

'Mighty Caesar, can I get you anything. All on the house for the honour you do my establishment.'

The general smiled warmly. 'A jar of whatever this gentleman is drinking, if you would.' He gestured at Fronto's cup, then winked at the legate. 'For just as you gravitate to the best bar, so do you usually find the best wine on instinct alone.'

'I was in the trade, remember,' Fronto laughed. 'Still am, if I ever get back to Massilia.'

A strange dark cloud passed over them for a moment, and Caesar actually contrived to look faintly guilty. In an apparent effort to drive away the shadow in the mood, the general looked around appreciatively. 'This reminds me greatly of a tavern we once frequented at Bibracte. You remember the one?'

Fronto did, and he blinked in surprise as he looked around. It was, in fact, remarkably similar. For a moment that shadow on his soul threatened to darken as his memory helpfully furnished him with the faces of those friends who had drunk in that tavern with him, who had mostly gone to Elysium now. It seemed as though most of those he'd called friend when they went into Gaul had passed on since then.

'Balbus was sitting here last time,' the general smiled, gesturing to a seat nearby. 'How *is* your father-in-law? I miss his steady hand among the staff.'

A flash of guilt shot through Fronto. He'd not given much of a thought to his old friend for months now, and he'd not even written to Lucilia and the boys, for the distance between here and the villa outside Tarraco, partially controlled by Pompey's allies, made sending missives touch-and-go at best.

'Balbus was good when I last saw him. With luck, once we trounce Pompey I will be able to return to him. My boys are growing all the time, and I've missed most of it. They will hardly recognise me when I return to them.'

A similar shadow now passed through Caesar's eyes, and Fronto remembered all too late that the general's only daughter had died a few years earlier. Damn this stupid dance of politeness: Caesar trying not to offend Fronto, Fronto trying not to offend Caesar. He bolted on a smile, forcing things back into the light.

'How is Octavian?' he said suddenly. 'That lad will go far, you know?'

Caesar chuckled. 'I quite agree. He will have changed a great deal since you saw him. That was seven or eight years ago, was it not?'

'Something like that.'

'I meet him periodically, and his mother keeps me abreast of matters. Sometimes he writes to me directly, for he is fourteen years old now, and with no males in his immediate family, I suspect he thinks of me as a father. He will don the toga virilis this year and be a man with whom to reckon. He tells me he already hankers after a place on my staff, but while he wears the bulla of childhood his mother will not let him.'

'You plan to adopt him, don't you?'

Caesar threw him a sly smile. 'The notion has some merit, I have to admit. Of what value is a man's legacy if there is no one to pass it to?'

Fronto nodded and fell silent, grateful that a moment later Brutus struck up a conversation with the general regarding their shared family, for something had struck Fronto at Caesar's last words and had sent a shiver through him.

How many times had friends and enemies alike accused Caesar of monarchic aspirations. Fronto had always known him to be ambitious, and there had, he had to admit, been times when he had foreseen the general moving in that very direction. It had been the brutal realisation that the only clear alternative in the current climate of the republic was Pompey that had sent him back to Caesar's side.

But now the man talked of a legacy, and Fronto could not help but suddenly worry what that planned legacy might be. He brushed the thought angrily aside. Adoption was hardly uncommon in the better circles of Roman society, and every family with any pride or aspirations planned for the future beyond their own demise. Still, suddenly he flashed back to a quarry in Hispania and the dying form of Verginius, begging him to put an end to Caesar before Caesar put an end to the republic.

The rest of the afternoon became rather sour for Fronto, who was unable to keep unpleasant thoughts from surfacing time and again. After a while, Caesar made polite excuses and returned to the business of state with the new archon of Metropolis. Other officers drifted off and even Galronus, who tried briefly but unsuccessfully to rid Fronto of the gloom so clearly settled upon him, eventually went back to the house.

Fronto took a brief wander, located a local scribe and purchased vellum, ink, stilus, wax and a scroll case at a somewhat inflated price, and then slowly made his way back to the tavern. There he sat alone in the shade of the trees with good wine and penned the first letter to his family in half a year. When he finally finished and tucked the missive into the scroll case, he slipped the signet ring from his finger, melted the wax over a candle and sealed the case. He would pass it in the morning to Hirtius, who dealt with Caesar's correspondence. Whether it would ever reach Tarraco he couldn't say in these uncertain times of war, but he had at least done his best.

His mood had improved with every line he wrote and, catharsis complete, he once more sought out Galronus, intent on spending an evening of social good humour. Within an hour word of he and the Remi laughing raucously in the tavern garden had spread and other officers joined them, including Atenos and Salvius Cursor. The evening passed thereafter in laughter and wine.

The following day the army seemed set in. Caesar had announced that they would continue to reside in Metropolis for at least the next few days. There had been no word of Pompey or Scipio in the vicinity, and scouts and outposts had now been set up all around the edge of the Thessalian plain to give adequate warning of any approach. Moreover, Caesar wanted to wait and judge from further reports the mood of the rest of Achaea. Mostly, Fronto suspected, the general was happy and comfortable in a place with adequate supplies and no apparent danger, and was less than willing to give that up. It was sometimes easy to forget that the general was not a young man. Fronto tried not to admit that he was not far off the general's age himself. He mostly failed.

Over the next few days, that tavern became the standard social meeting place for officers, though Fronto noted that his favourite table in the corner remained free at all times, awaiting him. The tavern's owner, who had likely never seen so much business and would end this campaign a wealthy man, could not do enough for them, constantly on hand and sourcing the very best food and drink for his customers. For a time, Fronto began to relax.

News began to drift in slowly over the following days, and initially it was all good. Calenus was succeeding in securing all of the south of Achaea from a base at Athens, and had even made overtures to the ancient cities across the sea in Asia. City after city across Thessaly sent diplomats or messages, guaranteeing their support to the Caesarian cause and offering both men and supplies.

Then, one warm and pleasant afternoon, came the first bad news. The city of Larissa, some forty miles to the north-east, had failed to send any sort of overture, and Caesar had been pushed to enquire of them from neighbouring states. It seemed that Larissa was menaced by the threat of Scipio to the north, and did not feel they could submit to Caesar with such a dangerous enemy close by.

The discovery that Scipio was close now changed everything, for it seemed unlikely that Scipio would be moving closer to Caesar without Pompey's main force in support. It would appear that the enemy was on the advance once more and this time of comfortable peace would soon be over.

That same afternoon, Caesar put in another appearance at the tavern, most of the staff at his heel. Praetorians pulled three of the tables together, and Hirtius produced a map of the region and spread it out, anchoring the corners with heavy earthenware cups.

'We're preparing to move?' Fronto prompted.

Caesar nodded without looking up. 'The time is almost upon us, gentlemen. Scipio threatens Larissa, which puts him no more than sixty or seventy miles from here. We cannot safely assume Pompey to be far behind him. I anticipate news of my old partner's arrival in Thessaly in a matter of days, now. On the bright side, the damage of Dyrrachium is healed, and I think we can all agree that we made the correct decision following the disaster.'

Fronto nodded as he rose, poured another wine and crossed to the map table with the others.

'Our objective when we retreated from Dyrrachium,' the general reminded everyone, 'was to find adequate time and space to heal our men's morale, while endeavouring if possible to lower that of the enemy, and to allow us to acquire sufficient resources to rebuild, ready to face him once more. Our army is now as spirited as it has ever been, it is well-equipped and well-fed, and now somewhat bolstered by the addition of Calvinus' own cohorts and of those bodies supplies as auxilia by the local cities. We are, I think, as prepared as we can ever truly hope to be.'

His finger tapped the northern edge of the map. 'By comparison, Scipio's forces have been almost constantly on the move and engaged since he left Syria, and our agents in Achaea have been stirring up trouble behind him, such that his supply lines must be disrupted at best. Pompey has been forced to move slowly in order to preserve his own supply chain from Dyrrachium and Macedonia, and his men will be impatient and tetchy from their own hardships. There will never be a better time to meet the old warhorse and his cronies in the field and finally dispose of them.'

He looked up from beneath grey brows. 'And make no mistake, gentlemen, I mean this to be our last engagement with Pompey. I will not retreat again, and I will not countenance such failures among my officers as we suffered previously. I want the calibre of service I remember from Gaul. That is why I have continually drafted the old guard back into my staff. When we meet Pompey this time, I want him beaten and with no opportunity to rebuild. It all ends this summer.'

He turned back to the map.

'All that remains is to decide upon our ground, for we are in the most advantageous position of being able to select at least *where* we will meet Pompey, if not when.'

'Given that we don't know how long we have,' Antonius put in, 'we could do with gathering all the provisions we can manage.'

Caesar nodded. 'Harvest time is upon us, and that plan has the added benefit of leaving little of use for Pompey and Scipio. Every mouthful upon which our men gorge helps starve Pompey's legions. Splendid. I shall send riders to every city that has now pledged to us to send their spare grain and supplies. We could even send a unit to gather from the dubious Larissans, as long as they are fast, long range men and can return at speed. All that remains then is to select our ground and have everything converge there.'

'We need a good commanding position which Pompey will feel obliged to contest,' Sulla put in, poring over the map. 'How about here? Orthis? The entrance to a valley with a road that seems to be a vital artery down to the plains beyond the southern range?'

Caesar shook his head. 'We have to assume that Pompey has connected with Scipio or is at least very close to doing so, and we know Scipio to be just north of Larissa. If they come from Larissa they will be in the east of the Thessalian bowl. There, they can take either main fork, southwest to the Ekarra Pass and beyond into Malis, or southeast, over the low hills and to the coast near Halos. Either way they could theoretically cut us off from Calenus and his army. If I were Pompey that would be precisely what I would do. So we need to hold him before he reaches the southern area, here, and make him commit to battle.'

Fronto frowned over the map, taking in all the salient points, then tapped his finger on Larissa. 'He will come through here, gathering what supplies and men he can from the Larissans, who are still nominally his. He's almost certainly going to have joined with Scipio by then, and if not, Larissa is the clear place to do so.' He drummed the fingers of his other hand on the map for a moment, then started to drag his forefinger southwards from Larissa. 'There's a road marked. Seems to be an important one – *arterial*, I suspect – that splits here and heads to both those routes you mentioned, General. But before it splits, it passes through a city on the south bank of the…' he paused and squinted at the map, 'the Enipeus River. If such a main road crosses a river big enough to be named on this map, then it's a critical crossing. And any critical crossing on that route is plainly your place to hold Pompey and bring him to battle.'

Caesar frowned at the map and began slowly to nod. The other gathered officers confirmed their agreement similarly. The general peered closely at the map.

'That is our place, then. Send to our allies and support and have all units and all possible supplies converge there. We face Pompey at Pharsalus.'

Part Two

Endgame

Pharsalus 48 BC

CHAPTER 18

Fronto paused on his way to the briefing, taking the rare opportunity to view the enemy between the long lines of tents. Still nothing had changed. Huffing irritably in the warm morning air, he thrust his thumbs behind his belt and plodded on towards the headquarters and the waiting officers. His spirits fell a little further at the sight of Salvius Cursor waiting at the end of the Tenth's lines, prepared to join him in the briefing as the legion's second in command.

The army had arrived at the bridge just outside Pharsalus on a pleasant afternoon six days ago. Thanks to excellent organisation and numerous cities keeping faith with Caesar, within a day of their arrival, already supplies and manpower were joining the large camp. There was a distinctly high spirit about the army as they prepared to meet the enemy, who scouts had said were now definitely moving just north of Larissa.

Then Pompey had finally reached Thessaly three days ago. His massive force had flooded the plain to the north and moved south with the swiftness of a general who was both competent and confident. He had come into view of the Caesarian pickets a few miles north of the bridge and had, upon receiving intelligence of Caesar's position at the crossing of the river, which was not large but possessed of difficult, steep banks, moved off the road to the west a little and made camp on a low rise between two higher hills, each of which was manned with lookouts.

There Pompey's forces sat, some four or five miles away on that low hill, visible from Caesar's camp only as a mass of dark movement on that distant slope, like an anthill viewed from a height.

Spirits among the army had taken something of a knock immediately as they watched the enemy arrive over the course of an entire day, flooding that rise like a dark swarm. Clearly Pompey's force outnumbered his enemy by at least two to one, a fact that caught in the throat of all present. Worse, though, than the discrepancy in numbers which, while worrying was hardly unexpected, was the clear level of their supplies. Caesar's army had thought themselves well provisioned and Pompey poorly-so, but it seemed that the old man was more adept at logistical planning than Caesar had assumed. The supply train that poured in behind the army was seemingly endless and bulging full. Clearly during the time Pompey had stayed in the north and Caesar's army had moved south across the hills and mountains, the old man had been doing more than threatening Calvinus. Somehow he had secured superb supply lines and extra troops.

Presumably much of his auxiliary manpower had come west with Scipio, for even at a distance the eastern and exotic nature of some of the units was clear. Pompey's camp, once complete, covered more than twice the area of Caesar's. The worry that local cities, such as Pharsalus for example, might suddenly decide that Pompey once more looked favourite pervaded the staff, and men were sent with each supply caravan to reassure allies that all was under control.

To Fronto, things didn't *look* particularly under control. The whole purpose of pulling back southeast had been to repair spirit and body in the army while diminishing those of the enemy, somewhat evening the scales. In the event, now that Pompey had finally arrived, it transpired that if anything the odds had become more tilted in Pompey's favour in the intervening months.

Yet oddly Pompey, with his massive force and excellent supplies, arrived cautiously and, rather than committing to battle, had pulled away and made camp. And more, he was seemingly unwilling even now to commit. As they had done every morning at Dyrrachium, Caesar marched out the army and mustered them on the plain before the camp and facing Pompey, and every morning the old adversary had brought out his own forces, but only as far as the slope below his camp, keeping them back from the plain and on terrain advantageous to him. As if daring Pompey, and giving something for his troops to concentrate on, each day Caesar paraded his force a little closer to Pompey, tempting the hot-tempered old bear into moving. Still he did not.

And so here they were: two armies facing one another, neither willing to move too close to the enemy's lair, daily daring one another to attack.

Fronto nodded at the guard, but the two praetorians outside Caesar's tent made no move to let him past. He frowned, and a cavalryman cleared his throat.

'Watch word, sir.'

Fronto's frown deepened, and the soldier shrugged apologetically. 'Sorry sir. General's orders now. All checkpoints and posts require the password, regardless of how well known you might be. The enemy are only a few miles away and they're Romans too, some of them veterans from this army.'

The legate nodded his understanding. It was eminently sensible, though it would hardly prevent the presence of any spy of talent, and Fronto was convinced there would be half a dozen of them in camp already. Conversely, they had no men in Pompey's camp.

'Venus Venetrix,' Fronto said, and the two guards stepped aside.

Venus Venetrix indeed. Caesar was nothing if not devoted to the cult of the self. Venus being reputedly the origin of his family, he was willing to play on his divine connections at all times.

Nodding once more to the twin guards, Castor and Pollux in chain shirts, he stepped inside.

The general's tent had been given a partitioned entrance lobby, where two more of Ingenuus' men took Fronto's weapons for storage. No chances were being taken, it seemed. Behind him, he heard Salvius Cursor complaining bitterly about being disarmed, but he ignored the chuntering tribune and pushed on into the tent.

The other officers were already there and many irritable faces turned his way as he moved inside.

'Don't you ever get anywhere on time?' Antonius snorted from close to the general.

Fronto raised an eyebrow. 'I didn't realise anything was so time-sensitive. Are we late to go for a stroll ten feet closer to Pompey?'

A variety of good humoured chortles and irritated grumbles greeted his comment, and he took a seat next to Brutus, Salvius sinking into the one next to him.

'Good,' Caesar said, standing. 'The purpose of this particular meeting, gentlemen, is to discuss the little intelligence we have on the enemy and to attempt to divine a way to move matters forwards. For my part, I have had the scouts moving as close as they can come to the enemy's camp and to try and identify unit insignia and the identity of the commanders.'

There were approving nods, and Caesar went on. 'The results are not especially thorough or enlightening, sadly. We know that in addition to Pompey and Scipio, Labienus is present. This has been ever the case in Achaea. But we also have identified Afranius and Petreus, who clearly wish to reprise their stubborn roles from Hispania last year, and Ahenobarbus. There are others there, too. Senators such as Junius Brutus, Casca, Cato and the like. They do not concern me on the field of battle, but their presence, I think, along with our Hispanic friends, explains a great deal.'

Fronto chuckled. 'You think Afranius and Petreus are failing to agree on anything again?'

Caesar nodded. 'More even than that. Our force is under my command. You all accept that. You are my officers and each strong and important men in your own right, but you all know that you serve your consul, and will accept my decision over all. Pompey, on the other hand, has accepted a mandate from the senate to lead their forces, which means he is beholden to them, and they will consider themselves to have a stake in command. Every decision made in that camp is made by committee, and we all know how well that works in an army. Undoubtedly, some of them want to charge into battle. Others will not.'

'The question is what Pompey wants to do,' Sulla put in.

Caesar shook his head. 'Given the difference in army sizes and the improved supply situation, I think now that Pompey would be content to try and starve us once more. We have adequate supplies for now, but if we remain into autumn and winter, they will diminish rapidly, while Pompey will still have his supply lines. No, I think Pompey almost certainly wants to watch us fade, but there will be others in his camp pressing for a victory. No, I do not think that what Pompey wants to do is the question. I think what their command as a whole will elect to do is the true question.'

'If only we had better information,' Brutus muttered.

'Pompey guards his watch word carefully, and his lines are well sealed. The chances of sneaking men into his camp are small. I am loathe to lose even a single man in such a futile effort when we are already so heavily outnumbered.'

Fronto nodded. 'Galronus is concerned about the cavalry issue. Latest estimates put them at six times our own number. Everyone's favourite Remi is a good commander and we have excellent riders, but even with Mars himself among us, six to one is horrible odds.'

'Where is he?' Antonius muttered. 'Surely he was supposed to be here for the meeting?'

Volusenus, the Prefect of Horse, cleared his throat. 'He is with the cavalry overseeing the new training. Every hour the gods send he's preparing. I can't blame him. I'm not looking forwards to having to kill six riders myself just like everyone else.'

* * *

Galronus was standing on the upper rail of a corral fence when Fronto found him, bellowing at someone called Kintugnatos and casting aspersions upon his parentage and species while suggesting that he could ride a horse slightly less well than another horse would.

'Going well, then?'

The Remi noble turned and sagged, dropping back from the fence to the springy turf. 'Actually surprisingly well, all things considered. I don't know whether it would work in battle as it does in practice, mind. Getting used to being among horses is one thing, doing it while spears are stabbing down at you is another entirely.'

The two men watched the new practice routine with interest. A thousand horse, with almost no Roman cavalry among them, the force they had at their command was mostly constituted of Gallic and Germanic units. They had been split into their individual tribal commands, the leaders of each unit agreed on the plan of action but each left to command his own unit, which allowed for both better spirit and greater mobility. Interspersed between the horse were a thousand legionaries. They had been selected from multiple legions for their speed and youth, each and every one. They had been stripped of all heavy kit and left with only chain shirt, sword and pilum. They were as fast and manoeuvrable a unit of foot as

Fronto had ever seen and, after three days now of this training, they were beginning to move among the horses with growing confidence and skill. It was impressive to Fronto's mind. Infantry did not react well to being among horses, and they had been extremely nervous at first. Now, after days of it, they were becoming comfortable. Whether or not they ever fought in battle like this, the simple fact was that their increased confidence among horsemen could be invaluable when battle was finally joined, for with such a large cavalry force Pompey would likely make sure to use them advantageously against the Caesarian infantry.

Fronto smiled. 'Well I think we're about to find out how well they manage. Caesar wants you to test them.'

Galronus frowned. 'That's Volusenus' job. He's the Prefect of Horse. I was just training them.'

Fronto laughed. 'Volusenus bowed out in favour of you. He's happy to command from a chair. You understand the men. You can read the Gauls' minds.'

Galronus nodded. No false modesty there. He was an excellent commander of native cavalry, and he knew it. 'Where then? Nowhere it stands a chance of bringing the entire force against us, of course.'

Fronto shrugged. 'Oh I don't know. It might be a good thing if you could get them to commit at last.'

Galronus gave him a scathing glare, and Fronto chuckled again. 'Water gatherers?'

The Remi paused for a moment, deep in thought, and then nodded. 'Good choice.'

Several times each day Pompey's army, residing on a hill as they did, sent a party two miles south across the plain to the river to gather supplies of fresh water. Naturally, they were mounted parties –they needed to be able to return to the camp at speed if they found themselves in trouble, and the sheer volume of water required demanded pack animals.

'We'll have to take them by surprise or they'll just run away.'

Fronto grinned. 'I shall leave the details to you.'

* * *

The late afternoon sun huddled just above the western plain like a sulking adolescent. The heat of the day was dying and the faint chill of evening was already beginning to make itself felt across Thessaly. Galronus sat astride his horse impatiently, willing the enemy to put in an appearance. It was the habit of Pompey's horse to make their last water gathering trip close to sundown, which would then see them through until the dawn. Locating their favoured place for gathering was far from difficult. The scouts had discovered it readily, for the mess made by three hundred horses churning the turf made it fairly obvious.

A copse of poplar, cypress and oak with abundant smaller vegetation lay to the west, on the far side of the area of crumbled banks and churned earth. It had taken a great deal of care to move two hundred horse down the steep bank further east and into the river, and then ducked low along the river and back up on the far side of the corpse where they could remain hidden, having approached in the gulley and out of sight of Pompeian pickets. It had taken almost an hour to move the cavalry into position where they could not be seen behind the trees, and there they would not be expected, on the far side of the watering place from the Caesarian lines. While the two hundred horse waited, ready to move at a moment's notice, the two hundred infantry remained standing in the cold water at the river's edge, hidden by the banks. The entire force, four hundred strong, would not be visible to the enemy until it was too late.

The first Galronus knew of the enemy's arrival was laughter. They were easy, overconfident and loud. He had expected unfamiliar voices: Syrian and Cappadocian and the like. What he actually heard was achingly familiar – the tones of central Gallic tribes. They were joking with one another.

He peered through the foliage and caught tantalising glimpses out into the clear ground beyond the copse. He was at the edge, with the best view, albeit still virtually obscured. Carefully, gingerly, he walked his horse slightly closer to the eaves of the woodland. Through the lighter foliage, he could see Gallic horse moving down to the water, roped lines of beasts each burdened with huge water barrels plodding along behind.

He counted under his breath, watching as the enemy all moved close to the river. The opening of battle would be clear and not chosen by him. He waved a flattened hand up and down, warning his men to be ready.

The signal came only a few heartbeats later. A cry of alarm, for the horsemen had reached the river and were suddenly aware of the infantry waiting for them below the banks. A roar of invective in Latin announced the attack of the light-armed footmen as they leapt swiftly up the bank and into the horsemen. Galronus and his horsemen were already moving when he heard, in a terribly familiar dialect, the order given to pull back to the camp.

He burst into the open, sword held aloft, his riders close behind. Just as he'd hoped, they had all passed the edge of the copse now and were gathered near the river, bellowing defiance at the sudden threat. Their voices rose in pitch and changed entirely in content as the rearmost of them suddenly spotted Galronus' cavalry bursting clear of the trees behind them, cutting off their path back to Pompey's camp on the hill.

Orders were called to form up, others conflictingly to charge the approaching infantry, yet more to abandon the pack animals and race east along the river. The bulk of the forwards horse decided that the infantry would be easy pickings, whether or not they'd heard the warnings about Galronus' men. But these footmen were no ready target. On almost any other battlefield, when faced with angry cavalry, the infantry will either flee or immediately close into a defensive formation. Galronus' infantry simply bellowed all the louder and charged the horsemen.

Even as the anvil of infantry crested the river bank and fell among the shocked cavalry, so the hammer of horsemen hit them from the rear. There was instant chaos. Galronus hauled on his reins and pulled off to one side, staying out of the combat. This was time for Roman style command, for he needed to be able to judge the capabilities of this mixed type of combat and he could not do so from within the melee.

Carefully selecting a place where he achieved an excellent view of the violent struggle, he peered into the mass. The first thing that struck him was that in any such future engagement, the mixed Caesarian force needed some sort of identifying mark. Almost every man on a horse was Gallic or Germanic, no matter what side he fought for. That was no issue for the riders, for they knew their tribes, their symbols, their marks, and could pick out who was friend and who was foe even amid the worst of the carnage. In fact, Galronus would be willing to wager that old feuds and hatreds were being played out now on the field of battle over and above the Roman cause.

The issue, though, was the infantry. They were legionaries, drawn from places that were predominantly Latin speaking, and all were citizens. They had been working alongside Galronus' Gauls and Germans for only a few days, yet to them there was no distinguishable difference between any of the riders. Consequently, though they were exhibiting no fear and were in among the horses attacking, they were lunging at Caesarian riders as often as Pompeian ones. The worst was avoided after the first few blows when the allies began to shout 'Caesar' repeatedly, allowing the infantry to better select their targets, but if he were to do this sort of thing again, Galronus would have them all tie some coloured scarf around their arm or suchlike.

Regardless of those setbacks they were doing well, and now that the legionaries were better able to choose a target, they were swiftly dealing with the Pompeian party. There would be an attempt at flight soon, for there was still an opening to the east, and many would be able to escape once they got out of the press. He would…

His train of thought screeched to a halt as his eyes fell on a figure amid the chaos, hammering down with his blade and bellowing curses in a Rhodanus-valley accent.

Egus and Raucillus.

In fact, he could see only Egus, but he felt certain the other chieftain would be there. The last time he had seen them was at that gate in the siege works at Dyrrachium as they rode for Pompey's lines, changing sides because they had been chastised by Caesar for their criminal activities. After only a moment, he also spotted Raucillus, tussling with a legionary. Even as the Remi's eyes narrowed dangerously, the treacherous Allobroge chieftain died, a pilum thrust upwards into his unprotected face. He shrieked and lurched back, though the legionary had jabbed with such strength that the pilum stayed lodged, dangling out of the dying man's face and pulling him forwards again with the weight. He disappeared from the saddle and Galronus knew without a doubt that he would never rise again.

He wanted nothing more than to ride into that mess and deal with Egus. To put down that other traitor would be a moment of supreme satisfaction. But he was not sure he could get to the man through the press, and over and above it all, a notion had struck him as he watched the confusion among the men fighting one another.

Should he?

Settling on a decision he sheathed his sword, pulled off his Remi torc and arm rings, tucked his pendant into his tunic and swept off the Roman style cavalry helmet he'd been wearing. Wishing he'd kept his beard longer – it had grown back out from stubble over the campaign – he gripped his hair with the fingers of both hands and rummaged, messing up and tangling the neat strands. At least he'd kept the traditional braids.

He detached the broach holding his cloak in place and let the thick wool garment fall, fastener included. He was almost done. One more thing. He rode to the edge of the combat, bearing neither sword in hand, nor clear sign of any tribe, and consequently he was largely ignored by everyone. He waited patiently until an Allobroge warrior nearby took a blow to the ribs and died, wailing, in the saddle. Then, as swiftly and subtly as he could manage, he closed on the dead man, whose horse was milling about uncertainly, and slipped the arm ring and the torc from him. Smiling weirdly, he pushed them both into place and then moved around the edge of the fight again, towards the east.

Now, disguise in place, he peered across the heads of the riders once more. It took him a moment to spot Egus. The man was moving his way, face lowered. As he watched, Galronus realised that the Allobroge was wounded. He was hunched forwards, clutching his side and trying to push for the edge to make it to freedom.

Galronus smiled an unpleasant smile and drew the dagger at his hip. He waited, horse stepping sideways impatiently, until Egus neared the edge of the mass. The chieftain had gone horribly pale. Almost certainly a death wound, then. He'd lost vast amounts of blood already in such a short time. Still, it would be good to help send him on his way to *Dubnos*, where his black spirit could writhe for eternity.

Galronus waited, trying to look inconspicuous.

Egus finally pushed his way clear of the crowd, not even casting a glance at the Remi, who walked his horse closer. As he came alongside the Allobroge chieftain, Galronus cleared his throat. Egus, pale and squinting, teeth gritted against the pain in his side, turned at the noise and frowned in incomprehension.

Slowly, like a pale sun dawning on an even paler sky, recognition flooded Egus' face.

'You!'

Galronus did not reply. He simply nodded even as his dagger jabbed out, burying itself in Egus' throat. The traitor's eyes widened in shock and he coughed, blood fountaining up out of the twin holes of mouth and neck.

Galronus just smiled, wiped his dagger on Egus' already soaked trousers, and then turned away, riding back to the mass.

'Pompey Magnus!' he bellowed as loud as he could. 'For Pompey and Rome. Retreat. To the camp.'

He was not their officer and none present among the enemy would know his voice, but it mattered not. All they had needed was a trigger, for they had been ready to break since the beginning. Moments later the Pompeian cavalry were disengaging, pulling away and racing east and then north, away from the river and towards the camp on the hill.

Galronus let a dozen or so pass, and then kicked his own horse and fell in with the fleeing riders. Many more died to derisive Roman pila before they could entirely disengage, and it was only once they had been riding twenty heartbeats that Galronus turned in the saddle and looked back over his shoulder.

The joint infantry and cavalry he had led were cheering and shouting foul and crude things after the fleeing horsemen. They had also, in the process of the fight, captured a good number of pack animals and cavalry steeds. The Remi noble smiled. They would celebrate well tonight, and probably together, Roman legionaries and Gallic and German riders drinking to their joint victory.

Not so: Galronus of the Remi.

* * *

Fronto watched as the horsemen approached. The infantry who had gone out with them on the attack had been forced to jog alongside when they left. Now, as they returned, the legionaries were mounted triumphantly on pack animals, swaying along in front of water barrels, or on captured cavalry horses, sitting amid the blood stains that remained mute evidence of a former owner.

The grinning unit gave the password of Venus Venetrix to the pickets before the gate and then swept on in to the camp. Fronto watched, initially elated, along with the cheering legionaries and the singing cavalry, but his worry and tension rose with each body that passed through the gate, for none of them were his friend.

As the last few men entered, including a Gallic nobleman Fronto vaguely recognised and was sure was an officer of some sort, the legate descended from the rampart top, his knee wobbling slightly with the speed and exertion.

'Where is Galronus?'

The nobleman, busy laughing at something with his companion, turned a surprised look on the legate. 'Sir?'

'Galronus. Remi nobleman. Commanded this force. Where is he?'

The man's frown deepened. In a thick Gallic accent loaded down with confusion, he pointed along the line. 'Somewhere here.'

'No,' Fronto said flatly. 'No he isn't. I watched you all return. He's not with you.'

Now the man began to look concerned. They stopped walking their horses and he had a brief exchange in his native tongue with the man beside him, who did rather too much shrugging for Fronto's liking. Finally, the nobleman turned back.

'It is very strange, Legate. He stayed at the edge. Did not fight. He was watching. Commanding. He was fine. We went through the fallen. Looted the enemy. Brought back our own. I know the commander was not among the dead.'

'Did they take captives?'

The man shook his head. 'They had no time. They ran home.'

Then where in Hades' name was Galronus?

'I am sure he will be here somewhere. He must be,' reiterated the nobleman, and then began to ride on once more, leaving Fronto standing worried and alone.

'Where are you, my friend?'

252

CHAPTER 19

The first half mile of the race across the plains to Pompey's camp was fine for the Remi horseman. Each rider was deeply in the grip of panic, and their commanders had both died in the melee, so there was little in the way of control. But after that half mile, once it was clear that the Caesarian force was not following, they had begun to slow. Galronus had tried to appear inconspicuous but had found himself, for a heart-stopping moment, riding between two men, both of whom who he remembered by sight as being part of that treacherous Allobroge breakout he had witnessed back at Dyrrachium. If *he* recognised *them* from the brief glimpses he'd had, then he, as a notable Caesarian cavalry commander they had seen most days, would be blindingly obvious.

He allowed himself to drop back towards the rear of the group where he recognised no one, and as covertly as possible rubbed his hands in the blood on his horse's flank – a vestige of Egus' spraying neck – which was already becoming sticky. He then reached up and rubbed it in places on his face and in his hair. Combined with the inevitable dust and horse sweat it stank and was filthy, but it would help hide his features from knowing eyes.

He knew this was about as dangerous as it got. Men caught spying in another camp were unlikely to receive any level of clemency, and possibly not even a clean death. Better to put things to the test here, where he might still be able to make a break for it and ride away, than in the camp. Swallowing his nerves, he slowly edged forwards until he was between those two men once more, and then waited until one of them turned towards him quite by chance. He then lifted his head and met the man's gaze before, with a calculated expression of defeat, lowering it again. When he peeked out to the side, the man had ignored him, facing ahead once more.

Good. If people who had reason to remember him were oblivious, then he was as safe as he could hope to be. They rode the remaining distance in silence, each man mulling over what had happened. Someone would have to take responsibility for the debacle and report it to the staff. At least it would not be Galronus.

The camp was well-constructed and took advantage of the land's contours. Initially, Galronus had wondered why Pompey made camp on the lower slope and not on one of the two high hills that flanked it. Arriving at the rampart, he now realised why: sheer size. Had Pompey camped atop one of those hills, his ramparts would have enclosed much of it and many of his men would have been billeted on a steep gradient.

It was strange to arrive at a Roman camp gate as an enemy, even if the defenders were not aware of that fact. The legions that occupied the camp were so similar to Caesar's, barring the insignia on their flags and shields – and even those were in the same colour, distinguishable only by design. The gate remained firmly closed as the column approached, and as the head horseman came close to the defences, he called out 'Hercules Invictus.'

The unconquered Hercules. Pompey clearly had as grand an opinion of himself as did Caesar. It was hard to suppress a smile as Galronus realised that he now had the password for Pompey's camp, which would be equally viable for pickets and scouts encountered out in the wild. That alone already made his dangerous mission worthwhile. So long as he managed to get home, that was.

With a start, he wondered how long he'd thought of Roman camps as home, and resolved to return to Durocorteron soon.

The gates swung open and the lead element of the tired and wounded column began to make their way in. A man in an officer's uniform with a tribune's narrow-striped tunic gestured at the lead man.

'Report to the headquarters straight away.' Then he raised his voice. 'The rest of you get back to quarters and clean yourselves up.' As Galronus passed, the man's nose wrinkled in distaste. 'Not you. You get to the valetudinarium and have a medicus look at that.' He gestured to Galronus' blood-smeared face. The Remi nodded meekly and continued onward. The man had mistaken the mess for a wound. That could be massively advantageous. The last thing Galronus wanted right now was to find himself in the cavalry quarters with the rest of the riders.

Though he had no idea where the medical section would have set up in the camp, he knew Roman thinking. Hygiene was of paramount importance. It would be at the edge of the camp somewhere, beside a slope that would carry away waste. And given that the nearest water source was the river, it would likely be this side of the camp. Consequently, not far from the gate, without a word to the other riders, he turned right into another alleyway between tents, heading down a gentle slope. He'd been right: at the end was a collection of huge tents which had to be the medical unit.

He had no intention of going there, of course, since he was unwounded. A score of paces down the alley he checked to make sure he was alone and slid from the saddle, leaving the beast entirely. The horse, tired and grateful to be left alone, simply stayed between the tents and began to munch on the grass.

Galronus hurried down the slope. While he had no intention of presenting himself at the hospital, he knew something of value lay there, and he needed to look less like a wounded Gallic cavalryman and more nondescript and invisible in a camp of thousands of legionaries.

It took only moments to find one of the huge water troughs behind the hospital complex. It was far from the cleanest water he'd ever seen, since it was used to dunk injured men to identify their wounds before admittance, and even though there had as yet been no battle, men on campaign acquired wounds and injury entirely by misfortune.

Ducking between two tents, he stripped down to his tunic and then lowered himself quietly into the cold water of the trough. It was the work of only moments to scrub off the worst of the muck. He worked quickly. The valetudinarium might be quiet in these pre-battle days, but sooner or later someone would come by.

Lifting himself back out, he kicked his stolen torc, arm rings, his own precious possessions and the rest of his clothing under a tent's outer edge, and in only a sodden tunic and boots, and carrying his sword belt, scurried off into the sea of tents. It was dusk now and men were busy preparing their evening meals. He hurried past two groups of soldiers who paid him no attention, and ducked into a shadowy area between tents, where he drew his dagger. With a sigh of regret, he ripped through his hair, taking it off at what he judged to be a hand width from the scalp. Away fell the sodden locks, braids and all. Then the beard, scraping it down to the chin.

In fifty heartbeats he was moving again. He paused at a washing line strung between two tents and stole a freshly laundered red legionary tunic. By the time he arrived at one of the main thoroughfares in the camp, he had the red tunic on and belted with his sword hanging to the side. It was a longer sword than the standard legionary issue, but with his camp-made Roman scabbard, it would be difficult to tell at first glance.

For the next half hour he strode around the central area of the camp, largely to test his disguise. He was badly shaven and his hair still long for a legionary, but they were on campaign, and men were generally scruffy at this stage anyway, and no one gave him a second glance. He came close to the command area with the headquarters tent, Pompey's own praetorian guard in evidence, each with a somewhat ostentatious leopard pelt atop their helm, in the manner of a standard bearer. He would not get close to the tent, clearly. He could almost hear the voices within, but to gain any clarity he would have to be close enough that the guard would take an interest in him. As he watched, a legionary appeared with a jar of wine and a tray of cups. The man was admitted swiftly, and Galronus took note. Dangerous, but possible.

Instead, he decided to tour the camp. For perhaps three hours he did so, ignored by every man he passed, whether legion or auxilia, soldier or officer. It was oddly liberating to be so invisible. By the time his stomach grumbled and his tired eyes told him it was time for sleep, he had gathered so much information it would be difficult to relate it all to the staff on his return.

He had taken note, of course, of legion numbers and standards, and wished he had one of the Roman wax tablets to record it in. He noted the various auxiliary units of native spearmen and slingers and archers, all of whom seemed to have come across the sea from the east. His interest fell naturally upon the cavalry, and their composition lodged more in his head. Galatians, Thracians, Syrians and Cappadocians, Some Germans who seemed somehow to have acquired eastern accents and deeply-tanned skin, Gauls in fewer numbers, Macedonians and various other smaller contingents. Interestingly, he noted that they did not seem to be quartered separately, but together as some homogenous whole. How had Pompey made that work, he wondered? If *he'd* tried to gather even Caesar's thousand riders together and make them work as one and not as their individual units, he was pretty sure it would fall apart swiftly.

As the evening truly closed in to night and the next watch sounded, Galronus began to form more of a plan. He would have to remain for the night, of course. And he would have to leave tomorrow. To stay too long was to tempt the fates. And he would have to be up as early as possible, for every hour in this camp would teach him things that could be of use.

Another hour of wandering, looking for likely places to hide out for the night, and he fortunately and gratefully happened upon a tent with a small cooking fire outside, a pot of some sort of stew bubbling up and a plate of bread, the owners temporarily absent. They would almost certainly be back any moment, so he hurriedly dipped half a dozen pieces of bread in the stew, tipped them onto a spare plate and ran off with them. It was neither the most filling, nor most exciting meal of his life, but it would stop the worst pangs of hunger and he devoured it with relish, hidden behind some other tent in the periphery.

He could do with more equipment. Perhaps a blanket or cloak, at least. Hurrying around the margins of the camp, he spotted a tent with sacks of grain stacked outside, legionaries busy ferrying it in for storage. Grinning, he hid himself and watched. It did not take long, and the eight men ambled off, rubbing sore muscles and complaining about officers who never had to dirty their hands or do a real day's work.

Once they were gone, he moved to a better vantage point. The granary tents had two guards, legionaries who sat huddled under cloaks in the dark, for no naked flames were allowed this close to the dangerously combustible grain. Ignoring them, he moved around the back of the tents. They were well put together but left little gaps, for it was important to keep grain dry, but also well ventilated. It took only three slashes of his dagger to slip through the leather flaps. Twenty heartbeats later he was nestled at the rear of the tent among relatively comfortable grain sacks. Fifty heartbeats later he was asleep.

* * *

It was, Galronus reasoned as he clambered back from blessed slumber, a good thing that he did not snore like Fronto, who sounded increasingly like a distressed ox as he grew older. He had passed the night unnoticed and it was only as the front of the tent was opened and exhausted-sounding voices cursed some tribune called Gaetulicus that he truly woke. With great care and slowness, he picked his way back to the torn flap at the rear of the tent, listening intently. It was pre-dawn, but these legionaries had been allocated the duty of disseminating the grain ration to the various unit representatives who would collect it to bake bread for their tent mates' breakfast.

Perhaps he was being overconfident, but Galronus actually grinned and chuckled to himself as he hurried away from the grain stores and paused to swipe a plate of cheese outside a tent. It was leftovers from the previous night and smelled like damp feet, but he ate it anyway and then stopped further along the same unit's tent lines. There had to be a line between daring and foolish, and he was fairly sure he was starting to walk along it, but the opportunity was too good to resist.

A legionary had been removing rust spots from his chain shirt and had paused, perhaps for a latrine break, leaving the tell-tale barrel of rough sand with the gleaming shirt inside.

Galronus simply could not help himself. Praying to Sucellos and to Jupiter, which came as something of a personal surprise, that the legionary would not return too swiftly, he removed the shirt from the barrel and shook the worst of the sand from it.

Then he ran. He did not stop until he was among the tents of another legion and, though he raised the odd eyebrow on his journey, legionaries running with a chain shirt were not *that* surprising. He cleaned the rest of the sand off in relative safety and then donned it over his red tunic. As the first golden streaks appeared over the mountains to the east, he found a group of legionaries at a water trough, washing and shaving. Finding a shiny bronze plaque there that was being used as a communal mirror, he began trying to tidy up his tufty hair. He had barely begun before a burly soldier with a tattoo of a Capricorn on his forearm interrupted.

'You're going to end up with a gouge in your head like that. Give me your knife.'

Heart pounding, aware of the potential danger, Galronus did as asked, saying 'thanks' in as Italian an accent as he could manage. It was perhaps testament to just how much he'd lost his regional tones that the legionary clearly accepted it. He sat patiently as the big man trimmed down his hair into a standard legionary cut. When he'd finished, the man ,dipped the knife in the water and passed it back.

'At least now you don't look like some sort of rodent.'

'Thank you, my friend,' Galronus smiled. He spent a moment tidying his shaven cheeks and chin, then left, hoping despite everything that the big legionary came out of the coming days intact and healthy. Sometimes it was uncomfortable to be reminded that the enemy were all too human.

He wandered on as the day began to dawn, and the moment that changed everything came quite by chance. He happened to have wandered back close to the headquarters in the half-light of dawn and passed what appeared to be a temporary wooden shack guarded by legionaries. He had picked up a small pile of dirty tunics outside a tent and was carrying them with purpose, for the first rule of being invisible is to be clearly involved in something menial and uninteresting. As he passed the wooden building, a voice emerged from the door that was at once totally unexpected and horribly familiar. He actually jumped a little, and the pile of tunics fell from his hands scattering across the grass.

'Pick 'em up, idiot,' grinned one of the guards, and Galronus did just that, slowly, carefully, keeping his face lowered as the owner of the voice emerged from the building. Labienus looked older than Galronus remembered. He was dressed only in an expensive tunic and boots, and with a towel around his neck, his hair wet. Another officer emerged who Galronus couldn't quite put a name to, though he remembered him from Rome upon a time. A senator, perhaps.

'I do not trust it,' the second officer said, rubbing his own hair with a towel as he walked. Galronus hurriedly grabbed up the rest of the laundry. Four soldiers followed the two officers, their personal guard, but Galronus took care to follow on, apparently on his own business, but close enough to hear.

'Pompey knows what he is doing,' Labienus replied. 'My only concern is how alike Caesar he can be. I worry that he will have some difficulty laying aside such power when the time comes.'

'Caesar is sharp,' the other man replied. 'He may have fewer cavalry...' *Oh? Cavalry? Galronus' ears pricked up.* '...but Caesar has a solid history of being prepared for the unexpected. Look how strong he is despite what happened at Dyrrachium.'

'We have six and a half thousand horse, Cato,' Labienus said impatiently. 'Caesar has at best a thousand. We will commit to the flank, and so will he. It is the way of things and he can do nothing else when he sees our formation. But through sheer numbers we will punch his horse aside and then fall upon the rear. It is far from foolproof, I will grant you, but it is a good, solid plan.'

'Caesar's army are clever. They are veterans.'

Labienus stopped suddenly, grasping at the other man's elbow. Galronus almost walked into them, and had to skirt around the edge and walk on.

'These are not the conquerors of Gaul, Cato,' Labienus hissed. 'Most of those veterans are either with us or have been retired or killed. This army is smaller, greener, hungrier and poorer than the great force we had in Gaul. Remember that you sat in the curia arguing, but I was there. I fought alongside *King* Caesar in Gaul and Belgica, and I've fought him in Illyricum. I know that of which I speak. They are not the same army. They can be beaten.'

Galronus was forced to keep walking. He was leaving them behind, but to stop would have aroused too much suspicion.

'You think you can command the cavalry?' Cato said uncertainly.

'I shall. You just need to persuade him to commit to a damn fight.'

The rest was lost. Galronus was out of earshot and moving. A flanking attack with vastly superior cavalry. Gods, but it was important for him to get back to Caesar now. Gaining the enemy's watch word was impressive. Identifying their units might be useful. But to know the tactics the enemy planned to use? That could change everything. And Labienus was entirely correct. Six thousand against one thousand was too much. Unless Caesar could pull off the impossible, Pompey's horse would flank the army and destroy them. Pompey's plan was good.

Only one flaw in it: Galronus of the Remi.

The problem that remained was how to return to his own camp. For some time, he wandered again, noting things of minor interest, all of which were largely lost against the enormity of what he'd learned. Leaving the camp with a water detail would be much more dangerous than arriving with a tired and wounded one. And shortly the entire army would move out onto the slopes and parade in front of Caesar's inferior force. Galronus could not go with them. He had no place in the lines and would likely end up unmasked. He contemplated losing himself among the scouts, but he was now attired as a legionary, and would have to change again, and very likely all the scouts knew one another.

Again, it was entirely chance that threw the opportunity into his lap. He passed the officers' quarters of one of the newer legions, where the senior centurion was busy bellowing at someone in his tent. Outside, by the door, lay a nondescript leather satchel. A capsa, of the sort used by field medics. And by couriers…

He snatched up the satchel, slinging it over his shoulder as he ran. Finding a horse was more troublesome, and he needed one as a courier. He found the corrals of cavalry beasts easily enough. It took careful planning from there, though. He waited near the gate of the corral as a small crowd of native scouts argued with the equisio in charge of the beasts. Their argument, in some eastern tongue, became gradually more heated, and the officer stormed off into his tent in a huff, waving at three horses being brought by a soldier. The scouts also waved at the beasts, though rather derisively, and then followed the man inside. Still shouting.

Galronus again threw up a prayer for good fortune in the next few moments. He almost directed it at Fronto's favourite Fortuna, but decided that he was all too readily letting go of his heritage, and instead implored sacred Epona, the lady of the horses, for her aid. Taking a deep breath, and aware that the argument raging in the tent was the only thing distracting them and buying him time, he helpfully opened the gate for the soldier, who thanked him and walked all three horses out. Galronus dutifully closed the gate and then reached out, grasping the reins of one of the three horses.

'Sorry?' demanded the legionary in confusion.

'Time's important,' Galronus grunted, trying to force his voice into an Italian accent again. 'General Libo needs these orders.' He tapped the satchel for emphasis. The legionary looked all too uncertain, his nervous gaze darting to the tent where the argument was still in full swing.

'I don't…'

'If there is a problem,' Galronus said wearily, 'tell your commander to speak to mine. Centurion Gobinius Adrastus.'

The legionary still looked unconvinced, yet he did not resist as Galronus plucked the reins from the man's hands and nodded his thanks, walking the beast away. As soon as he was out of sight, Galronus mounted swiftly and rode the horse via a complex route towards the north, an area of the camp he had scouted last night where there was less activity that the south and east, which faced Caesar and the river.

As he moved out into the main Via Praetoria, he could see the north gate. As he'd hoped, it was already open despite dawn still being little more than an indigo glow. Wagons and beasts were already arriving, part of Pompey's excellent supply system. Praying he managed this last stage safely, Galronus trotted his horse past the wagons and to the gate, where four legionaries peered at him in a bored manner as they checked the arriving carts one by one for anything untoward, surreptitiously syphoning off bits and pieces they could personally consume or sell.

Adopting a similar sense of ennui, Galronus reined in.

'Where are you bound?'

'North,' he replied calmly. 'Then east, to Byzantium.'

'Long ride.'

'With a lot of mansios and wine on the way,' winked Galronus.

The soldier gave him the bitter look of a man condemned to battle while Galronus rode to safety. 'Password?'

'Hercules Invictus,' Galronus said confidently.

The soldier nodded and waved on the lucky courier.

Galronus did not dare look back until he was away from the hill and on the flat ground. Nothing untoward was happening back in the camp. He had seemingly got away with it. He resisted the urge to laugh maniacally, and bent over the horse, riding around the northern edge of the next, higher hill. There he would meet the main Larissa road, and could turn south for home.

Two miles distant, he found a picket post by the side of the local road he travelled, though they let him pass without trouble when he gave the password. A second encounter with a small group of scouts was similarly easy and uneventful, and it was with vast relief that the Remi noble turned the edge of the hill and laid eyes upon the distant dark mass of Caesars camp.

It was full morning light when he finally approached the pickets outside the camp. The sun hung pensively over the eastern horizon.

'Password?' muttered the pickets suspiciously.

'Hercules Invictus,' Galronus said confidently, then laughed out loud at the men's expression. 'Oh, yes. Wrong one. Venus Venetrix.'

Still with narrow, suspicious eyes the pickets let him pass, though one of them escorted him to the camp gate, where he this time gave the correct password easily.

'Name and unit?' the centurion above the gate said carefully, even as the gates began to creak.

'Galronus of the Remi, Praepositus in charge of allied cavalry under Prefect Volusenus.'

There was a brief, urgent confab, and the centurion leaned over the gate as the locking bar was removed inside. 'Galronus? Thank the gods. Legate Fronto has been giving us all earache for the best part of a day.'

* * *

'Before you say anything…'

Fronto turned at the voice, his face drawn and pale with worry. 'You mad, dangerous, stupid shitbag.'

'I said *before* you say anything…' Fronto took three paces and threw his arms around the Remi, who had the grace to look a little embarrassed at the episode. 'Marcus, I'm sure you were worried but we're both grown men, officers and warriors.'

'I know that, you arsehole, and I've buried more friends than I care to remember, but you do not get to do that. Ever. You don't vanish without word, and you don't go off doing what I think you've been doing where I think you've been doing it.'

'Men like Atenos…' tried the Remi, but was mercilessly ridden down.

'No. You don't get to compare like that. It's not the same. You are betrothed to my *sister*.'

'And here was me thinking *you* were worried.'

Fronto's expression slid more from worried to angry. 'Don't be bloody facetious. You know I was worried. But I've already lost Verginius on campaign. It took her decades to get over that. Can you imagine what she'd be like if I let you die? She'd never recover.'

Galronus nodded. 'I recognise that it was perhaps selfish, Marcus. But the simple fact was that I saw an opportunity that may never have arisen again, and I had to go for it if we were to have any hope of getting through this.'

Fronto simmered for a while, fists still clenched, then nodded reluctantly. 'In truth, I would probably have done the same. You went with the survivors back to Pompey's camp?'

Galronus nodded. 'I have learned things, Marcus. Things that can help us turn the tide.'

A hundred heartbeats later they were in the headquarters and the majority of the staff were there, called in for an emergency evening briefing. Caesar welcomed them all, and then opened the floor to Galronus, who cleared his throat and looked pensively around his audience. He had never addressed such a meeting before. He was no Roman orator. And his dirty, crude look as an overly-hairy legionary did little to boost his appearance. Yet the moment he began, relating his combat first and how well the men had done, what needed to be looked at and what went well, he realised he was fine and his audience was rapt.

He went on to tell them of his sneaking into the enemy camp, his intelligence gathering on units and nationalities, his tense night, the password, which could be important, and finally the conversation he had overheard between Labienus and Cato. Fronto and Caesar shared a look with Marcus Antonius over the mention of their old political rival in Rome. Finally, he described his escape and flight.

A long, heavy silence followed, during which Caesar and Antonius seemingly managed a huge conversation with only their eyes. Finally, the general nodded and broke the silence, straightening.

'Pompey has a good plan as to how to break us. It will take cunning and subtlety to counter that plan without giving it away too early. I believe I have an idea how to achieve that, but it will take excellent tactical skills, experience and timing, and I will require the very best from the best of my officers. However, in order to test their plan and any counter-plan I develop, we still need to bring Pompey down from that hill. Ideas, gentlemen?'

Salvius Cursor rose. 'In Hispania, we had a similar reluctance from Petreius and Afranius, but the moment we moved to take a critical position, they committed in response.'

'Quite so,' Caesar replied, 'but we have no such position to take this time. We might consider cutting off access to the river but there are streams to the north. They are smaller than the river and further afield, but they would keep him fed. No, I do not think we can trust to making a move and pushing him into it. It must be something else. Something that even the most recalcitrant senator with a voice in the staff might fall for.'

A smile spread slowly across Fronto's face.

'I might have an idea.'

'Go on?'

'When,' Fronto said quietly, 'is the only time Pompey has committed instantly and without consultation?'

There was a mutter of uncertainty in the tent. 'He hasn't,' Antonius said finally. 'He hovered in the east when we arrived. He camped across the river and wouldn't commit. He pushed the siege lines only when it suited him, and then he dallied in the north while he combined with Scipio and set up adequate supply lines.'

'You have such a small memory for failure,' Fronto chuckled.

'What?'

'The only time Pompey has ever committed in an instant in a reaction was when we left Dyrrachium. You didn't see because you were far ahead. Sulla probably didn't see because he decided very helpfully to announce our departure with a fanfare and then legged it and left the Tenth to catch up.'

The equine face of Sulla turned an unpleasant look on him, but Fronto ignored him. 'The moment Pompey realised we were running and he was in danger of missing the chance to catch us and stab us in the back, he ran like a pox-ridden peasant to the nearest latrine. Sent his cavalry to catch us, with his army heartbeats behind. And he kept trying to stop us right up to the moment we outstretched his supply lines.'

Caesar nodded. 'When we decamped, then.'

'Yes. Perhaps if he thinks he will lose you again and you are heading south to join up with Calenus he might feel compelled to try and stop you?'

Caesar nodded again, with a smile. 'It would have to be sudden enough to make him panic. And it would have to be very swift. And he would have to already be comfortably lodged in a sense of security.'

Sulla, still glaring at Fronto, put out his hand. 'Overnight, level the defences. Use the ramparts to fill in the ditch. That way, when we make our move, we will be able to do so a full cohort at a time, and not be restricted by the gate.'

'Good,' Caesar smiled.

Brutus rose. 'He needs to be as settled into this stalemate as possible, so that he has stopped thinking of alternatives. Stay for several more days and keep presenting for battle as though nothing has changed.'

Again Caesar nodded. 'Good, because that will give me adequate time to put the finishing touches to my idea and run it by you all.' He straightened. 'Congratulations, gentlemen, and you have my thanks, not least Senator Galronus here, whose quick wits and bravery have won us the information with which we shall win the war.'

He folded his arms. 'Well done everyone. After a distressing six days of uncertainty and worry, I believe for the first time that we have the makings of a plan to come out of this in victory. No matter Pompey's odds, we shall beat him, for grey matter beats iron any day.'

And yet blood-red beats all, thought Fronto.

CHAPTER 20

Fronto stood at the north-west corner of the camp on the remaining full true stretch of rampart, straining to see into the distance. There *was* movement on the hill, but it was so difficult to tell what precisely was happening this far away. The scouts were still in position, as close as they dare come to Pompey's lines, but they themselves were not visible from this distance either. He glanced over his shoulder.

The army was almost ready. The striking of the camp had been carried out as slowly and obviously as possible. In order to make it most visible to enemy eyes they had not begun work until dawn began to streak the sky with gold. As soon as any hidden Pompeian watchers could identify what was happening, a couple of cohorts of auxiliaries left the camp with the baggage train and began to move across the bridge, heading along the road south as if making for Athens. Once they were clearly on the move, as the light level gradually rose, the legions began to take down their tents and stow them, gathering their full kit and arming up. Conveniently, apart from their furca pole that bore all the marching and living kit, their gear for the march was more or less the same as their gear for war.

Now, all the tents were down and the legions beginning to mass in their ranks, ready to depart. In fact, the leading elements of the Eighth were even now filtering through the east gate and making for the road, forming up there. It would take precious time for any sizeable army to issue from the camp, of course, even using all the gates. And that was why they had utilised the hours of darkness in filling in the ditch to the south and east and flattening the rampart a little. The palisade remained in place, though the ropes that kept the posts tightly bound together had been removed and their bases, where they were driven into the ground, loosened. All was as ready as could be.

Of course, Fronto had continued to espouse his belief that Pompey undoubtedly had eyes and ears in the camp, and that nothing done here was safe to assume a secret. But all that could be done to maintain security had been done. There were no unescorted visits to the river, and all patrols and posts were doubled in manpower and drawn from multiple units. The chances of anyone leaving Caesar's camp and carrying word to Pompey had been drastically reduced. Fronto was still convinced that there would be enemy agents in the camp, but they would be impotent to do anything with the information they had, unable to leave. This was as good as it was going to get.

Fronto's eyes raked the enemy hill. Definite movement, and not just ordinary camp life. Pompey's army was moving. They were starting to emerge from the gates, but as yet that could mean nothing more than that they were performing their usual daily deployment on the hillside facing Caesar, as they had done each day since both armies had made camp on the plain of Pharsalus. Fronto realised he was holding his breath with the tension and forced himself to relax.

He watched for some time as the enemy cohorts settled into their lines before Pompey's camp, willing them to do something more. Every now and then he would glance over his shoulder and see the legions of Caesar exiting the camp and forming up by the road. Was Pompey calling their bluff? Surely the old bastard wouldn't let them just leave? He couldn't afford to do that. There would be dissenting voices in his council calling for combat, surely? But if the enemy didn't move soon, Caesar would have to make the decision whether to keep moving for real or return to camp and settle in while searching for a new gambit.

Pompey's legions formed up on the slope as per usual, and Fronto chewed on his lip.

'Come on you bastard.'

'He will,' said a quiet voice next to him.

Fronto turned to see Galronus join him and lean on the fence. 'What makes you so sure?'

'His deployment. He lines them up the same every day, but today it's different.'

Fronto squinted. 'I know my eyesight's not that good, but surely even *you* can't see insignia from here?'

The Remi laughed. 'Hardly, but look to the cavalry. Thus far each day he has had the cavalry split into two wings flanking the infantry on both sides on the lower ground. This morning they're concentrated to the north, on his left flank. Today he's lined the army up with his horse ready to make a concerted push, and on the side of his forces where they will not get trapped against the river. He's ready for battle this time.'

'That's fairly thin evidence,' Fronto said, though he could certainly see the logic of it. 'I believe you're right, but we can't do anything until he moves and we know he's committing.'

And that was the meat of the problem. The moment the Caesarian army turned and made it clear they were ready for battle and not, in fact, on the run, Pompey might realise he had been tricked into committing. At that point it would come down to a decision among their commanders. If Pompey's side won, they could pull back to their camp. If not, they would fight anyway. But if they actually marched forth and made it perhaps a quarter of the way across the flat plain towards this place before it became clear that Caesar's army was ready for them it would be too late. They would have to commit, for if they turned to retreat, Caesar's forces would simply harry them as they ran, and the enemy would be battered into submission.

'Best get to your cavalry, then,' Fronto murmured.

'And you to your cohorts,' replied Galronus.

Still, Fronto stood at the rampart, watching. Tense. The enemy were on the lower slope. Were they beginning to move? It was so damned hard to tell when they looked like a sea of ants on the brown-green slopes. His breath caught in his throat. There *was* movement, but it came elsewhere. His peripheral vision had picked up riders. Horsemen racing alone or in small groups for the Caesarian lines. The scouts and pickets were coming back, and they were coming at speed. That could mean only one thing.

The tension suddenly spilling over into excitement, his eyes climbed from those racing figures back up to the hill. They *were* moving. They were *definitely* moving now. This was no daily show of strength, but a commitment to battle. Pompey was coming at last.

Fronto had to shove aside a minor doubt over the fact that the force flooding down that slope was perhaps twice the size of their own. This fight would not be won on numbers alone. This was about outthinking Pompey and using his own tactics against him. Caesar had a plan. They just had to hope it would be enough.

'Come on,' Galronus said, and was suddenly moving. Even before Fronto turned and strode off after him the calls went up across the legions. Battle was about to be joined. Fronto's men were at the rear of the army, the last to leave the camp, and it took him but moments to reach them. Six cohorts, numbering some two thousand men between them, drawn from every legion present. A second reserve. Caesar's hidden knife in the back-alley fight to come.

To some extent, Fronto regretted that he would not be in direct command of the Tenth in this, which promised to be the final battle, and the one that would see Caesar or Pompey total master of Rome. The honour of leading the Tenth would fall to Salvius Cursor, though Caesar himself would be stationed with his favoured legion, too, so at least hopefully the general's presence would curb his tribune's most dangerous instincts. Salvius, then and not Fronto, who would have a specific role to play and, if everything went according to plan, a critical one, too.

Galronus paused as they reached the reserve command, and grasped Fronto's hand. 'Be safe,' he said, then 'and be lucky.'

'You too. See you on the field.'

He watched the Remi nobleman race off and leap up onto his horse as though born in the saddle. There was no better man to lead Caesar's cavalry in the coming conflict. Volusenus was with him, too, along with Quadratus, each leading one component of the horse, but it would be Galronus who held the disparate groups of Germanic and Gallic horse together and gave the critical commands. And then there was that force of infantry

Counting off in his head, Fronto decided that the time had come. By now Pompey's army had to be at, or close to, the point of no return. Now they would be committed whatever the situation, and even the dissenters in his command could no longer turn around. Battle was inevitable.

Another signal was given, and the already feeble palisade was pushed flat, a simple job since their bases had been loosened and the ropes removed. In heartbeats, what had been a solid set of ramparts became little more than a hummock around two entire sides of the camp circuit.

Whistles blew and standards dipped, and Caesar's army flooded out of the camp en-masse and with a swiftness that could not help but take the enemy by surprise. Crossing the ramparts and thundering over the fallen timbers and across the in-filled ditch, they raced at their centurions' commands around the fort lines to the northwest, just beyond where Fronto had recently stood watching, and there fell into their lines. Fronto's unit was the last to move, and he could imagine the consternation and arguments that would now be going on among the Pompeian officers. The more nervous or cautious among them would be shouting that Caesar had tricked them and demanding a return to the camp. Others would be worrying that they had committed to something they were not adequately prepared for but gritting their teeth and readying themselves. Whether they wished to press forwards or run back, there were two facts that would be inescapable for every mind among that force, officers and men.

That they had not the time to retreat or to change their deployment. And that Caesar was not fleeing along the road to the south, where they could catch him from behind and cut his army into manageable chunks to deal with. Instead, Caesar was entirely prepared for them and his army was out and moving rather than being restricted in emerging from the camp.

Fronto's cohorts moved out, bearing no flags and no standards, the only concession to the usual system of command and operations a single musician with a buccina who stayed close to Fronto. He had only three calls memorised, as did each man in the reserve line, for they had to react only to their own commands and not those of any other unit in the lines.

They crossed the low rampart with ease to the northeast, then raced as fast as they could around the edge, preparing to fall in at their allotted position. Being the last to emerge, the bulk of Caesar's army was already settling into position. At the rear as he was, Fronto could not see the enemy, but he could see the deployment of their own forces in the traditional *triplex acies* formation.

On the left, at the southern edge of the huge army lay a small force of auxiliary archers, slingers and spearmen, guarding the flank and bound on their left by the river. Beside them, the somewhat depleted Eighth and Ninth legions had been combined to form one solid, strong legion of veterans, and they, the auxilia and the powerful Seventh came under the command of Marcus Antonius, his main duty to press the attack on the left and deny Pompey any hope of collapsing that flank.

At the centre of the formation Calvinus had overall command, with the Sixth, Fourteenth and more recently raised Twenty Seventh. This would be the heart of the press, where traditionally the worst of the fighting would occur, and despite having one of the youngest legions there, he could claim the most intact legions with full manpower. An army usually collapsed when a flank gave, but the centre was always critical. If the centre fell, the army would be broken up into smaller pieces, easier to destroy. Calvinus had to hold, and he had to press the enemy hard.

On the right flank, the Tenth, Eleventh and Twelfth were commanded by Caesar himself, with his point of command at the rear of the Tenth. Three of the best legions ever to fall under Caesar's command. Three of the best legions in Rome's history entirely, in fact. Units that had fought the Belgae, had been at the Sabis, at Aduatuca, at Gergovia and Alesia, at Uxellodunum and Ilerda. Veterans and heroes all.

Pompey's army should quail at the very sight of them.

Nine legions of veteran killers, flanked to the left by strong auxiliaries and the uncrossable river. Each legion was split up into three lines, the first two of which would press into the attack, while the third line would remain in position at the rear, ready to react to any failing along the front. A traditional formation and one that without doubt Pompey would be following. Fronto's heart skipped a beat as he realised how widely spaced the legions were, not in the traditional tight order. The sheer difference in numbers between the two armies had forced Caesar to space his men adequately to match Pompey's line, which would present a front almost two miles across.

Then there was the right. Not the right flank of the infantry, but the counter to Pompey's cavalry. Sweeping down from that hill, on the north side of Pompey's vast force was a unit of horse some six thousand strong. And Galronus' thousand cavalry sat at the Caesarian periphery, ready to meet them in dreadful six to one odds.

Heart racing at the knowledge that on parchment this battle was almost certainly Pompey's victory and that only Galronus' intelligence, Caesar's plan and the reactive ability of his officers could hope to carry the day, Fronto fell into his allotted position at the rear. Each commander would feel the pressure weighing down on their shoulders today, though the heaviest weights would definitely be on Galronus and Fronto.

Horns blew, followed by a shrill chorus of whistles, and the army of Caesar began to march northeast, parallel to the river, to meet the forces of Pompey. As Fronto's musician blew the call to advance and his cohorts marched off behind the army, Fronto reached into his scarf and produced the twin figures of Nemesis and Fortuna that hung around his neck. Nemesis, the Goddess of Vengeance. Her favour would allow Fronto all sorts of opportunities today, for among that enemy force were Pompey himself, Labienus, who had betrayed his oath and gone over to the enemy, and Ahenobarbus, that bastard who had commanded Massilia and escaped justice aboard the last ship to leave when the city fell. *Lady of Vengeance let me have at least one of them*, he thought as he kissed the figurine. And then there was Fortuna, whose favour would be very much sought throughout the army today – *both* armies – but whose presence would in particular be make or break for the right flank. He kissed Fortuna, and then tucked the figurines back into his tunic. Finally, as he fell into the easy pace of the march, he drew his sword.

Across the lines the legions of Caesar began to chant and to slam their blades against the edges of their shields in time with their stomping feet, a rhythm to break the confidence of the finest of enemies. Not Fronto and his reserve, though. They marched in silence. They had a job to do.

* * *

Lucius Salvius Cursor twitched. He had been a tribune both junior and senior. He had led cohorts in battle and fought under Fronto for whom, despite his early misgivings, he had attained a grudging respect. And now in the role of *praepositus* in command of the Tenth, he was finally beginning to *understand* Fronto. How a man of action, who lived for the weight of the sword in his hand

and that headstrong rush that only came with facing an enemy blade to blade, could survive standing at the rear, nominally directing things and taking no direct part, he could not understand. That, he saw, was why Fronto was always where he shouldn't be, in the thick of it. And probably why he was so perpetually grumpy and miserable. Salvius would be at the front too, but unfortunately Caesar had chosen this legion for his command, and he sat astride his white horse in his scarlet general's cloak but twenty paces behind Salvius. How could he find a way to actually fight without earning Caesar's anger?

But he *would* find a way. The last moment information the scouts had delivered to Caesar, which was even now being disseminated among the officers, had located the senior generals among the enemy force. Afranius, with Petreus beside him like a hound, commanded the enemy's right flank, down towards the river and facing Antonius. The centre, who would meet Calvinus in the brutal melee, was commanded by Scipio, who had proven himself a vicious and capable general. The cavalry, a huge and critical force on the left edge of the field was under Labienus, who deserved to die a thousand traitor's deaths, may the gods favour Galronus' sword to find his heart. But the left flank of the enemy infantry, directly facing Salvius' men, while it lay under the control of Ahenobarbus, was the direct command position of Pompey. The two great figures of the republic faced each other directly.

And Salvius would find a way to get to the front once the fighting started. He would carve a path through the enemy First and Third legions, alone if necessary, to plant his blade in Pompey's heart. And when he had done just that, he would take the blade he'd used and he would wrap it in linen and place it in the vault with the funerary urn of his father. Damn Pompey's black heart but Salvius would skewer it this day, Caesar or no Caesar.

Despite the dry ground, this land had been farmed and irrigated periodically, and consequently at least they were free of the worst of the cloying dust cloud so often kicked up by a legion's marching feet. This meant that from horseback – tribunes were expected to be mounted, let alone legionary commanders – Salvius could see the enemy lines.

It struck him suddenly that there was no dust at all around the enemy. Despite the relatively small cloud building beneath the Tenth's feet, there was still a faint haze of grey in the air. There was no such cloud around Pompey's army.

He turned to Caesar.

'The enemy have stopped marching, General.'

Caesar frowned, and squinted into the morning light. 'So they have. Standing still and waiting for us. Interesting.'

'They will lose all the rush and momentum,' Salvius said in bafflement. He knew, as did any veteran commander of infantry, how much of any conflict was won by the attitude of the men. A unit that charged into the fight with a roar and smashed into the enemy shields built up a certain spirit in the blood that gave them an edge without which any fight was much, much harder. To stand still meant they lost that build-up of vim and, worse still, it gave the men far too much time to think, and thinking when there's a man running at you with a sword and screaming generally leads to panic.

Caesar seemed to be weighing up the revelation, then he pursed his lips and nodded. 'I think I understand him.'

'General?'

'Pompey seriously outnumbers us, but many of his soldiers are green and untested. He will undoubtedly have bolstered their numbers with his precious few veterans, but he perhaps does not feel he can rely on their mettle if they charge. He is keeping them tight and ready, their spirits lifted by the veterans and the knowledge that they outnumber us. It is not what I would do, but I understand the logic. We shall take this opportunity to slam into them with a charge and break that fragile morale.'

'Do you think we can win through here, General? The Tenth, I mean.'

'I doubt it,' Caesar replied quietly. 'But then here is not where the battle will be won or lost. That honour-and-curse lies with the cavalry. We must simply hold and not break.'

But Salvius Cursor thought otherwise. If they did not break Pompey's legion on this flank, then the old bile-sack would escape Salvius' vengeance, and that could not be permitted. Regardless of how critical the cavalry were to the plan, Salvius would break Pompey's left flank and he would kill the general personally.

* * *

Galronus glanced left and right. He commanded the heart of the Caesarian cavalry, but he had given over the left to Volusenus and the right to Quadratus, and each knew precisely what to do, each leading their men from the front, just as Galronus was. They had to make things look good, but they had to actually fight and do damage. They needed to kill as many of Pompey's horse as they could before their position became untenable. And to that end, he had devolved command so that each man led an ala of three hundred and some, and each of *them* had allowed free command to the regional tribal commanders of the units within that ala. Each man was fighting for his own leader and each of those leaders for a prefect, and each of those prefects for Galronus. He would be the one to give the critical signals, but until the signal was given, it would be down to each man to do what he could.

A glance across the field of battle showed Pompey's infantry lined up from here right the way to the river bank, two miles away. A vast array of men. A truly breathtaking force to behold. And since there was no sign of the cavalry on the flank, Galronus might have doubted his own information had it not been for two things. He could see the cloud of dust behind the enemy, whence the cavalry were coming, and the scouts had already noted their approach and the identity of the man who led them.

That was one thing Galronus did not relish: the possibility of meeting Labienus face to face. The man had once been a friend and ally of Fronto and Caesar, and Galronus had liked him. He had been one of the few of Caesar's officers who showed the remotest consideration for the Gallic and Belgic peoples who were suffering throughout the general's wars. And because of all that, Galronus had no desire to rob him of life. He doubted that either Fronto or Caesar, or indeed anyone in the Caesarian rank at all, would relish that opportunity.

Still, they would be lucky to achieve even holding the enemy horse for a hundred heartbeats, let alone scattering them and attacking their commander. He scolded himself. Concentrate on the matter at hand: kill as many of Pompey's horse as you can, and give the signal the moment it looks as though you're doomed.

There they came. Finally, the enemy cavalry rounded the legions' flank and burst out into the open on the northern edge of the field. Gods, but there were a lot of them. In fairness this must have been what it was like back in Gaul or Hispania when enemies had looked on Galronus or Varus' approaching cavalry. It gave him a new insight into fear, for certain.

He could see the makeup of the enemy cavalry now. All the colours and shapes and compositions, from white-skirted Illyrians with crested helmets to cloaked and trousered Galatians with long, ribbed shields, to Syrians in fish-scale shirts of bronze and light spears, to Cappadocians with their high conical helmets, and so many others. All pushed together to fight like some homogenous collection. Conversely, Galronus' men were almost entirely Gallic, Belgic or Germanic, and those few regular Romans among them had been working alongside the former for the best part of a decade now. A command given in either Latin or Gaulish was comprehensible to all, and they invoked the same gods on the whole. Moreover their weapons, armour and fighting techniques were more or less the same even at home, let alone serving together for Rome. They fought as individual units but were naturally perfectly able to work together. It would be fascinating to see, even in the midst of the fight, what Pompey's strange cavalry were capable of. Were they even able to work together? It would be testament to Labienus' control if they did.

* * *

Fronto tromped along, his two thousand strong unit of veterans drawn from nine legions keeping pace in open order. Each man left a full two arm-lengths between himself and the man beside him, and each of the five lines kept two arm-lengths from the line in front. It was the most open formation Fronto had ever adopted for a fight. And this would be a *real* fight. He turned and looked at the men along the front line beside him.

Each man had been selected on four criteria, carefully and over days in the camp. The result was that each man in this entire unit was a veteran of at least five years in Caesar's legions. That meant that they had fought through Alesia and beyond at the very least, which proved their strength, tenacity and skill and bravery. Each

277

man had also shown skill with a spear. Not the throwing of a pilum, but at using it in the manner of a spear. There had been plenty of opportunity to practice such things in sieges over the years and each one had talent with the fighting style. Thirdly, each man had no fear of horses and was willing to face them. Again, these were men such as those who had formed the defence on the hill near Ilerda, facing Afranius' horse. One of the centuries was that very same century that Fronto had found fighting for their lives near Lissus when he was looking for Antonius and the ships in the spring. Finally, each man had shown himself to be capable of acting on his own without the need for commands when the shit came flooding in. In fact, many of the force were those same men who had practiced among the cavalry with Galronus and had fought at the river skirmish. Such were Fronto's men: the best of the best.

As well as moving in such open order, they were very specifically armed. Each man wore his chain shirt and helmet, and each man had his sword and dagger belted at his middle, but each had been relieved of his shield and instead given a *dory* spear taken from the auxiliaries' supply carts. A seven or eight foot length of ash with a flat, leaf-shaped blade at the tip and an iron spike at the butt end. A Greek weapon of antiquity, but one that had helped unite the east and conquer Persia, so one with a history and a reputation for efficiency.

Fronto swallowed.

No pressure. Just the hinge on which the battle, and all their futures, swung.

Ahead all he could see was the back ends of horses: Galronus' cavalry moving at a walk. Horse sweat, horse shit, hairs of a dozen colours swirling in their wake and the most dust to be found on the battlefield, for while the legions were not stirring the well-irrigated land too much, the horses were a different matter. All Fronto could see was horse. Somewhere beyond them, of course, on the far side of the field, were yet more horses. *Lots* more horses. But from this position behind the cavalry he could see nothing of them. The first he would know of his time in the fight would be Galronus' signal. His glance left told him all he needed to know. He could see Caesar with the other staff, following the Tenth Legion close by, and the general's signaller had gathered up his purple flag and was making ready.

It was starting. That flag was the signal to begin it all. As soon as Caesar gave his signal, the legions across the two mile front would break into pace and a half, and then at a signal from the centurions, they would stop and cast their pila. Then they'd move once more, into double time, and then into the enemy like a runaway cart on a steep hill.

And when that signal was given, the archers and slingers at the far flank near the river would run until the first pilum cast, then settle into position and loose their deadly hail, the spear men and auxiliary infantry protecting them from the enemy.

And when that signal was given, Galronus and his horse would meet an unstoppable force in the form of Labienus and his six thousand cavalry. They would have to hold for as long as they could to make this work. The traitor had to think it was working. He had to believe he was breaking Caesar's cavalry and closing the door to flank the Tenth.

Good luck to you, Galronus.

Off to the left, the purple flag rose, and then fell.

The battle had begun.

CHAPTER 21

Salvius Cursor peered across the open ground to the Pompeian forces awaiting them. They still were not moving. Whatever Caesar might say, Salvius could not countenance the very notion of standing still and waiting for the enemy to run into you. He did note, peering back over the ranks of enemy heads, since there was no haze of dust hanging over them to obscure the rear, that Pompey had made another adjustment to the traditional deployment. Rather than keeping the third rank of the legions as a reserve as Caesar, and all the great Roman commanders through history, had done, Pompey had committed them to the solid block of waiting men. Perhaps he believed that the increased strength in the battle lines would counterbalance the lack of momentum? Salvius doubted it.

No, the man's tactics were all wrong, and whatever Caesar said about understanding the decision, a single look at the general's expression revealed a level of derision and disagreement with it. Caesar was no more a fan of the plan than was Salvius.

A coughing noise drew his attention and he looked across to see one of the men almost bent double as he marched, hacking up dust. His forehead was lathered with sweat and he was panting. So were the others. The men of the legion were tiring of marching across the dry ground under the already hot morning sun in full kit. An idea occurred to him, and one that might have useful aspects. He turned to the general.

'Sir, might we not take the opportunity for a pause to rest the men? The enemy are not coming for us, after all?'

Caesar frowned, but his eyes raked the legions and slowly he nodded. The enemy cavalry had not yet put in an appearance, though the cloud of their passage was visible behind the enemy legions on their flank, and they were racing into the fray.

'A count of thirty,' the general said, and turned to his musician. 'Give the order.'

Salvius nodded. Blaring horns and shrill whistles rang out along the lines and the men came to a halt, lowering their shields for a moment and breathing deeply as their officers told them to catch their breath. They would have to move again straight away or the cavalry would engage early and everything could go wrong, but that count of thirty would make the difference between a row of tired, sweating men charging and a line of vigorous, enthused ones. Another failure of Pompey's strategy.

Caesar was busy monitoring things among the enemy and, grasping the only opportunity he was likely to get, Salvius took the chance to slip forwards through the ranks. Caesar would disapprove and no doubt make his feelings clear later, but Fronto had survived decades of doing things like that, so why not Salvius Cursor?

He threaded his way between legionaries, a journey made easier by the open formation they'd had to adopt in order to stretch the army to meet the length of Pompey's line. Salvius counted off the heartbeats as he moved. In thirty they would be advancing again. By twenty he had reached the front rankers, and he settled in four lines back from the front line, not for safety or any sort of propriety, but for purely practical reasons. The front two ranks carried pila and would pause to throw them, and if Salvius was among them not only might he get in the way but, crucially, he would take the place of a man who otherwise would be throwing a pilum into the enemy. No, better to be in line four, where he could get to the action, but not get in the way of the initial attacks.

Two centurions stood in the front row, one on either side of him and perhaps ten men away along the line. He recognised Atenos to the left and nodded his approval. The big Gaul led from the front like all centurions, but Atenos was more than a simple officer. He was a warrior born, and the sheer power of the man seemed to radiate and affect those close to him. He was like a human standard on the battlefield. Plus, he was seemingly immortal. In the past two years Salvius had seen him take so many wounds, but all were minor and had not even slowed the man down. The other centurion was a man named Crastinus, who had been rousing the men in the camp before they left, geeing them up for the fight. Another veteran and another good man. Hopefully with men of their calibre in the front, and the veterans of the Tenth, too, they could surpass

Caesar's expectations and carve their way through the enemy legions like a hot knife in butter, clearing the way to Pompey himself.

The signal was given, dragging him from his hopeful reveries. The legions gathered up their shields once more, and at the next whistle began to march forwards, determined.

'Pace and a half,' bellowed Atenos, and more whistles shrieked across the battlefield. The men began to jog, Salvius keeping up with the shush of chain and the clonk and rattle of arms and armour.

'At twenty five paces, first row pila,' bellowed Atenos. 'Second at twenty.'

Salvius watched the enemy lines getting closer with every step, preparing himself with his invocations to Mars.

'Ready,' roared the centurion again.

'Now.' Another blast of whistles.

The legion came to a sudden halt, the front rank, having levelled their weapons easily in the open order, launching them even as their leading foot stamped into the ground. The added momentum of the sudden drop in pace gave the missiles an extra burst of speed, and hundreds upon hundreds of iron points hurtled out along the battle lines, falling with pleasing accuracy among the Pompeian lines.

The result was instant and gratifying. All along the line shields were punctured, the pila punching through the boards and lodging there. Others managed to sneak between shields and drive into chain shirts or even flesh, given the more densely-packed ranks of Pompey's larger force.

An answering whistle chorus broke out along Pompey's ranks, and the men of the Caesarian legions raised their shields in response.

But Atenos was shrewd. He had calculated effective distances for the weapons in his head as they marched into battle. The added momentum of the run had given the Caesarian missiles just that little boost in distance and made them truly effective. Pompey's men had no such additional power and the enemy pila launched along the lines with far less efficiency. A few of the better shots from the stronger men struck legionaries in the front ranks, but the vast majority fell to earth just in front of Caesar's army. The legionaries roared and, at a series of swift commands, the front two ranks rotated. Another whistle and they were off again.

Five more paces, this time at standard march, and another call. The ranks stopped and the second volley of pila hurtled out, this time without the momentum but at an acceptable range. Once more, they punched deep into Pompeian soldiers, creating carnage and chaos. But the cries of agony and terror among the green recruits there were brief, the lines moving forwards to fill the gaps, while their answering volley was more effective than the first, striking Caesar's legionaries all along the line.

Again, Caesar's men shuffled forwards, filling the ranks, and Salvius now found himself in the third row, replacing a man who had taken a pilum to the side and now lay, thrashing on the floor next to Atenos, who calmly leaned down and used his sword to finish the poor bastard off swiftly.

Another whistle. The line surged forwards. Only three paces and the call came for double time.

Three more paces and the 'charge' was issued. With a roar, Caesar's legions hurled themselves over the last dozen or so paces and into the waiting arms of Pompey's forces. Salvius swiftly found himself moving forwards and into the melee. The familiar surge flooded his veins as Mars possessed him and he gave himself over to the war god in his entirety, surrendering himself to the urge to kill, mercilessly.

His sword bit into flesh and he exulted.

This was where he was meant to be; what he lived for.

* * *

Galronus watched the two infantry forces close, exchange pila, and then clash, but only out of the corner of his eye, for he had his own problems to attend to. Even as the two armies met, the huge throng of Pompeian horse raced for his own meagre collection of cavalry. He knew nothing of the enemy's mettle but, even assuming they were poor at best, still it was a lost cause. At best he could hope for a three to one kill ratio, and even that was pushing the boundaries of credibility. Realistically, he figured his men could manage to shrink the enemy force by a thousand or even fifteen hundred before his own losses became so heavy he would be forced to flee or fight to extinction, and the plan called for the former.

'For Caesar,' Galronus bellowed, a cry repeated by Volusenus and Quadratus, though not one that would resonate too strongly with the horse. Yes, they were Caesar's men, but they were still, in truth, Gauls and Germans before anything else. There was a surge of noise in support. They might not roar at serving the republic, but a powerful general could earn their respect, and Caesar was most definitely that.

'For Taranis and Thunor and Mars. For victory!'

This time the noise rose to a roar. He could hardly invoke national pride with so many disparate peoples serving side by side, but each man would know the gods of war and thunder, and all would respect them, and every warrior could throw his voice into a cry for victory.

As they rode at the vastly superior enemy, bellowing invocations to a dozen different gods but all uniformly to victory, officers among the enemy were shouting things about Pompey and the republic, and the lack of response from their men spoke volumes. Labienus of all people should know better than to try to appeal to their *Romanitas*, for they had none.

A moment later the two forces met.

Galronus, at the front as any good leader should be, slammed his spear into a charging figure in gleaming bronze scales, angling the tip at the last moment so that it aimed dead centre at the man's chest. The easterner had aimed his own spear out to the side, trying for Galronus arm or ribs, where the chain shirt would provide less protection. The Remi simply leaned slightly in the saddle as the two clashed. Leaning was not easy in a four-horned saddle, but there was just enough give that the easterner's longer spear brushed past his arm, drawing a thin line of red but doing no real damage. Conversely, Galronus' spear could not hope to penetrate that fish-scale armour dead on, but that had not been his aim and he had leaned heavily into the blow.

The spear tip slammed into the man's armour and failed to punch through, but the simple momentum plucked the rider from his saddle, his useless spear falling from twitching fingers, his strange eastern saddle lacking the support of the rear horns. The screaming man disappeared into the press and a moment later

Galronus was fighting for his life. Swords came at him from every side and his Roman shield, oval and bearing painted designs of gods, took a relentless beating as he shifted it this way and that, preventing those deadly points from digging into him. At the same time his own sword arm twisted and shifted, lashing out with the blade and then parrying. Mostly parrying, in fact. There were so damn many of them.

He could feel his arms numbing and tiring with the constant fighting even only fifty heartbeats into the battle. The effort of swinging and stabbing, along with the battering on his shield arm, were wearing him down. His knees guided his horse, Roman style, though in truth there was precious little guiding to do. In this thick press he was barely moving.

His sword bit into a man in leathers who shrieked, but a moment later he was gone and replaced by two more men. Swords and lances, shields and daggers. Something punched into his left leg and he didn't even have time to look. There was a momentary flash of extreme pain and then a worrying numbness. He could not move or even feel his left leg, but there simply was no chance to look and see if it was wounded, broken or even still there. A spear grated off his helmet with a noise that made him shudder and would certainly leave a dent. Pieces of his shield were flying like airborne kindling, and he knew it would offer precious little protection now, for it was little more than a collection of shredded boards, loosely held together with torn linen and ruptured bronze edging.

He felt a score of pain across his right arm, but managed to swing his heavy blade and respond to the blow with a slash that divided the man's face in two. In a worrying moment the enemy surged around him, but the unexpected arrival of several warriors of the Senones at his side gave him a chance to breathe.

He looked down even as he discarded the ruined shield and drew his dagger as paltry parrying protection. His leg was still there but was soaked red from mid-thigh downward, so drenched that he could not make out where the wound was. Damn it, but he'd have to do something or he'd bleed to death in the saddle.

'Get to a medicus, sir,' shouted one of the riders, and Galronus almost nodded. But no. He couldn't. This was the critical fight. No matter what else happened on the field, this fight had to go right.

Pompey had to see his cavalry win convincingly and sweep on to flank the Caesarians.

Allowing the fresh riders to take the fore Galronus retreated, backing up his horse through the press with the skill that only a life-long rider could attain. Once he was out of the worst danger, his men protecting him, he jammed his twin blades under his armpit and with some difficulty removed his neck scarf. He couldn't manage the brooch that fastened it without dropping the weapons, so he simply tore the scarf free, losing the expensive pin that Faleria had given him somewhere in the press. Gritting his teeth, he pushed the scarf under his wounded thigh and briefly discovered how welcome the numbness had been as the wound opened like bloody lips and agony coursed through him again.

Tears streaming down his cheeks, he forced the scarf into place above the wound and tied it so tight it made him wince. He couldn't see any visible difference, but with luck it would keep enough blood in him to see him through the next hour or so.

Time to take stock.

He gripped his weapons once more, and made the mistake of trying to rise in the saddle to see better, which caused a little extra blood loss and an awful lot more pain. Sweating and gritting teeth, he looked around. His men were doing better than he'd expected. Losses seemed to be relatively low, all things considered. Of the empty saddles he could see, more than two thirds were eastern ones, and more of the bodies on the floor wore odd bronze scales or white linen than Gallic chain. Still, they were being thinned out, and they wouldn't hold for much longer even if they fought to the end.

He resisted the temptation to give the signal. Not yet. He had to fight until they could not realistically hold. If only he had those infantry he'd trained fighting in among the cavalry, it might have made something of a difference. But those men were now with Fronto, and they had their own task.

Turning, he moved forwards into the press once more. Briefly, he caught sight of Prefect Volusenus struggling with a Cappadocian. He felt the pang of dismay as he saw the easterner's sword come down and slam into the prefect's shoulder, separating his sword arm, and cleaving deep through bone and muscle and into organs. Volusenus died in the saddle but remained there, flopping about horribly amid the press. His killer lasted only moments longer before he too was gouged deep with a Gallic blade.

All was the stench of death and bowels, overlaid with fairly strong equine odours. Briefly, the Remi noble wondered how things were going with the infantry. Then his attention returned to his own task. He had to fight on until he judged they could hold the line no longer. With a roar, Galronus launched himself into the fray once more.

* * *

Salvius Cursor was blind. Blood from his latest victim had sprayed free of a terrible neck wound and covered the tribune's face with warm, wet, iron-tinted life. He could feel it running down his cheeks and when he blinked, which he was doing repeatedly, it filled his eyes. He felt, as he did occasionally but would never admit out loud, a tiny thrill of panic. Blind was not a thing to be on the battlefield.

Something knocked into him from the left and he staggered, Reaching down with his free hand – tribunes were not expected to fight and so did not habitually carry shields – he grasped the cloth he kept tucked into his scabbard's fasteners for cleaning his blade after a fight. Lifting it, he wiped the worst of the gore from his face and blinked a dozen times to clear his vision.

He was just in time to parry a powerful blow from a grizzled legionary whose face was more scar tissue than skin. One of Pompey's few true veterans. Roaring defiance, Salvius slammed the man's blade down and let his cloth fall away, gripping the edge of the veteran's shield with his left hand and head-butting him with every ounce of strength he could muster. He felt the man's face shatter beneath the elegant and elaborate embossed brim of his helmet.

Before the howling, broken veteran fell away, Salvius gripped the shield all the harder. He had to hack at the dying man's wrist twice before the shield came away, hand still gripping the cross bar. It was even more work to prise the severed hand from the shield, but he managed, gripping the thing just in time to block the next blow.

He had lost all sense of time and place. Deep down he knew several important facts. First and foremost that he was committed to driving a wedge through the First Legion to get to the treacherous general at its rear. Secondly that he was countermanding Caesar's orders by doing so, and unless he fell back into his position at the rear, the Tenth were effectively leaderless. Thirdly that he was so caught up in the fighting that he might well be ahead of his own men now.

The simple truth, though, was that he didn't care about any of that. He knew he *should*. He knew that it made him both a bad tribune and a potential liability to the army. But the truth was that he had no control. Once he surrendered himself to the war god everything else, no matter how important, necessarily slid into the background.

With an incoherent cry of rage, he dispatched the legionary who'd just struck his shield, then put the great board in the path of another blow while he dropped low and drove his sword point into the groin of a man to his right, scything through muscle and organ under the hem of his chain shirt.

Mars flowed through him once more, driving out all other concerns.

Briefly, he was aware of other scenes around him, though, as he killed and maimed.

Atenos was there in the surge, just for a moment, seemingly larger than life – a Titan rising above the press with a gladius in one hand and a vine staff in the other, simultaneously driving the point of the former into a man's neck while smashing another round the side of the head with the latter, denting the bronze of the man's helmet agonisingly into his ear.

To the far side, Crastinus was less lucky. The impressive centurion, who had infused his troops with the desire to fight, had killed so many men that his soldiers called him 'Bloody Flux' behind his back, but his reign of terror among the Pompeians came to an end in that moment. A legionary caught him a lucky blow, punching a gladius into the centurion's face so hard that the sword slid into Crastinus' mouth and burst out through the back of his neck. It lodged there, the gagging, dying centurion falling away into the press, but the man who let go of his sword, thrilling at having killed one of Caesar's infamous centurions, went to Hades only a moment later, punched into the torso with three different blades by a handful of vengeful legionaries.

Similar scenes were playing out everywhere but Salvius Cursor caught them only peripherally, like some sort of dance routine at the bath house while he was personally more intent on scraping off the dirt with a strigil.

He punched, stabbed, sliced, kicked, butted, and even bit his way into the press of Pompey's men. With every step forwards, he half expected to burst from the rear of the enemy lines and find the fat old general standing in front of him. That vision spurred him on and he continued to carve a path, hoping that his men were following and that he was pressing a wedge into the enemy rather than being cut off within them.

His advance ended suddenly. His blade slammed deep into the side of a legionary and he took two more blows on the great, heavy shield, but then something smashed into his helmet and everything went red and then white and then black in agonising flashes. The battle disappeared entirely as his hearing was flooded with an all-consuming shrill whining sound. As those flashes vanished, all he could see was blackness with occasional hints of colour. His head felt as though he had stuck it inside a bell just as someone rang it.

For just a moment, Salvius wondered if he was dead. Then his strength failed and he sank to his knees.

* * *

Galronus knew his force was on the cusp. He had been pushing forwards and fighting like a madman periodically, then pulling back when the effort became too much, the pain in his leg intense. But every time he pressed forwards there were fewer of his men around him, and every time he withdrew it became clear that the enemy were gaining ground. Briefly, he caught sight of the infantry off to the left and the sight confirmed how far back they had been driven. Those legionaries were fresh and neatly lined up, as yet untested. At the initial clash of horse they had been level with the army's front line.

Pompey's cavalry were succeeding. Their remit, as he'd heard from their officers in their own camp, no less, was to hammer through the Caesarian horse and then turn upon the infantry's flank, massacring the Tenth and then ruining the army until they broke and lost.

They were remarkably close to doing just that.

He resolved not to personally move forwards once more. The time was almost upon him, and he needed to be ready. Leaving the press of struggling horsemen, he deftly angled his horse out obliquely. He'd had to discard his dagger and take to using his left hand on the reins, since guiding the beast with his knees had become impossible, every press of his left leg causing blood to well up into the agonising wound.

After what felt like half a lifetime of guiding his steed through the struggling cavalry, he reached the southern periphery of their fight and surveyed the general situation.

Caesar's infantry were hard pressed, but the fight must be going well enough, for the third line had not yet been committed. Certainly they were in a terrible melee. The cavalry were in trouble, though that was only to be expected. Had they fought enough?

Just for a moment, he caught sight of a man in a senior officer's uniform across the far side of the field, bellowing rage, exhorting his men to greater martial feats. Oddly, it was easy to see now, from this peripheral viewpoint, how much of a difference the styles of command and organisation had made.

His men had survived better than he could have hoped for at this point. He couldn't take an accurate count, but from what he could see, he'd be willing to wager that between six and seven hundred of his thousand men still remained in the saddle. More than half, certainly. And it was impossible to tell the difference in the enemy numbers, given how huge the force was, but just from what he'd seen in the press, his men must have on average killed at least two Pompeians apiece. So the enemy must have lost a thousand. Possibly more.

He should pull his men, he knew. From here the more he lost, the less feasible mere survival became. But he also knew that unless he thinned the enemy out by at least two thousand, then Fronto's job would be nigh on impossible. They had to hold.

The one bright side was that he could see the failures in command among the enemy, and how it was leading them to a much higher casualty rate. The units fighting under Galronus were in their own national bands, fighting for their chieftains, which meant that they kept together and fought as units. Gaps appeared here and there between those units, but really it mattered not, because there was still not room for the enemy to navigate such a deadly maze in force. By comparison, Pompey's horsemen had been forged into one massive fist of cavalry and consequently there was little in the way of individual unit command in the field. Their horsemen were each doing what they could with no view of the whole, their men pushing independently into the gaps between Galronus' units, where they were being cut down easily.

That was it. That's what he had to do: the equivalent of a legionary defensive square. He had to have each unit become such a formation and gradually give ground, fighting as they went. That way he could minimize his casualties and use the enemy's lack of cohesion to maximise theirs. For a moment, he gave a wry smile at just how much he'd started to think like a Roman in the saddle.

Close by were his outriders, a small unit of lightly equipped couriers he'd kept from the main force to pass commands if he had them. He'd not expected to need them, but now was the time.

'You men. Deliver this message to each commander in the field: form a defensive square and give ground slowly, killing as you go, and await my signal.'

Saluting, the riders hurried into the press, risking their lives to deliver the messages.

He became aware suddenly of something brushing his left leg, and almost swung his sword at it out of instinct. The capsarius flinched where he had been examining the wound.

'What are you doing?' the Remi frowned.

'My job, sir. Sit still.'

'I haven't got time for medical attention yet.'

'Then you'll be dead before you do. Sit still.'

The Remi had spent long enough among the legions now to know how their medical personnel considered themselves almost a different species to the rest of the army, and that their skills gave them the right to issue commands even to officers. The sad truth was that they were more or less correct.

Galronus sat still while the soldier tore open a stretch of his ruined trousers and carefully probed the wound, wincing and hissing every time the medic's fingers caused him fresh waves of pain.

'Bite down on this,' the man said, handing him a piece of well-chewed thick leather. Bracing himself, knowing what was coming, Galronus did as he was told, and spent some time weeping and whimpering as the soldier none-too-carefully stitched his wound. As the soldier tied off the last knot, the Remi noble heaved in a sigh of relief and spat out the leather, handing it back to the man, who took it delicately in two fingers and dropped it into a bag. He then washed down the leg, mopping it gently dry with linen before liberally slathering it with a compound that smelled of honey and vinegar and spices. Then, the man expertly bound the upper leg tight and finally pinned the wrappings in place.

'Have someone help you dismount and don't try to walk on it without a crutch,' the capsarius said authoritatively. Galronus nodded. Given how much it hurt, he could barely imagine even *falling* off the horse, whether with or without help.

His attention returned to the fight. Such was the efficiency of the Roman medical corps that he had had the entire treatment in less than a quarter of an hour. The gambit seemed to have been successful. His units were gradually pulling back, but they were killing with every step they took, and the number of the enemy had dropped visibly, while he had lost at most a hundred more men.

Yes, a fresh count suggested he had now lost half his men. The time was upon them.

'Good luck, Fronto,' he muttered under his breath, and then found his musician sitting alone to the side and waved his arm. The man nodded and took a deep breath before bending and blasting out a triple cadence.

The Caesarian horse broke and ran for it, heading at an angle away from the army and towards the hills on the northern edge if the field, opening up the flank for Pompey's horse to press home their advance as they had planned.

This was it. The critical moment.

May Fortuna be with the legate of the Tenth.

CHAPTER 22

Three notes rang out across the field of battle, and though they were much the same as many other legionary or cavalry signals and could easily have been lost in the cacophony of war, they rang out like the tolling of a doom-laden bell, summoning Charon and his boat to cross that final river. For those three notes placed the weight of Caesar's world squarely on Fronto's shoulders. He swallowed nervously, the worry born not of the dreadful conflict to come – he had fought the most dreadful of all battles in the world at Alesia, and no man could fight worse – but of what it meant, and how much rode on its back.

As he rose and then dropped his own hand in signal, off to his left, he could see the third line of the legions, as yet uncommitted, which meant that things were bogged down at the heart of the fighting, but at least Caesar's legions were not being forced back and losing ground, else those rear ranks would by now have been sent in to supply extra strength to weakened sections of the line. On the other hand there was no exultant roar, and no calls for the melee that would inevitably result when one line or the other was completely broken. The fighting would be thick and dreadful, still, then. His thoughts went briefly to Atenos and to Salvius Cursor, deep in the press of it, but he swiftly dragged them back. He had other matters to deal with.

It was impossible to see Pompey's cavalry from here. They were on the other side of Galronus' horse, and he had absolutely no idea how strong or depleted that enemy force now was. He remained confident that his Remi friend would not have put out the call until he had done all he could, and Galronus' certainty that his men were individually far stronger and better than Pompey's gave him heart that his thousand horse could give considerably better than they got. At worst, they would have killed a thousand, by Fronto's reckoning. At best no more than three thousand, though.

And that left Fronto with just two thousand foot against anywhere between three and five thousand horse.

No pressure.

Now, the Caesarian cavalry were leaving the field. Pulling back, they angled north, breaking for the hills, looking for all the world like a force determined to save their skins and flee the carnage. Of course, Fronto and his men were already running. He had given his own signal the very moment he had been certain that Galronus was on the move, mere heartbeats after those three notes. He could see the horse and, as the six cohorts under his command broke into a run, the back of Galronus' cavalry became their whole world, all they could see. They were swift, and Fronto estimated that they had taken perhaps a fifty per cent casualty rate. Galronus had fought as long as he could, but had given the order at precisely the right point, may the gods bless him.

For heart-stopping moments, it looked to Fronto as though his timing had been wrong. It appeared for all the world as though they were about to hit the rear of their own fleeing Caesarian horse. Then, like a drape being swept back from a window to reveal the view, Galronus' cavalry were gone.

In their place, Pompey's horse were revealed in all their dreadful power. Perhaps four thousand horse now at an initial blind estimate, yelping and whooping their exultant victory, for they had won and would please their general. They had driven Caesar's cavalry from the field and now the way would open for them to turn the flank, smash into the Tenth and begin the process of utterly collapsing the lines of Caesarian infantry.

For important moments the oncoming cavalry, spotting Fronto and his men suddenly revealed by the exit of the Caesarian horse, couldn't figure out what it was they were looking at. Fronto could imagine what was going through their minds. They knew that Caesar had a third line that had not been committed, and that line would be their main concern at this point, but they had to be wondering where this fourth line of reserves had come from. They would be wondering why it had been stationed behind the cavalry and, critically, at the last, they would be wondering why they were armed like some sort of bizarre auxiliary spear unit.

Then Fronto's men let out a roar. It had not been planned. Fronto had given no signal and called for no such thing, and he marvelled as perhaps a hundred voices bellowed out the name of Mars, then again, with perhaps a thousand, and then a third time with two thousand, every voice hoarse and straining with the effort.

As though their voices alone had the power to wound, the enemy cavalry faltered, panic rippling through them.

Then Fronto's cohorts hit Pompey's cavalry.

The legate himself was armed with his sword alone, not one of the spears like his men, yet he was among them in the second line as they hit the horse like a low wave breaking on high, black rocks. His eyes went to a horseman before him in some sort of antiquated linen armour, and then so did his blade. His gladius punched up. The ancient-style linothorax was strong enough to turn a blade straight on, but not from beneath, an angle unanticipated for such a panoply. The point sank up through the hanging pteruges and plunged into the man's pelvis. Fronto was forced to rip his sword free swiftly and dance out of the way, for there was still momentum in the cavalry and he really did not want to get crushed.

Spinning to select a second target, he could already see his men pressing into the swathe of horsemen. The selection process for his unit had been more than merely successful. The legionaries, showing no fear of the horses in a most un-infantrylike manner, were moving among the Pompeian cavalry and using their short spears to truly deadly effect. Even as Fronto swung left and right, he saw one Thracian horseman howl for the briefest moment before the cry became a clotted gurgle, a spear thrust from below ignoring all the protection of helmet and shirt, the lead-blade slamming into the man's neck, piercing his throat apple and punching into his spine before being expertly hauled back out by its wielder. Then, to the right, a horseman learned the danger of looking down to target one of the dreadful footmen among them. A spear slammed into his unprotected face directly between the cheek pieces, ruining his nose before skipping off bone and burying itself in his eye. He lurched back, already dying and the soldier yanked on the shaft, hauling the spear back out with blood, eye and brain still clinging to it.

Good. One thing that had been drilled into the men was the need to keep hold of the spear, as it was a valuable weapon in this situation, giving the men the perfect reach to deal with the riders, and from an unexpected and less-protected angle.

Of course men were losing spears. Some were snapped, some lost still buried in a victim, and it was here that their mettle, adaptability and expertise as legionaries of Rome came to the fore. Losing their primary weapon, those men simply drew their swords and went to work on the horses or on any rider's leg that presented itself.

It was carnage.

Legionaries were dying, of course, but the vast toll of death was being dealt to Pompey's cavalry, unable to react adequately to this unexpected and horribly efficient attack.

It had been Caesar's plan, of course. Ever the great tactician, the general had reasoned that they had to meet cavalry with like, but that there was simply no way to win with the odds as they were. Galronus' force was doomed, but if they could weaken the enemy and at the same time make them overconfident, then deliver them into the arms of a second unit, then their job was done. The general had planned to meet the cavalry with unexpected auxiliary spearmen, deploying them hidden behind the cavalry rather than on the flank by the river where they in fact ended up.

It had been Antonius and Galronus both who had suggested legionaries instead. Antonius because he feared the inability of the auxilia to carry out the task. Galronus because he believed that the tactics of the mixed infantry and cavalry he had trained and seen at work with the water carriers would be the one to carry the day. Such a force, he argued, could destroy the Pompeian cavalry, as long as his own horse wore some identifying mark to avoid a repeat of the river bank. Caesar had agreed, but not to field them as a mixed unit, but just the legionaries, equipped as spear men, behind the cavalry. If they could show the same skill and spirit as they had against the water party, they might just be able to break Pompey's horse.

And it would appear that the general's belief was being borne out.

'Forwards, push deep!' he bellowed. They could not allow the cavalry time to recover from their shock and panic. Indeed, they needed to increase that terror and prevent the rear ranks of cavalry rallying. Close to him a legionary fell with an agonised cry, a

Syrian blade cleaving his neck. Fronto turned in the press, sword raised, and brought it down with all his might, severing the Syrian's arm just above the wrist. As the legionary fell away, Fronto reached out urgently and grabbed the spear with his free hand, tearing it from the man's dying grip. The Syrian was staring in horror at his stump, and the expression froze on his face as the spear buried itself in his armpit.

Fronto nearly lost the weapon. He was totally unfamiliar with the use of a spear, as well as using it in his off-hand, and he hauled it out so inexpertly that he pulled a muscle in his arm doing it. The Syrian fell from the horse and Fronto had to leap out of the way to avoid being flattened beneath the corpse. He felt his knee give and for precious moments dropped to the ground amid the pounding hooves, before gritting his teeth and forcing himself back up. Casting a quick prayer up to Aesculapius, he wondered momentarily whether it might be worth obtaining a figure of the healing god for his neck, but dismissed the idea in a trice. If he had every god he'd need to call on hanging around his neck, he'd walk with a permanent stoop.

Hoping against hope that his knee would hold up for the duration he stepped forwards, ducking a spear that had not been aimed at him but merely flailed this way and that in the press, its owner finding great difficulty in using the weapon from horseback against the man beside him in this press.

For a moment, just a tantalising moment, Fronto caught sight of a familiar figure. Labienus was dressed in the uniform of a general, complete with red cloak and knotted ribbon, an honour Caesar had accorded him on more than one occasion. The defecting officer had a face filled with a difficult mix of hope, fury and uncertainty. His career would ride on this action, if not his life. For the briefest of moments, Fronto considered pressing hard through the mass of horsemen to reach Labienus. Of course, that would carry the most dreadful mortal danger, but killing a commander, especially when their unit is a strange, disparate one only held together by the chain of command, could change a whole battle. Still, at the base of it all, Fronto was less than convinced that if it came to it he could plunge his blade into Labienus. The man might currently be the enemy, but he had long been a friend before that, and somewhere deep within would surely still be that thoughtful, incisive and noble Roman Fronto remembered.

He turned his gaze from Labienus. If the man died on the field today it would not be by Fronto's hand. His spear lanced out at an Illyrian rider, finding an easy target in the unarmoured horseman, plunging deep through white wool and into giving flesh before Fronto yanked it out once more with only a little more skill than last time. The rider howled and Fronto almost fell as a sword blow slammed into his back. He felt the heavy strike across the bronze shoulders of the shaped cuirass he wore and thanked Fortuna that he'd plumped for a traditional officer's armour this morning and not for the chain shirt he had taken to wearing at times for ease. The chain would have stopped the blade, but the bruising and possible broken bones would have knocked him out of the fight for sure. The cuirass was considerably less practical than chain in so many ways, but when turning a slash of a blade, it won out every day. He felt the blade skip across the bronze, ding off the neck guard of his helmet and disappear into the air. Instinctively he turned and thrust, not with the spear in his left hand but with the gladius in his right. His aim was true. He'd understood simply from the direction the sword had gone, how the rider had opened up one of the true attack points for a swordsman. The gladius plunged into the unprotected flesh of the armpit and was immediately and expertly twisted and withdrawn.

It was not a killing blow as it would be against a foot solider, because of the angle. He had pierced neither organ nor artery, but the damage would be crippling and agonising, and would certainly remove the man from the fray. Similar stories were being played out among the entire mass of cavalry. The enemy simply did not know how to effectively deal with this unprecedented threat that moved among them with impunity and without fear, striking up from unseen places and, where unable to do so, felling the horses and then falling upon their panicked riders.

It was at that moment, deep in the press and at the heart of the battle, that Fronto knew he'd done it. The weight of responsibility that had weighed him down like a yoke about his shoulders suddenly shattered and fell away. Whatever happened now, he knew he had done that which he had been tasked with doing. He had beaten the Pompeian horse. There were other roles to play, of course, for Caesar's stratagem was not yet done with, but the one part that Fronto had been uncertain would work had done so, and admirably.

Around him, riders were dying so fast and in such quantity that they fell in waves and the legate could almost identify whole areas amid the cavalry that were opening up, their only occupants corpses, both human and equine. Riderless beasts milled, and they were becoming more of a danger to the legionaries than were the Pompeian cavalry who, having been exultant in the belief they had broken Caesar's horse, were now only a hair's breadth short of complete rout. Confusion had become fear and fear had become panic. Few of them pressed forwards now, and Fronto estimated that more of the riders he could see on the field were attempting to get away than to fight.

A sword from nowhere smashed into his spear and cut it in half, making his hand throb with the impact, and Fronto turned and dispatched the man with no ceremony and little thought. He was more concerned with the battle as a whole now. There *was* still a danger, after all. If the enemy could somehow recover their wits, they likely still had two thousand men intact. They could fight back, and possibly even beat Fronto's men, but only if they managed to master their terror.

The best way to guarantee a fight against cavalry was, of course, to remove the horses from the equation. If they could somehow feed the panic of the beasts, it would spread further among the riders. As Fronto parried and killed, he pondered how to spook the enemy's mounts. Loud noises sometimes frightened horses, though that seemed rather redundant in the middle of the monstrous din already filling the air.

Taking a deep breath, Fronto began to chant.

'Caesar... Caesar... Caesar...'

Turning, he thrust his blade into a target of opportunity, and spotted two men with spears back to back. He nodded meaningfully as he continued to chant. The two men took a moment to understand, and by the time one of them had joined in, the other had fallen to a Cappadocian spear.

'Caesar... Caesar... Caesar...'

But it began to spread, and rapidly. In moments the chant was rising like a tide among the press.

A horseman close to Fronto made to swing his long blade at the legate, and Fronto moved his own sword forwards to parry, but the necessity disappeared in a heartbeat as the nervous horse backed away from him and then reared and threw its rider.

Fronto frowned for a moment and then slowly a possible explanation dawned on him. Some time ago, in camp, Bucephalus had encountered a snake in the grass. The hissing reptile had terrified the great black horse, who had thundered off to the far side of the paddock to get away. When Fronto had laughed and told the equisio, the man had shrugged and replied that most horses didn't like snakes, and that Bucephalus' panic was far from unusual.

Could it be the hissing? The drawn-out S in mid-chant? Certainly there was a growing wave of nervousness among the horses, and it rose exponentially as the chanting neared fever-pitch. It was one of the strangest, and yet grandest sights Fronto had ever witnessed on the battlefield. The chanting legionaries, their rhythmic devotion now so loud that it suppressed almost all other noises, moved among the Pompeian horse and killing like wildfire. Horses and riders fell with every heartbeat, and Fronto could almost see the depletion of the massive cavalry force happening. Their numbers had been drastically reduced and continued to be so. Now, even if they managed somehow to regroup and push through the spear men, they would be unlikely to have adequate strength to turn the flank. Labienus had failed, no matter what happened next.

As Fronto grinned his victory, he spotted the enemy commander once more, Labienus in his red cloak rising above the press, his face a stony visage of hate. He clearly also knew that he had lost.

Fronto watched, hawklike, his old friend and current adversary. Labienus raked his irritated gaze across the sea of men and snarled. For just a moment he locked eyes with Fronto, and his brow furrowed. Then the man turned in his saddle, red cloak hanging limp in the summer heat, and gestured several times to his musician. Moments later the call echoed out across the cavalry. Labienus had signalled the retreat. It was all his riders needed. As though they had only been waiting for permission, the entire Pompeian cavalry exploded in panic, wheeling their horses in the press and pushing for open ground.

Fronto was impressed with just how quickly the rout happened once it began. He wondered whether it was a symptom of having tried to form so many disparate peoples into one tactical unit, but unlike the orderly withdrawal of Galronus' cavalry so recently, Labienus' horse simply bolted as fast as they could, every man out for himself and racing for freedom. By the time the bulk were clear of the spear-wielding legionaries, they had spread out like wildlife fleeing a conflagration. They swarmed away in the direction of the hills and their own camp, to the north-west and a great cry of triumph rose in successively noisy waves from the victorious legionaries, replacing the chanting of their general's name.

The last detail Fronto saw of the Pompeian cavalry was Labienus, roaring his anger at his men for fleeing so ridiculously and not forming a careful withdrawal. The commander suddenly realised that he was largely unprotected and that Fronto's spearmen were hurtling towards him, and he too, wheeled his horse and raced off, musicians and personal guard alongside and following on behind.

Pompey's entire cavalry had fled the field.

In a strange parody of their own action, the next line of Pompey's forces became visible as the cavalry fled, just as Fronto's men had appeared when Galronus' cavalry had pulled away. There were two important differences between the two scenes, though. Firstly, while Fronto's men had been a complete shock, and a dreadful one, for the waiting cavalry, Fronto had been expecting this. It was a standard tactic and the obvious play to follow the cavalry's attempt to turn the flank. Once Pompey's horse had destroyed Caesar's they could move into the poorly defended rear and begin smashing the Caesarian legions and, with the auxilia following on in support, arrows would then begin to rake the Tenth. A good plan, but only if the cavalry succeeded, because the other difference lay in the horse. While Labienus' riders were now fleeing en-masse for their camp, Galronus had stopped at the edge of the field, and there re-formed his remaining half thousand riders.

The Pompeian auxiliaries did not know what to do, the entire battle plan having failed before their eyes. For a moment, they looked as though they would charge Fronto's men, and in fact some of the archer units among them did pause to release a rather paltry flurry of missiles. But they were dithering, uncertain of whether to press on despite the failure of the cavalry and hope for a miracle, or whether to flee and by doing so more or less consign Pompey's entire army to the funeral pyre. It was not a position Fronto would have revelled in occupying, for sure.

Their decision was made suddenly as, with a whoop of fury, Galronus and his horse put heel to flank and raced back onto the field of battle, fresh and recovered and making directly for those lightly armoured Pompeian auxiliaries on the flank. Still they dithered for precious moments and, with that, sealed their doom.

Fronto shouted his orders and the musician relayed the commands. His spearmen-legionaries began once more to form into their cohorts, and he was impressed to discover that he had not lost much more than a quarter of his men, even against such a massively superior force. May the gods bless Caesar, Antonius and Galronus for their tactical insight, although Fronto allowed himself something of a quiet smug smile in the knowledge that *whoever* had planned such a thing, it had been Fronto that had carried it to its conclusion in the field.

The enemy auxiliaries began to pull back, their command devolved to individual prefects and their professionalism therefore showing through better than the mass debacle that had been the cavalry. In fact, Fronto was impressed. Rather than break and flee, despite the clear fact that death rode whooping at them, they retreated in good order, the infantry units shifting to protect the archers in the withdrawal.

It was professional, and nicely done, but it was too little and too late. Galronus' cavalry hit them like a brick against old plaster, dashing them to pieces. The auxilia simply disintegrated. A unit of spearmen tried their best, pausing in the withdrawal to create a hedge of spears that would deter horses, but the cavalry, victory in their grasp, simply rode past, ignoring them, and then over and through units of swordsmen and archers, pulverising and mashing bodies beneath hooves and hacking and hewing with blades. The enemy's orderly withdrawal lasted perhaps fifty heartbeats before it too became a rout, each man running for whatever perceived safety he clapped eyes upon.

As the cavalry carved their way mercilessly through the auxilia, and Fronto's infantry reserve began to run along the periphery, supporting them and making a push for Pompey's own flank, the Tenth Legion roared their approval and their own struggle against Pompey's infantry redoubled in intensity, strengthened in the knowledge that not only had Pompey failed to flank them, but it would appear that that was exactly what was about to happen in reverse.

The ebb and flow of battle had changed. It had become a tide, and that tide was flowing Pompey's way. Cut off from all allies, that single unit of Pompeian spear men who had formed up against cavalry took one look at Fronto's roaring cohorts pounding towards them and broke, fleeing off to the north, into the only open space left to them, escaping the field of battle.

For the briefest of moments, Fronto considered giving chase. It was bad strategy in general to allow an intact enemy unit to survive behind you, but three things decided him against the idea. Firstly, given the way things were going, the rest of Pompey's northern edge would soon begin to disintegrate, and no competent commander would take his unit back into that mess without good reason. Secondly, the battle teetered in the balance. They had won out on the northern flanks against massive odds, but they were still outnumbered by Pompey's infantry and any lag in momentum now might give Pompey time to rally and change the situation, so Fronto had to press on behind the cavalry. And thirdly it was clear, at the very least from the dark swarthy skin tones of the fleeing spearmen, that they had come from some distant eastern land, perhaps even Arabia, and their commitment to any Roman cause would be very easily shaken and broken. It was extremely unlikely, while it looked like Pompey was going to lose, that they would commit to his support any further.

Dismissing them as no longer important, Fronto kept his eyes ahead. Galronus and his cavalry had made minced meat of the auxiliary. Those who were not lying on the ground with dreadful sword wounds or covered in hoof prints and with pulverised bones, were running as fast as their legs could carry them. It mattered not where, so long as they were away from the dreadful Caesarian cavalry or the vicious legionary spear men even now thundering towards them.

They had done it. They had withstood the hammer of Pompey's vast cavalry and then broken them, and followed up by shattering the enemy's auxiliary reserve. The main struggle of the battle still raged along a two mile front across the plain of Pharsalus, but the opening to a most unlikely victory lay ahead now. Pompey's flank was bare, and racing towards it were five hundred murderous horsemen and fifteen hundred exultant legionaries. Wars had been won on less.

The flank was theirs and, if they played the next moves right, so was the battle.

CHAPTER 23

The auxiliary units – or what was left of them after Galronus' cavalry rode through them anyway – melted away from the battlefield in moments, and Fronto could now see only the flank of the Pompeians. The din of battle had given way, as the action on the northern edge of the field unfolded, to a surge of victorious cheers from the Caesarian legions, even as they continued to fight a superior enemy. A quick glance back across at their own lines made it clear to Fronto that the general was capitalising on the change in fortune across the field. Signals blared out, followed by choruses of whistles, and the third line marched forwards. As they filtered with relative ease through the spacious Caesarian formations, they fell into the front lines, hacking and stabbing and barging, fresh and energetic even as the tired former front liners fell back through the press to take up a relief position at the rear.

Pompey's flank lay open.

Gods, but they had a chance now.

Fronto could see the men of the First Legion lined up, three ranks compacted, each one having taken their turn at the front, all tired. And now that they were exposed to danger, the centurions were blowing shrill calls, urging their optios to re-form the legion. Men were turning to create a flanking shield wall in a desperate attempt to preserve their lines.

Fronto turned to the men marching alongside him. Grim expressions of determination filled every face. This was perhaps the worst aspect of the war: the men awaiting them had once been allies. Friends, even. At Alesia, the greatest battle any man could ever know, the veterans among these soldiers had fought alongside the First, the consular legion that had then returned to Rome and to Pompey's hand and now stood arrayed against them. Many of Fronto's men would have shared wine and a joke with those gleaming eyes that hunkered down behind shields.

It mattered not. The men of Caesar's legion had pushed aside all traces of sentimentality in that desperate press of horses. Fronto's own gaze strayed further still. Behind the enemy lines would be the senior officers. Somewhere was Labienus, who had raced away at the rear of his cavalry. Would he have fled back to camp with the horse? Fronto somehow doubted it. He would stay and fight, no matter how bitter the struggle became. But also, somewhere out there was Pompey – the prize for all of them. The capture of the opposing general would not only signal the end of the battle, but the close of this entire war, for if Pompey fell, who might the senate be able to persuade to stand and command in his place?

Miraculously, Fronto saw him then. Far off, out on the plain some distance back from the First Legion, a grand figure on horseback who could only be Pompey. As Fronto watched in growing incredulity, that single figure trotted his steed further and further from the lines, several other officers and his personal guard joining him, and then, in a move as unexpected as it was pathetic, the great general ripped free his red cloak and let it fall to the ground. The symbol of his command of the army, fluttering down to the dust. In a heartbeat the general who had routed them at Dyrrachium and who had stymied Caesar at every turn was on the run. With his cronies and a detachment of his praetorian guard, Pompey raced away to the northwest.

There was a groan of dismay from the rear ranks of the First and Third, the two closest legions, but otherwise the fighting went on with no pause in intensity. It would take precious time for word of their general's cowardly departure to reach them and even then, if they were good, solid legions as the First and Third had been, their commanders would keep them fighting.

But it was another blow. Their great weapon, the cavalry wing that was supposed to win them the battle, had failed dismally. Now their general had fled the field in disgrace with his staff, leaving the legions to fight on in his absence. Their morale had to be faltering, dipping to an almost critical level, especially with so many green, untried troops in their lines. One more failure could be enough to end it all.

There *were* veteran units among the Pompeian army, though. On the far flank were those men who had fled Hispania and joined their former commanders Afranius and Petreius. These would be good, solid soldiers – the ones they'd faced at Ilerda and others from Further Hispania. And at the centre were the Syrian legions brought west by Scipio. And then, of course, on the northern flank were the First and Third. If just one of these bulwarks of professionalism were to collapse, it would likely be the end of the army as a whole.

Ahead, he could see now that Galronus had brought his cavalry in at an angle and was adopting the time-honoured tactic of harrying the enemy at speed. Those men who had retained their spears prepared to use them. Skipping the first two ranks of the legion, the cavalry turned and angled in towards the third, who were already shaken by the disappearance of their cavalry and auxiliary support and the flight of their general from the field. Their confidence would be wavering critically now.

As he and his men veered off to move against the second rank, Fronto watched his friend's force. As the cavalry pounded in, they formed a column two riders wide. The stratagem was well-chosen, and better than any wedge or Cantabrian wheel. Galronus had carefully organised his men and the first dozen or so pairs were the ones still bearing spears. With the expert skill of veterans, they cast their missiles as they neared the enemy and then peeled away to the sides, the next men coming forwards and casting *their* spears, veering off and so on.

At the heart of the hastily-formed legionary shield wall in the third rank, the spears did their job, punching through shields and men alike and creating a crucial gap. Then as the spears ran out those men who'd already cast theirs or lost them earlier in the fray, with swords drawn, raced into the hole their companions had made, driving into the legionary lines where they began to hack down at the soldiers in the tight press. It was terribly dangerous work for the cavalry, who would be easy targets for the infantry, but Galronus had two advantages. Firstly they were deep in a thick press of men, for Pompey's ranks were in tight formation unlike Caesar's, which meant that there was little room for the men below to effectively wield a sword, while the cavalry had open space above to hammer down with their blades. Secondly, morale among the legion was at its lowest possible ebb and more soldiers were concerned with pushing through their mates away from the horsemen than attempting to take out the riders among them.

As it had been ever since Galronus' signal, the critical factor now remained pushing forwards, delivering blow after blow not only to the physical forces before them, but also to their spirits. Given the continued horrible odds that outweighed Caesar's army, they had to break the enemy before they could hope to beat them in combat, and each blow to their spirits brought them a touch closer to that moment. If this went on for much longer, Galronus and his horsemen would be cut down and the legion would recover.

Bellowing incomprehensible shouts, Fronto and his cohorts hit the side-facing shield wall flank of the First. He could only imagine the bafflement and worry among the enemy, for the legionaries attacking them bore no shields, barring one or two who had taken shields from their Pompeian cavalry victims, half of them gripping sword and dagger, the other half carrying bloodied spears.

Fronto had given no commands, for he had no idea what tactics might be successful in such unprecedented, peculiar circumstances. Moreover, he had given no encouragement to his men, who had needed none, for their blood was up and nothing short of a stone rampart was going to stop them now.

His cohorts simply waded into the First, those with spears using them expertly, jabbing them into any gap between shields they could find, certain of a wound delivered in the press of men. Screams echoed along the line, and the swordsmen capitalised on those small gaps created by the victims of the spears. In any other fight, the front man, when he fell, would be replaced with a man from the second line shuffling forwards. It was an old and serviceable system. But not when this was the flank and those men behind were as often as not facing another direction and trying to feed the front line against the Tenth. Their formations and careful lines began to disintegrate immediately, for no square block of men can feed a shield wall to both front and left simultaneously without confusion reigning and gaps inevitably opening up.

Fronto grinned and, with a brief prayer to Fortuna, threw himself into the nearest gap.

He could feel the atmosphere in the First Legion even as he pushed his way in among them. They were broken. Their morale had drained away and every man there knew the day was lost. They only fought on through a strange combination of ingrained professionalism and the discipline of their centurions, who were still driving them on, continually exhorting them to battle.

Fronto let go of his need to command and control and threw all his concentration and spirit into the blade in his right hand, proving once more that age need be no barrier to a soldier if he kept up his physique and training. That being said, once or twice he felt his knee going in the press and was forced to pause and recover, men from his cohorts clustering around him unbidden, keeping him from the worst of dangers in the press. Then, mere moments later he was up and fighting again, his sword parrying with bone-quivering metallic grating noises, stabbing into flesh and iron and painted wood.

He felt swords tear at his tunic, ding and scrape off his cuirass, felt a worrying lance of pain as a shallow cut opened up on his thigh, then another on his left arm. He noted with interest in passing that Pompey's legions, as well as their identifying shield designs, had dyed their scarves a purple blue – the eastern dye *indikon*, no doubt brought by the Syrian legions. A blue scarf for them indicated an ally.

It turned out to be a lucky realisation, for twenty heartbeats later he shoved a gurgling, dying legionary out of the way and raised his blade to strike the next, realising only at the last moment that the man wore no such blue scarf. As the soldier turned towards him, also raising his sword and realising that Fronto wore no blue, the legate grinned, recognising the shield design of Caesar's Equestris Legion.

In the press of men, he had met the Tenth pushing forwards.

The man grinned back and then shoved off in another direction. Fronto hacked and stabbed once more, being careful to make sure his target was blue-scarved before delivering the blow.

* * *

Salvius Cursor knelt and whimpered. His head felt as though someone had parked a cart on it. How long he had blacked out, he had no idea, but he knew instinctively that he had done so. He reached up and ran his left hand over the surface of his helmet, half expecting to find a squishy bit where his own brain was exposed. What he *did* find was a dent, and it was no small ding, but a sizeable crease. Gingerly, he probed it and almost passed out again at the intense pain that washed through his head at his fingers' pressure.

Carefully he reached up and untied the leather thong beneath his chin that held the cheek flaps together. With dreadful slowness, he began to lift the helmet from his head. He winced as he felt his hair being pulled taught at the dent, where blood had matted into it and some had caught in the metal. He tugged lightly and felt the hair tear as the helmet came free. Turning it over, he looked at the dent in the bowl and his eyes bulged. How he had survived such a blow he would never know. The dent had to be a full thumb-width deep. He could see the contour of a slightly curved blade in the impression it had left in the bronze. Turning it over and looking inside, he quickly wished he hadn't. The bronze had slammed inwards through the felt liner which had probably been the thing that had saved his life. But despite that, the once grey liner was now a purple-brown-black mixture of blood, sweat and hair. He let the helmet fall away. It had been a fine and expensive purchase some years ago, but he would never wear it again. Even if he had that dent hammered out, the bowl would forever have a weak spot there. Reaching up, he very gently touched that spot on his head and was instantly sick the moment his finger entered the wound. The bronze had presumably cracked his skull. He wondered if what he had touched was brain. When he looked at his hand it was covered in blood. Would it have been grey if it was brain?

Slowly, he rose, then collapsed again. While he was down there the second time, gathering sufficient strength to stand, his questing fingers found his sword and he gripped it gratefully.

The reality of his situation sank in and he peered about himself. Every figure he saw was a legionary of the Tenth, and they were all pushing in the same direction. So, he was in no further danger, but farther and farther removed from the action. More carefully this time he staggered to his feet. His legs felt wobbly. Not as wobbly as his vision or his head, but still wobbly.

His vision was slowly clearing, and thinking becoming less baffling and woolly. He needed medical attention, of course, but he was not going to seek it. He was not done here yet. Eyes narrowing at unfamiliar calls across the battlefield, he tucked his sword into his belt for a moment, reached down and removed his scarf and then tied it carefully about his head as some sort of cap. It would hardly protect him from a blow, of course, but he reasoned that the wound had been protected until he removed the helmet, and the last thing he wanted was random flying muck getting into his brain through the wound. At least the scarf might keep it clean, if you were kind enough to label the gore-streaked scarf clean itself, of course.

He pulled his sword back out of the belt and took a deep breath. He had something to finish yet and nothing short of death would stop him. Snarling what were supposed to be obscenities but probably came out as mumbled rubbish past his swollen tongue and baffled mind, he pushed into the crowd, hauling his own legionaries out of the way in an effort to reach the front of the fighting once more.

'Out. Way. Move.'

Legionaries ducked aside at the sight of the gore-encrusted, wild-eyed, crazed-looking tribune, and he was surprised how easy it was to move forwards when people were startled at the mere sight of you.

A soldier in front of him suddenly turned out to be an enemy. He'd forgotten about the scarves in his state and he only knew of it when the legionary tried to kill him. He parried somewhat inexpertly, realising only now that his strength had drained away, presumably through the hole in his head. He felt surprisingly feeble. His counter blow, a jab to the belly with his gladius, went horribly wrong. It seemed he didn't quite have the strength for the blow, and the point of his sword dropped. He narrowly missed skewering the man's knee and instead of stabbing him neatly and efficiently with steel, he fell against him and then liberally coated him in a fresh wave of vomit.

Shit, this was no good. How was he going to kill if he could barely lift his sword.

Another figure swam into his wavering view as the vomit-covered legionary was helpfully dispatched by one of the Tenth beside him. The tribune frowned at the figure, trying to determine in the muck and press whether the officer was wearing a blue scarf.

'Salvius? Salvius Cursor?'

He frowned, then squinted at the figure. 'Fronto?'

'Gods, man, what happened to you?'

In answer Salvius reached up and pointed at the scarf, which he was fairly sure was already soaked with the blood leaking from his head.

'Jove, that must be bad. You need to get to a medicus.'

'No.'

'Salvius, your life is on the line.'

'No.'

Fronto straightened in front of him, and Salvius tried to do so too, which resulted in yet another wave of nausea. He vomited onto Fronto's boots.

'Tribune,' the legate snapped in a surprisingly authoritative tone, 'get to a bloody medicus before you cough out your own brains.'

'No. Can't.'

'Don't be stupid.'

Salvius ground his teeth, not savouring the taste in his mouth. 'I can't Fronto. Pompey. He's here. He has to die.'

Fronto gave him a look that was so oddly sympathetic that Salvius couldn't quite understand and wobbled a little more until a legionary helped him. 'What?'

Fronto's brow furrowed. 'Pompey's gone.'

'*What?*'

'Threw down his general's cloak and fled the moment his left flank collapsed.'

'No.'

Gone? No, this was the chance. The last battle. The opportunity to actually meet the man face to face and stick a sword in him. 'Where?'

'Back to the camp, no doubt,' Fronto said carefully.

'To camp,' Salvius nodded, instantly regretting it. 'Come on, then.'

'In good time,' Fronto said, then gestured to two of the soldiers. 'Get the tribune to the medical section and tell them to take care of him. And if the tribune argues, you have my permission to poke him in that dent on the top of his head. That should stop him fighting you.'

Salvius stared. 'No.'

'Get well, Salvius,' Fronto replied, and suddenly Salvius was being helped back out of the press by the two men with an odd mix of courtesy and forcefulness.

* * *

Fronto watched Salvius being helped away and shook his head in disbelief. The tribune was a lunatic. He half expected, when this was over and they got to Pompey's camp, to find Salvius already there, his brains slopping out all over the place and Pompey's head in his hand. Oddly the image did not entirely displease him.

He turned his attention back to the fight that still surged, but he became aware a moment later of another change in the general atmosphere of the legion around him. The disheartened fear had turned into something new: despair.

Their leaders had fled, the wing collapsed and now Caesar's legions were in among the ranks of their men and killing with impunity. His ears caught the sound of a strong voice exhorting men to kill and fight on, and his searching gaze picked out a tableau not far through the thinning press. A centurion with a crest of blue feathers was shoving at men and pushing them back towards the enemy. His men were in a full panic and were trying to push past him, but the centurion and his optio nearby were stopping them fleeing with powerful tones and words of undefeated strength, and turning them, sending them back into the fray. Fronto gave a grim little smile. It was clearly a small island of command and vigour in a sea of despair.

That ship of hope had to be sunk.

Ignoring everything else, Fronto set his sights on the man and pushed forwards. The fight surged around him like the sea, lapping and splashing, crashing and flowing, men bellowing victoriously and men crying in agony and horror, the stink of blood and faeces almost unbearable. Fronto shut himself off from it. He had smelled those appalling stenches a hundred times over the years. It never became better or more acceptable, but it did become easier to ignore it and rise above.

It did not take long – perhaps only five steps – before he lost sight of the heroic Pompeian centurion, but every now and then as he strained to look over the heads of struggling me he could see the

315

tips of those blue feathers and knew he was heading the right way. A man lunged at Fronto unexpectedly and out of the blue, and it was only then that he realised he was not alone. Half a dozen of the men from the Tenth had spotted their legate in the press and flocked to support him, and he still had two of the men from the cohorts he had led into the battle, too. Between them, those eight men were doing an admirable job of keeping the danger out of the way and allowing Fronto to move with purpose. The man who had lunged was parried, then mercilessly run through and pushed away into the throng.

Other men tried, leaping forwards to tackle this determined Caesarian officer, and each one was caught by a veteran of Fronto's, parried, turned, killed with an almost mechanical efficiency, and still they were with him. He spotted the centurion again now, not just the feathers but the man in his entirety. The Pompeian officer looked faintly familiar and Fronto realised bitterly that he'd probably fought alongside the man for years without ever knowing his name when the First had served Caesar in Gaul.

The centurion bellowed at a cowering legionary and as the man made to push past him, grasped him by the hooks of his chain shirt, lifting him clear of the floor, turning him and throwing him back towards the fighting. Another man, panic overriding his sense and his discipline, made to stick the centurion with his knife in an attempt to get past. The knife punched into the chain shirt, catching on the harness of medals the officer wore, and failed to penetrate the armour. The centurion, lip curling in distaste, delivered his would-be killer a vicious blow with his vine staff, and then threw him away. He was an impressive specimen, even among centurions, and the entire breed were as hardy as Titans.

Damn it but he hated the idea of having to kill such a heroic and powerful legionary officer. Men like him were too valuable to throw away. But unfortunately, as the Roman army had learned to their cost more than once, centurions also made valuable targets. Their deaths robbed their entire century of both discipline and courage.

Two men who rather unpleasantly simultaneously killed one another fell out of the way and Fronto's path to the officer was clear. The centurion caught sight of the officer stomping towards

316

him, no blue scarf in evidence, nodded his understanding and drew his gladius, swapping his vine staff to his off-hand.

Fronto would be at a disadvantage with just a knife, so as he closed on the man, he reached up and unpinned the cloak he wore – a russet-coloured utilitarian wool garment. Under normal circumstances he would have hated to use a good cloak as a parrying weapon, but the shredded nature of the garment, cut by several blows in the battle already, hardly made it worth saving. He wound it round his wrist.

'Deal with the optio,' he said to his men, then broke into a run.

His first blow at the centurion was knocked aside easily with the ancient, hardened vine stick, but Fronto had hardly expected it to succeed. This man would, by the very nature of his rank, let alone the impressive array of medals on his chest, be an expert and a veteran. He threw out the arm wrapped in the cloak on an assumption and was rewarded with a jarring thump as the centurion's sword thudded into it. Fronto swore. Another blow like that might just break his arm.

He had danced past the centurion with the blow and turned now to find that the man had also spun to face him once more.

'Go back to your tent, sir,' the centurion said. 'I don't like killing officers.'

'Me neither,' Fronto said quietly. 'But times are hard.'

The centurion moved without warning, and fast as a striking snake. His sword swept up to the left, then down across Fronto in a diagonal sweep, then back in an impressive slash before he pulled it back and jabbed hard for the groin.

Fronto's blade caught the first blow and somehow managed to be back in the way of the second. The third only failed because he had twisted out of the way. He responded with a stab that the centurion turned, but with a little difficulty. Another flurry of blows came, a stab, a slash, a low jab. Fronto smiled quietly to himself. The man was fast, and he was damn strong, but he was also horribly predictable. They were all moves taught by any training centurion. He had watched Velius hammer these sequences into stunned legionaries every other day for years, especially in that camp at Cremona over the winter before they all marched into Gaul.

He parried and danced out of the way again, this time feeling the ache in his knee as he planted a foot badly. He waited. He did not attempt another strike. This fight was going to be won with the brain, not the hand. He watched. The centurion's sword came up high. Fronto closed his eyes for a long blink, picturing Velius all those years ago and praying to Fortuna he was right.

He opened his eyes to see the blade descending and took a step right, dropping his cloak-wrapped arm to a low position on his left, readying his blade, point-downwards.

His memory paid off. The centurion's descending blow missed entirely. It became a slash, sweeping up and was caught at a comfortable angle on the thick cloak, bounced away and was knocked out of danger by the blade. Fronto grinned.

'Hades, you're quick. But you know what's better than quick?'

'What?' growled the centurion.

'Unpredictable,' Fronto said as he let go. While he had been speaking, he had been surreptitiously unwinding the cloak from his hand. The centurion had been intent on his eyes and mouth and had not noticed the subtle move. The cloak flew out, billowing as it did, and engulfed the centurion's head and torso.

Fronto knew what would come next. The centurion, enraged, cast aside his vine stick and reached up to remove the cloak, simultaneously jabbing out with his blade as he stepped forwards. But Fronto knew the move, and knew what was coming. The man's blade met only empty air as Fronto stepped lightly past the centurion and then, with little in the way of panache, reached up with the sword as the cloak came free and cut the man's throat.

The centurion's eyes bulged and he turned in shock, bubbles of crimson forming at neck and mouth.

'Sorry,' Fronto said. 'Low trick, but this is war and it's all about the winning, not about the how.'

He kicked the centurion behind the knee, sending him to the ground, and then delivered a mercy blow, putting the man out of his agony. He felt his own knee wobble and was almost on the floor with him for a moment. He rose to see his men mobbing the optio, who was clearly out of it. The soldiers of the First were already running. Fronto turned with a frown of satisfaction as the field around them began to empty, enemy legionaries finally running.

'Bastards aren't so brave without their centurion,' he noted.

'Sir?'

He turned to the speaker, a legionary from the Tenth. 'With the centurion dead, they flee,' he repeated.

'They're answering the call sir. Can't you hear it?'

Fronto frowned and cocked his head, ear raised. There it was over the din: the retreat. It was an elaborate version, probably the First's own call, but it was clear as a variant on the standard legion signal. Now that he was listening, he could hear similar calls in the distance. Pompey's army was on the run. He felt a curious mixture of elation and disappointment. The enemy were fleeing the field. Caesar had won, even against ridiculous odds and, despite the calls, this was not an orderly withdrawal, but a full-fledge rout. The men of the enemy legions were running for their lives, some even dropping shields and helmets to make them lighter and able to run all the faster.

He should be elated. He should be revelling in the victory for certainly a strong part of it was his own to celebrate. Yet somehow the knowledge that he had pitted himself against the centurion and essentially cheated to achieve a victory totally unnecessarily rankled badly. He hated having killed a good, strong Roman officer for, in the end, nothing.

Fronto stood there, recovering, feeling his knee throbbing as the army fled. Caesar's victorious legions responded well to the signals that followed, calling them to their standards rather than letting them run after the enemy, which often heralded disaster. He watched the legions pull into ranks, depleted by the battle, but not so much as he had expected. They had, he decided, got off remarkably lightly at Pharsalus, but then they were due it after that mess at Dyrrachium.

He was standing there, amid the stink and the corpses, watching his faithful Tenth forming ranks on their standard, when he became aware of the arrival of the staff. Somehow he had sensed Caesar's approach long before he heard that familiar clearing of old, scratchy throat or saw the shadows of a dozen horsemen in cloaks and plumes. He did not turn.

'Congratulations, Caesar. A decisive victory.'

'And one owed in no small part to yourself,' the general replied.

'Forgive me if I'm having trouble celebrating. I'm not sure I'm so pleased.' He threw out a hand, indicating the numerous dead around him, some wearing blue scarves, others not. All Roman.

'I understand your woe, Fronto, and I do share it. But we must look to the army. If we present a face of regret and sorrow, we will do little for our men's morale. Our force will now be more or less on a par with the enemy, but we have the advantage in that our morale is high and we have not paused to take stock. The enemy has. They will be despondent and while I desire the death of Roman citizens no more than you, Pompey is still at large, as well as most of the other officers. As long as they evade our grasp, we must accept that this may not be our last fight. We must move on, while spirits are high. We must pursue and engage. We must force those legions into surrender and we must capture those fleeing officers. It is the only way to be sure that this is over.'

Fronto nodded wearily. He hated the thought of fighting any more. Of chasing a terrified legion into their own camp and butchering until they all fell to their knees. But Caesar was right. Pompey had to be captured, as did Scipio, Ahenobarbus, Afranius, Labienus and all the others, else they remained at liberty to raise further armies. And those legions had to be made to take Caesar's oath. Only then would the victory at Pharsalus be truly complete.

'Alright, General,' he sighed. 'Let's go finish Pompey.'

320

CHAPTER 24

Fronto peered up at the low rise upon which Pompey's huge camp sprawled. The defences were, of course, of a very familiar and standard design, just like their own back towards the Pharsalus bridge, though without a ditch given the sloping rocky terrain. The mass of fleeing legionaries from Pompey's army were pouring into that massive camp by the nearest gate, still in the grip of panic and dismay. They had something of a head start, partially because they had fled straight there from the battle, and partially because it had taken Caesar's legions precious moments to prepare themselves for pursuit.

'How many, do we think?' Fronto asked, guiding Bucephalus closer to the other officers.

Antonius turned to him. 'Survivors from the field or reserves in the camp?'

'Both.'

'The scouts reckoned about seven cohorts had been left in camp, mostly legionaries, but with some Thracian auxiliaries. As for those fleeing the field, it's anyone's guess, but if I had to pluck a figure from the air, I'd say about twenty five thousand.'

Fronto whistled through his teeth. He'd had a very specific and narrow view of the battlefield while he was on it, unlike Antonius who would have been able to see more and estimate numbers. 'And we're chasing them with, what, eight thousand?'

They had left most of the army on the battlefield and taken only the reserves who were still relatively fresh and energetic up the slope towards Pompey's camp. The rest were slowly marshalling and would be following on, but were simply too depleted and exhausted to go marching up a hill. Yet the officers knew they had to press for a full defeat and swiftly, lest Pompey rally his surviving force and turn on them.

'We'd better hope the panic is still running strong through them,' Fronto said darkly. 'Charging at a fortified camp containing maybe thirty thousand men with only eight is a little worrying.'

'Momentum,' Caesar said quietly. 'We cannot let them stop to take stock. They must continue to run and fear. Send out the auxiliaries with the bows and javelins and any units with pila. Clear the ramparts swiftly so the legions can push into the camp without stopping.'

Ahead, the last of Pompey's survivors disappeared into the gate and the timber leaves slammed closed. Fronto peered at the defences over the heads of the men in front. The camp was surrounded by a rampart that was topped with only a makeshift barrier formed by the sudis stakes that each legionary carried on campaign. The hill itself consisted of only a thin layer of grass and soil over rock, which meant that a ditch had been impossible, and gathering up sufficient earth and turf for the rampart had been so difficult that the mound was only low. Added to that, the lack of local timber sources – the only real one would be the small copse near the river where Galronus had hammered the water gatherers – meant that no stockade or fence could reasonably be created. Not the most daunting of defences, and the soldiers manning it were not too worrying either. It was what awaited them inside that mattered. Twenty five thousand legionaries. If they could be persuaded to surrender then all would be well. If not...

Caesar's instructions were being followed, now. The heavy infantry had slowed the pace of their ascent, while the light auxiliary missile units and the few centuries of legionaries who'd retained their pila jogged out ahead. Fronto watched as those units raced up the hill, urged on by their centurions and prefects. He could almost feel the nervousness of those defenders on the ramparts from here, and something occurred to him as he peered at the interspersed legionaries and Thracian spearmen.

'Why aren't the rest of the legions helping to man the ramparts?'

Antonius shrugged. 'Panic.'

'That's not enough of an explanation. Even in the worst rout there are men who recover. And there will be officers among them trying to pull them together. It makes no sense for them to cower in their camp protected by just seven cohorts. If they really are frightened of us, then why make for the camp, yet not hold it?'

Caesar nodded thoughtfully. 'It is puzzling, I admit. But we will no doubt understand when we seize their camp.'

The lead elements were even now reaching missile range. Units of auxiliary archers fell into formation in three positions along the length of the rampart and began to loose arrows in deadly clouds. The few legionary defenders on the walls answered as best they could with their pila, but their range, even down the slope, was nothing compared to the archers, and few of the missiles found a target. Conversely, arrows raked the south-eastern rampart, thudding into flesh, chain and shields, thinning the enemy ranks in mere moments.

A second flurry of arrows followed, then a third, and then the legionaries reached position and hurled their pila. The beleaguered defenders took the barrage hard, many of them falling away in agony. Men began to leave their posts now, simply disappearing, fleeing the brutal attack. It was perhaps telling that it seemed to be the legionaries running, rather than the Thracian auxiliaries. The latter, of course, would be an experienced native unit, while the legionaries were almost certainly recent recruits with little or no true combat experience.

At the commands of their officers, soldiers were now hurrying out around the other sides of the camp, and a quick look over his shoulder confirmed for Fronto that the rest of the legions were on their way from the field below, having re-formed into their units and left the wounded to be dealt with. Galronus and his cavalry were with them, following on.

'Something just isn't right about this,' Fronto said again. 'We're taking the camp far too easily.'

Truly, they were. The Thracians soon joined their legionary counterparts in fleeing the ramparts and leaving the camp defences bare. Officers turned to Caesar. The general gave the signal and with a roar his legions raced for the empty defences, up and over them, pausing briefly to disassemble the sudis fence lines.

The officers began to trot their horses slowly up the last stretch of hillside towards the claimed ramparts of Pompey's camp, and Fronto continued to fret. Pompey would be in there, as well as many of the other officers. And many thousands of legionaries, and yet Caesar's paltry force was meeting virtually no resistance.

His attention was caught by a call from off to the left and his eyes picked out soldiers waving and pointing off to the west. Fronto called across to the others and Marcus Antonius exchanged a brief word with Caesar, then nodded to Fronto and the pair of them rode off along the hillside, parallel with the rampart, towards the beckoning legionaries.

Fronto didn't need to reach the soldiers to discover what they had seen, though. As they rounded the corner of the great camp and the hillside fell away to the west, he could see what the men had spotted: many thousands of legionaries on the move. For a dreadful moment he thought Pompey had managed to rally and re-form his army and that there would be another great fight among the hills, but in moments the truth sank in: the legions were still fleeing. They had run for the camp under the watchful eye of Caesar and his army, but they had not stopped there.

What had happened, he could not say. Perhaps the officers had managed to urge them back to the camp but had failed to make them stay and defend with Caesar's legions in close pursuit. Or perhaps they had simply planned from the start to rush straight through the camp and out the other side, using it as a rear-guard to hold the Caesarian forces that little bit longer and give them a better head start. Whatever the case, they had clearly not stopped at the camp and had fled straight through it, out the other side and then up the slope of the high hill beyond, which would be a more difficult proposition to assault, with rocky outcroppings jutting up at places around it.

'You think they went through the camp to pick up desperate emergency supplies?' Antonius mused. Another possibility, Fronto admitted.

'Who knows. The big question is whether they're just running over that hill on the way somewhere, or whether they're planning to hole up and make a stand there.'

'Jove, but I hope not.'

Fronto nodded. The place was a little too reminiscent of Alesia for comfort in Fronto's opinion. He had no wish to repeat that dreadful siege, especially against other Romans.

'Either way,' Antonius said with a heavy sigh, 'we can't let them get away. We have to force a full surrender and disarmament, else we'll be fighting another battle soon. There's bound to be officers up there among them who harbour a grudge.'

Fronto nodded. 'The camp will fall with the men already assaulting it. We don't need the other legions below.'

'Agreed,' Antonius replied. I'll gather those legions and get them moving at speed to seal off that hill. You secure the camp and let Caesar know what's happening.'

With that, the curly-haired commander wheeled his horse and raced back down to the mass of tired legions stumping along behind, waving at their officers and pointing at the hill to the west. The army would be exhausted, but every man would still be riding the crest of victory, and Fronto knew they would do whatever was required of them without question or argument. If Antonius could head off Pompey's fleeing forces and trap them on the hill, they could maybe still end this here. Especially if Pompey was up there. Finally, he would be in a disadvantageous position and might consider a deal.

Turning, Fronto rode back towards the gate that now stood wide. The two legions' worth of soldiers they had brought up the hill were still pouring into the vast camp. There was no sign now of the small group of mounted officers, and they must have moved inside. Kicking Bucephalus' flanks, Fronto pounded off across the slope and made for an area of the rampart where the sudis stake defences had been dismantled. He crossed it with ease and spotted Caesar in the main thoroughfare of the camp, deep in discussion with Hirtius, still both mounted.

The legions were pouring through the camp, and as Fronto closed on the officers, he peered down the roads between the ordered lines of tents. Fights were in evidence all over the place as the Caesarian forces swarmed through the camp, putting down any resistance they came across. Moments later, Fronto reined in beside the general.

'Pompey's legions are fleeing up the big hill to the west, still on the run,' he said. 'Antonius is gathering the legions back down on the plain and taking them to seal the enemy in.'

Caesar nodded. 'They will not be able to hold out for long.'

'I'm not sure that's a good thing, though,' Fronto replied. 'With inadequate supplies and no water source, if we've got them pinned down they'll either have to agree terms or fight. And if Pompey's there with them, he's unlikely to want to come to terms. We might just be facing a bitter siege.'

'I do not believe so, Marcus,' Caesar smiled. 'Venus walked the field of Pharsalus with us and brought us an excellent victory. I do not believe the great goddess would offer me a gift like that and then snatch it away with such a change in fortune.'

Fronto nodded quietly, fighting the urge to point out that he'd not seen the goddess in the press and that it had been he and Galronus who had brought Caesar his victory.

'Pompey could still rally his men,' he reminded the general. 'He has the gift of the silver tongue.'

'Pompey is not on that hill,' Caesar said, his smile still in place.

'What? How do you know?'

'Because his personal vexillum and the standards of his praetorians are up there at his headquarters. Pompey did not flee with his men. Perhaps even now he awaits us in his quarters. Come, Fronto. Let's not disappoint him.'

The general began to ride slowly along the main thoroughfare towards the small collection of impressive tents that marked the quarters of the enemy senior command and their headquarters. Urging Bucephalus on, Fronto fell in with the small collection of officers, Aulus Ingenuus and his riders pulling in defensively, keeping Caesar from harm.

The camp had fallen to them easily, with a paltry defence, but there were still struggles and fights occurring throughout the huge installation. Each side street Fronto glanced down, he could still see legionaries and auxiliaries fighting between the rows of tents. Those men who had remained in camp were not selling their lives cheaply, and the advance through the place was sporadic, meeting resistance at almost every corner.

Still the main road had been cleared and, ahead, a century or so of men were engaged with a small unit of Pompeian soldiers in front of the command section. Though he could see no insignia from here, Fronto was sure they would be Pompey's own bodyguards, performing a last ditch defence of their commander's headquarters.

Their defence was heroic, but as doomed as every other struggle going on throughout the camp and, as the officers approached, the last four of Pompey's veterans shuffled back to back, dying by the swords of Caesar's legionaries. The officers passed the struggle and the gurgling corpses and reined in close to the tents. Fronto frowned as his gaze took in the principia and the officers' quarters. He'd never seen such opulence or decadence on campaign. The four officer's tents he could see from this position were fronted by pergolas upon which grew ivy and vines. In their shade sat dining arrangements on fresh, springy turf, tables bearing silver bowls and cups and jars of expensive wine.

'Who lives like this in a war?' he snorted in disgust.

'Senators,' Caesar replied in a disapproving tone. 'Not soldiers, but fat oligarchs who were only here because they thought Pompey would protect them.' He gestured to the command tent, and four of the praetorian horsemen slid from their saddles and hurried across and then in through the great tent's door, shields up and blades drawn ready. Other men fanned out and began to check the other tents. Gradually they reappeared, shaking their heads. All empty, as was the headquarters tent, confirmed by the four riders who reappeared, sheathing their swords.

Caesar, Fronto and Hirtius slid from their own horses, handing the reins to legionaries and then striding across the turf to that huge command tent. The interior was gloomy, but visible by the light of half a dozen oil lamps.

'Someone was here recently enough to have the lamps lit,' Fronto noted.

'Pompey,' Caesar confirmed, strolling around the interior. The tent showed signs of being abandoned hurriedly, and recently. The huge table had been swept clear, maps and scroll cases and wax tablets all cast down to the floor where they lay in heaps.

'Seems he was looking for something. I wonder what.'

Caesar, nodding, moved to the dividing wall and pushed aside the flap that led from the public area to Pompey's private quarters. This was more like what Fronto had expected of the officers, he thought as he followed the general in. Pompey's quarters were decked out much like Caesar's. Utilitarian and efficient, with the minimum of glamour and pomp. Here, again, lamps were lit, and checking the small bed chamber off to one side, the same there.

And once more everything had been left scattered and upturned. Had Caesar's legions reached the headquarters before them, Fronto would have assumed that the victorious attackers had ravaged the tent in the search for loot. But the officers had been the first here, and silver and gold accoutrements still lay around, mute evidence that nothing had been looted. The mess here had been left by the tent's owner searching for things and gathering his critical belongings before fleeing.

'So he's gone.'

Caesar nodded.

'And he probably *is* on that hill now, regrouping.'

Caesar shook his head. 'No. Pompey is not with his army. Likely other senior officers are, but not he. Remember, he cast off his general's cloak in front of his men. He knows that they saw him do so. To all intents and purposes he gave up his command in that moment. He cannot trust the legions to obey him now.'

Fronto sighed. 'I cannot fathom why he would do that, you know? He's a lunatic, but I never had him pegged as a coward.'

Caesar paused, frowning, and shook his head again. 'Not cowardice, Marcus. Remember that he had only taken on this command against me because the senate asked him to. And I would suspect that he has ended up fighting those same senators for control of his own army. His one gambit had failed on the battlefield, and Pompey will have been well aware that in the aftermath his influence will have diminished to almost nothing. If the senate no longer trust him to lead the army, then he is done.'

'If he's done, why do we still chase him, sir?' Hirtius put in.

Fronto answered for the general. 'Command or no command, Pompey is a powerful symbol and there are men who are still fanatically loyal to him. He might have given up his command of this army, but men like Ahenobarbus or Afranius will be up there trying to gather the legions back together and form a new command, and there are men like Attius in Africa with an army of his own, too. As long as Pompey is at large, he can be used to rally men against us. Legions don't care about the needs and desires of senators like Cato, but if those men speak through great successful generals like Pompey, the armies will listen and obey. We have to stop Pompey as well as his legions and senior officers. And if we don't do so here, it'll come back to bite us on the arse somewhere down the line.'

He turned to Caesar. 'Which leads me to my next question. If Pompey's not here, and he's not on that hill, then where in the name of Hades is he?'

'A good question indeed. He needs to retreat to somewhere where he is still in favour.'

The officers spent a short while searching the rooms in a fruitless attempt to ascertain what it was Pompey had taken, in the hope that it might provide some sort of clue, though in the end the answer came from an entirely different source. The main door of the tent swung inwards and Ingenuus dipped inside.

'Sir?'

'What is it?'

'Pompey's been spotted, sir.'

The officers broke off their search in an instant, turning and paying sudden attention. 'What?'

'Pompey has been cornered by our scouts with some of his praetorians near the north gate.'

'Come,' Caesar said simply, and hurried from the tent, mounting his horse with an agility that belied his age.

* * *

It was clear from the moment the officers rounded the corner of a huge tent complex and were treated to a view of the sloping northern reaches of the massive camp that the incident, such as it was, was over. A small group of men were gathered in a cluster near the north gate, but though one was clearly holding aloft a Pompeian standard, they were definitely men of Caesar's legions, with no blue scarves, and instead the bull motif on their shields.

The officers, the wind somewhat knocked from their sails, slowed to a walk as they neared the scene. There had been a short but very vicious conflict here. Half a dozen of Pompey's guard lay dead, one with a spear rising like a flag pole from his back. Their standard was clearly the one now being handled by a soldier from the Ninth. But alongside the six dead Pompeians several dozen scouts.

'Pompey?' the general prompted as they stopped.

The legionary with the standard looked up and saluted. 'Gone, sir. He'd gone by the time we got here.'

The officers moved across to the gate nearby and peered out. Far off, to the left, they could see the beaten legions of the Pompeian army gathering on the high hill top. To the right, some of Caesar's scouts had just taken a small lookout station from the enemy. And ahead...

Pompey was on the road north, along with perhaps thirty horsemen. They were already some distance away, though Fronto noted with some excitement a detachment of Gallic cavalry cutting across the slope in pursuit.

'We might get him yet,' Fronto murmured.

'No,' said a familiar voice nearby, and he turned to see Galronus on his horse, one leg soaked crimson to the boot, the thigh wrapped tight.

'You alright?'

'I'll live,' Galronus replied quietly. 'But Pompey's gone.'

'Your men?'

'They'll not catch him. My riders and their mounts are all exhausted after the battle while Pompey and his guard just sat at the back throughout, so they're well rested. They have the edge and my men simply will not be able to keep up with them.'

Caesar nodded. 'You are correct, of course. And Pompey makes towards Larissa where he still has some control. He will find succour, aid and supplies there. But he will not stay. He has no more military strength there. He must flee for now.'

'Then we must catch him,' Fronto said.

'Yes, but not now. Firstly we must finish off his former army, accept their surrender and deal with their commanders. We cannot afford to chase Pompey and leave an enemy force behind us with the freedom to recover and rebuild. We will follow Pompey, and before this season is at an end. But first: the legions.'

Fronto could not tear his eyes from that rapidly disappearing group of horsemen, though.

'Where will he go? Back to Dyrrachium?'

'No,' Caesar replied with a sigh. 'His fleet disintegrated and he brought the bulk of his forces from there to Pharsalus. He has no power any more in Illyricum, and it is too close to lands loyal to us.'

'Then Africa.'

'Perhaps. But not directly. He dare not travel west. But the lands to the east will likely still owe him loyalty. My wager would be Asia. Or Syria perhaps. He will travel swiftly and put a sea between himself and us, for he knows we cannot transport the entire army across water quickly. No, we deal with his legions here, rest and consolidate, and then we will follow Pompey and then, Fronto, you can be my terrier once more and root out the man for me.'

Fronto sagged. Caesar had taken his wish to pursue as a personal desire to hunt the man. Nothing could be further from the truth, though. Pompey could still cause trouble, yet Fronto would happily let the man go. He had agreed, though, despite everything, to command legions for Caesar until they had beaten Pompey and brought order once more to the republic. With Pompey in their grasp, the notion that he might be able to sail west and see Lucilia and his sons had felt real and close. Now, watching that rider disappear north, he could feel that hope slipping away. He would not be going home yet. At least not until they had caught and finished Pompey.

* * *

They found Marcus Antonius sitting on a low spur, peering up at the hill. The legions of Pompey were massed up there, and their number still sufficient that they resembled an army of ants. The dependable officer had split his legions into individual cohorts and spread them out around the hill.

'What news, Marcus?' Caesar enquired as they arrived on the low rise.

'We're in the shit,' Antonius replied.

'Oh?' Caesar said with a hint of disapproval. 'How so?'

'We have fewer men than them and I have a massive hill to surround. I considered simply marching up at them, but our men are tired, for all their enthusiasm, and the hill is steep. I fear we would lose, and that would be a poor result on the back of our recent victory. So attacking them is out as an option, I fear.'

'But you're surrounding them,' Fronto noted, 'and they can't have much in the way of supplies. And no water source.'

'Fronto, look how thinly we're stretched. If that force up there suddenly decides to go for a drink at the river, then we'll be hit by the better part of twenty five thousand men. Where along our lines do you think we'd hold them for more than a couple of heartbeats?'

Fronto nodded silently. The only reason Caesar's army was still ascendant was because of morale. The opposition were tired and defeated and had not yet managed to rally their spirits. If they came together as an army once more, they would roll over the cohorts below in short order.

'Then get them to work,' Caesar said flatly.

'What?'

'Start siege lines. We did it in days at Alesia and this place is far smaller.'

Antonius stared at the general. 'It's also dryer, harder and rockier. And the men have just fought a battle.'

'The men will appreciate having a rampart and palisade to stand behind if that army decides to, as you said, come down for a drink.'

Fronto looked up at the hill once more. This afternoon was going from bad to worse. From the extraordinary high point of having beaten a superior enemy in the field and achieving a phenomenal victory, they had lost the enemy's general and with him Fronto's hope for a quick resolution and a journey home before winter, and now the hill began to look more and more like Alesia. The last thing he wanted was to live through a repeat of a siege that had left him with years' worth of nightmare fodder.

He chewed his lip. Their best hope was to keep the enemy at odds with one another so that they failed to come together as a force and turn upon Caesar's legions once more. A smile spread slowly across his face. No, this was not Alesia, with a focused king like Vercingetorix and an army that shared one heart and one goal. This was an army in chaos and their one commanding figure had gone, leaving them as a force run by a committee.

'Afranius and Petreus,' he mused out loud.

'Pardon?' prompted Caesar.

'What? Oh, I was thinking that this looked like a repeat of Alesia, and I think we all want to avoid a repeat of that nightmare. But now I think again, it's more like Ilerda. More so, even, because some of the men up there were actually *at* Ilerda, and I think we might safely assume Afranius and Petreus to be up there among them.'

'You are suggesting a disparity in their command?' Caesar enquired, eyebrow arched.

'Something like that. At Ilerda things were a mess for the enemy because those two couldn't agree. This time there's those two, but since we've found no sign of corpses, I think we can assume others like Cato and Scipio and Ahenobarbus to be there also. Imagine how difficult an agreed-upon course of action will be with *those* men.'

Caesar nodded. 'We pressed Ilerda repeatedly and in concert. Eventually they broke and ran and we caught them only after some pursuit across the hills of the region.'

'The same, I think, is going to happen here. They will not be able to gain enough focus to launch an assault. I think if you pressure them, they'll break. And when they do they'll go north, because that's the only area they're familiar with, and where they might find aid. And once they cross a small valley to the north they're in the only damn range of hills to be found in this plain. We need to be ready in advance this time and not spend a month trailing them across the hills. We need to block them off each time they move, and you need to offer them a good deal.'

'Sorry?'

'You, Caesar. You need to reprise your famed clemency of the Italian campaign. You need to present them with an offer they cannot refuse.'

'Fronto, that army has fought us in the field as an enemy. They should be disbanded, their eagles and standards confiscated, and they should be scattered across the republic in veteran colonies where they cannot hope to stand together once more. And as for their commanders…'

But Fronto was shaking his head. 'No, sir. Most of those men were fighting for their officers and their eagles, because that is what a legionary does. They took an oath and they kept it. Make them take a new oath. Then they can keep that. Bind them to you. Offer them retirement or assimilation into our legions. The gods know how short of manpower we are. The Tenth has a nominal strength of near five thousand and we can't in truth muster half that. There are still enemies to beat – in Africa if nowhere else. Bind those men to us.'

'Though their commanders…'

'Bind *them* to you also. Many of them are senators and could be our allies if we only play things right.'

'Perhaps you are right,'

'I am. And you know it. But we have to put enough pressure on them first to make them want to talk.'

And then, when the army here is finished, we can deal with Pompey.

His memory treated him momentarily to an image of Labienus racing away with the cavalry. Those units were drawn from various eastern allies and would even now be deserting back to their lands of origin. They would be no further trouble.

With luck he wouldn't have to deal with Labienus, either.

CHAPTER 25

The hill, known locally as the 'Priest's Hill' for some unknown reason, was an entirely different proposition to Alesia, as were the works being constructed around it. Alesia had been considerably larger, of course, calling for many more miles of siege works and while this place was only a minor hill, for all its rocky outcroppings and vertiginous slopes, the conditions were far less conducive to a siege. The ground was soft enough, as the plain itself was extensively farmed, but timber was just as hard to come by for Caesar's army as it was for Pompey's. It had taken less than six hours to depopulate the three copses they had located within a mile of the hill.

Still, though it took longer, especially with troops exhausted from a recent battle, they had at least begun a solid investiture of the hill. The rampart went up swiftly, built with the earth taken from the ditch. It was dry, dusty, filthy work, for this was arable land and not grass, so there was no good turf surface to apply to the rampart. Just dirt.

The scouts had done an excellent job over the day following the battle and into the next morning, checking the surroundings with a view to the changing situation. Fronto's initial fears that the beaten army might spend a month leading their pursuers through hill country as they had at Ilerda turned out to be groundless. The small range of hills of which this was the southernmost stretched only a few short miles and then gave way to the flat plain once more. As long as the enemy could be kept on those hills, they would remain thirsty and trapped. And while they could move freely from hill to hill, the terrain made them slow in doing so, and even the most cautious of Caesar's officers was content that they could easily outpace the enemy on the flat ground and keep them penned in. Thus it was that there was little urgency to the siege works, as long as they did the job of sealing off the enemy from the nearest water source, which they did admirably.

And while the legions worked with spirit and vim at starving the enemy on their hill, Galronus and his riders came into their own. The plains of Thessaly were prime cavalry terrain and the Remi noble and his men could move with impunity to any quarter in a short space of time. Scouts and pickets had been put in place, and there was little chance of moving across the flat ground without bumping into a roving patrol. Thus it was that small units from Pompey's beaten legions – especially the young, barely-trained recruits – had already begun to sneak away under cover of darkness that first night. They had made it down from the hill heading northeast, away from the siege works. They had thought themselves lucky and safe, right up to the moment they bumped into a hundred veteran Gallic cavalry.

So far several hundred deserters had been brought to Pompey's old camp, where they were kept, under minimal guard. In fact, they came to consider themselves the lucky ones soon enough, for they were fed and watered as Roman prisoners of war, while their 'free' colleagues on the hill went thirsty and starved. Caesar had begun once more his conquest of hearts and minds.

Later in the second day it had become clear that the army atop the hill was on the move. The beleaguered legionaries on the heights shifted north, along the ridge that kept them relatively safe from Caesar's horse and his infantry. But as they moved north, so did Caesar begin to seal them in, leading four legions – all he could spare – out across the easy plains and to the north.

Fronto walked his mount alongside the Tenth, peering up at the range of hills to his left. There was no visible sign of the enemy, but they were definitely up there – the scouts had confirmed it. The small range of hills ended after perhaps three and a half miles and, as the legions arrived at that northern perimeter, Fronto heard the general's signal. Scouts sent ahead had located a second watercourse, more a stream than a river, but one that could in theory feed the enemy. Already the engineers who had moved ahead with the vanguard were marking out the lines to fortify and seal off this second source of water as they had the first.

Fronto turned to give his orders and was momentarily taken aback once again at the absence of Salvius Cursor. He'd never particularly liked the tribune, that was for sure, but over the last year or two he had become strangely accustomed to the man's presence, and not having him there to question Fronto's orders seemed strange. It would be some time before the tribune would march or ride with the legions, though. He languished now in the hospital section under the scrutiny of a medicus and his orderlies. He was expected to survive, though no one seemed confident that there would be no ongoing ill effects from such a bad head wound. Fronto had found it hard not to smile when the medicus had voiced his concerns over Salvius after a brief conversation with his patient, and Fronto had had to explain to the physician that the language and bile he'd encountered were entirely normal for the tribune.

Ignoring the hopeful-looking young junior tribunes, Fronto waved over to Atenos, himself sporting an arm splinted and slung tied to his chest.

'Have the Tenth Cohort join the others in constructing the works. The remaining nine can line up nice and shiny, facing the hill.'

Atenos saluted and issued the orders to his men. Similar commands were given out across the legions, and soon four cohorts of engineers and pioneers were at work constructing the rampart to block off the stream, while the bulk of four legions stood silent, waiting, watching the hill. Already, by mid-morning the late summer sun was searing hot, the landscape abuzz with insects and smelling of dust and flora.

It was a tedious wait. The scouts had only been able to estimate roughly the speed of the enemy in the hills, given the terrain they would have to cross, and therefore only the rough time of their estimated arrival. Five hours the legions stood, sweating in ordered lines while the four burly cohorts dug and heaved, constructing the rampart with all speed to block off the water.

As the trapped Pompeian survivors finally put in an appearance, swarming up to the northern edge of the hill and beginning to gather atop the slope above Caesar's waiting force, Fronto was struck once more by how many there still were. Caesar had brought four legions. It was all they could spare, with the others committed to the siege works around the other end of the hills, guarding prisoners, protecting both camps and the ever-busy medical complex, and gathering supplies and forage.

Four legions. Four *understrength* legions, Fronto corrected himself. Thank all the gods that the enemy still seemed to be under the nominal command of a senate of arguing civilians. Had a man like Pompey or Caesar, even Fronto, been up there in control, he might have just taken his chances with a fight. The men down here on the plain, for all their shiny veteran impressiveness and high morale, numbered perhaps twelve thousand men all told. Maybe half the number that now massed on the hill above. Of course conditions – hunger, morale, lack of equipment – might even it out as far as parity between the two forces, but that could still be enough for the enemy to triumph.

Clearly that was not going to be the case. Instead of gathering into ordered units, raising standards and rushing down the hill in response to a well-given command, attempting to crush Caesar's army and reach the precious, life-giving water, the enemy simply milled and massed on the summit.

'Why don't they at least try for something?' Atenos murmured, standing close by.

'Partially, I think, because they will remember something similar at Dyrrachium. We cut off their water supply there and they tried to rush us and ended up with disastrous losses. That little escapade will loom heavily in their thoughts. But mostly because there is no clarity of command. No army works well run by a committee.'

Atenos laughed, then became serious once more. 'But there are strong men up there. Good military men, surely? Can they not take control?'

Fronto shook his head. 'Afranius and Petreius cannot agree on the colour of shit let alone how to command an army. We learned that lesson well at Ilerda. Labienus and Pompey have both gone, escaped straight after the battle. Scipio might be up there, I'll admit, and Ahenobarbus, probably, but I cannot see either of those two deferring to the other, and none of the four of them would willingly let another take sole command. The rest of the officers will be senators like Cicero and Cato. Men with a little command experience, but far more at home in a courthouse than a battlefield. And it was the senate who, through Pompey, supplied the pay for the legions, so I doubt any of those remaining commanders will be able to charge up the blood of the survivors without the support of all of his peers. It'll be a mess. And I for one am bloody glad, because that chaos is probably the only thing stopping a second fight breaking out.'

Atenos nodded and they both peered up at the heights. More and more figures were massing at the crest, but as a mob rather than a military force. They had lost cohesion and all hope of solid command. They were little more than hungry bandits now, led by a committee.

'Will they turn back again, sir?' asked one of the junior tribunes.

'They might, but I doubt it. It took them half a day to slog their way across the rocks and dips to get here, and they're increasingly hungry and thirsty. No one will relish the thought of repeating that, especially since at the other end are just siege lines blocking them off anyway. They're trapped.'

He straightened in the saddle. 'The way I see it, they have four choices. They either try and make a break for it east or west, though they must realise by now that we can simply get ahead of them and be in the way wherever they go. Or they seek terms. Of course, if they do, Caesar will have a fine line to walk. He doesn't want to give them everything, but he must be magnanimous in victory and not push them too far, else he might break them and end up in a fight anyway. That's their third choice, of course: fight. But there will be enough leaders up there unwilling to start that, let alone tired and hungry legionaries.'

'And the fourth choice, sir?'

'Continue to dither and slowly starve to death. Not the most sensible option, but one upon which they seem intent at the moment.'

'Can you see what they're doing?' Atenos said in a surprised tone.

'What?'

'They seem to be making camp.'

Fronto stared. The centurion was right. Some of the refugees had brought tent materials with them when they fled through the camp and had begun to put up shelters. Others had used pilum and cloak to create a one man sunshade. They appeared to be settling in for the duration.

'Ridiculous. Caesar's going to have to do something soon.'

Atenos nodded. 'Maybe not 'til tomorrow, though, I'd wager. Another night of starvation and thirst will turn a lot of hearts towards the idea of reconciliation.'

* * *

Galronus squinted into the darkness. The campfires of the army at their new siege line below the slope burned bright, dancing and flickering in the dark, making the four legions' strength and their defences a visible reminder to the enemy even in the middle of the night. No fires had been lit atop the hill – there would be precious little up there to burn, after all – but the army of Pompey was still visible as a dark mass atop the peak, occasionally shifting around in the night.

The cavalry, on the other hand, were active. It had been a simple decision to split the entire remaining force into turma of thirty two men and set up a system of shifts, such that each unit did one night patrol and one day patrol and rested or slept in between. At any given moment there were more than two hundred riders out in bands, watching for men fleeing the lines. Some of the officers had argued that it could have been worth simply letting them go. They were deserting from the enemy, after all, and Sulla for one thought they should be encouraging such behaviour. Those men were overruled, though. The potential value of adding the deserters to the Caesarian manpower was too enticing, and though Caesar had initially displayed some scepticism over the idea, he had swiftly come around to it, once he had spoken to some of the prisoners being held in Pompey's old camp.

They were Romans. They were soldiers. They had followed their eagles until they fell to the dust and they had held true to their oath to support Pompey until he ignominiously abandoned them and fled the field, leaving them to die in his wake. It was becoming clear that the survivors were less than proud of their former commander, an attitude no doubt enhanced by other officers up on that hill who saw themselves as his successor.

And so the cavalry continued to rove the plains, and continued to capture small bands of fleeing individuals. The numbers on the hill would be dwindling, not enough to make a difference if it came to a fight, but their noted disappearance could only be further weakening morale there.

Galronus gestured to a low line of shrubs suddenly.

'What was that?'

The riders to either side of him peered into the dark, eying the line of bushes that looked little more than a lumpy hedge in the night. After a while, one of the riders shrugged. 'Nothing. Leaves in the breeze.'

'What breeze?' Galronus said in low tones.

The rider frowned. The night air was as still as a gnat's breath and had been for many days now, the day's heat still captured in the soil. All the three men squinted at that line of bushes. There was definite movement among the foliage, and had there been even the slightest air current it would have entirely escaped Galronus' notice. Without resorting to further spoken commands, he motioned to the men beside him to lead their riders both to left and right, around the ends of that line of bushes. Each officer did so, taking ten men and drumming off at a good pace, and Galronus gathered the remaining ten. All the men of this turma were Lingones, a tribe of central Gaul, their homeland lying roughly between his own Remi and the Aedui. They were good riders, and he had chosen them for his own unit based on their regular displays of skill and cohesion.

With just two hand signals, he directed the men to join him and walked his horse towards the bushes. Hunting men was sometimes so similar to hunting animals. Beat the undergrowth and send them the way you want, onto a spear point, preferably.

The other two units rounded the line of bushes and suddenly there were shouts in both Gaulish and Latin from beyond the foliage. Just as Galronus had suspected. He lowered his spear tip and gestured for the men to line up. They did so, their own spears coming down to form a deadly pointed hedge that moved slowly, inevitably towards the bushes.

He was not the least bit surprised when a small group of lightly equipped Romans burst from the hollow in a panic, though he was a little perturbed by the number of them. Perhaps two dozen men were running towards him, more than the usual half dozen nervous looking deserters they came across. These men wore no armour, just their russet tunics and boots and a sword belted at their side.

Their faces and arms were darkened with dirt to make them less visible in the night.

The deserters yelled in shock as they emerged to see eleven riders clopping slowly towards them with spears couched and ready. Desperate, taken aback by a trap they'd not anticipated, several of the men decided that they might fare better on their own and veered off left or right. Unfortunately for them, both the other cavalry officers had been bright enough to anticipate their quarry's attempted flight, and half the riders emerged back around the end of the line, five at each side, closing in on the escaping soldiers.

There was an assortment of reactions to the trap. More than half the men dropped to their knees, throwing their hands in the air. Only two drew their swords. The rest were still trying to run for it. Carefully, Galronus angled his horse so that his right side was more exposed, his left hidden. His leg still throbbed day and night and hurt like Hades when he mounted and dismounted, no matter how much help he had or how careful he was. One experimental prod had confirmed how much it hurt when anything touched it. He couldn't risk exposing his injured leg to an enemy.

One of the running legionaries – and he was brave, Galronus had to admit – made a valiant attempt to evade his captors, throwing himself to the ground and attempting to roll underneath Galronus' spear to relative safety beyond. Almost negligently, the Remi noble dropped the point of the spear and the man rolled straight into it. He hit it hard enough that Galronus felt the impact up the shaft right to his shoulder, and the point snapped off the spear.

He let go of the weapon and drew his sword as the moaning Roman tried to stand, got as far as his knees, and then coughed blood. The wound had not been an instant kill, but it had entered through his back and had clearly done something permanent and critical inside. The soldier went pale, eyes bulging, and coughed again, a mass of dark liquid dropping to the grass.

'Surrender and the consul may show clemency,' Galronus said, a line he had trotted out more than once in the last day or two. Staring wide-eyed at the dying man in the dirt, the other legionaries gave up the fight and dropped to their knees with their fellows, hands raised.

'I told you he would cock it up,' grunted one legionary.

Before Galronus could enquire further, there was another commotion at the far side of the bushes. A haughty, aristocratic voice in Latin demanded his release. There was a thump and then silence. Galronus, intrigued, sat quietly and waited. There was a long, tension-laden pause, and eventually half a dozen riders, led by a Lingone nobleman, emerged around the western edge of the bushes. Galronus' brows knitted as he saw that they had a prisoner amid the horses, hands bound and the other end of the rope tied to the officer's saddle horn.

As the riders came to a halt the Roman, a tall, thin man with short hair and a clean-shaven face that had been smeared with dirt, straightened with a haughtiness that seemed ridiculous in his situation. Galronus looked him up and down. He seemed vaguely familiar, but that was all. Perhaps it was because of the dirt.

'Let me go,' demanded the Roman, and Galronus' brow rose in surprise.

'Do you truly believe you are in a position to give orders to *anyone*, let alone your captors?'

'You have no idea who you are dealing with. I am a man of import. Caesar will have you slit from chin to balls if you mistreat me.'

'With who am I dealing that Caesar will be so concerned?' There was, of course, a standing order among the cavalry to treat officers with respect and deliver them to the staff rather than straight to the internment camp. So far they had taken a legate, a tribune and three centurions. This man was clearly in a different league, though, or at least believed himself to be.

'I am Lucius Domitius Ahenobarbus, acting praetor in the field on behalf of the senate of Rome.'

Galronus almost laughed. 'Ahenobarbus.'

'Yes, and Caesar will want…'

'Caesar is not here.'

'No, but Caesar…' the man began.

'And if Caesar *was* here, I doubt the mercy tree would bear you much fruit, Domitius Ahenobarbus. You stand accused of numerous crimes that warrant the sword.'

'I am ready to affirm a vow to…'

'I think not.'

The Roman stared at the Remi prince. 'How dare you, you barbarian oaf. Just because you know how to ride a horse…'

'I,' Galronus said with a smile, 'am Gaius Julius Galronus, a senator of Rome and senior cavalry commander in the field serving the consul. Perhaps you would care to rethink your insults?'

'Caesar will hear…'

'Yes,' interrupted Galronus. 'Yes, Caesar will hear about this. I shall tell him myself. You may have the chance to speak to him. It depends partially on how much your gods love you and partly on how sprightly you are.'

Ahenobarbus' brow creased in bewilderment and Galronus nodded to the officer as he reached out and took the other end of Ahenobarbus' rope. 'Take the other prisoners to the camp, then return to patrol. I shall deliver this creature to the general.'

The other riders saluted. The captured soldiers rose at their bidding, hands on their heads. Galronus was interested to note one of them risking a beating to step out of line and spit a huge wad of phlegm at the bound officer.

'Prick,' the man said under his breath and then joined his mates for the march south to the prison camp.

Galronus sat for a moment, surrounded by his ten men, then he took a deep breath.

'It is just less than a mile to Caesar's camp. I know from long experience that my horse can comfortably cover ten miles in an hour without breaking a sweat. I wonder: can you?'

'What?' snorted Ahenobarbus. 'I…'

'Fronto is always trying to prove to me how civilised Rome is by quoting old stories. Idiotically, as often as not they are about Greeks. Have you heard the tale of Pheidippides?'

'What? Of course I have.' Realisation dawned slowly on the man, and his eyes bulged.

'Fronto tells me,' Galronus continued, 'that Pheidippides ran twenty six miles to deliver news of some battle or other. I doubt you would manage twenty six, but I shall be interested to see if you can keep pace with me for just one.'

'Now listen here…' Ahenobarbus said, though this time with rather more panic than haughtiness.

'I think not. Take a deep breath Lucius Domitius Ahenobarbus.'

'I have information…'

'Good,' was Galronus' only reply as he kicked his horse's flank with his one good leg and urged her on, looping the rope over one of his own saddle horns. The other riders spaced themselves out so that they created a mobile circle around the commander and his prisoner.

Ahenobarbus stood his ground for mere moments until the rope jerked him into motion. He began to jog, keeping up with the horse. Galronus turned an unpleasant smile on him.

'Can you jump?'

'What?' gasped the Roman again, then made a strange, panicky strangled noise as he noticed the gulley coming up – irrigation for the fields hereabouts. Galronus jumped his horse easily. Ahenobarbus made the jump with some difficulty, landed badly on the side of his foot, and somehow, miraculously, managed to stay up and running. The other riders cheered.

'Well done,' smiled Galronus. 'Get used to it. These fields are well-irrigated.'

* * *

Fronto heard the commotion outside, scrambled from his cot, and poked his head out of the tent. A soldier was at Caesar's headquarters, knocking respectfully but urgently as a small group of horsemen approached up the Via Principalis. He recognised his friend leading them with a sigh of relief. Galronus was laughing with one of his officers.

Caesar emerged from his tent at the same time as Fronto, though where the legate of the Tenth was busy shuffling into unlaced boots and belting his tunic, fresh from sleep, the general was fully dressed and alert. Antonius was with him, a folded map beneath his arm from where the pair had been working into the night.

'Senator Galronus,' Caesar smiled. 'You have important pickings from this night?'

'Pickings full of their own importance, General,' grinned Galronus. He walked his horse forwards, and the gathered officers could now see the shape on the end of the rope behind him.

'Explain?' Caesar said, a dark tone inflecting his voice.

'One Lucius Domitius Ahenobarbus. I had it in mind to simply do away with him when caught, but he seemed insistent upon speaking to you.'

Caesar looked unimpressed, but Antonius snorted with laughter. Fronto stared at the thing that had been Ahenobarbus. He'd have been happy to order the man's death, for few Romans, and none of Pompey's officer corps deserved it more, but this tortuous method seemed too much. It was then that he realised with shock Ahenobarbus was still alive, groaning and twisting this way and that.

'He survived the trip,' Antonius said, dropping his maps into the hands of a nearby legionary and coming out front.

'Yes. He made it almost half a mile before he tripped on a rock. He was noisy for a while.'

'I'll bet,' Antonius laughed. He approached the dusty, bloody heap on the rope's end. 'So you have something to say?' he asked. The ruined officer coughed up dust and blood and murmured something in a low, scratchy voice. Antonius leaned close, putting his ear close to Ahenobarbus' lipless mouth.

'Talk.'

Ahenobarbus did. For only a moment, and it was clearly painful to do so, but Antonius nodded. 'Your information is received with gratitude, Ahenobarbus. Now let me help you in return.'

Swiftly, Antonius drew his sword and plunged it into the broken officer's heart.

'What did he say,' Caesar asked, quietly.

'It would appear that both Cato and Scipio fled ahead of him. Cicero is now the most senior man up there.'

Caesar nodded. 'Cicero is too sensible to fight on. Good. This is almost over, gentlemen.' He gestured at the body on the rope. 'Someone get rid of that before it starts to smell.'

* * *

The deputation came the next morning with Cicero at the head. He looked tired and lean. Behind him was a small group of senators who looked utterly out of place in just tunic and boots, dirty and hungry. A few tribunes, too, and a small honour guard of

346

legionaries under a centurion. None of them managed to stand with any real pride.

'What are your terms,' Cicero said, with no preamble as he came to a halt thirty feet from the rampart.

Caesar rubbed his hands together and then hooked them over the fence in front of him.

'There will be an amnesty for all commanders,' he said in a loud voice. Cicero had the grace to look surprised. 'I have no wish to make further enemies within the republic when all of this could have been avoided by simply granting my request for the consulate a year ago. How selfish of men like Pompey, and yourself, to waste a sea of Roman blood in dreadful civil war simply to keep me from a consulate which I rightly deserved. But I am not here for recriminations. Pompey will fall into my hands soon enough, and then this entire disaster can be put right. For now, all officers will lay down their commands and retire from any public position they currently claim to hold. They will become private citizens once more. If, when this war is fully concluded and we all return to Rome, the senate then votes those men fit to hold such positions once more, they will of course be allowed to do so.'

Fronto nodded. Not only clemency, but the most generous terms he could hope to hear. Perhaps men like Cato who had snuck away at night might come to regret not seeking the general's terms, after all.

'And what of the men,' asked another voice: Marcus Junius Brutus, cousin of the man who still served as Caesar's naval expert and once a close friend of the general's. Caesar's face took on a sad expression at the sight of his old friend.

'Each man on that ridge will come down to the plain before the defences and will throw down his arms. They will then be given the choice of amnesty and freedom to return to their former life, or continuing service in the forces of Rome, though taking a new oath and joining the legions that won the field at Pharsalus and were depleted in doing so.'

A ripple of surprise ran through the entire deputation then. None of them had expected mercy on this scale.

'Let this be an end to this bloody and destructive civil war,' Caesar announced. 'Pharsalus is not a victory to celebrate with a triumph. It was a field of blood that should never be repeated. Let us *heal* the republic.'

Fronto smiled and nodded, though he was under no misapprehension that this was the end of the war. Attius still held Africa with his legions, and Pompey was at large somewhere, as were Labienus, Cato and Scipio. The war was not yet over. But at least the *battle* was.

CHAPTER 26

Fronto finished fastening his belt and pinned his least limp and stained cloak about his shoulders. For a moment he considered taking his helmet, but this was not war, and the day's heat was already building. A sweaty head was not to be sought for no reason, after all. Examining himself in the slightly warped bronze mirror, he nodded. He looked like he always did: like a soldier, not a nobleman, of a warped, bronze, wobbly one..

Leaving the tent, he was surprised to see Salvius Cursor standing nearby, similarly attired though less crumpled and stained. The tribune still had pink-stained bandages wrapped around his head, though the bruising to his upper face and ear was now fading rapidly. Fronto had visited the man in the sick tents several times, noting with a mix of irritation and pride how desperate Salvius was to get out of the hospital and back into the ranks of the legion. But the medicus had been adamant that it would be half a month yet before the tribune was fit even for the lightest of duties. His skull was still slowly knitting together, even though the bleeding had long since stopped.

'Sir.'

'Medicus relented has he?' Fronto asked, though he already had an inkling that this was not the case.

'Not quite, sir. Discharged myself. I'm fine so long as no one pokes me in the head.'

'Why now?' After all, it had been two days since the surrender of the army on the hill and, though Fronto had received a summons from Caesar, there were no signs that the army was preparing to depart.

'There's a rumour going around that Caesar is going to march off and chase down Pompey.'

'Ah yes. I might have guessed. The faintest chance that you might get to strangle the old bugger and even beheading wouldn't make you lie still.' He looked the tribune up and down with pursed lips. The man seemed perfectly compos mentis, at least as he *ever* did, and was the right colour again, at least. And it felt odd not having the lunatic there to disobey his orders, too. He shrugged. 'Try not to get yourself in trouble. I'm on the way to see Caesar.'

'Yes.'

'I was summoned.'

'Yes.'

'You were not,' Fronto added, pointedly.

'I shall wait outside.'

Shaking his head in faint exasperation, Fronto stomped off towards the general's headquarters, with Salvius at his side. He rolled his eyes at their approach, noting the somewhat ostentatious sign of their total victory. In the open area before the headquarters tent, the captured standards and eagles of Pompey's army stood, planted in the ground. It was like a glittering metallic forest. One hundred and eighty standards and nine eagles made for a lot of silver in the bright sunlight, and the men of Ingenuus' praetorian guard around the tents had been trebled, protecting the precious standards and eagles, should any legionary drunkenly wonder whether he could get away with swiping one and living easy for the rest of his life. They strode through the narrow path between the gleaming prizes and reached the headquarters tent, where two more guards waved Fronto in and eyed Salvius suspiciously, as he stopped outside and began to look around the standards with interest.

Inside, Caesar's great table was spread with a huge map of the region. Wooden markers had been placed all over the map indicating units, generals and other points of interest. Other than Caesar, three other figures occupied the tent: Marcus Antonius, Decimus Brutus and Galronus. An odd, but interesting trio.

'Good,' Caesar said, fingers drumming on the elbows of his crossed arms. 'Fronto, we have made decisions as to our road onward from here. We cannot ignore Africa now, it being the strongest enemy garrison remaining, and equally we cannot forget Rome, and the prize it will now become for our opposition. Additionally, there are numerous Pompeian elements surviving that we need to take care of.'

Antonius nodded. 'The beauty is that we are much stronger since the addition of Pompey's legionaries to our own forces.'

'Quite. I am therefore dispatching Antonius here with your legion, Fronto, the Tenth. They and the Ninth are by far the most depleted and deserving of rest after Pharsalus. In Italia, Antonius will pension off the older veterans into key positions for the potential defence of Italia and Rome, and keep the legions at the heart of things, ready to rebuild, probably at Cremona or Aquileia.'

Fronto felt a strange mix of elation and disappointment. If the Tenth were to be garrisoned and partially disbanded, then his command was gone, given to Antonius. Perhaps he was done. He could go back to Tarraco, see his family at last. But a nagging little irritation at the base of his skull urged him on, to see this whole storm of shit through to the end, and the republic restored to peace.

Antonius laughed out loud. 'I must play dice with you for money, Fronto. Your face is an open book. I could read your intentions so easily. Panic not. You will not return to Italia with me. I am charged with the defence there, because I am glib and likeable, and I can play a part in the senate as well as on the battlefield. You, on the other hand, are a warhorse and of little use in the nicer social circles. No, you're not done yet, my friend.'

Again elation and disappointment, though this time the other way around. No going home, but a chance to finish this. Caesar nodded.

'Antonius is simply my rear-guard. We must move, and we must do so decisively, if we are to keep our momentum. We have had word of Pompey. It seems he is in the north, now. He has been seen near Amphipolis, on the coast up near the Bosphorus. I had assumed he was making for Syria initially, but perhaps he now has other ideas. Because he still has something of a power base in Syria, I am sending Calvinus with three legions thither, where they will impose control and prevent any support for Pompey. With luck he will still go there, but we cannot be certain. One thing that concerns me is word that Cassius and a sizeable part of Pompey's now-fragmented fleet were bound for the Hellespont. If Pompey can link up with a section of his navy we will almost certainly lose him.'

'So you head to Amphipolis?' Fronto said. 'And with all speed, hence the cavalry commander.' He nodded in Galronus' direction.

'Quite. If at all possible, I would like to catch Pompey while in that place, before he can begin to form an army again. Word of his ignominious actions at Pharsalus will not precede him, and quite possibly his reputation remains intact in the east. If he can gather men at Amphipolis and ships from Cassius, then we face a further test. Our advantage currently lies in the fact that our opponents' forces are fragmented and widespread. We can overcome them all, piece by piece, and put an end to this, but we must act upon them before they can combine into strength once more.'

'The potential involvement of the fleet also explains Brutus,' Fronto noted. 'None of this explains my presence.'

'Can you not guess, Marcus? I need my terrier. With or without the Tenth, I need the man who won me the flank at Pharsalus. I have appointed Canuleius to the gathering of warships in the Adriatic, since it is beginning to look as though we might need them, and he has ties that might be of use in that respect. So, with his departure, the Sixth is without a legate. The Sixth is one of the few legions that is still relatively strong and fit and energetic. They will be my armoured fist, while the cavalry are my spear. We shall chase down Pompey, I with the cavalry riding ahead, the Sixth following on by forced marches as we once did in the lands of the Belgae if you remember? You are the man to lead them on, Fronto. Bring the Sixth to Amphipolis with all speed.'

Fronto nodded with only a slight frown, his eyes straying to the huge map. 'Amphipolis must be two hundred miles from here. Certainly not far off that. With the cavalry you can do it in six days?'

'Five, Galronus here assures me.'

Fronto rolled his eyes. Damn it. 'Alright, five. I can get the Sixth there in five days too, but that it at forty miles a day. That's a lot, as you know. With campaign kit they will be tired at the end. If you intend us to fight a battle at Amphipolis we need to march slower than that and preserve our strength.'

Caesar shook his head. 'Speed is the concern here. If we have to fight a battle, then we have failed in our goal, which is to catch Pompey before he can gather a force. Five days it is. We have brought in extra allied horse units, and we now have eight hundred horse. The able, hale manpower of the Sixth is three and a half thousand. That should be adequate to deal with one man and his personal guard.'

Fronto nodded. 'As long as nothing goes wrong. I have one request.'

'Oh?'

'Salvius Cursor is standing outside, almost chewing through his own lip with worry that he will not be allowed to face Pompey. I would like him to accompany us as senior tribune of the Sixth.'

'I thought you were rarely keen on Salvius' somewhat violent and unorthodox approaches?' Antonius said with a strange smile.

'He has proved himself, and if it's terriers you want, for Pompey hunting, then Salvius is your man.'

'He was sorely wounded at Pharsalus,' Caesar said, brow furrowed. 'Is he well enough?'

Fronto shrugged. 'I think so. I can't guarantee that he won't go all funny if you poke him in the head, but that's what helmets are for.'

Caesar exchanged a look with Antonius, who paused for a moment and then nodded. 'Very well. Salvius and Fronto with the Sixth. Go to your command and prepare them. We leave in an hour.'

* * *

In fact, it was day six when Fronto and his new legion finally laid eyes on Amphipolis. Not because they could not keep up the pace upon which he had agreed, but because travelling with the cavalry meant inevitably travelling in the cloud of dust they created, and it was enough to ask the men to march forty miles a day in full kit under a hot sun, without having them do it in a dust cloud.

Caesar had not been overly pleased but had eventually agreed and on the second day of the journey the Sixth slackened their pace a little and let the cavalry pull far enough ahead that the dust had settled before the legions passed through.

The lands they traversed were something of a catalogue of ancient names for Fronto. He had received a good education, of course, like any good Roman boy of a patrician house. He'd enjoyed the tales of gods, heroes and war and ancient Greece was full of those, and the names of the places they passed by and through resonated with him.

Crannon, where, following the death of Alexander the Great, Macedonian forces under Antipater had crushed the Athenians, slid by on their left as they approached Larissa, which had now thrown open its gates to victorious Caesar and foresworn its former allegiance to Pompey. Mount Olympus, home of the gods, passed by on their left in its lofty majesty, while they made their way from Larissa to the coast. Pydna, scene of two great Roman victories over the Macedonians, languished now in happy obscurity near the sea. Other names: less famous but equally evocative, lands of ancient battles and homes of heroes now legend. For days they passed such places, passing the great city of Thessalonike and its peninsula and finally bore down on their destination.

Amphipolis lay on a rocky spur nestled into the curve of a river, between two ranges of high hills. Encircled by strong walls that had already been partly consumed by the extending urban sprawl, the city of red roofs spread up the slope to a high rocky acropolis bearing an ancient temple.

Leaving the Sixth on the western side of the river to make camp, judiciously away from the city itself, Fronto told Salvius to settle the men for the night. The tribune all-but vibrated with the desire to join his commander in the city and pursue news of Pompey, but grudgingly followed orders and Fronto, with just half a dozen guards, rode across the bridge and into Amphipolis. He was pleased to discover that Caesar had clearly done the same with his horsemen, as Galronus' cavalry were encamped on the green between the river and the city, though there was no sign of the commanders.

It was not hard to locate the Roman officers in the city. Moving up through the ancient curving streets, Fronto reached the agora below the acropolis' buttressed walls, presuming the general to be somewhere in the city's political heart. Half a dozen of Caesar's praetorian guards sat on their horses outside a grand looking building, with several riderless animals. Fronto and his men rode over to them and slowed.

'The general is inside?'

One of the guard nodded and gestured to the door, so Fronto slid with only minimal difficulty from his saddle and, handing his reins to one of his own men, strode in through the door into a cool, dark interior corridor. Following voices speaking in Latin, he found the other officers in a large room with a balcony overlooking a pleasant garden with a view across numerous roofs to the river, beyond which the Sixth was busy making camp.

'Ah, Fronto. About time,' Caesar said.

Fronto nodded to Galronus and Brutus and saluted the general in such a casual manner as to be almost insubordinate.

'It would appear that we have missed Pompey,' Caesar said with just a tinge of irritation. 'By only a few days. It appears that he sought to drum up support here, in lands that had long held an allegiance to him, but the people of Macedonia and Thrace have seen sense and thrown their support behind the true senate and republic of Rome. Pompey lingered as long as he dared and tried everything he could, to no avail. I have already thanked the boule of Amphipolis for their steadfast attention to duty and their loyalty and made it known that they will be remembered for it.'

'But still we missed Pompey. Do we know where he went from here?'

Brutus nodded. 'He took ship. I made some enquiries and it is clear that he was bound for Mytilenae.' He noted Fronto's bafflement and clarified. 'An island city off the Asian coast, some two hundred miles southeast of here.'

'Oh good,' Fronto grunted. 'Another two hundred miles.'

'But these should hurry by,' Brutus smiled, 'by ship.'

Fronto fixed him with a withering glare, and Brutus gave a guilty chuckle. 'Ah yes. I forgot how bad a sailor you are. Can I suggest you load up with ginger and mint to ward off the worst of it?'

'Better to empty my stomach and try and shit myself inside out so there's nothing to bring up on board.'

Brutus chuckled again, and Fronto tried to make his glare a little more angry.

'Fear not,' Caesar said with a smile. 'We shall march from here to the Hellespont tomorrow and cross there with what few ships Brutus can gather.'

'I've already begun acquiring them,' Brutus winked.

Caesar nodded. ' Brutus will take the ships up to the Hellespont to meet the army, after which we shall cross, and then march fast down the Asian coast, hopefully catching our quarry at Mytilenae, which lies just off the coast. And given the rather open nature of sea travel and our lack of definite knowledge of Pompey's plans, I shall dispatch a fast ship to Athens and instruct Calenus to send his cohorts from the Twenty Seventh to Cyprus, where they can be on hand to move in any direction as required.'

* * *

Thus it was that three days later Fronto eyed a boat suspiciously, but grudgingly acknowledged that even he was unlikely to vomit his organs out in a distance of a little over two miles. Brutus had done an admirable job as always, acquiring any vessel large enough to carry a century of men or a turma of horse, and the better part of a hundred ships and boats now bobbed at the jetties of Callipolis or out in the water just beyond. An odd haze had settled on the region, born perhaps of a combination of heat and moisture, and the air was not as clear as it should be and smelled damp and slightly cloying.

Off to the southern edge of the harbour the first load of vessels were already moving out into the channel, full of eager legionaries, while others moved into their place, ready to load the first consignment of cavalry.

Fronto climbed up the plank onto the sleek yet heavy liburnian, one of few military ships that had been acquired, and felt his guts churn even at the motion of the ship at the dock, swaying slightly with the strong currents of the Hellespont. This ship held Caesar's praetorians, the First century of the Sixth, and Fronto, Brutus and Galronus. If this weird fleet could claim a flagship, this was it.

On Brutus' advice they waited a while, as the first cavalry transports were loaded, and once all the ships were occupied they moved out into the water. It was better planning Brutus had said, since they did not know what might await them ahead, to land in full force and move on from there.

Fronto moved off to the rail, his accustomed position on board ship, where he could unburden himself of his stomach contents with the minimum of fuss. As they pulled out into the middle of the Hellespont, where the current was strongest and ships were known to be torn apart in bad weather, the captain angled his ship along the channel, with just a slight angle to cut across, making little headway. The other ships behind did the same, and slowly they pulled their way across the dangerous stretch of water.

It was purely due to his position there that Fronto saw them first. The officers and most of the men and the sailors were amidships or to the rear, or below with the horses. Fronto, very much on his own at the port rail near the bow, looked up from his latest culinary evacuation and peered unhappily at the horizon, despite the many times he had been told that this only made it worse.

The Bosphorus stretched away northeast towards Byzantium, green and grey slopes to each side, making it even more forbidding. The surface of the blue water looked deceptively calm. It didn't *feel* it. Less than a mile up there, he could see the narrow channel opening out into a wide stretch of water: the Sea of the Propontis. It was hard to make out a lot of detail at this distance because of the haze. Then, suddenly, shapes began to coalesce. He stared. Ships. And not just any ships... warships.

'Shit,' he shouted, wiping his mouth and staggering back away from the rail. A moment later he was battering his way between angry sailors and waving at Caesar, who was deep in conversation with Brutus.

'What is it?' Caesar said.

'Warships,' he gasped. 'A fleet. Cassius at a guess.'

Caesar huffed and rubbed at his temple. 'How far?'

'Less than a mile.'

'Then we will not get our troops disembarked before he is upon us, and half the army will remain cut off on the north bank. This could be a disaster. He cannot yet know who we are. Perhaps he will ignore us and think us a merchant fleet.'

'No, sir,' Brutus replied. 'Too many. And we're clearly crossing the straits. We cannot go in disguise.'

'Have we got one of Pompey's flags with us?' Fronto said quietly.

'What?'

'Any flag that could be of Pompey's allies? Maybe if we display it we can slip past them as friends?'

Caesar nodded. 'We have several vexilla that bear simply an eagle and SPQR.' He turned to one of the praetorians. 'Fetch an eagle flag and have it displayed prominently at the prow. Quickly, now.'

As the man hurried off about the task, Caesar spat out further orders. 'Get the First Century up on deck, but without their shields or vexillum. Nothing that gives them away as mine. Let's look like one of Pompey's ships.'

'What if he wants to know what we're doing here?' Galronus said.

'Then we're in for a fight,' Fronto replied. 'We can only do what we can, eh?'

He hurried along the rail towards the bow once more, where a sailor was stringing the flag. Behind him, he could hear the jangle, clunk and clatter as the legionaries made their way up onto deck and fell into lines.

Fronto watched the approaching ships. There were only twelve visible. He'd expected more. It had to be Cassius' fleet, or at least part of it. There would be no other naval forces in the region. Perhaps the rest were further away, invisible as yet in the haze? They were coming on, straight for the flotilla crossing the channel. Of course, that same haze would make identification more tricky until they were close, but they had to be at least interested now. The lead vessel began to pull out in front, slightly faster than the others. Fronto could see a flag fluttering on that ship, a crimson one with... yes an image of Hercules. Definitely Pompeian ships.

They were coming fast. Fronto knew his eyesight to be far from the best, but even a below-average lookout on that ship must have seen the flag by now. What were they doing? They were clearly too interested to simply leave the flotilla alone, else they would not have picked up pace. But they were not coming armed for war, for the rest of the ships simply ambled along behind.

What did they think: friend or foe? He fumed and turned to the flag, which was now fluttering and waving in the strong mid-channel wind. It snapped straight momentarily and Fronto stared in horror. The damn soldier had picked up the wrong flag. The golden 'Taurus' bull emblem of Caesar gleamed in the sun above the 'VI' that identified its legion owners.

'Oh, shit.'

He turned and ran to the officers. Caesar had retreated inside and left Brutus in rather nondescript armour as the senior officer on board. The general himself was, after all, fairly recognisable.

'General, the daft sod sent up the wrong flag. We're displaying the Sixth's bull.'

Caesar leapt up and stepped out of the shade. 'Gods, but what a mistake. They are close enough to see, yes?'

'Beyond a doubt.'

'Are they arrayed for war?'

Fronto frowned. 'Oddly, not. What do we do?'

'Our ruse is blown, Marcus.' He turned to the rest. 'Issue the standards and shields to the men. Fly all our flags and have the order given to the other ships. If we have announced who we are, then let us meet these men in the open. Perhaps we can persuade him that we are more than we truly are.'

Moments later the insignia was being raised on standards above the men of the Sixth and flags rose on the various other ships of the fleet, all displaying Caesar's bull. Fronto took a deep breath. The general was quite right. They had failed to sneak past, so they must brazen it out.

They kept to almost the same course, steering very slightly into the current, almost head-on with the approaching warship. With men lined up in gleaming ranks and banners snapping and fluttering, they waited for the ships to close. As they neared, the lead Pompeian ship began to slow, oars back-watering and then, as the trireme slipped to a stop, barring the pull of the current, the oars were shipped.

Fronto glanced back at the other officers and shrugged. Caesar gave the order to come to a full stop, and the liburnian slid close to the lead warship, similarly back-watering and then shipping oars. Fronto joined the others, trying to look much more impressive and much less ill than he felt.

A figure in a senior officer's uniform approached the bow of the other ship and stopped at the rail. He looked familiar, but it was only as Caesar's voice rang out that Fronto realised why.

'Gaius Cassius Longinus, well met.'

Fronto frowned. This was Cassius, who had been the only officer to leave the field of battle at Carrhae with his men when Crassus fell to the Parthians. This was Cassius the war hero, supporter of Pompey and former tribune of the plebs. But what surprised him more was that Cassius had both arms extended, palms up and his sword laid across them.

'On behalf of my sailors and officers and the ships of the Euxine Fleet, Caesar, I surrender all to you and seek only your clemency for those deserving men who have done nothing more than serve both Rome and their conscience.'

Fronto stared, but Caesar was less taken aback, clearly, for he strode across to the rail and threw up his hands in greeting. 'Gods, but it is good to see you, Cassius. Your brother, who as you know has served me faithfully as proconsul, has been worried about you. Perhaps now the pair of you can retie your familial bond.' He smiled easily. 'Never has it given me more pleasure to grant clemency, to the entire fleet and every man therein. Come, Cassius, sheath your blade, for I have need of men of your wit and skill. Join us.'

Fronto shook his head in wonder at it all. Caesar bowed only truly to Venus, while Fronto spent his life honouring Fortuna, yet it was the general who the goddess continually threw her cloak about. Would the man's luck never fail?

* * *

They arrived in Cyprus on a sunny late afternoon to find more ships and the cohorts of Calenus encamped near the port, awaiting their general. Caesar's small army had travelled down the coast of Asia, with Cassius and his ships keeping pace out to sea. They had called at Mytilenae only to discover that Pompey had been there a short time, gathered a small flotilla at great expense and then left, heading south once more, bound, it was said, for Cyprus. That critical island being the logical stop before Syria, it made a lot of sense. The army had paused in places down the coast, often encountering signs of Pompey's passing or influence. At Ephesus, Pompey's creature Ampius had attempted to strip the Temple of Diana of all its wealth to hire men in Pompey's name. He had failed, though largely due to the news of Caesar's approach that set the whole city against him, so that he fled south in fear. And so the Caesarian force had moved on, bound for Cyprus.

The ships docked swiftly, and the army disembarked, the Sixth and the cavalry combining with the Twenty Seventh to create a much more formidable force. Fronto heaved his usual sigh of relief as he stepped onto dry land, still dimly and uncomfortably aware that Cyprus was just a very big island and that the only way off it was once again by ship. At the dock, he mounted and joined Caesar, Brutus, Galronus and the now-trusted Cassius, and made for the camp of the Twenty Seventh.

They were greeted at the gate of the camp by a tired-looking tribune, a centurion and an honour guard of legionaries. The tribune threw a salute out at the approaching officers, and Caesar waved the niceties aside.

'Tribune?'

'Sir. Titus Orfidius Bulla, commanding a vexillum of the Twenty Seventh. We have eagerly awaited your arrival.'

Caesar nodded impatiently. 'Thank you, Tribune. What news of Pompey?'

The man sagged a little, and Fronto knew then that they'd missed him again.

'Pompey came to Cyprus and spent some time here, sir. According to my information, the Cypriot cities closed their gates to him as a whole, but he roved the countryside with his men, causing trouble. He managed to waylay and steal a considerable amount of money from the local tax collectors and used it to recruit a small mob of criminals, refugees and the disaffected. Before the local authorities could put an end to him, and they assure me that they tried, he took ship from a harbour near Kourion.'

'Syria?' Fronto muttered, but the tribune shook his head. 'Our last intelligence has him bound for Aegyptus, sir.'

'Good work, Tribune,' the general said, straightening. 'Pompey has links with Aegyptus and with the ruling family. He was close to the previous king, Ptolemy the Twelfth. Ptolemy had five children and I gather there is something of a complicated civil war going on at the moment, but that could be just the sort of situation that plays to Pompey's strength. Likely he will ingratiate himself with a favourable faction and begin to build his reputation and strength once more.'

He turned and peered back out to sea, then his gaze slid to Fronto. 'Do not bother with a hearty meal, Marcus, for your digestive system's issues are not yet over. Gather the entire fleet. We take ship for Aegyptus in the morning.'

CHAPTER 27

Aegyptus, October 48 BC

Fronto greeted the approaching line of green and gold shore with the last of his stomach contents, hurled out into the water with gusto. He was fairly sure that if the sea remained calm enough, a good ship could track Caesar's passage by the copious trail of vomit all the way from Cyprus. His relief at seeing the approaching city was muted somewhat by the churning pain in the pit of his stomach.

'Magnificent, isn't she?'

He turned to see Salvius Cursor standing beside him at the rail, looking well and happy.

'Who?'

'Alexandria, Queen of Cities. I cannot say what awaits us there, but I have a love of this place.'

Fronto frowned. 'You've been here before?'

'I've been over quite a lot of the east under Pompey. I had a lot of friends here.'

'You might find more enemies now, especially if Pompey has been here for some time insinuating himself into court circles.'

'Perhaps,' shrugged Salvius. 'We are making for the Great Harbour, for that is where the royal palace complex lies at the landward end of the Diabathra – the long breakwater you can just see end-on. We shall pass between that and the great lighthouse and make directly for the Royal Harbour, a walled sub-port of the Great Harbour.'

'Aren't you just a fountain of information,' grunted Fronto.

'Fountain is a poor choice of word, I think, since that more or less describes you for the last few days.'

Fronto lifted his eyes to glare witheringly at the tribune.

The two men fell silent and Fronto shifted slightly as Galronus arrived and leaned on the rail at his other elbow. 'I am intrigued,' the Remi murmured. 'I have become used to the parched landscapes of Italia, Hispania and now Achaea after the lush green of home, but what I have heard of this place makes it sound like nothing I have ever imagined. Like a beach that extends forever.'

Salvius leaned across Fronto, gaining another glare. 'Actually, you'll find it reasonably green here,' he said. 'The city will be hot and dry, but it has a lake on one side, the sea on the other, and it is bordered by the green delta of the Nile River. The sands of the desert are far from here.'

Galronus managed to conceal his disappointment quite well, and the three men watched one of the world's greatest cities slide towards them. At the head of the small fleet, they slipped between the famous lighthouse and the breakwater into the harbour. Despite himself, Fronto was intrigued. The huge oval of the harbour was subdivided, with three individual ports lined up to the left and shipyards and slipways to the right. There were relatively few ships he could see in the ports, and their own vessel seemed to be heading for the shipyards for some reason.

'Why are we going this way, and where are all the ships?'

Salvius smiled. 'We have to curve wide with the wind three quarters astern and then turn sharp and row for the ports. There are hidden reefs, you see.'

'Reefs in the port?'

'Yes.'

'Typically Aegyptian planning,' grunted Fronto.

'Macedonian. These were built by the Ptolemies. And the lack of ships is because this is the harbour for the military only. With the current political situation many of them will be at sea somewhere across the delta or up the river. The other harbour off to the west is the commercial one.'

Another grunt issued from Fronto, and he watched as they turned, bringing fresh waves of nausea, and made for the easternmost docks. This sub-harbour lay beneath the walls of a huge complex of rich golden stone and white marble, sporting defensive ramparts and grand colonnades, obelisks jutting up and great stone lions and sphinxes regarding the sea with cold disdain. It was the oddest mix of Greek and Aegyptian Fronto could have imagined.

Most of the navy might be absent, but they had been here recently and were regular visitors as was evidenced by the condition of the quaysides. The warship that bore the general, his senior officers, his praetorian guardsmen and two centuries of the Sixth pulled towards the left most free jetty, which sat below a great gate with a carving of some broad-winged bird above it, vividly painted in bright colours. The gates themselves stood open, though a few native soldiers were on guard at the sides. Beyond, as the ship slid to a halt, Fronto could see a lush green garden and a wide, white square with the palace buildings rising behind it.

Caesar gave the orders and by the time the ship was stationary and the sailors were throwing out ropes and securing the vessel, the passengers were lined up and fully equipped, ready to disembark. All along the port, any jetty not being occupied by a Ptolemaic ship was now host to one of Caesar's small fleet, legionaries lining up by ranks to disembark.

A huge ramp was run out and Fronto noted with amusement Caesar's lictors lining up to move out first. The general, of course, was often preceded by his lictors in public as was traditional, especially when in Rome, since they proclaimed the status of the man who followed. On campaign, those men went about other duties, for it simply was not practical for the general to prosecute a military campaign with a dozen men in togas bearing their bundles of rods in front of him wherever he went. The fact that he was to be preceded by them here announced that this was a political and very official visit.

The twelve men traipsed off down the ramp and reassembled on the dock, hefting their heavy bundles of rods and axes. Next came Caesar himself, followed by his officers. Then, the praetorians and finally the First century of the Sixth. The other century was to remain on the ship, partially so as not to flood the city with soldiers, which might send entirely the wrong message, and partially to protect the vessels from harm.

Crowds had begun to gather at the edge of the port, watching and tense. There was no applause and no petal throwing. This was, after all, a foreign nation, for all its reliance upon Rome to help solve its troubles from time to time. The arrival of a consul in state and with a sizeable force of both men and ships would not be welcome in every quarter.

Once they were assembled, the general gave the command once more and they began to move at a stately pace towards that bright, intricate palace gate. They had passed through much of the port and were closing on the complex when it became clear that a welcoming committee was assembling.

Soldiers were massing in the courtyard beyond the gate and, while that portal remained open, there was a tangible air of menace floating around. Fronto frowned at the gathering men. There were three distinct units assembling in lines, quite efficiently, and they were all individually odd, let alone as a group standing side by side.

To the right a unit of darker-skinned Aegyptians wore only an ornately-decorated white tunic and no helmet or armour, brown shields with pointed top and bottom showing an eagle standing atop a thunderbolt, strange curved swords belted at their sides and tall Macedonian-style lances in hand.

In the centre, men with brown tunics and blue cloaks and sporting long beards, carried white shields of a very Celtic design with the same eagle motif, clad in ornate bronze helmets and bearing Greek-style blades

To the left stood a unit of what appeared to be legionaries, although bearing once again that Ptolemaic eagle design, blue tunics and what looked to be leopard pelts over their mail shirts. While they were probably very impressive, what struck Fronto as he sweated beneath the searing Aegyptian sun was how damned hot they had to be under all that.

'Who are they all?' Galronus asked from horseback, next to Fronto.

'The ones on the right, I've no idea. Some native unit, clearly. The ones in the middle I think must be part of the royal guard. The ones on the left are the Gabiniani, I presume. They were stationed here about seven years ago to support the old king, Ptolemy the Twelfth, after a revolt. They've never been recalled, and I'd heard they had even stopped drawing pay from Rome, taking their wage now from the Aegyptian rulers. I don't know a lot about them, but I suspect they will be Ptolemy the Thirteenth's men now. Whatever the case, they don't look very pleased to see us.'

The lictors marched up to the very threshold of the palace gate and looked set to march straight into or over the waiting soldiers until Caesar gave the command to halt just short of them. For a few tense moments the two forces stood opposing one another, not a jocular face in evidence. The atmosphere could have been cut with a knife. Fronto eyed up the Alexandrian units. They were roughly equal in number to Caesar's force outside the gate, but that was without most of the army, which remained on ships or mustered on the docksides. Combined, they would seriously outnumber the Aegyptians.

Finally, a man in a curious uniform stepped out ahead of all three units. He wore a gleaming bronze muscled cuirass embossed with a weird combination design that included both Greek and Aegyptian elements. His blue tunic was of rich linen, banded with gold, and his helmet was of a strange eastern design. His long blue cloak hung limp. When he removed his helmet and tucked it under his arm he was clearly a local, though he sported a short, curly beard in a more Greek fashion.

'Such a foreign display of military might is not welcome in the realm of the Mighty Warrior of Horus, He of the Two Ladies of Upper and Lower Aegyptus, Divine Beloved of Gold, Lord of Two Lands of Sedge and Bee, Father of the Black Land and son of Ra, Ptolemy Theos Philopator the Thirteenth. This is an infringement of the royal authority of the house of the Lagidae. I command that you embark once more and leave these shores, lest the wrath of his Majesty be brought down upon you.'

Caesar's face rippled through several expressions, including downright disbelief and genuine amusement, but finally settled into a cold glare. Fronto could imagine how the Alexandrian officer felt. Few men could meet that look and not quail. It was one of Caesar's strengths. After a deliberate pause, the general walked his horse slowly forwards between the ranks of lictors until he was directly in front of the officer, then stopped.

'I am here as a consul of Rome, which has a vested interest in the ongoing stability and fortune of your nation and its rulers. Accords were agreed between the senate of Rome and the former pharaoh, Ptolemy Auletes, which give me every right to attempt to mediate in any situation that could have a direct effect on the republic. Unless you are willing to be the man who breaks sacred accords between our two nations and opens a conflict with the legions of Rome, then I very much suggest you return to your barracks, stand down and desist from interfering in the affairs of your betters.'

He took three steps forwards, so that his horse was almost standing on the officer's foot. The officer looked somewhere between astonishment and horror, now, and was probably wishing he hadn't removed his helmet.

'I presume,' Caesar continued, 'that the Mighty Warrior of Horus, He of the Two Ladies of Upper and Lower Aegyptus etcetera etcetera, Ptolemy Theos Philopator is not currently in residence, or does his send lackeys while he hides in the dark?'

The officer tried to straighten and take back some control. It was a valiant effort, if doomed from the start. 'His Majesty is encamped with his army in the delta where the cursed usurper and witch Cleopatra sits with her hired force of easterners.'

'Good,' Caesar said in a businesslike manner. 'Then we shall quarter ourselves in the palace with his assured hospitality until his return. You may go.'

The man stared in shock, and Caesar simply turned and gestured the column across to the steps of the palace.

* * *

In fact, despite what Caesar had announced to the officer, who had quickly led his soldiers away, the general had consulted with one of the palace's senior eunuchs upon their arrival and had quite happily accepted quarters for he and his officers in a guest wing. Within an hour of the officers settling in, the common soldiery quartered close by within the ramparts, they had been made very welcome, food and drink brought, baths prepared and beds plumped up and made ready.

Two hours after that the officers had assembled in a common room with a balcony that looked out over the port and strange columns carved to look like some ribbed plant with a burst of colourful petals at the capital. The floor was covered with soft animal pelts and the furniture was of dark wood, inlaid with gold designs. The level of opulence was staggering.

A master trader had been located in another part of the guest quarters and was now in attendance as the most sensible available source of information. It was an accepted thing in strange lands –

scouts could learn a lot, but traders already knew everything they could find out about their local market. If you were new to a place and you wanted to find out about it, ask a trader.

'So the queen is encamped at Pelusium?' the general frowned. 'On the far side of the delta, yes?'

The trader nodded. 'Very far. Perhaps one hundred fifty, perhaps two hundred of your mile.'

'And Ptolemy is?'

'His army many place. Blocking Alexandria to Queen. Main camp at Sais, perhaps fifty mile, yes?'

'There would appear to be little chance of reconciling the royal couple.'

The trader laughed. 'He hate her. She hate him. Much hate.'

They had been listening to his breakdown of the political situation in Aegyptus for quarter of an hour. They'd tried several times to steer his account, but he was intent on rambling at his own pace. What he had told them, though, was gold dust to any strategist.

'And you mentioned that the queen had Syrian and Nubian generals and a mostly Syrian and Palestinian army. Who leads that of Ptolemy?'

The man grinned. 'Achillas is general for king. Powerful. Wise. He is soldier. But king also rely on eunuch called Potheinus. He regent and politic.'

'Thank you,' Caesar gave the man a few coins and gestured to Ingenuus, who stood by the door. Take the man out of here and buy him a few drinks. See if there is anything else he forgot that we might need to know.'

The praetorian officer saluted, and the trader waved goodbye and went out happily with him.

'We seem to be in a somewhat difficult and very unusual position,' Caesar sighed. 'In attempting to put an end to our own civil war we have stumbled into another, in which we have a very important stake. There will come a difficult decision, I fear, very soon. Do we throw our support behind Ptolemy, who seems to be rather unfriendly to us and I understand may be the weaker candidate, but who, being male, will find it greatly easier to gather the support of his nation. The Aegyptians are traditionally wary of powerful women, unless they are married to kings who can

369

overrule them. So that is our other choice. Cleopatra, who remains an unknown quantity, but will be a more difficult candidate to put on the throne without resistance.'

'Or do we let them fight it out and see who wins?' murmured Cassius thoughtfully. 'This problem is not our main priority after all. We are not here for them, remember?'

Before the conversation could progress, though, raised voices drew the attention of all present, and their eyes slid to the doorway. The guards there did not move to block the entrance, but Fronto did note that most of them put their hands on their sword hilts and loosened them in the scabbard, all the same. The officers arrayed themselves so that they all faced the door in concert just as the source of the voices appeared.

Salvius Cursor stepped into the room and Fronto was astonished to see that he had managed to get his chest and one arm covered in blood somehow. The man was a damn miracle when it came to seeking violence. Behind him several other figures lurked in the shade of the portico.

'Tribune?' Caesar prompted, looking him up and down.

Salvius frowned, then looked down at his chest in surprise as though he couldn't understand where the blood had come from. 'This, sir? Oh we've had a few run-ins between our boys and the less careful members of the local garrison. I've made sure that none of our men start any trouble, but I've made it clear that they have full permission to end it when someone else does.'

Caesar nodded his approval, and Fronto studied Salvius. There was something about him that looked odd. Nervous. Twitchy.

'There's a deputation here to see you, General,' the tribune announced. 'Say they've come from Sais.'

'From Ptolemy?' mused Caesar. 'But not the king himself. We have been here less than three hours and Sais is fifty miles away. Someone broke a horse or two to get here as fast as they can. But then, if Ptolemy is, as I suspect, harbouring Pompey, then our arrival might prompt such speedy action.'

Salvius stepped aside and beckoned to the men without. They entered slowly, four men in those slightly altered Roman uniforms that identified them as members of Ptolemy's Gabiniani cohorts. Two of them wore centurion's crests, and the other two were ordinary legionaries. The man who was clearly their leader stepped

370

forwards and essayed a curt bow, his leopard pelt slumping forwards as he did so.

'Lucius Septimius, sir, commanding Second Century, First Cohort of the Gabinianus legion.'

Caesar nodded. 'Greetings, Centurion. To what do we owe this honour?'

The centurion stepped aside, as did the other more senior officer, and the two soldiers behind them carried forth a box and placed it on a low table. Caesar frowned at the container, which was perhaps two feet long in each dimension and made of good wood.

'A gift,' the centurion said, 'from the pharaoh Ptolemy Theos Philopator the Thirteenth for the consul of Rome.'

Caesar's eyebrow rose a little. He gestured to one of the praetorians, who still had their hands on their sword hilts, watching these foreigners like hawks. 'Open it.'

The man let go of his weapon and stepped across to the table. With a brief, suspicious, look at the Gabiniani, he carefully undid the catch and lifted the lid. Fronto watched the man's face fall into an expression of horror and disgust. He already knew with a sinking feeling what it was, before the man reached gingerly inside and lifted out the contents.

The legate was grateful that whoever had embalmed the head had at least cauterised the neck. The soldier holding it aloft by the curly hair was clearly having trouble keeping in his stomach's contents.

Pompey did not look dead. The embalmers had done an excellent job. It was, after all, something the Aegyptians were noted for. Pompey's broad face even managed a slightly constipated smile. Fronto shivered. His hand shot out instinctively and grasped Salvius' wrist just as the tribune made to step forwards. Salvius turned to him, a weird and awful expression on his face, and Fronto simply shook his head.

'What is the meaning of this?' Caesar asked, his tone so cold and hard it felt like marble flowing through the ears. Centurion Septimius frowned. 'Behold, mighty consul of Rome, the head of your enemy. His Majesty presents you with a gift to end your war.'

Fronto looked from the centurion to the head and back, and then again, and suddenly, frowning, he turned to the other centurion.

Three of the four Gabiniani were facing Caesar, their expressions hopeful. The other centurion, though, was favouring Salvius Cursor with an unreadable expression, and there was something about him...

Caesar stepped just one pace forwards. 'A gift? The head of Pompey Magnus a *gift?*'

Septimius, confused and more than a little uncertain now, nodded. 'Yes, Consul. Your enemy is vanquished.'

'My enemy remains scattered around Africa and the east, you fool. My enemy is all those senators who sought my prosecution and who took up arms against me. Pompey? Pompey was the man they chose for a general, but he was vanquished on the field of Pharsalus. Pompey might have faced me in battle,' Caesar hissed, his voice bearing an edge like a gladius, 'but he is still a Roman hero, the victor over the pirates, thrice feted with triumphs, a consul, a general, a senator.' He took a deep breath. 'And my son-in-law.'

Septimius finally seemed to realised what had gone wrong and he blanched, as did his companions. Not, Fronto noted, the other centurion, who was still looking at Salvius.

Caesar pinched the bridge of his nose and lowered his head, eyes closed. There was a long, worrying silence, and then he straightened, his face stony. 'You two,' he pointed at the two legionaries who had borne the head. 'Take this and locate the rest of my son-in-law's body. Makes sure it is as well preserved as possible and reunite the two. Then have it delivered to the palace while I try and decide whether to accord him appropriate funeral honours here or to send him back to Rome as is.'

The two legionaries hurried forwards and the praetorian gently placed the head back in the box, fastened it, and let the two men take it. They hurried out.

'You. Septimius. You are responsible for this deed?'

'I wielded the blade, General, I and my companion here. It was the command of the pharaoh, though, delivered through his regent Potheinus.'

'In my experience, regents rarely consult their charges before issuing orders,' Caesar growled. 'You are both under arrest for the murder of a Roman citizen. You may be in service to Ptolemy and he may issue your wages, but you are still soldiers of a Roman legion in service. You shall be given the right of a proper trial, as you are citizens, and until that time you will be incarcerated in the palace barracks.'

Septimius bristled angrily, though his companion simply seemed to accept the judgement. The two were bustled out by Ingenuus' men swiftly.

'I shall see to their imprisonment, sir,' Salvius said suddenly, and began to walk out before Caesar could comment on the statement. Fronto frowned after his tribune, then turned to Caesar, who also wore a suspicious, curious expression. The general nodded, and Fronto turned and hurried out after the prison detachment. He caught up with Salvius Cursor at the bottom of the wide steps, the tribune following the two prisoners and their praetorian escort at a short distance.

'What is going on?' said Fronto.

Salvius failed entirely to react and so Fronto reached out and grabbed his upper arm, dragging him to a halt. To his shock, the tribune turned with a pugio in his hand and the most dreadful expression on his face. He did not lunge with the dagger, but Fronto felt certain he'd at least weighed it up as an option.

'Talk to me, tribune,' he said, trying something more official. It had the desired effect. Salvius lowered his dagger and seemed to deflate slightly.

'Pompey is dead.'

'Yes,' Fronto said.

'Caesar is not happy about it, and neither am I.'

Fronto frowned. 'Caesar might not appear happy on the surface but I suspect that, whatever he wants people to think, the next time he's alone he'll jump up and down with bloody glee. What to do with Pompey when we caught him is a thorny problem that's been weighing us down for a long time. He's a Roman citizen and hero. We couldn't kill him, except on the battlefield, yet he couldn't be allowed to go free, as he'll always be a threat. Those two men did Caesar an enormous service. We just can't make it look that way in public.'

'I'm not happy, because it was meant to be *my* blade that did it, and not my *brother's*!'

Fronto's jaw fell open. Now he suddenly realised why the other centurion had looked faintly familiar. Why the man had spent his time looking at Salvius, slightly removed from the scene.

'Him?'

'Marcus. Marcus Salvius Aper. Last I heard he was serving under Gabinius in Syria. Not a surprise to find he's still with the Gabiniani, though he never sticks to anything, so I suppose it should be.' There was, Fronto noted, more than a touch of bitterness there. Something else connected to Salvius' untold story, clearly.

'Can you not simply be grateful?' Fronto said. 'You wanted Pompey dead. He's dead.'

Salvius pulled away and marched off after the men who were even now being led into a small barrack block. 'Oh no you don't,' Fronto grunted, and hurried after him.

Salvius was moving at speed now, and he had reached the door of the barracks by the time Fronto caught up again. The tribune stopped in the doorway, took the keys from the man who was messing with the lock, and turned. 'Dismissed, the lot of you. I'll put them inside.'

Fronto was tempted to countermand those orders, but desisted. As the guardsmen dispersed, he followed Salvius inside. The two centurions were standing by separate doors. Fronto felt the need to say something, and cleared his throat.

'I will make sure your trials are soon, and I think you need not worry about the outcome. You will almost certainly both go free.'

'In,' snapped Salvius, opening a door and gesturing. Septimius shuffled inside. In moments the tribune had the door locked behind him and shook his head at his brother, motioning to a door at the far end, some distance away. Moving the padlock, he attached it to this other door, but motioned for the other centurion to enter and, when he did, followed him in. Fronto hurried after them and slammed his foot in the door just as it closed. He was fairly sure a toe broke in the pressure and he winced, but withdrew his foot as the door opened once more.

'This is private,' Salvius said quietly.

'Bollocks, frankly,' Fronto relied. 'You had murder in your eyes a few moments ago and you almost drew a blade on me. If you think I'm leaving you in here alone with him, you've another thing coming.'

Salvius glared at him but said nothing, and so Fronto closed the door and sat on the edge of a bunk opposite them. Now that he looked at them he could see the definite family resemblance, though the centurion was more sun bronzed and sun-bleached.

'It was you,' Salvius Cursor said quietly.

'Yes.'

'Not that other man.'

'No. He wanted the glory, that's all.'

'How in Hades did you do it?'

Salvius Aper shrugged. 'It was easy. The queen knew that if Pompey lost he would come to Aegyptus, because of his old ties with her father. Part of the Gabiniani had already served with him against Caesar, and he would probably now want the rest.'

'Wait,' Fronto held up a hand. 'The queen?'

'Is he trustworthy?' the man asked his brother. Salvius Cursor eyed Fronto as he replied. 'On so many levels, no. But you can talk in front of him.'

'The queen, Cleopatra, set me the task of planting a blade in Pompey. But there was so much to it. We had no idea where he would put to shore, once we'd heard he had been moving down the Asian coast. And I had to make it Ptolemy's fault, you see? I spent a month in the pharaoh's camp planting the idea in the mind of his idiot eunuch and enlisting a fellow centurion with more ambition than sense. Pompey knew Septimius, you see? They'd served together. He would not remember me, and if he did, he'd hardly put himself in my hands. But I've changed over the years. I look different. And Septimius was his friend.'

'But how?' Salvius urged.

'Pompey landed at Pelusium, perilously close to the queen's camp. He sent overtures to Ptolemy, and we carried the reply. We persuaded him that it had to be a clandestine meeting. We would sneak him past the queen's camp and to Ptolemy. Once we had him alone in a boat it was easy.'

Fronto shook his head in disbelief. 'It's a bloody master stroke. She rids Caesar of a difficult enemy that he doesn't know what to do with and manages to plant the blame with her brother, making him look like a murderous fool. This woman is sly.'

Salvius Aper gave him an odd look. 'The queen is the sole rightful ruler of Aegyptus and a thousand times brighter than Ptolemy.'

'Did Pompey not take his guards?' Fronto asked.

'He took a couple. But we had Achillas and half a dozen men too. They were swiftly overcome and dumped in the river.'

Again, Fronto shook his head. 'Brilliant. And now Caesar gets to look forgiving and noble and mourn Pompey's loss, and the queen will have set Caesar and Ptolemy at odds. The pharaoh will have to work to maintain any hope of peace now.'

But he was more or less talking to himself now. The brothers were in discussion once more.

'You said you would have nothing to do with it,' Salvius Cursor muttered. 'You said I was on my own.'

'Times have changed, brother. *I* have changed. You went back west for revenge, but I stayed out here.'

He turned a meaningful look on Fronto, who suddenly felt very out of place. He was still fascinated as to what lay at the root of this family's attitudes, but this was clearly not the time to pry. Besides, he had his own problem to look to now. Should he tell Caesar about the queen's part in it or not?

Whatever the case, he was now sure that Cleopatra was the clear choice in this war.

CHAPTER 28

Caesar leaned on the table and shook his head. 'Not the army, the king himself.'

'Why would the king come without his army?' Cassius mused.

'Perhaps he wants to avoid the danger of conflict? Perhaps he feels he has the right. This is, after all, his city and his palace, and we are but foreign visitors. Whatever the case, the king will be here within a matter of hours. What we must do now is make some decisions before he gets here. The first being a matter of military strength.'

'Estimates put Ptolemy's forces at somewhere between twenty and thirty thousand,' Fronto put in as he poured himself a drink. 'Though the estimates come from civilian traders and observers, so we have to allow a strong margin for error.'

'We still do not know whether they present a threat to us or not,' Cassius pointed out. 'At the moment we are neutral visitors in a civil war. It may be that Ptolemy is our friend. After all, his father was. Perhaps it is Cleopatra that we should be wary of.'

Fronto shook his head. 'Cleopatra is clever.'

'All the more reason to be wary,' Cassius said. 'And how do you know?'

'I have heard things. From trustworthy sources. From what I understand, Ptolemy is enthusiastic and arrogant but with a somewhat childish mentality. His court is administered by Potheinus and his army by Achillas. All he does is preen. Cleopatra, on the other hand? Well put it this way, from what I've heard, I'd far rather have her as an ally than as an enemy.'

'The fact remains,' Caesar pointed out, 'that we are outnumbered once more. We can boast three and a half thousand infantry and eight hundred horse. We have to assume that Cleopatra's force is similar to her brother's, else there would not be the stand-off there is. And with our four thousand, we cannot face an army of twenty thousand, no matter which side we come down on. We cannot, after all, rely on any support from the other.'

Cassius made an irritable huffing sound. 'I still do not understand why we care. Pompey is dead. Aegyptus is now unimportant to us. In my opinion we should be leaving them to their sibling squabbles and marching off to Africa to put down Attius before he becomes any stronger. You can guarantee that half the surviving officers from Pharsalus are flocking to him. The last stronghold against you grows in power and instead of dealing with it we dally in Egypt watching an effete brother arguing with his inbred sister-wife.'

Fronto turned to Cassius. 'You are awfully intent on pushing against the other senators, considering you served them a couple of months ago against Caesar.'

'Don't try and test my loyalty, Fronto. I gave an oath to the general, and I just want to see this war ended so we can all go home and things can be put to rights.'

Fronto nodded his acknowledgement of the point. It was very much what he wanted, in fact. Lucilia...

'Aegyptus must be settled,' Caesar said firmly. 'This place is such a pivotal player in the east, we need her alliance. We always have. That is what led the senate to send Gabinius here. We garrisoned half a legion here to protect their king, remember? No. We must have Aegyptus settled. I want a message sent to the queen at Pelusium, demanding that she stands down her army on the condition that her brother agrees to do the same. Send it with your fastest rider. I shall make the same demand of the king when he arrives. Then Cleopatra can come to Alexandria without fear, for we will impose the rule of law. With a little intuition and skill, and a healthy dose of good fortune, this conflict can then be brought to a close with talk and law rather than swords and shields.'

'Yet you worry about our numbers?' Fronto prompted.

'Law does not always win the day, Marcus,' Caesar replied. 'That is why swords exist. I shall send the fastest riders in all Alexandria to the queen, but also beyond her, all the way to Syria. I want Calvinus to force march the Twenty Eighth and Twenty Ninth Legions from Damascus to Alexandria to more than double our strength. They are, after all, in Syria to guard against a

Pompeian rising, which is now somewhat redundant. At the fastest legionary pace they should take no more than sixteen days arriving. Allowing for a courier with horse relays delivering the orders, the entire thing should be possible within twenty days, to get the message to Calvinus and for him to bring the forces here.'

'That's pushing it,' Fronto noted. 'Possible, but hard. They'll be worn down, and that's assuming there are no delays. Remember that Cleopatra and Ptolemy both have armies in the way. Can they not come by ship? It can't be more than three day's sail.'

'We do what we must,' Caesar replied. 'The Etesian Winds made our journey south from Cyprus easy, but they make leaving Alexandria and heading north more or less impossible during the autumn. Thus our messenger must travel by land. And we took our entire naval capability when we came south from Cyprus. There are not enough ships available for Calvinus to use. No. Forced march it has to be.'

* * *

Ptolemy the Thirteenth, he of the many and very tedious names, was little more than a boy. The way people had talked about him, Fronto had formed the impression of a young man, but one whose mentality was still in the juvenile stage. In fact, the king was probably around the age when a Roman son would lose the bulla of childhood and take a man's toga. He had not yet spoken, but Fronto was already imagining him to have one of those teenage voices that was on the verge of breaking, hovering somewhere between scratchy falsetto and warbling baritone. His nose was too large for his face, which gave the instant impression that he was coming at you, leaning forwards all the time, and his eyes heavy lidded, which made him look half asleep. It was not overall an awe-inspiring look for a man who was ruler of one of the world's most ancient nations and supposedly the incarnation of a god.

Perhaps Fronto's impression was rather ruined by his entourage, too. The legate had never been a fan of glittering ostentation, preferring the good ascetic nobility that was the very heart of Romanitas. So he did not find a solid basis for respect when the king arrived, preceded by lithe, naked Nubian dancers, a full orchestra of musicians playing a tune that sounded like a cat being slowly tortured by a man with a rattle and a lyre, jugglers, acrobats, four cameleopards, sixteen white bulls wearing ornate headdresses, a gang of weird looking priests with fake beards and shaved heads carrying a wooden god, and finally the fifty or so burly slaves that were required to pull the throne.

The throne itself was clearly solid gold, intricately worked and inset with every coloured stone imaginable, including much lapis lazuli – the Aegyptians seemed to love bright blue and gold together. But it was not the seat that was the eyesore and the sickening sight. The seat was settled amid a small bright garden of colourful flowers that itself sat on a wooden sledge some sixteen feet long, inlaid with yet more gold, which was being dutifully dragged along the cobbles.

Behind the king came a small collection of functionaries in white robes and a weird looking guard unit wearing various exotic animal skins and carrying swords that were so oddly-shaped that Fronto couldn't work out how you would swing one, and which must have weighed the same as a small cart. At least they weren't gold, like everything else.

Caesar, by comparison, sat astride his white horse in just his leather subarmalis with the handing pteruges over a red and white tunic, belted military fashion and with a general's red cloak. His lictors were in evidence again, and the various officers were gathered. It felt like a curious reverse to be standing on the steps of the royal palace to greet the arrival of the man who owned it.

The giant sledge slid to a halt, the slaves breathing deeply, leading Fronto to wonder whether the Aegyptians were aware of something called 'the wheel' and if so why they dragged a sledge around the streets. King Ptolemy rose with some difficulty, which Fronto suspected was something to do with the weight of the enormous, ostentatious and weird looking crown-hat thing he wore. At least the fake beard made sense with the king, for he undoubtedly could not yet grow his own. Still wobbling his head to balance his ridiculous headgear, the king stepped forwards into the open air, and a slave was suddenly there, bent double, forming a step for him. The same happened again, and again, repeatedly until the last slave was lying prone next to the sledge and the king reached the ground. That was apparently not the end of it. The king's sandals were, needless to say, gold. Two more slaves ran out with armfuls of white linen rugs, which they placed in a line in front of the king so that he could walk without dirtying his sandals.

The king stopped in front of the Romans, some twenty paces away and Fronto frowned as he realised Ptolemy was not looking at Caesar, but somewhere at his horse's chest. Having to stifle a chuckle, he realised that the king would not look up at someone, so absolute was his power. Consequently, he couldn't look Caesar in the face and had to content himself with the horse. It took only a moment for a steed to be brought for him so that he could meet the consul on a more level ground.

'Greetings, Ptolemy, son of Ptolemy, son of Ptolemy ad infinitum,' Caesar said, somehow managing to keep a straight face.

One of the white-clad functionaries ran up and stood next to the king.

'His Majesty cannot recognise a foreign ambassador who is standing in his home, while the king is in the street, Consul.'

'And you are?' Caesar prompted.

'I am Potheinus, regent and servant of the great king.'

'Ah, *you* are the regent. You must be looking forwards to ending your tribulations and relaxing when the king comes of age.'

Ptolemy began to turn a funny red-purple colour, and Potheinus waved his hands urgently. 'The King is already a man, Consul. I retain my rank only as an advisor, not a true ruler.'

'My apologies,' Caesar smiled. 'However, I am not here as an ambassador, but as a consul of Rome, and a mediator in your current dispute. In your name I have had a feast prepared for your arrival.'

The colour began to fade on the king's face and he smiled at last. 'It has been a long, dry ride,' he said.

Fronto ducked behind the other officers to hide his silent laughter at the king's alternating falsetto and baritone warbling. By the time he had recovered, they were moving. Caesar and the king both dismounted, their horses taken for them, and the Romans and Aegyptians alike moved into the palace. As they walked, Caesar opened up conversation with the king politely.

'What of your siblings, Majesty? I am aware, of course, of Cleopatra, but there were five of you, I believe.

The king's lip twitched at the mention of his nemesis, but he recovered well, if briefly. 'My oldest sister, Berenice, died at the hands of your general Gabinius, of course, during her ill-advised revolt against our father.'

'Oh yes, how remiss of me,' Caesar said politely and with an impressively straight face. 'And the others?'

'My younger brother, also a Ptolemy, is in Memphis, and my younger sister Arsinoe follows in my retinue.'

'Good to see that your quarrel is not wider spread than with Cleopatra.'

Another lip twitch.

They reached the great dining chamber with a view of the theatre below and the port beyond, and took seats by tables laden with food and drink.

'I'm afraid I must get business out of the way before we discuss more pleasurable matters,' Caesar said suddenly, earning a frown from the king. 'Your father, I am afraid, ran up certain debts with Rome during that dreadful revolt, and with an army to support in the midst of all these troubles, I must, unfortunately, call in that debt.'

'How much?' asked Ptolemy in surprise.

'You cannot, you foreign animal,' snapped Potheinus, then recoiled as Caesar glared at him.

'Seventeen and a half million drachma,' Caesar said pleasantly.

'That much?' replied Ptolemy, still surprised.

'I am sure your man there can confirm it in records, but that is definitely the figure.'

'You may have my throne,' the king said airily.

'That would account for perhaps a quarter of it,' Caesar replied. 'But I was intending to donate a sum to each of the former king's children in recognition of their friendship to Rome. You may keep your throne and supply only thirteen million drachma.'

The regent, his eyes narrowed, nodded at his king. 'I will see to it Majesty, but be aware that this is a debilitating quantity of money at a time when we are in need, and this leech of a Roman will never stop sucking.'

'And one other piece of business remains of importance,' Caesar said, one scathing eye on the eunuch.

'Mmm?' the king managed around a mouthful of peach.

'The matter of your little war.'

'Well, I...'

Caesar rode over his words. 'It is becoming the norm in your land for civil conflict. Firstly your sister challenged your father's rule, and Gabinius had to step in and help. He had to leave troops that I believe have come down to you somehow. And then he dies, leaving clear instructions that you and Cleopatra are to co-rule, and now the two of you are at war.'

'I think you are hardly entitled to stand the high ground there,' snorted Potheinus, and Fronto was amazed when the general didn't even look at him this time. Such insolence rarely went unpunished.

'While we are involved in our own conflict, I can see the dreadful effect it is having on our people. War is not to be sought, but to be avoided where possible. A good general knows that. So I have to ask you, in the role of mediator which my position as consul and the accords between our nations allow, to lay down your arms. Stand down your forces and dismiss them.'

'Never, I...'

'I have made the same demand of your sister, and invited her here. With the armies disbanded, we could solve this under law, I am sure.'

'I will never share the throne with that hag,' Ptolemy spat.

'The queen treats the king like a fool,' Potheinus put in.

Fronto had to suppress another chuckle. He was beginning to like this Cleopatra, even if he hadn't yet met her.

'You should take your cue from Rome,' Caesar said quietly. 'The republic is governed by the senate, but the senate elects two consuls each year, and we effectively run things, with our senatorial brethren. It is a rare year when the consuls are in full agreement on all matters, but we are still capable of administrating side by side. If we can do that, with new men in power each year, then you should be capable of the same, especially when you know you do not have to relinquish that power.'

Fronto thought there was a touch of wistfulness about that last comment, and his eyes narrowed.

'Frankly,' Caesar said with fresh energy, 'I would be looking closer to home than Pelusium for your enemies.'

'You are my enemy?' whispered Ptolemy, clearly confused.

'No, Majesty. I think certain members of your court may be unfairly attempting to influence you. Anyway, I say again, disband your forces and I will mediate a conclusion.'

For a long time Ptolemy said nothing, his brow working this way and that, deep in thought, with Potheinus making angry faces. Finally, he nodded. 'I think you are correct. And I think that when you meet my sister you will see how impossible that is. I think you will realise that I can be the ruler who Rome would find favourable, while Cleopatra will lead you a merry dance. But she will not come. She will not trust me.'

'She will come,' replied Fronto suddenly.

* * *

Two hours later, in response to a summons, Fronto rapped on the general's door. He was interested to note the increased number of praetorians in the complex and the fact that they were now in almost every corridor.

'Come in.'

He did so, to find Caesar sitting on his bed, massaging his calf, boot off and foot in a bowl of steaming water.

'Ah Fronto. Good. I have been making some enquiries and observing matters carefully throughout the day. Tell me what opinion you formed of Potheinus?'

'I wouldn't trust him as far as I could shit a trireme.'

'Colourful. But accurate, too, I would say. I believe the eunuch has grown too fond of ruling the country when his king was still a boy. I do not think he intends to relinquish that power.'

'You think he wants to be pharaoh himself?'

Caesar shook his head. 'He cannot. The Aegyptians are very superstitious and extremely rigid about their rulers. Potheinus would never survive the year if he tried, and these people have some horrible ways of dealing with such things. You only have to look at what they do to their dead to realise what they can do to the living if they have a mind to. But as long as he has a dribbling young fool to talk through in a red, white and gold hat, the people will listen. Ptolemy is little more than Potheinus' mouth as, I suspect, Achillas is his blade. The king might agree to disband his army, but I would be extremely surprised to see it actually happen. They will play for time. And Cleopatra might wish to come, but she is clearly no fool. Ptolemy has the navy and they control the coast. He has his army spread across the delta, and he has forces here. She cannot come to us without risking everything.'

'What do we do, then?'

Caesar pursed his lips. 'We bide our time. Twenty days. In twenty days, Calvinus can have two more legions here, and then we will have sufficient force to intervene properly. Until then we must be careful. And bear in mind the ways of such eastern courts. Be circumspect in everything you do, Marcus. Only eat food that you prepared yourself or your most trusted men did. Hire a taster, even. Watch for knives in the dark, snakes in the bed, a scorpion in your boot. We must all do so. It would be quite convenient for Ptolemy if we expired quietly.'

Fronto nodded, looking faintly uncomfortable. 'Understood. I think there is something you need to know.'

'Oh yes?'

'It concerns the centurions who killed Pompey.'

'Yes?' Caesar's expression was not the one of a man who sought revenge for an unjust killing. More a matter of intrigue.

'I think you need to set them free.'

'Fronto, they murdered a Roman citizen.'

Still a veneer of righteousness. No real feeling.

'They solved a huge problem for you.'

Caesar gave him a warning look, but Fronto ignored it. 'You know that's true. And there's no one here you need to impress. We both know that Pompey was always going to end up dead somehow. This was the best thing that could happen for you.'

'They need a trial.'

'Give them one, then. But a quiet and private one. And then acquit them and release them. You see, Septimius is one of Ptolemy's Gabinian centurions, and it will be a good gesture to release him. Sooner or later the king will discover that you have him locked up. Better to let him go now.'

'Perhaps.'

'And the other centurion, for all his uniform, is one of the queen's men.'

Caesar's eyes narrowed. 'You are sure?'

'Most definitely. It seems that, despite what we see, it was Cleopatra who arranged the death.'

Caesar's frown deepened. 'I shall not ask how you know this, but you are quite certain?'

'Yes.'

'Then this other centurion. Perhaps he can get the queen to Alexandria?'

Fronto shrugged. 'I suppose it's possible. She's clever, and he appears to be, too. He is...' Fronto paused. He wasn't sure this was something he should be revealing. With a deep breath, he said: 'He's Salvius Cursor's brother.'

* * *

The next day was a strange one for Fronto. It began with a visit from the camp prefect of the Sixth Legion. The man appeared at Fronto's door in the palace only an hour past sun-up, with a disapproving look under the wide wicker hat he had adopted to keep off the glare of the Aegyptian sun. Fronto was in his sleeping tunic, scratching, yawning and rubbing his eyes.

'Sir.'

'Prefect, what can I do for you?'

'Could you procure replacement rations for us, sir?'

Fronto frowned. 'Why?'

'The grain the legions have received from the city granaries this morning is of the poorest quality. It is, more or less, the sweepings-up. Not fit for a beggar's bread, let alone a soldier.'

'I wonder why.'

'If only we could set up a supply fleet, sir. Our own grain waits in Cyprus and beyond.'

Fronto nodded. It was a difficult job getting ships out of the harbour and north with the Etesian Winds against them, but there were ways to do it. Ships would have to transfer from the Great Harbour to the commercial one via the channels through the heptastadion mole, which would require royal consent and the aid of the port authorities on every occasion. It would probably cost them dearly, and the administration would make it all as difficult as possible, but if they got ships into the other harbour, the winds would be less troublesome. And there were not reefs there, either.

'I will see what I can do about setting up a supply run to Cyprus and back. If we can get even half a dozen ships doing so, we can keep everyone fed well.'

'Thank you sir, but in the meantime?'

'Yes. It's frankly bloody ridiculous that a country that provides more grain than half the republic put together cannot supply us with enough food to feed four thousand men. I will speak to the king's sycophants about it. I will return to you shortly.'

'Thank you, sir.'

Once the prefect had left, Fronto garbed himself in his best gear and then left his quarters. As he passed through the large dining room, he paused, brow furrowed. Slaves were collecting the gold, silver, copper and glass cups, bowls and platters from the room and replacing them with dull earthenware and wooden alternatives.

'What's this?' he asked a slave, who turned a blank look on him.

A man in the corner in a court official's costume, tapped a stilus on his list. 'Your consul has bled us dry of wealth. To pay his avarice we must make sacrifices.'

Fronto stared. He had seen enough gold in the past few days to build a damned city out of it. He refused to believe that the king was so poor he needed to melt down his plates. This was petty prods from the regent, no doubt. Well Fronto would not rise to it. He preferred a good low-born soldier's cup anyway, and Caesar was quite comfortable dealing with such fare.

He found the unpleasant Potheinus with a gaggle of other officials, doling out orders.

'Potheinus?'

The man turned, his habitual sneer sliding into place at the sight of the Roman. 'Ah, yes. One of the parasites in the consul's army.'

Fronto forced himself to relax. Their situation would not be improved by punching the regent in the face. 'I need to speak about the grain rations for the legions.'

'I do not see what there is to speak about. We delivered exactly the agreed-upon number of sacks, and on time.'

'But the quality is so poor even the rats are shunning it.'

The regent shrugged. 'We agreed on a quantity, not a quality. The food does not belong to you and is being given to you against my better judgement. Your men will learn to like it, or they will starve, for there will be no other.'

Fronto took a calming breath.

'Listen to me, you obsequious little turd, I want proper grain for my men, or I will take this up with the king himself.'

'You do that,' snapped Potheinus, and stalked off.

The rest of the morning was spent in an equally fruitless series of meetings with members of the king's administration. No better grain would be forthcoming. The king refused to meet with a lesser, and when Fronto went through Caesar, the king was mysteriously too busy to meet a consul of Rome.

'We're going to have to secure our own supplies,' he said to Caesar. And by sea. By land they would have to go past two armies, neither of which we can count on to be wholly allied and trustworthy.

Caesar nodded. 'While we are here, we are largely at the mercy of Neptune. Our ships are our lifeline. While we are outnumbered they are our only chance of getting away and they are our sole possibility for supply runs. I take it you plan to pass the heptastadion and use the commercial harbour?'

'Quite. It will take some work to get the agreement of everyone involved, and if you can somehow arrange a meeting with the king, we might be able to get more than replacement grain. He could clear us to use the passages between the harbours.'

Another irritating couple of hours followed dealing with various administrators from the ports and harbours.

The bad news came in the early afternoon. The king had sent two of his most noted ambassadors, Dioscorides and Serapion, to the army with orders for Achillas to stand his men down. The escortrider who returned was wild-eyed and horrified.

'He had them put to death,' Potheinus reported to Caesar and Fronto after he had personally dealt with the man. 'Achillas has refused to stand down the army. He believes the king to be in danger and all of this to be some wicked Roman plot to cheat him into disbanding his army so that you can put Cleopatra on the throne. I can understand why he would think this,' the eunuch sneered. 'It sounds eminently plausible. I suspect something like this myself. Your twisted plots will fail, Roman.'

Once the man had gone, Caesar, Cassius, Galronus and Fronto sat at the table with guards keeping everyone else out of earshot.

'Things are coming undone here,' Caesar said. 'There are more forces at work here than the two monarchs. Achillas and Potheinus are influential and they are changing the game. We are outnumbered and, with the winds keeping our fleet in the harbour, effectively trapped in Alexandria. I have no wish to fight another war here, gentlemen, but that very possibility is looming.'

Fronto nodded. 'Send the centurion.'

'What?'

'Send the centurion. Cleopatra's man. Thus far we have only one side of everything. All we hear is the king's drivellings, the eunuch's bile and the general's refusal. I think we need the queen's impression on all of this.'

Caesar nodded. 'Then it's time. Release the prisoners.'

CHAPTER 29

Cleopatra fretted and paced, which was irking her almost more than the reasons she was doing so. For her entire life she had presented a public face of confidence and pride, which was usually genuine. Even when her brother had raised troops and moved to oust her from her throne, and she knew she could not withstand them, she had taken the bit between the teeth, withdrew with self-assurance and style and gathered her own force in exile to return.

Yet now she paced nervously. The game was changing and she had cast her die, but she could not see the board at the moment. She had just over ten thousand men, hired mercenaries from the east, encamped near Pelusium, but her brother had twice that number between her and Alexandria, as well as the bulk of the navy patrolling the coast and the larger channels of the delta. She was effectively pinned and unable to move west without entering into a conflict with a considerably larger force and, while she was clever, she knew Achillas to be an excellent strategist and commander, for all his other faults. How long could she maintain a mercenary army without access to the royal vaults, which lay, of course, in Alexandria?

And Caesar was in Alexandria. She had no idea how he had reacted to Pompey's death. She could guess of course, but there had been no confirmation. Ptolemy was in Alexandria, too. Of what were Ptolemy and Caesar speaking? She had to be there, to be involved, to play her side. She had received the summons from the consul this morning. A summons? The arrogance of the man, to summon a foreign country's queen. Yet she knew his reasoning. He sought resolution at the earliest possible time in order to pursue his own war without leaving a festering ally/enemy behind him.

But she knew her brother. It mattered not that Caesar had invited her and that Ptolemy was with the man, still he would not issue orders to grant her passage. He would keep Cleopatra in Pelusium as long as possible while he secured the Romans' support for his cause. And Rome was a patriarchal state. They would naturally side with Ptolemy through basic misogyny. Unless Cleopatra could put her case to the consul.

That was simply it. She had, she was sure, weakened Ptolemy's standing with the head of Pompey, whether Caesar knew it was truly her doing or not. Had she not so weakened it, likely Caesar and Ptolemy would even now be drawing up pacts that placed him on the throne in return for exceptional concessions for Rome. But Caesar was not entirely sold on the king, else he would not be inviting her to seek a peaceful solution.

She had to get to Caesar, yet with an army in the way it seemed unlikely.

'Show me the map again,' she said, finally stopping her pacing and leaning over a chart of the entire delta region.

'The sea is completely forbidden us,' Apollodorus said in his strange, western accent. 'Ptolemy's navy is strong and our lookouts say that no matter where you stand, you cannot pass a quarter of an hour without seeing one of his ships. It would have to be by land. But the ships also cover all three main channels of the Nile, as well as smaller boats patrolling the narrower channels. He has garrisons at Buto, Sebennytus, Tanis, Bubastis, Athribis and Naukratis that we know about, and likely more besides. His patrols cover every road through the delta, his men guard every ferry landing and he has eyes behind every tree, Majesty.'

Cleopatra looked up at him disapprovingly. The details were important, his hyperbole wasn't. Still, Apollodorus of Sicilia was one of the few clever military minds who had been with her since this entire conflict had begun, all the way to Syria and back, and remained staunchly loyal. Such loyalty bought a great deal of latitude with minor irritations.

'Is it likely a small unit or skiff could make it across the delta? I presume not, from your description.'

Apollodorus shook his head. 'I cannot see any likelihood of success, and failure would mean the end of it all.'

392

She nodded. 'Travelling south, then? Past Memphis and crossing the Nile beyond the delta to come back to Alexandria along the far edge of the floodplain?'

He pursed his lips. 'It would be a long journey. It stands a higher chance of success but still not one upon which I would wager. Your other brother remains in Memphis, and his loyalty is suspect at best. Passing through or by Memphis will put us within the grasp of his own forces, and he might well just sell us to his brother just to put you out of the way. And if we did pass Memphis, we would still have to pass Naukratis and any forces that Ptolemy has outside the city. No, it is not safe enough to try. Your brother may be a fool, but Achillas is not and he has every route to Alexandria sealed against us.'

Again, she began to pace. This was ridiculous.

'How about launching a small assault against one of his garrisons and slipping past with the distraction?'

'It would have to be done repeatedly with each garrison we passed. The chance of failure would rise considerably with each attempt. And there is every chance that committing to a small conflict would trigger a full scale fight that we know we cannot win.'

'Infuriating.'

She heard the pounding of feet long before the guard at her door entered, bowing deeply.

'Yes?' *Heart pounding. Something important was happening, to summon such urgent, running feet.*

The guard remained bowed. 'Commander Sosibius, my queen.'

She nodded and bade him enter, and a moment later the commander of her own personal guard stepped inside, flush from his run. Her heart beat even faster.

'A ship, Majesty.'

'Explain?'

There is a small ship, little more than a boat, heading for Pelusium. Our watchers say it came along the coast from the east, like the other ships of Ptolemy, but this one has dared to enter our branch of the Nile, making for the city.'

'You say it is small. Not large enough to present a threat then, surely?'

Sosibius spread his hands wide. 'In normal circumstances I would say not, my queen but, Achillas notwithstanding, it would not be beneath Potheinus to send us plague or poison.'

Cleopatra shook her head. 'He would not believe we would take in the ship, I think. His devious mind will not allow for simplicity. No, this ship is not from Potheinus, for he would not believe we would allow it to land. And it is not from Achillas, for it bears too little military importance. But it is definitely of my brother's fleet?'

'Most assuredly, my queen.'

'Let it dock. I shall meet with it.'

It took only moments for the queen to array her finery and leave her headquarters, climbing into her litter and giving the order for the slaves to bear her to the dock. They moved down the street from the fortress with her litter preceded by her guard under Sosibius' command, Apollodorus riding beside her and the functionaries of her court behind, followed by more guards. Pelusium was flat, surrounded by equally level salt lands and water, the highest thing for miles around being the buildings of the city or the trees outside, and so it was not possible to see the dock or the river until you were there. Consequently, Cleopatra's heart continued to pound, the feeling that something was happening, for good or ill, building.

As they emerged onto the dock side, she knew immediately which ship it was, even without Ptolemy's eagle on the sail, for her soldiers had formed a solid wall of muscle and bronze at the end of the jetty. At her arrival, the force split and parted for Cleopatra and her entourage, and in moments she came to a halt, still seated above her bearers, guards around her. She did not examine the sailors, for it would make no difference. She could hardly identify them. And there was no sign of a military force on the deck. She felt the hairs rise on the nape of her neck as the boarding ramp was run out to the jetty.

A single figure emerged from the ship, a soldier bearing the armour and uniform of the Gabiniani.

'Salvius,' she said, relief flooding through her.

'My queen,' he replied, striding along the jetty and falling to a knee before her.

Cleopatra had her slaves lower her to the timbers and she stepped out to greet the centurion. At her nod, Sosibius dismissed the bulk of the troops at the jetty's end, leaving only a small bodyguard.

'How did you come here in one of my brother's ships? And tell me. How do things stand? How did Caesar react?'

Marcus Salvius Aper rose and rolled his shoulders. 'Caesar was, of course, morally outraged at Pompey's death.'

'Of course he was,' smiled the queen. 'A Roman hero, and his own son-in-law? Of course he was.'

'I suspect quietly grateful on the inside. Or at least so I was led to believe by friends in their camp.'

'You have friends in their camp? How innovative and useful.'

'Caesar, I think, sees Ptolemy only as something to control and manoeuvre, like a young horse. There is clearly no love lost between he and Potheinus, who works every moment to undermine the consul. The court is a mess of intrigue and distrust.'

'Excellent. Better even than I hoped.'

Salvius bowed. 'Caesar wants to resolve this problem. I believe he sees the two of you reunited, despite your brother's violent protests.'

'He has not yet reckoned with me,' the queen said with quiet determination. 'Caesar may be able to force Ptolemy to some deal against his will, but he will not achieve such with me.'

'He sent me to bring you to Alexandria. It is a dangerous proposition, my queen, for though we may slip past his navy, bearing his flag as we do – I requisitioned one of your brother's ships from the port in Alexandria, of course – if we reach the city we still have to get you inside without falling foul of Potheinus' watchers. He has eyes and blades everywhere in Alexandria. I had to kill three men to take the ship.'

'Where there is a will, there is always a way,' Cleopatra smiled, 'and I have no shortage of will. When do we depart?'

'Such stealth is always improved by darkness. The journey will take two days even if we sail through day and night. If we depart within the hour, then I would estimate our arrival at Alexandria around midnight the day after tomorrow.'

'Perfect. Have you quarters for my men?'

'My queen, you cannot take a force with you. If we are boarded by other ships, which is entirely possible, you could be hidden, and I wear an allied uniform. A small force of your troops could not be sneaked through. It must be just you and I. No army. This is not a military operation, after all.'

The queen nodded hesitantly. She trusted Salvius, but…

'I will take just one man: Apollodorus.'

Behind her the big Sicilian nodded. Commander Sosibius, on the other hand, shook his head. 'It is too dangerous, my queen.'

'It is our only option,' she replied. 'I will be with two men I trust implicitly. Keep the army ready. We know not how the dice will fall if I meet with Caesar.'

Reluctantly, and with clear disapproval, Sosibius bowed and stepped back with his men.

'Well, Salvius Aper,' the queen smiled, 'show me to my quarters.'

* * *

The journey was one fraught with dangers, and Apollodorus' concerns about sea routes seemed to have been well founded. In two days of travel, not an hour passed without coming dangerously close to another of Ptolemy's vessels. Had they not been one themselves, then they would most certainly have been boarded without making it ten miles along the delta's coastline. Even bearing Ptolemy's eagle they attracted the attention of one warship late that first night, who called them to a stop and questioned them. Fortunately it seemed that Salvius was conversant enough with the enemy to be able to mimic them sufficiently, and they went on their way without being boarded.

During the second day it became clear that something else was happening. That first day they had seen ships passing back and forth, east and west along the coast in roughly equal numbers, patrolling far and wide. The second day it became clear that more and more vessels were heading west, in the same direction as they. So as not to draw too much attention and be visible constantly to the same ships, they slowed occasionally and periodically picked up pace along with the others.

Ptolemy's fleet, it seemed, was concentrating back towards Alexandria.

The tension built as they passed Bolbitinum on a projecting mouth of the Nile, the last major channel before their destination, for the sun began to sink into the west and, by the time the city was out of sight behind them, there was nothing left of Ra's eye but a gold-red glow that rippled across the water. By the time they slid past Canopus on its promontory, the night had become truly dark.

Cleopatra stood at the rail as they finally approached Alexandria, watching the flickering lights of her home, the palace where she had been born, dancing on the shoreline at the end of the diabathra. Four other ships were visible around them now, in the night, all heading for the city. The fleet was returning, for certain.

'You had best get out of sight, my queen,' Salvius Aper said quietly, and with a nod, she did so. She had entered this harbour so many times in her young life, she could have navigated the reefs blindfolded, and her mind's eye provided her with the view she could not see below deck. Every tiny turn she recognised. She felt the wind catch three quarters astern and knew they had turned to make for the harbour entrance. Artillery would be trained upon them from both the end of the diabathra and from the defences on the Pharos island, for nothing could pass within the Great Harbour without the will of the place's ruler. Despite their vessel being one of her brother's she still felt the tension, still expected the twang and thud of artillery launching at them. It was a distinct relief when she heard the sail being furled above, the power of the wind abating as the oars were run out and the vessel leaned, beginning its turn to the northeast.

They were passing the reefs now, and she could almost count the oar strokes as they pulled towards the easternmost port, lying below the walls of the palace. As they passed within the welcoming arms of that last stretch and made for a free jetty, she heard Salvius Aper curse in the Roman tongue above. She turned to Apollodorus. 'Go and ask what is happening.'

The big Sicilian did so, clambering up the ladder and crossing the deck. She heard muttered conversation, and the man returned in a moment.

'We are pulling up to the jetty, my queen, but perhaps this ship has been missed, for there are many of your brother's soldiers on watch. They guard the closed palace gate and stand at every corner and on every wall and tower, at the end of each jetty and on the harbour walls.'

'Then we are undone.'

'I fear so, Majesty.'

There was a familiar scrape and thud as the ship touched the jetty and sailors began the work of tying her tight. In moments, Salvius Aper was sliding down the ladder his hands and feet gripping the sides. As he hit the lower deck, he turned to his passengers.

'How tied are you to propriety, my queen?'

'I will do what must be done. Why?'

'There is simply no way you can walk into the palace. Even in disguise you will be checked over. There might be a way, though. It is demeaning, uncomfortable, and extremely dangerous and stands only a slim chance of success, but I simply cannot picture another way.'

'Explain,' she said.

Salvius turned and walked over to a heavy duty sack, one of a dozen or so on board. 'You go in one of these.'

Apollodorus frowned. 'A grain sack?'

Salvius nodded. 'The Roman forces here are doing all they can to acquire good grain, for Potheinus is distributing to them only the poorest available. It will come as no surprise for a sack of grain to be entering the palace.'

'What happens if they look inside?' the queen said, genuinely curious.

'You will need to curl up in the bottom of the sack. We will stuff a couple of empty bags above you and then fill the top with grain. It's not perfect, and if you can think of another way, then I'll happily concede.'

The queen shook her head. 'It is a fine plan,' she smiled. 'Often the most brazen lie is the easiest to tell and the softest to hear.'

Moments later, Apollodorus and Salvius had emptied one of the sacks in a dark corner and the queen climbed in, curling up at the bottom and arranging herself so that no limbs or joints protruded, becoming as smooth and rounded as she could. She was not tall in stature, was lithe and supple and, though she could not see the results from her hiding place, she was content that she was as well-hidden as she could manage.

'It is not convincing,' Apollodorus said.

'Leave it to me,' Salvius replied, then leaned over the sack. 'Apologies, my queen. We will get this over with as fast as possible.'

Two rough sacks were pushed down above her and pulled this way and that to cover her as much as possible. Then she heard grain being shovelled in.

'Quickly,' Salvius said. 'If we are too slow leaving the ship we will arouse suspicion.'

More grain was shovelled in and then she heard and felt the sack being tied.

'You carry it,' Salvius said. 'It would look odd for a centurion to do so, and you look, if you'll forgive me, very forgettable.'

She heard the Sicilian grunt and felt herself lifted from the deck. The next fifty heartbeats were some of the least comfortable of her life as Apollodorus shouldered her and then climbed the ladder to the upper deck with difficulty. The movement shifted the sacking above her and a steady trickle of grain began to drop down into where she was curled. She wondered in a moment of near panic how much grain they had shovelled in on top. Enough to suffocate her if it all sank down?'

She felt the change of temperature as they clambered up onto the deck, and the creak and groan of wood as they walked across the ship to the boarding ramp and down it to the jetty. She could hear their footsteps, the hobnails of Salvius Aper clacking and scraping on the stone as they left the jetty and moved onto the dock, Apollodorus' hard leather boots slapping.

She could almost feel the eyes of the world upon them as they approached the palace gate.

'Stop,' called a voice in Greek, the language of the Aegyptian court. One of her brother's men, then, clearly. 'Who are you and where are you bound?'

Salvius replied, his voice taking on a tone of authority, haughtiness and irritation that was impressive to hear. 'I am Marcus Salvius Aper, centurion of the Third Century, First Cohort of the Gabinius Legion, stationed here, as you damn well know. Stand aside and let me in.'

'What is that?' asked the voice.

Cleopatra could feel her panic rising. There really was a lot of grain now, and it was beginning to make her chin itch. If it got to her mouth and nose... She reached down as carefully as she could, with tiny movements, and pulled from her belt the small knife she habitually carried, then gave the sack below her a tiny jab. She was rewarded with the sound of grains hitting stone below in a steady trickle. She could not risk any further movement, and so kept the knife in her hand and sat still. The danger of suffocation receded as the level of grain around her drained slowly.

'This is good grain for the Roman forces,' Salvius told the guard irritably. 'If Potheinus keeps feeding them rubbish, then the consul is going to turn against the king. Now stand aside.'

'Better move fast,' one of the guards murmured, 'it appears you have a hole in the sack.'

'Damn it,' Salvius Aper spat, and the queen felt his fingers probing the hole in the sack beside her left foot.

With immense relief, she heard the palace gate being opened, and Salvius rather gruffly thanked the men and hurried inside with Cleopatra bumping along against Apollodorus' back. She tried to maintain calm as she heard the footsteps changing as they climbed steps, moved from stone to marble and entered a building. Finally, she heard Salvius' nailed boots clack off ahead. Worry thrilled through her, but then she heard him at the far end of a corridor in low conversation with someone.

She heard another door open and then, ten heartbeats later, she felt her porter come to a halt.

'Is this true?' an unfamiliar voice asked in Latin.

'Perfectly true, sir,' Salvius replied. There was an odd silence, and then she felt herself lowered to the floor and the bag above her began to rustle and shake. She felt the ties loosened and the sacks were removed from above her.

'My queen,' Salvius Aper said, encouraging her.

Stiffly, rolling her neck and shaking out the discomfort, Cleopatra rose from the sack.

The room was one reserved for accommodating high status guests. She knew it well, and had met many people in the place at one time or another. Half a dozen Romans in the uniforms of senior officers stood around a table, though her eyes fell immediately upon only one. She had seen portraits of Caesar, of course. He had always appeared a little too aquiline and sharp-angled, with receded hair and high cheekbones. He looked arrogant even on coins and statues. She had expected someone who radiated power and confidence, and she was not disappointed. What she had not expected was for that strangely aquiline and increasingly elderly face to be disturbingly handsome. The combination of heady power and attraction made her shiver slightly, and she felt goose flesh rise upon her. She was acutely aware that she was not at her best, and would be dusty and smell of old grain. Hurriedly she brushed herself down and smoothed her apparel into place.

'Queen Cleopatra, daughter of Ptolemy Auletes, welcome to Alexandria at last,' the consul said with a smile that appeared to contain genuine mirth. She felt a quiver of irritation that the man seemed to be laughing at her and in a way she had known she could since her earliest teen years, she switched on that part of her that exuded languid attraction. Few men could resist her when she did so, and it had bought her a great deal of power over the years. She knew there were more handsome women in the Ptolemaic court than her, and yet she knew how to make herself desirable with barely a move. Indeed, she felt an instant change in the atmosphere among the Romans.

'This is Apollodorus of Sicilia,' Salvius introduced her other companion, 'the queen's trusted man.'

'Well met, Apollodorus,' Caesar replied, 'and you too, Salvius. Please, help yourselves to food and drink. I suspect you have not had an easy journey.'

The queen eyed the other Romans, and Caesar noted her roving gaze.

'Forgive me. This is the admiral Cassius Longinus,' he said, indicating a tall, thin man with black neat hair and a serious expression. 'This is Orfidius Bulla of the Twenty Seventh Legion,' a shorter, stockier man with a scarred face and a shock of red hair. 'Marcus Falerius Fronto, of the Sixth,' a man of a similar age to Caesar, with a tired, veteran face, favouring a bad leg, she noted. 'Galronus of the Remi, my cavalry commander,' a strange pale man who seemed oddly out of place among the others, though impressive all the same. 'And Salvius Cursor.'

Her eyebrows rose and she turned to Salvius Aper, who nodded. 'My brother.'

'My apologies for the manner of my arrival,' she said. 'I was somewhat inconvenienced by my brother.'

Caesar chuckled, and she realised now that there was no insult in his laughter, which made her relax a little more. 'I fear your brother has little to do with your difficulties, Queen Cleopatra. It is the rodent Potheinus who infects this city and palace with suspicion and keeps eyes and blades at every door, and it is Achillas who floods Aegyptus with soldiers seeking to apprehend you. I suspect your brother has had little to do with it other than complaining that he doesn't like you very much.'

'He is quite right to complain,' the queen said flatly. 'If the opportunity arises I shall not hesitate to open him up for the carrion feeders.' She flattened her palm to display the small knife in it, and then tucked the blade back into its place at her belt. She saw disapproval in several Roman faces, especially Cassius', but the one called Fronto nodded his approval, and Caesar simply arched an impressive eyebrow. Damn it, but she was finding it hard to take her eyes off the old man.

'And here was I seeking to reconcile you both and settle once more into your joint rule,' Caesar said.

'I doubt that would be possible now,' the one called Fronto said, 'even if they didn't hate each other.'

'Quite right,' Caesar agreed. 'I'm afraid that your daring and ingenious arrival might have been sadly mis-timed, your Majesty.'

'Oh? How so?'

But her mind was already racing ahead. The fleet coming back to Alexandria. Ptolemy's soldiers at every door and wall. She narrowed her eyes. 'You are at war?'

'Not quite yet,' Fronto said, leaning on the table, 'but it looks to be looming. We have less than four thousand men here, only four and a half thousand even with the palace guards, and that's if they can be trusted. But we have just received word that far from standing down his army, Achillas has martialled them and drawn them together.'

She shook her head. That was hard to believe. Or was it? Achillas was a clever man, and ambitious. Could it be that their little civil war had just gained a third player?

Caesar nodded as if reading her thoughts. 'Achillas marches on Alexandria and his forces outnumber us at least four to one. His ostensible reason is that he believes your brother to be in danger, held by us, though I think we can all safely discount that as genuine concern. If I send your brother back to his army, I rather suspect he will be dead in a ditch by nightfall with no witnesses, and the army will continue to march. I believe Achillas intends to take Alexandria for himself.'

Cleopatra sighed. 'I have a force that could bolster yours, but they are on the far side of Achillas' army, and therefore of little use.'

The one called Fronto nodded. 'And we have two more legions coming, but they are at least ten days away and they will pass your army before they get here. The winds will not allow our fleet to leave in worthwhile numbers, so we are effectively trapped. I am very much afraid that we must fortify ourselves in Alexandria and prepare to repel Achillas' army. We need to hold them off long enough for our support to arrive.'

Damn it, the queen fumed. She had thought that with Caesar's aid she could force down Ptolemy, but she had not reckoned with Ptolemy being unimportant and Achillas taking the fore.

There would be war. But at least she was in her palace. The Romans were known for siege warfare and they had good strategic minds, and Cleopatra knew both Alexandria and Achillas well. Together they would weather the storm. She looked up into Caesar's eyes and felt that tingle again, her flesh prickling as she approached the map and leaned on it.

'Then here is what we must do…'

The end.

HISTORICAL NOTE

I'm going to begin at the end, here. I'm going to explain my decision to end this on something of a cliff-hanger, which I have been refusing to do throughout the series. Hopefully it won't have irritated you, but I have good reasons. I had pondered, when planning the book, where to cut off the story. Clearly I was going to be telling the tale of Caesar's second year of civil war, focusing on Dyrrachium and Pharsalus. The natural cut off seems to be in the aftermath of Pharsalus with Pompey on the run and Caesar once more victorious, and I expect that's what the reader has been anticipating. But I had several reasons for moving on a few chapters and taking us to Egypt.

The notion was born when I got to the end of my first read of this year's work in Caesar's own campaign diaries. In that, he talks of both Dyrrachium and Pharsalus, but also takes us to Egypt and shows us the first moves in the war there, including some serious combat in Alexandria (no further spoilers). The very last line of Caesar's civil Wars, which deals with this year's events, is "This was the beginning of the Alexandrian war." And so, in the spirit of Caesar, I agreed. Let us finish book 11 with the feeling that the Alexandrian war has begun, perhaps in the same spirit as George Lucas' second Star Wars prequel with Yoda saying 'begun, the clone wars have.'

But that is only the trigger. The reason it appealed. The reason finishing this on a tense note rather than in the pleasing downtime largely revolves around Pompey. Had I finished book 11 after Pharsalus, there would be the thread of Pompey hanging around, and yet he could not be the focus of the next book, disappearing as he does from history with a brief squeak off-stage. And I felt that beginning the next book with a short couple of chapters leading to Pompey's rather disappointing end would hardly be an exciting build-up for book 12. No, I think Pompey had to go in book 11.

Linked to that is the tale of Salvius Cursor. His inclusion a year ago in Spain and Massilia is no accident. In Plutarch's life of Pompey, he names three assassins of Pompey on the boat in Egypt: Septimius, Achillas, and Salvius. Of this Salvius, nothing else appears to be known. I won't go into the details of my reasoning, but Salvius and his brother are instruments of my will, and I didn't want to end book 11 without a little closure for our favourite tribune.

I wrote the first chapter of MM11 and decided almost straight away that I needed some kind of disconnected prologue to create perspective beyond the two warring parties. Cleopatra loomed in my plans, and I just could not resist having her and her brother make a brief appearance. Having done that, I realised that one of those all-time great historical moments fell at the end of this year's events: Cleopatra being snuck into the palace in a mat. Somehow, I just had to frame the book with her.

And finally, With the Gallic wars, when I was writing them there is generally a simple cut-off at the end of each year. Though some important events occur over the winter, in military events, the campaigning season generally stops in autumn and I followed suit with each volume. Now we are in the complex civil, Alexandrian, African and Spanish Wars and the events of Rome in the last years of Caesar's life, things tend to snowball and become constant. Those periods of winter downtime are not as convenient as they once were, and it's becoming difficult *not* to end a book on a cliff-hanger. So that's my reasoning. Hopefully you won't have long to wait until book 12.

I will come back to Cleo in due course.

Firstly: Dyrrachium. From the point of view of a fiction writer, I have to say that Dyrrachium is a royal pain in the butt. Though the sequence of events is laid out in Caesar's own writing, and the terrain and locations are still there to be seen, the whole thing is something of a jumbled mess. There are so many things that happen and decisions that are made that do not bear too much scrutiny, or the reader begins to question the wisdom. There is a lot of running around, arguing, faffing, posturing and the like. When the fighting does happen it tends to be sporadic and happen all over the place at the same time. Much of the siege is quite irritating to study, I have to say, and there are elements of farce in there, with the two sides fighting to enclose one another in an ever-lengthening wall, officers mistaking one rampart for another and attacking the wrong place and so on. Really, Dyrrachium was a mess. But one with some diamond scenes in it, I'll admit.

My main concern with Dyrrachium was going to be the big push at the end, where it all goes wrong. In accounts, Caesar's army flees. He tries to stop them doing so and the standard bearers throw their standards at him and run past in the panic. Caesar's own withdrawal from the battlefield is not recorded, and I did it the way I did simply because it had more fictional impact than simply having him saddle up in desperation and ride off in the wake of his fleeing army.

Pharsalus was a much nicer proposition. Where Dyrrachium was a mess of toing and froing and arguing and pushing and shoving that lasted months, Pharsalus was a nice clean battle that lasted hours. Even if you include the earlier cavalry engagement(s) that I had Galronus involved in, it was days rather than months. A pitched battle is much easier to relate, I have to say. And the very nature of the battle and how it unfolded gave me my perfect viewpoints: Salvius presenting the clash of the legions, Galronus the pivotal turning of the battle with the cavalry, and Fronto the surprise hammer blow that crushes Pompey's plan.

There is, of course, no record in Caesar's diary of a man sneaking into the enemy camp and learning everything he can. I'm sure there was a great tradition during Roman civil wars of spies in each other's camp. It was portrayed beautifully in Asterix the Legionary, in fact, with the secret agent codenamed H_2SO_4. And I don't care how secure the generals made their camps, with the watchword 'Venus Venetrix' for Caesar and 'Hercules Invictus' for Pompey, covering their entire force, security must be laughable. It is the Roman military equivalent of using your date of birth as your password, or setting your PIN to 1234.

But to me, there has to have been intelligence reach Caesar's camp about Pompey's plan. There is simply no credible reason for Caesar to have put in that fourth line behind the cavalry (niftily explained earlier with the new mixed cavalry/infantry move that is recorded in his diary) unless he knew precisely what Pompey was planning. And Pompey and Caesar each in a matching position on the field, facing one another with their best legions? That was no accident. So someone apprised Caesar of Pompey's plan for a cavalry sweep to flank him. I had it be Galronus. And why not?

I somewhat curtailed the long, drawn-out aftermath with the starving legions on the hill, and I somewhat embellished Ahenobarbus' death scene (did you know he was the emperor Nero's great grandfather by the way? So he probably deserved a gruesome death for that alone. His grandson appears in my Caligula novel, and he is a dirtbag too!) But in accounts, Ahenobarbus was caught and killed by cavalry while trying to flee the hill in the aftermath of Pharsalus, so I only amped up the detail a little. Ahenobarbus is not the only larger than life character who gets screen time in MM11, though. Labienus is back. I had him back in around books 2-4 I think, being a very reasonable man and a sympathiser of the human plight, despite also being a very capable commander. I had wondered years ago how I would feel about portraying him after he turned against Caesar. Back in MM10 I didn't have to, for he was an absentee villain. But at Dyrrachium and Pharsalus he was a principle character, and I decided the only way he could possibly have gone was to be bitter and adamant in his opposition.

Fronto has been far removed from his loved ones now, too. I am to some extent missing the familial connection at the moment, but it is simply not possible to bring the rest of the familia into this period of the action. Fighting brutally across Greece, Asia, Egypt and Africa is not conducive to creating scenes of family harmony. But they will be back. We are engaged in a huge circle here, that will eventually bring us back.

If you're reading this book, by the way, with a copy of Caesar's diary to hand and wondering at how many strange events I have simply plucked out of the air and are not recounted there, particularly towards the end, that is because I have, in previous volumes, stayed largely true to Caesar's own writings and eschewed too many external viewpoints. This is the story of his campaigns as he told them, in essence. But with the complications towards the end of this year and the simple boredom of telling the tale of Caesar racing around the eastern med, staying always a few days or more behind Pompey, I wanted to add something to make it a little more interesting. Thus I lifted more scenes from other biographers. The crossing of the Hellespont, for instance, is from

Appian, though the flag escapade was my own addition. I do find it hard to give credence entirely to the notion that Cassius, in command of a sizeable portion of Pompey's fleet, simply saw Caesar in a boat with a bunch of other skiffs and immediately surrendered.

Similarly, my events in the final two chapters are informed considerably more by a few paragraphs of Plutarch than Caesar's own (at this point quite convoluted) account. I chose to put aside Caesar's heroic fights and assign them to the next book. We'd done enough battle here already. But it is Plutarch who relates the arrival of Cleopatra at Alexandria. He says 'as it was impossible to escape notice otherwise, she stretched herself at full length inside a bed-sack, while Apollodorus tied the bed-sack up with a cord and carried it indoors to Caesar.' I changed this to a grain sack and added Salvius, as I couldn't see any realism in vigilant guards happening to let an itinerant Sicilian with a bed-roll into the palace complex. Given the grain issues, that seemed far more appropriate.

And so we have lost Pompey, but we have gained Cleopatra and Ptolemy (and their sister Arsinoe and brother, er…. Ptolemy.) Begun the Alexandrian war has (he says in his best Yoda accent.) And beyond that other exotic wars in exotic locations. And while their account might have been the work of different writers (including almost certainly Hirtius), they are all part of the civil Wars, for now the survivors of Pharsalus wait with Attius in Africa.

This particular episode of the story, though, will conclude with Marius' Mules XII next year.

Until then, vale and thanks for reading.

Simon Turney, June 2018

If you enjoyed Marius' Mules XI, please do leave a review online, and also checkout another great book that was also released this month:

LEGIONARY: EMPIRE OF SHADES

By Gordon Doherty

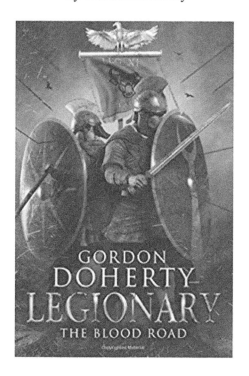

381 AD: The Gothic War draws to a brutal climax, and the victor's name will be written in blood... The great struggle between the Eastern Roman Empire and the Gothic Horde rumbles into its fifth year. It seems that there can be no end to the conflict, for although the Goths are masters of the land, they cannot topple the last of the imperial cities. But heralds bring news that might change it all: Emperor Gratian readies to lead his Western legions into the fray, to turn matters on their head, to crush the horde and save the East! The men of the XI Claudia legion long for their homeland's salvation, but Tribunus Pavo knows these hopes drip with danger. For he and his soldiers are Gratian's quarry as much as any Goth. The road ahead will be fraught with broken oaths, enemy blades... and tides of blood.